WE THAT ARE LEFT

LISA BIGELOW'S life revolves around story-telling.
Her career as a journalist and communicator has focused
on building and delivering compelling stories about people,
environmental sustainability, climate change and the events
that shape our lives. She recently completed a Masters
Degree in Communication and aims to use her writing to
illuminate important issues and make them accessible to a
wide readership. Lisa has been an avid reader from age five
and now as an adult she's delighted to be adding her voice
to the bookshelves. *We That Are Left* is her first novel.

WE THAT ARE LEFT

LISA BIGELOW

ALLEN&UNWIN

SYDNEY·MELBOURNE·AUCKLAND·LONDON

First published in 2017

Allen & Unwin
83 Alexander Street
Crows Nest NSW 2065
Australia
Phone: (61 2) 8425 0100
Email: info@allenandunwin.com
Web: www.allenandunwin.com

Cataloguing-in-Publication details are available
from the National Library of Australia
www.trove.nla.gov.au

ISBN 978 1 76029 700 8

Internal design by Romina Panetta
Set in 12.5/17 pt Adobe Garamond by Post Pre-press Group, Brisbane
Printed and bound in Australia by Griffin Press

10 9 8 7 6 5 4 3 2 1

The paper in this book is FSC® certified.
FSC® promotes environmentally responsible,
socially beneficial and economically viable
management of the world's forests.

CHAPTER 1

March 1941

GRACE FOWLER STEPPED OFF the tram and stared for several moments at the granite façade of the newspaper building. It looked like a film set, like something from a Torchy Blane movie. The four-storey building loomed over the railway yards and a busy intersection, its bulk covering an entire block at the edge of the city. Soaring columns and huge windows added to the sense of stately grandeur above the brass entry and three garages, now swallowing a fleet of trucks returning from delivering *The Gazette*, the biggest-selling morning tabloid in Melbourne. In a few hours, those same trucks would emerge with the first editions of *The Tribune*, just in time for the lunch crowds. The final editions would be printed for people catching trains and trams home from work.

Somewhere behind the loading bay, giant presses ran around the clock, ten or maybe twenty times the size of the press at her father's paper in Benalla. Right now, teams of printers would be turning gigantic rolls of blank newsprint into papers and magazines. It was magic, just like the morning milk and bread deliveries; people hardly ever thought about the work that brought them to their doorstep, but they noticed if they weren't there.

Grace smoothed her best maroon gabardine suit and gripped her brown leather handbag extra tightly as she stepped off the footpath and crossed the road. A man in a dark green uniform doffed his cap and smiled as she entered the building.

After signing in and pinning a visitor's pass to her lapel, Grace stepped into the lift with half a dozen men of different ages. No one spoke but she wished they would, anything to distract her racing thoughts. *Mr Barton. News Editor. Mr Barton. News Editor.* She was sure of his name and title, but she worried her mind would go blank when she met him. Not that it had ever happened before, but she'd seen it in a film once—which one was it? No matter. *First impressions count for everything.* The teachers at secretarial college had drummed that into her.

The lift operator slid the metal door open then pushed aside the grille, and she and most of the men exited. Grace followed the men around the corner and through the door marked *Editorial* to find a sea of desks covered in typewriters, paper, books, newspapers and telephones. A few near the back were occupied by older men who looked rumpled and tired, as if they'd been there all night. The air smelled of stale cigarettes and sandwiches.

'Miss Fowler, I presume?' A man looked at her across a clutter of papers on a desk twice the size of the ones in front of her. His desk was just inside the entrance, right where he could see everyone in the newsroom and, more importantly, within shouting distance, if he was anything like the news editors she'd met before. At her nod, he said, 'Sam Barton.'

He looked pleasant enough, more like a businessman than the dishevelled, big-bellied newsmen she'd grown up with. His neatly combed light brown hair had just a hint of grey near the temples. He looked a bit younger than her father but of a similar vintage, mid-forties or so. FATHERLY NEWS EDITOR GREETS NEW SECRETARY. Her headline for that moment.

'You'll be sitting behind me.' Mr Barton waved to a smaller desk with several overflowing in- and out-trays, two telephones (both ringing) and a typewriter. A bank of filing cabinets lined the wall behind her desk. 'My secretary's on leave and we don't know if she'll be back. Until we can arrange something more permanent I'll need you to handle all the usual things; answering the phone, managing my calendar, checking the wires, filing, keeping people out of my hair. You'll get to know which people as you go along. You've done this before?'

Grace nodded, trying to quell her disappointment and focus on what her new boss was saying. Of course she would have preferred a reporting role, and for just a few exciting moments, before she'd understood why he was phoning, that's exactly what she'd thought he was offering.

'Any questions?'

She shook her head. 'That all sounds quite straight-forward, Mr Barton,' she said, surprised that she managed to sound so professional. *I can do this*, she told herself as she removed her gloves and placed her handbag in her desk drawer. She sat and opened a notebook, retrieved a pencil from a holder and answered the first of the ringing telephones.

'Newsroom. Miss Fowler speaking.'

Was that right? Should she give the name of the organisation first? No, these calls were all coming through the switchboard. Maybe she should answer with Mr Barton's name? After all, that's probably who people were calling—but they'd need her name so they knew who to address in the first place. She tried without success to remember what she'd been told at secretarial college. She took a different approach with the next call.

'Good afternoon—oh, I mean morning, sorry. Mr Barton's office, Grace Fowler speaking.'

NEW SECRETARY DOESN'T EVEN KNOW THE TIME OF DAY. *Take a breath, slow your speech, annunciate more clearly while callers get used to your voice,* she reminded herself. Writing down the second caller's message and preparing to answer the next call, Grace glanced across the newsroom, straight into the face of—Gary Cooper? Well, not quite the movie star, but close enough. Nodding slowly, his broad smile revealed pearly teeth and creased the corners of his sparkling eyes. He was leaning against a desk, arms folded casually across his chest. His suit jacket outlined the shoulders and torso of an athlete, perfectly triangular.

He pushed himself away from the desk and walked towards her, his gaze fixed on hers. At least she thought it was, but perhaps he was looking at someone behind her? She quickly turned her head; no one there. As he approached, Grace blushed harder and faster than she ever had at school when Mick Foster walked past.

'Phil Taylor, senior sports writer,' he said, offering her his hand. His grip was warm and firm.

'Grace Fowler,' Grace replied, a little breathlessly.

'Sam's been looking forward to your arrival. I hope you don't mind working long hours.'

'Not at all,' Grace said. 'Newsrooms are my favourite place in the world.'

'That's right, he said you'd been a secretary for a country paper.'

'Reporter.'

'A reporter? Well, well. That's something you don't hear every day—a girl reporter.'

'I have every intention of changing that,' Grace said shyly. 'Hearing about women reporters, I mean.'

'I look forward to watching your progress, Miss Fowler. Meanwhile, if you need to know where anything is, just sing out.'

Grace watched Phil walk back to his desk. He hadn't seemed to be mocking her, but maybe she'd been a little too forthcoming. She'd dreamed of a reporting career on a city paper for most of her life, but none of these people knew that. Best to keep her ambitions to herself, at least until she'd learned to properly answer the phone.

CHAPTER 2

March 1941

THE WOODEN DOOR OF the cuckoo clock in the lounge room flipped open and the mechanical bird tweeted seven times. The maniacal cuckoo, Harry called it. Mae Parker smiled as a motorcycle approached the cottage and growled to a stop outside. Exactly on time, as though he'd waited up the street to make a grand entrance.

Mae had spent the day cleaning and dusting the cottage from cupboard top to wooden floor. The previously overflowing bookcase in the hallway was now sorted, with extra books stashed in boxes beneath the bed in the spare room. That room would become the nursery when the baby was old enough to leave her bedside, but for the moment it was filled with Harry's tennis racquets, golf clubs, easel, canvases and paints. Cradling her enormous belly with one arm, she waddled to the kitchen, lifted the roasting pan into the oven then glanced down to check she was wearing shoes rather than slippers.

Finally she whipped off her apron and smoothed her blonde hair. Perfect.

'There's my Sunny,' Harry said, bounding through the back door a moment later and hugging her close.

She filled her lungs with his scent; leather riding jacket mingled with hair oil and cigarette smoke. She'd be perfectly happy to stay in exactly this configuration—lips together, his arms holding her tight against his chest—until they both shrivelled to dust, she thought.

'It's true,' he said, loosening his hold and leaning back against the kitchen sink. 'All those comments about a mother's glow. I wouldn't have thought it possible, but you've grown even prettier than when we met.'

'You'd flatter any woman cooking your favourite dinner.'

She kissed him again and smiled, trying to appear carefree, but searching his expression for any hint of disappointment with her shape.

'You're the pin-up girl of expectant motherhood, Mrs Parker. I'm going to draw you this weekend, capture you in all your splendour.'

'Now, you're just teasing,' Mae said, stepping away and shelling peas into a saucepan.

He leaned over and stroked her stomach. 'Clothes on or off, I don't mind.'

Mae shivered. He'd asked so many times to draw her naked, but she'd never allowed it. Once she'd let him draw her in bed, while she was naked under the sheets, yet even though she trusted him completely, she couldn't bear the thought of him studying her body that way. Seeing all her flaws; her broad hips, her swollen ankles, her enormous bosom.

'You can draw me in my new smock,' she said. 'I've given up letting things out.'

'You'd look beautiful in a potato sack,' he said, arching backwards to stretch against the sink.

'Sore?'

'Just tired from hunching over the handlebars. Nothing to slow me down.'

Mae eased her hips forward to stretch her own back. Harry watched her carefully, his expression serious. It was exactly the look she'd been dreading—the look that always accompanied news about a new posting. The first time she'd seen it they moved to Sydney; the last time they'd moved back to Melbourne.

'Darling, did you hear that Jim's ship is home?' he asked slowly.

Mae held her breath for a moment before answering. 'I saw it on the newsreel with Et. Alice wrote that she expects him any day now.'

'They're all pretty exhausted, I hear, after all that action in the Mediterranean.'

'Alice says he thrived on it,' said Mae, turning to rinse the peas under the tap. 'A real *Boy's Own* adventure, he called it.'

'Well, the Italians certainly won't forget the ship that sunk one of their best. And that crew—a real red-hot bunch.' Harry plunged on. 'But some of the more expe-rienced men are leaving. The new fellows in the engine room need training.'

In the six years they'd been married and their two years courting he'd had three sea postings. Last time he was at sea she'd lost their baby. She'd lost two more before that one. Each time she'd only been a few months along but it had still been devastating. This pregnancy she'd been much happier having Harry training engineers at the naval college about seventy-five miles away, well clear of battles on the other side of the world.

Mae carefully sliced the carrots and potatoes and arranged them flat edge down in the roasting pan. Harry loved his roast vegetables slightly burned on one side only; he said they reminded him of toffee apples. The smell of lamb filled the kitchen while a jug of mint sauce steeped on the freshly wiped windowsill. Dinner was still an hour away.

'I—I received my orders. I'm heading to Perth to get the blokes up to speed. Just for six months. A year at the most.'

Mae started washing dishes. 'When are you leaving?' she asked without looking at him.

'There's a train on Monday night.'

She stopped washing and let her head drop forward. 'Europe or Africa?'

'Neither . . . for the moment, anyway. The ship copped a bit of damage overseas. They're fixing her up then we'll do some escort work up the coast and into Singapore.'

Moving in behind her, Harry pulled Mae towards him so that her head nestled under his collarbone. 'You know this posting is a dream come true for me,' he said softly.

'It could lead to promotions and a wonderful life for all of us.'

Mae turned to face him and tilted her head to look at his straight black hair, his sea blue eyes. She forced her lips into a smile. 'They'll be lucky to have you aboard.'

'Now we have three things to celebrate,' he said. 'My posting, our anniversary and our lovely daughter.'

'I thought you wanted a boy,' Mae said, trying to sound bright.

'I've changed my mind. Do you think it's too late to put in an order for a girl? Of course I don't really care, but if we do have a girl, we could call her Myrna, after Myrna Loy in the films. I think Myrna's a lovely name, don't you?'

'Didn't we agree on Ronald for a boy and Katherine for a girl?'

She tried to relax as he ran his fingers slowly up and down her spine.

'Well, since you're doing all the hard work, you should choose any name you want, although I'd prefer we didn't call our son Gareth. There was a dreadful bully at my school with that name.'

'I don't think *all* Gareths are bullies.'

'Can't risk it. Look at that Hitler fellow. How many nice Adolfs do you know?'

'I'm not sure you've proved your point but I promise not Gareth—oh! He just kicked me. I think he's upset.'

'Maybe he's tired,' Harry whispered in her ear. 'Perhaps we should lie down while dinner's cooking.'

Later that night Mae sat on the bed with Harry's head in her lap. As she stroked his hair, she tried not to think about him leaving.

He traced his finger across her stomach.

'Are you sure you'll both be all right?'

The clock seemed to tick more loudly than usual in the lounge room. She silently reminded herself never to criticise or make him feel guilty, to make sure he always had every reason to come home. 'We'll be fine,' she said, sealing her words with a reassuring smile.

'Et wrote that the family's terribly worried about you being here on your own,' he said. 'You must promise you'll stay with them after I leave.'

'Claire's just up the street. She knows much more about having babies than Et does. She's expecting another, in September.'

'Even so, I'd rather you were with your family,' he insisted.

'All right, in a few more weeks,' Mae said. 'But we need to get a cot and a pram organised for when we come home.'

'Goodo. Let's go into town tomorrow. We can order the cot and pram in the morning, then we'll go to a matinee. What do you want to see, Sunny? Anything you like.'

'There's a new production of *Madame Butterfly* at the Regent. The paper described it as witty and colourful.'

'Like your husband?'

'Of course! Well, colourful, anyway.'

'Any more cheek and there'll be no ice-cream sandwiches for you.'

'You've been practising Daddy talk in the mirror, haven't you?'

'I have, and I think I'm getting the hang of it. Don't make faces or the wind might change and you'll look like that forever. Wash your ears or you'll get potatoes in there. Sticks and stones . . .'

'That's very good,' said Mae, laughing. 'You're a natural.'

Harry looked stern. 'Any more cheek and there could very well be a spanking.'

'Do you talk to your crew like this?'

'Only the more junior men. I don't think it would go over too well with the officers.'

Mae relaxed into their cosy banter, trying to forget that he was leaving the day after next. It might be months before they had another night like this and probably no more on their own. Everything was about to change.

'Sunny, darling, you look upset.'

'Just missing you a little bit already.'

❧❧❧

The next morning they walked slowly along the shaded cobbles of Degraves Street. After leaving school the day she turned fourteen, Mae had trained as a tailor in a nearby workshop. The rag trade was centred around Flinders Lane and the best fashion and furniture in the city was still to be found there. Sometimes, as a girl, she'd imagined she was walking through an arcade in Paris or London or some other exotic city where you could window-shop all day, looking at antiques that were hundreds of years old, the finest embroidered linens, the most expensive silks from the Orient. But Melbourne was much younger than those other cities. There were lovely things here but there was little chance you'd stumble upon candlesticks from a castle or a cruet set once owned by a lord of the realm. That morning they'd chosen a thoroughly modern pram and cot, arranged delivery, and now they were on their way to the theatre.

'From behind, you'd never believe you were expecting,' Harry said, patting her lightly on the bottom.

Mae caught a side-on reflection of herself in a shop window. She was perfectly round with no sign remaining of her waist.

'I look like a hippopotamus.'

'A very pretty hippo in that get-up, I must say.'

'How will I get through doors in two months' time? I might have to get Et to wheel me to the shops in the pram.'

Harry laughed and kissed her cheek. 'I don't doubt for a moment that your aunt would be up to the task. When my mother was expecting Mim, she could only get out of her chair if one of us was around to haul her up.'

Mae gasped. 'What if I get stuck? I could be there for days.'

'You know the answer to that. Go and stay with your family. Set my mind at ease.'

She stopped in front of a furniture shop. The window display featured just one item: a buffet made of the most lustrous wood, shimmering with copper and ivory and ebony hues. 'Darling, look at this.' Mae looked across and saw that Harry was already admiring the buffet.

An elderly gentleman stepped into the window and arranged a pair of silver picture frames on top. He looked around and smiled then walked outside to greet them. 'Walnut,' he said.

'It's got such beautiful lines—and the wood tones . . .' Mae said, barely able to tear her eyes away.

'Come inside,' the man suggested. 'Costs nothing to look.'

They entered the cool darkness of the shop. Mae immediately went to the buffet and ran her hand over its silky, curved doors. 'It's gorgeous,' she said.

The man sighed. 'Such a shame,' he said. 'The couple who originally commissioned it have had to move to a smaller house. There's no room, so now I'm stuck with it. It's too big to fit in the shop so I had to put it in the window.'

Mae, whose feet had swollen in the heat, sank into a chair. 'We're saving to build a house. I'm afraid we can't afford furniture yet, Mr . . .'

'Jeremiah Johansson, madam.' Mr Johansson pulled a polishing cloth out of his pocket and wiped his hands, then bowed slightly towards her. 'I think it's the best I've ever done.'

Harry was carefully opening and closing every door and drawer in the buffet. 'As my wife said, we're saving, but just so we know for the future, how much are you asking?'

Jeremiah moved over to his desk and opened a leather-bound ledger. He ran his pencil down a column then tapped it on the page. 'They paid a non-refundable deposit of fifty percent.' He paused a moment as if deep

14

in thought. 'People are scared about the war so no one's spending,' he said. 'It could be taking up space in my window for months. I really need to display the smaller pieces that bring in the customers.'

Mae held her breath as he wrote a figure on the page then subtracted the deposit and added ten percent. She knew he was being extremely generous.

'Not many people appreciate handcrafted furniture. It would make me happy to think it was the centrepiece in a room rather than tucked away behind a door.'

'Harry, there'll be no space after the cot and pram arrive.'

'How about the bedroom? You could put the baby's clothes inside it for the moment.'

Mae smiled tightly at Jeremiah then turned to Harry. 'It's a wonderful offer, but maybe we should think about it a little more, darling. Over the weekend, perhaps.'

'Sorry, mate. Might have to give it a miss for the moment.' Harry shook Jeremiah's hand then he and Mae left the shop.

'We don't need to furnish our home right away,' she said, trying to sound bright as they walked away down the lane. 'We'll have years to make it perfect.'

'Of course,' he said, squeezing her hand. 'He'll have something else in the shop when we're ready. It doesn't have to be this one. Just think of the fun we'll have, finding the right pieces for every room. Meanwhile, we can camp like gypsies.'

'I could cook over an open fire in the middle of the hallway,' said Mae.

'Perfect, I can see it now,' Harry enthused. 'Our children running naked and laughing through the canvas tent flap we'll have in place of a back wall.'

'And I'll be washing and cleaning from daybreak to dark, because we won't have doors to keep the dust out.'

'Details, dear Sunny, details. You'll get Sundays off to enjoy the rustic vista of our own back garden.'

'Which I'll also be tending while you're gallivanting from port to port.'

'Steady on. I always make sure everything's in order before I leave. And before I leave this time, I need to make sure you're both in order.' He lifted her hand and kissed it softly. 'It won't be long now until you're the best little mother in the world.'

'And there's no question about who'll be the best father,' Mae said, certain that Harry would be wonderful but not at all convinced of her own abilities. As she said the words, she sensed something large crushing her chest, a feeling that had gnawed at the edges of her mind for as long as she could recall. She'd tried to push it away, yet the bigger the baby grew, the closer the feeling came to forming, to taking on colour; reds and oranges and yellows, like fire, like danger. As though rocked by a rush of wind, she felt her legs wobble beneath her. Her thoughts swam and swirled then arranged themselves into recognisable words: *What if I hate being a mother? What if Harry thinks I'm a failure? What if he goes away too?*

CHAPTER 3

HALF AN HOUR AFTER leaving Mr Johansson's shop Mae sat squashed between Harry and the train window. She was already regretting being talked into the second sandwich. Sitting directly opposite, with his knees almost touching hers, an older man scratched his belly and yawned. Reeking of stale beer and clothes that hadn't recently seen the inside of a copper, he balanced a tobacco pouch on his leg then slowly rolled a cigarette and lit up. Her stomach lurched as the smoke hit her nostrils.

She glanced at Harry, but he was oblivious, reading the afternoon paper and chortling over the funnies.

Mae's dress was plastered to her skin as perspiration crawled down her back. The temperature outside must have been well over ninety degrees, she thought, but inside the crowded carriage it was at least ten degrees hotter, with hundreds of bodies crammed together in a fetid fug of body odour, cheap cologne and smelly feet. Diesel fumes poured in through the open windows as the train left North Melbourne station, pitching from side to side as it changed tracks and gathered speed. The swaying motion continued as they passed the abattoir, the smell of rancid animal fat from rendering vats hanging thickly in the air. She fumbled in her handbag for a handkerchief and held it to her nose and mouth.

Harry lowered his paper. 'Are you all right?'

Breathing deeply again, Mae was thankful she'd used lavender water to press her linen. 'Just regretting the egg sandwich for lunch,' she said glumly.

'Your face is rather a green sort of hue, like the ratings on their first outings at sea.'

'Just wait till we reach the tar works.'

Harry removed his hat and placed it upside down on her knee like a bucket. 'Just in case.'

Mae breathed deeply. The trip from the centre of Melbourne to Williamstown normally took about thirty minutes but today it seemed to be taking much longer.

'We're almost there,' Harry whispered softly.

Mae closed her eyes. *Breathe the lavender*, she told herself. *Breathe*.

'How do you stop them being sick?' she asked. 'The ratings, I mean.'

'Sometimes, if they're really bad, we put them on the bridge and let them steer for a while. Have you noticed how drivers never get motion sickness? Nor do helmsmen. Something about concentrating on the horizon.'

'Do you think they'd let me drive the train?'

'We could ask.' Harry leaned forward to speak into her ear. 'I can't bear going away and leaving you like this.'

Mae took another breath through her hanky in answer.

'What if something happens and you're all alone? We don't have a telephone. How will you manage to get to the hospital?'

The train slowed and Mae opened her eyes. They were at Yarraville. Only Spotswood then Newport and North Williamstown to go. Mae moved the handkerchief from her nose and quickly dabbed her brow below her straw hat. She loved her family but hated the thought of going back to their house, back to her childhood room. She was a grown woman and wanted to stay in her own home, with her own bed and clothes and books around her.

At last the train reached its final stop, Williamstown Beach. Harry retrieved his hat from Mae's knee.

'Let's just wait a minute,' Mae said, 'till everyone's gone.'

Harry nodded, then, when the carriage was clear, he led her out onto the platform.

Mae felt her dizziness grow, the bile rising in her throat. Pulling away from Harry, she dashed to a nearby flowerbed and threw up on the stationmaster's geraniums.

Harry stood beside her, whistling through his teeth. *What shall we do with the drunken sailor . . .*

'Oh, you meanie,' Mae gasped, wiping her mouth with her handkerchief.

Harry whistled a few more notes. 'I'll see if I can find you some water,' he said. There was no one at the ticket office, so he went into the men's toilet, emerging a moment later with a wet handkerchief that he used to wipe her face and neck.

'Are you well enough to walk?' he asked.

'I think so, but we'll need to take it slowly.'

❧ ⁂ ☙

They were nearly home when a little boy dashed out of a driveway and ran towards them, arms in the air, the braces from his rompers trailing behind.

'Nicholas, careful, you'll trip,' their neighbour, Claire Barton, called out from her verandah.

Harry lifted the toddler into the air. 'My goodness, you get bigger every time I see you. What's your mother feeding you?'

Nicholas giggled as Harry flew him through the air like a plane.

'Mae, Harry! My goodness, what a day to be out walking. It's far too hot!'

Mae smiled at her friend. 'Hello, Claire. Nearly home. You've got the right idea staying here in the shade.'

'Just letting lunch settle and hoping Nicholas eventually gets tired enough for an S-L-E-E-P.'

Claire's husband Sam appeared from the garage. He held his hand out to Harry. 'It's been too long, mate. How is everything? And Mae, how are you coping with the heat?'

'All good thanks, Sam,' Harry answered. He put the little boy down and Nicholas ran over to lean against his mother's legs. 'We've been ticking off our chores before I ship out.' He lit a cigarette then leaned against the fence.

'How's the news business?' he asked. 'Interesting developments in Jugoslavia.'

'None of us can quite believe the news coming out of Europe,' Sam said. 'The way they're trying to stop the Axis forces getting to the Aegean—it might just halt the Kaiser's march on Greece.'

'Let's hope it's a turning point, hey?' Harry said. 'Get a few fellows back from Europe.'

'We'll need more than a few if the Japs don't settle down, especially in China. Their alliance with the Germans is growing stronger by the day. Sharing ports and the like.'

Harry glanced at Mae, trying to reassure her with his eyes. 'The Krauts have their hands full at the moment. They won't build up around Australia.'

'But they're smart trying to cut off our supplies to England. The Poms'll have a terrible time if they can't get our coal, not to mention our foods.'

'They're not likely to invade, though.'

Sam shrugged. 'Probably not. They might try to bomb our ports though. Menzies toured London this week. He was pretty rattled by the bomb damage. Said we have to increase our preparations, start building public shelters—'

Claire interrupted. 'Sam, we don't want to give everyone nightmares. Sometimes I think you forget that little ears take everything in.' She hugged Nicholas against her.

'Harry's heading back to sea next week,' Mae said, trying to keep her voice light.

'Yes, off to Perth on Monday,' Harry said, stubbing out his cigarette and kicking it onto the nature strip.

'Then out to sea?'

'I imagine we'll be spending a fair bit of time in port, at least until she's repaired; then a bit of patrol and escort work. Hopefully nothing too taxing—unless the Jap situation changes.'

'Which ship?'

'The *Sydney*.'

'Mate, that's fantastic! Especially after their victory in the Mediterranean.'

'It's a dream come true, mate, an absolute dream come true. Mae's a bit nervous about me being away, but I couldn't pass it up.'

'Don't you worry—we'll take care of Mae, won't we, Claire? I'll look forward to hearing all about your adventures when you return. I almost wish I was going too.'

CHAPTER 4

May 1941

GRACE SAT AS FAR as she could from other people in the movie theatre. She didn't want to hear people chewing their crisps or slurping their lemonade. She didn't want to hear the murmur of their conversation or hear them wriggling in their seats. Her Saturday night movie time was sacred, especially when it was a Torchy Blane movie. Torchy was everything Grace aspired to be: a sassy, blonde, fast-talking girl reporter working for a big city newspaper. Grace had dull brown hair and too many freckles, but her grandmother always said being clever lasted longer than looks, so Grace had focused on her studies.

Growing up in a small town one hundred and twenty-five miles north of Melbourne, she'd spent her spare time working for her father's newspaper, the *Benalla Star*. On weekends and during the school holidays, Nev let her report on the farming field days and regional agricultural shows, and when she turned fourteen he let her write movie reviews. That's how she discovered Torchy Blane. Watching Torchy's first film, *Smart Blonde*, Grace could scarcely breathe. Torchy was sensational. Somehow she managed to look like a magazine model while she talked and reported and solved mysteries like a man, all the while knowing exactly what to say to her policeman boyfriend, Steve. And best of all, there was a whole series of Torchy movies: *Torchy Blane in Panama*, *Torchy Gets Her Man*, *Torchy Blane in Chinatown*—films that showed a woman could be just as good a reporter as any man, if not better. Of course, that was in American newspapers; things seemed to be different here in Australia, with women's by-lines almost non-existent.

Since she was twelve, Grace had spent her weekly allowance on America's *Life* magazine, poring over the astonishing photo-essays of Margaret Bourke-White and Dorothea Lange. Seeing their work, she couldn't under-stand why her father refused to let her work as a reporter on his paper when she finished school; why he insisted that reporting was no job for a woman. 'There's not enough soft stories to keep you busy,' he'd said. 'I need a reporter that can cover anything—a real reporter who eats, breathes and sleeps news; someone who sees headlines in everything around them.'

'Send me to the cattle sales, the meatworks, I don't care. Bushfires—I'm not scared. I'll even do footy training.'

'Yeah, the footballers'd love that. I'll be chased out of the pub if you start swanning around the change rooms. Besides, you can't take a job away from a feller, someone with a wife and kids to support. It's just not right.'

'But it's all right for me to work as a teacher or a nurse. Men do those jobs too. How is that different?'

At this point in the argument he'd always huff and turn his attention back to his work. 'Anyway, work's just till you're married. Then you'll make way for another girl.'

As soon as she'd finished her leaving exams, Grace enrolled at secretarial college in Melbourne and set off for a new life. At college she learned reporting skills by stealth; growing particularly proficient in typing and shorthand, which she'd need when she applied for the next round of cadetships on *The Tribune*.

As Grace stepped out of the theatre into the evening gloom, she began composing a film review in her mind.

Torchy loses her spark. Miss Jane Wyman was sweet as Torchy but she was no Glenda Farrell. The story hit all the familiar plot points as Torchy exposed a counterfeit ring, but Wyman brought none of the sass and brass Torchy fans expect. A serviceable attempt but not a patch on the originals.

Although the film was disappointing, Grace had just spent ninety minutes *as* Torchy Blane, and no new actress could spoil that for her. She'd probably go back and watch the film again next weekend and the one after that.

Leaving the cinema, Grace continued to explore her new home: the narrow lanes, the food markets, the hospitals, hotels and restaurants. But no matter where she walked, she was always drawn to the true centre of the city: the Fields emporium and its five storeys of style. It was unlike anything she'd seen in Benalla. Fields sold every type of outer and underwear, shoes, handbags, hats and cosmetics, and anything you could possibly need to furnish a home. She rarely bothered looking at price tags. Apart from a pair of stockings or a hanky, Grace knew she couldn't afford to buy anything; it was enough just to look at the scarves and perfumes and the elegant salesmen and women dressed in black and white with their perfectly coiffed hair. Being a Saturday night, Fields was closed. But that didn't lessen its appeal. As she examined the window displays, Grace pulled her coat closed over her home-made skirt and blouse, determined that one day she'd be able to afford smart dresses and suits like the ones on the mannequins.

Grace walked another block up the hill to the Georges department store. While she'd often walked through Fields, Georges was another prospect entirely. Its windows gleamed and giant crystal chandeliers were visible through the doors when the shop was open. Sometimes she stood on the opposite side of the street at lunchtime, watching women with elegant shopping bags dangling from their wrists swishing in and out of the gleaming entrance. She'd never been told she didn't belong in that world, but instinctively she knew you had to grow up shopping in a place like that to feel comfortable.

She walked back down the hill alongside the *Tribune* office and stood at the corner to wait for her tram home to Richmond and the rooming house she shared with twelve other single women. Most of them were secretaries or teachers, some seeing boyfriends, others waiting for their fellows to come home from the war so they could marry.

Grace had never had a boyfriend, never wanted one apart from Mick Foster, Benalla's star footballer who'd lived next door to Grace. All the girls loved Mick, especially on the football field. He didn't have movie hero looks, like Gary Cooper in *Mr Deeds Goes to Town*—or Phil Taylor from the newsroom, for that matter; Mick was a pink-skinned redhead who'd shot up to six foot three when he was just fifteen. But his smile was enough to set a blush racing from her toes to the tips of her ears. No one else had ever had that effect on her, so she figured it was probably love.

Sometimes she'd found herself glancing at Mick's lips, imagining how kissing him might feel, but apart from holding hands, she had no idea what else she was supposed to do with a boyfriend. She knew about the birds and bees, but had no idea how things progressed to that stage. What do you talk about with a boyfriend? she'd once asked her mother. *Whatever they're interested in, dear*, had been the reply. No help there! So, unless she met a nice boy soon, someone with enough gumption to make the first move, it was likely that she'd turn nineteen in October without ever having been kissed other than in her imagination. OLD MAID CELEBRATES FIFTY YEARS AS NEWS SECRETARY. What an epitaph! She had no idea how, but somehow she was going to become more like Torchy, starting with making some new friends.

❧❧ ❦ ❧❧

The next morning, Grace woke as the church bells chimed seven. She made herself a cup of tea and two slices of toast then returned to her room to get ready for church. Each week she tried a new church to see which one she liked best. Today she was heading away from the city and out to Hawthorn. The same tram that brought her home from town continued into the suburbs, so it would be an easy ten- or fifteen-minute trip. She combed her hair, powdered her face and applied the lightest hint of mascara, just enough to widen her eyes. She blotted her lipstick, pinned her hat in place and grabbed her handbag.

Hurrying out the front door, Grace saw a tram gliding slowly past her stop. Waiting for the next one might make her late, so she ran as fast as her shoes would allow, hoping to catch up with the tram before it crested the hill and started to gain speed. Several boys leaned out the window and urged her on. When she was close she leaped, two men grabbing her arms and helping her up onto the running board. She hung on to a leather strap and caught her breath.

Shops and factories melted away as they crossed the river, the road instead becoming a boulevard lined with golden-leafed trees and large Victorian-era homes. When the tram finally reached the bluestone Anglican church, half the passengers stood and filed off. It seemed this was one of the more popular churches in town. With fifteen minutes to spare, she wandered along the path towards the crowd gathered around the doors.

'Miss Fowler?'

Grace turned and came face to chest with Phil Taylor, dressed in a dark grey suit and a black coat. His arm was held by a woman almost exactly his height, with platinum blonde hair and Chanel red lips.

'Miss Fowler, I didn't know you came to this church. I've not seen you here before.'

'Good morning, Mr Taylor. It's my first visit. I'm trying a different church each week.'

'That's very ecumenical of you.'

The woman beside Phil held out her unoccupied hand. 'Caroline Strickland. It's lovely to have you with us, Miss Fowler.'

'Sorry, Caro. Grace—I mean Miss Fowler—is our secretary at work. Well, Sam's secretary, I suppose. She's new to town; she's come up from the country.'

'How lovely. Well I do hope you'll choose our little church as your regular. We have all sorts of activities for young people too. You never know who you might meet.'

'I'd ask you to sit with us, Miss Fowler, but Caro and I are part of a christening this morning—godparents and all that. We have to sit with the family.'

'That's fine. Maybe another time. Enjoy the christening.'

Phil and Caroline walked towards a crowd of particularly shiny, well-dressed people, the women in furs and pearls, the men in tailored suits.

Grace felt a pang of loneliness as she watched the parishioners laughing and greeting each other, reminded of what she'd taken for granted living in the country. She'd never known what it was like to be an outsider, yet here she was, working long hours and spending her time lost in movies. It was a far cry from Phil's glamorous life. Caroline was stunning, her green eyes sparkling even early on a Sunday morning. The pair of them looked like they'd be just as at home on the silver screen. SCREEN GOD AND GODDESS SPOTTED IN HAWTHORN. GOLDEN COUPLE

OUTSHINES PARISHIONERS. SECRETARY SEES WORLD IN HEAD-LINES, JUST LIKE A REAL NEWSMAN.

Her father had had no idea how much of a reporter she was inside, how much she longed to tell stories—stories that mattered. But as much as she dreaded telling her father she'd ignored his wishes, she knew she'd have to tell him the truth when she got a cadetship. She hated lying. Once, when she was about ten years old, her mother had sent Grace to the shop to buy a canister of tea, and Grace had stolen some of the change to buy lollies. Normally the type to make a bag of freckles last an entire week, she scoffed a penny's worth behind a bush on her way home. But instead of enjoying them, she was overcome with anxiety, worried that she had chocolate between her teeth or hundreds and thousands melting into her cheek. When her mother questioned the change, Grace had burst into tears and admitted everything. She'd never eaten freckles again. Her mother still teased her about the episode and Grace still felt guilty.

So, no, lying wasn't an option. And she shouldn't have to lie. *The Tribune* was one of the best papers in the country. But if she got a cadetship her father would think she'd disobeyed him and that might put him into one of his tempers. She was far enough away now that she didn't have to fear his temper anymore, but he could still take it out on others—her mother, for instance. Grace imagined Nev's angry, red face, his hand swishing through the air and walloping the side of her head so that her ears rang for days after. He left bruises but rarely drew blood, that was one good thing, but her mother was getting frailer as she got older. If she fell the wrong way when he struck her, she could easily hit her head.

Filing into the church behind the crowd, Grace sat in a pew at the back. She looked at the sea of contented faces around her. Maybe she should settle for what she had. If she married a nice reporter, she'd still get to live in the world of the newsroom through her husband without risking her father's wrath. But would it be enough? And why should she have to give up without achieving any of her dreams? GRACE FOWLER QUITS BEFORE SHE BEGINS. No. She looked towards the pulpit. *Sorry, God, but:* GIRL REPORTER DOESN'T GIVE A DAMN ABOUT MARRYING!

CHAPTER 5

May 1941

HARRY HAD BEEN GONE just over a month when Mae packed for the move to her family's house in Yarraville. She'd filled her own suitcase with loose clothing and nightgowns, and a smaller case with tiny baby clothes, nappies, bottles and blankets. *Only a few more weeks*, she thought, as her heart pounded from the exertion of walking along the street to Claire's house. Here she was, the size of a house with feet like melons, but she was grateful that this pregnancy had been different from the last three. Mae held on to the handrail and hauled herself up the four steps to Claire's front door. As soon as she knocked she heard footsteps running along the hallway, followed by a thud against the door then the wail of a young child.

'Who's a duffer then?' Claire said, rubbing Nicholas's head as she opened the door. 'He was so excited when I said you were coming.'

Nicholas looked up at Mae with huge blue eyes full of tears. 'Bump!' he said as he rubbed his forehead.

Mae examined the red mark on his head. 'Yes, I expect you will get quite a bump.'

Nicholas took Mae's hand and tried to pull her along the hall.

'He wants to show you something in his bedroom,' Claire said. 'I hope you don't mind.'

Mae smiled. 'Not at all.'

As Nicholas led Mae along the hallway, Mae admired the wide, light-filled space that had no clutter, just a low line of bookshelves along one wall and framed newspaper pages above. The headlines screamed the big news events of the last twenty years: the stock market crash of 1929, Britain declaring war on Germany in '39.

'Sam's best front pages,' Claire said. 'We've just had them framed. He won awards for both of them.'

'Quite an achievement,' Mae said, thinking she'd love a gallery like this for some of Harry's drawings, when they had a bigger home. Claire and Sam's house was at least twice the size of their cottage, so it was easier for Claire to keep it neat, but Mae wondered if it might be possible to tidy any more of the clutter at home before she left. Stepping into Nicholas's room reminded Mae of *Alice's Adventures in Wonderland*. Everything was child-sized: the small bed, the small desk and chair, the rocker covered with cushions and two soft bears. A wardrobe and a small chest of drawers completed the furnishings. Nicholas pointed at a rug strewn with wooden blocks.

'Falled down!'

Mae wondered whether he was about to cry again. Instead he plopped down on the floor and started building, working quickly to finish the tower while he had an audience. Mae realised that she'd soon be doing this every day: sharing her home with a little person, playing games, teaching him or her to read, to eat. She'd be soothing scrapes, sewing tiny outfits, mashing vegetables. Claire said looking after Nicholas took all day, that sometimes there was barely time to dress herself or eat a meal. Mae wondered how that was possible. Surely babies just slept at first, and then when they could walk you'd send them off to play in the yard. She'd have plenty of time to read and take in some tailoring; that was how she planned to earn extra money for the house while her children were young.

The baby somersaulted in her stomach, digging a tiny hand or foot into her bladder.

Claire appeared at her side just as Nicholas placed the last block on the wonky tower. Willing the block to stay in place, Mae clapped enthusiastically. The sound must have startled Nicholas, as he kicked his foot forward, sending the tower tumbling to the mat. Anguish creased his forehead and his lip trembled again. 'Your fault!' he sobbed, looking squarely at Mae.

'Nicholas!' Claire said. 'Mrs Parker was being kind to you. Say you're sorry for being so rude!'

The boy looked at his mother but refused to look at Mae.

'It's all right, Claire. I scared him.'

'No, it's not all right. Nice little boys are not rude to

visitors. And if they don't apologise when they're naughty, they don't get lunch.'

Mae saw Nicholas's little shoulders slump. 'Sorry,' he muttered to his shoes.

'All right, Nicholas,' said Claire. 'Your sandwich is on the table.'

He raced out of the room towards the kitchen.

'I'm sorry he was so naughty,' his mother said with a sigh.

Mae smiled. 'Don't be silly. He was fine. Anyway, it was my fault. I never know how to behave around children.'

Mae often found Nicholas's behaviour unfathomable. One moment he was all smiles and chattering happily, and the next—for absolutely no reason—he was lying on the footpath crying and refusing to move. It had made some of their recent Wednesday walks to the beach nearly twice as long. Claire assured Mae that it was all quite normal and that every three-year-old had tantrums, but Mae couldn't believe any child of hers would be so poorly behaved, especially in public. *There must be something wrong with the little poppet*, she'd told Et after an incident involving a dropped apple slice. It was so bad that Mae and Claire had to pretend to walk away and leave him outside the butcher's shop. Quite a crowd had gathered across the street to watch, tittering behind their hands. Eventually he noticed his mother had moved away, and he leaped up and ran to catch them, wiping his eyes and nose on his jumper sleeve. *It's terrible, you just never know when he's going to erupt*, Mae had said. Et had just laughed and nodded. *Yes, quite shocking, indeed.*

As the women walked to the kitchen Claire explained that dealing with toddlers was all about bribery and coercion. 'It's not hard, but sometimes I feel like he only behaves so that I'll feed him. I'm told that only gets worse as they get older.'

Pausing in the kitchen doorway, Mae laughed at the sight of Nicholas standing beside his chair eating a sausage sandwich with his nose, mouth and chin coated in tomato sauce.

'Nicholas gets his table manners from Sam's side of the family,' Claire quipped.

'Does Sam have a large family? You never say much about them.'

'I never got to meet them. They all died when he was a boy, just twelve. His brother Geoffrey was killed at Pozières, in France, in 1916. His mother died a few months later from a heart attack. Sam says it was from a broken heart. The next year his father succumbed to the Spanish flu. After that, Sam was alone. An aunt raised him for a few years, then he got a cadetship at the paper and moved to Fitzroy. The aunt moved to Tasmania and he never saw her again. She died a few years later.'

'How awful for him. It's lucky that he met you and got to start his own family.'

'He took a bit of convincing though. He was so sure that everyone he loved would die, he refused to court anyone. Then, when we married, he was reluctant to have children in case he lost them too.'

'How did you change his mind?'

'I was his secretary, as you know. He'd been a police

rounds reporter for many years and I met him when he was just starting his time on the news desk. He started getting invitations to the theatre, to restaurant openings, to awards dinners. He refused to go at first, saying he wouldn't know what to do, what to say; that he didn't have a spouse. The paper's editor-in-chief, Mr Gordon, ordered him to go along to represent *The Tribune*. So Sam said that if he had to go then I'd have to go with him.'

'That sounds very glamorous! A lovely way to start a romance.'

'It was a terribly slow process. He kept things completely professional for two years, only accepting invitations to the things Mr Gordon couldn't attend. He still preferred to drink with the police after work rather than dressing up and hobnobbing. We always had a lovely time on our outings, so when I wanted to move things along, I figured my best plan was to make him miss me. I went away on holidays with my parents for a few weeks and that knocked some sense into him. He said 'yes' to every invitation after that, as long as I was free to accompany him.'

'Ingenious.'

'I thought so. Then, of course, I launched an assault on his stomach. I started baking scones and pies and cakes and bringing them into work.'

'Well, he wouldn't have stood a chance after that,' Mae said, eyeing the cinnamon teacake in the centre of the table.

'His favourite,' Claire said, slicing portions and placing them on plates. 'He'll be happy to see this for his supper.'

'If we leave him any.'

Mae felt another twinge stab her belly. Growing pains, she thought, shifting her legs to the side in search of a more comfortable position. Through the open window Mae caught a waft of salty air. That was one of the reasons she and Harry had moved here instead of closer to her family. Williamstown was the perfect location for them: only two train stops from Mae's aunt Et and uncles Albert and William, and close to the sea for Harry, who hated living anywhere he couldn't smell salt spray. She loved breathing the sea air, knowing that he'd be breathing in the same scent thousands of miles away.

Mae leaned forward to scoop a teaspoon of sugar for her tea. Her hand was halfway to the caddy when another pain gripped her stomach. She gasped and dropped her hand to her belly.

'Mae, are you all right? Your face has gone deathly white.'

Mae looked down and saw blood splashes on the floor beneath her chair. The stain slowly spread and her heart began to pound as she realised something was very wrong. *Oh, Lord, please no—not like my mother!*

'Claire?' she whimpered.

'Here, let's have you lying on the floor. We need to get your legs up.'

She let Claire help her lie down then Nicholas began to cry.

'Mumma, she's bleeding.'

'I know, darling,' Claire said calmly. 'Get Mummy some towels, please.'

Mae clutched her stomach as more pain gripped her belly. It felt like something was trying to tear her open. The floor beneath her dipped, the walls swayed.

She could hear Claire's voice speaking faintly, as if from a long way off.

'Mae, can you hear me? I'm leaving you for a minute to call an ambulance. I'll be back soon.'

Mae tried to reply but exhaustion overwhelmed her. Fear ebbed away. She was cold, she needed a blanket. Most of all, she needed Harry.

When Mae awoke in hospital the next day, Et was by her side, knitting something small and white. Mae lay very still, watching the needles clacking. Her aunt's expression was a mixture of concentration and tiredness, the circles beneath her eyes closer to black than their usual purple smudges. Knowing Et would start to fuss as soon as she realised Mae was awake, she waited a few moments before drawing attention to herself. Without moving she took in as much of her surrounds as she could. She was lying on her side. She couldn't feel anything from her waist down. She had flashes of what she assumed were memories: lying on Claire's floor; swaying and rocking in the ambulance; feeling pain and cold; then nothing— until now. It was impossible to tell whether the baby was still inside her or not. She lifted her hand and moved it towards her stomach.

'There you are, dear. Don't fret; you're safe now.'

'Et, the baby?'

'Fit and well, down in the nursery. You can see her in a couple of days, when you feel stronger.'

'Her? She's a girl?'

'Yes, dear. Quite the dramatic arrival, but she's doing very well. You will too, when you recover from the surgery.'

'Surgery? What do you mean?' Mae tried to sit up, conscious again that she couldn't feel anything below the waist. 'What's happened? Where are my legs?'

'Settle down. You had a hysterectomy, to stop the bleeding. They had no choice. You'll be fine in a month or two.'

'A hysterectomy? But that means no more children!'

'No dear, no more.'

It took several moments for Mae to realise that she was crying. All that time expecting the baby, all those lost babies, and now, no more. Harry would be devastated. He'd always said he planned to have a football team. Each time she'd lost a baby he was every bit as upset as she was—not tearful, but painfully quiet, serious, for weeks at a time. He'd tried to be cheerful for her sake, bringing flowers, rubbing her feet, even cooking eggs on toast a couple of times for their dinner. But it seemed he took as long to recover—to find his smile—as she did.

❧❦❧

In the days following the birth, Mae hardly slept. She was in pain from the operation and was constantly poked and prodded by the doctors and nurses. All she wanted to do was curl up with Harry, somewhere quiet away from the bustle. He'd make her feel better. Because it seemed nothing was going right. Being four weeks early, the baby spent her first week in an oxygen tent as a precaution. She was ten days old before Mae held her for the first time. The nurse tried to help her feed the squawking and fidgeting child with a bottle. It ended with mother and child in tears and the nurse taking over.

'She just needs time to get used to you,' the nurse said brightly. 'You'll get the hang of it.'

While the other mothers in the ward cooed and smiled at their babies, Mae tried to comfort the angry-faced infant that seemed to hate her. Mae couldn't understand why the baby wouldn't settle.

'Some of them are just like that, especially when they come early,' another nurse said.

A small stream of visitors—women from church, neighbours and Harry's family—brought booties and bibs and lots of advice. As each visitor dispensed wisdom on subjects like how to soothe a crying baby, how to avoid colic, how to wash nappies, Mae began to dread taking the baby home. There was so much to remember; her visitors were overwhelming her with information. But she smiled, thanked them for their gifts and nodded politely when they said her life was complete now she had a child.

'You're both doing well, Mrs Parker,' the doctor said during their third week in hospital. 'The baby has put on weight. You'll be ready to leave in a few days.'

Mae wept.

'That's right,' he said with a smile, 'your ordeal is nearly over. Now you can get on with things.'

41

But they weren't tears of joy.

Mae watched rain pouring down the windows and whitecaps whipping across the bay, wishing she could turn her life back to the way it was before Harry left.

The bell rang for afternoon visiting hours and within minutes Mae saw her aunt striding towards her.

'How are you feeling, my dear?' Et asked. She reached into a large shopping bag and pulled out a stack of clean, pressed nightgowns. She laid them on the shelf in the cabinet beside Mae's bed.

'The doctor says I should be ready to go home later this week.'

'That's wonderful news; everything's ready,' Et said, sitting down in the chair beside Mae's bed and pulling from her bag the baby blanket she was knitting. 'William's put the pram in your room. She can sleep in that for the time being. I'll wash and starch your old layette. It's big for the pram but it will suffice.'

'Thank you, but please don't go to any more trouble. I can just wrap her in blankets.'

'Nonsense. No child of this family will be treated like a foundling.'

Mae sank back into her pillows, not caring about winning the argument. 'It's just for a few weeks, Et. I'll be going home soon.'

Et tutted as her needles flew at lightning speed. 'It makes no sense to waste money renting a house when you could easily stay with us. Harry will be gone for at least six months and you're trying to save for a house.'

'It's important to me, Et.'

'You get your stubborn streak from your mother, dear. She'd never be told anything and she made some terrible decisions over the years.'

'Like marrying my father?'

'Well, in a way, but if she hadn't married him we'd never have had you, would we?'

Mae had only ever seen one photograph of her parents together: their wedding picture. She'd never heard much about her father, just that he'd left to find work up north when her mother was expecting. As far as she knew, they'd never heard from him again. Her mother, Katherine, moved home to be with her sister and brothers then died giving birth. As a girl, Mae was drawn to stories of single children and orphans, but she also wondered how it would feel to be part of a real family; a mother and father, brothers and sisters. She was so close to finding out, but what if Harry had changed his mind and didn't want to be a father after all? He seemed pretty keen to be at sea. Maybe he only liked the idea of fatherhood. Or what if he thought she was a bad mother, a bad wife, now she couldn't give him more children? He might leave, just like her father had, with no explanation. She'd have to go home to her aunt and uncles for good. Mae knew better than to ask about her father; Et refused to talk about him. But she suddenly needed to know much more about her mother.

'Do you think my mother would have been good at raising me?'

'She'd have been very good; she certainly would have made a much better job of things than we did. It took three of us to muster half the ability your mother had in her left hand before you were born. She mothered all of us, you know, especially William when he was injured.'

'You didn't do too badly with me.'

'We did what we had to do, and now you will too.'

Mae dropped her voice so the other patients wouldn't hear. 'I don't know if I can. I think the baby hates me. All she does is cry when I go anywhere near her.'

'Don't be silly. They all do that.'

Mae reached for her hanky. 'Do you think Harry will mind only having one child? I couldn't bear it if he thinks I've let him down.'

'Mae, there's nothing more you could have done. It's very likely that what happened to you is exactly what killed your poor mother. Besides, Harry adores you. Just count your blessings. People dream of having a life like yours—especially now, with the war on.'

Mae looked out the window and sent another silent plea for Harry to return. There'd be no one to help when she and the baby left the hospital. Et would be working at the shop all day, and William and Albert were too old.

'Have you thought any more about a name for the baby?'

'I've decided on Katherine—Katie for short—after my mother. Harry and I talked about that name for a girl.'

Et smiled and set her knitting aside to pat Mae's hand. 'She would have been terribly proud. What about a second name, dear? Elizabeth after Harry's mother?'

'I suppose we'll have to, since there won't be any more,' Mae said. 'But I'd prefer to name her Esther, after you.'

'Oh no! You know I hate being called by that name.'

'You used to let *him*!'

Et closed her eyes momentarily. 'How do you know that?'

'I saw it on the back of the photograph you showed me.'

'Of course,' Et said, looking back to her knitting; a white blanket with cables done on the finest needles. Et had already finished a matching cardigan. At least the baby would leave hospital in style.

'This is nearly finished. What else do you need? Singlets? More hats? We don't have much time to get ready.'

'She has more than she needs. We might have to start giving things away.'

'They don't tell you how much mess babies make. She'll use it all.'

Mae pictured the baby's cot in the spare room of their cottage, the pram in the hallway. She imagined Harry carrying the baby down the hospital steps to a taxi, settling her on Mae's lap, then tucking a blanket around them for the trip home. Then they'd begin life as a family, Harry smoking a cigarette and reading the paper as she fed Katie. After the baby was asleep they'd eat dinner and snuggle in front of the fire, just the two of them, as though nothing had changed. Everything will be so much better when Harry's home, she told herself. It will be just perfect.

CHAPTER 6

September 1941

SAM'S TELEPHONES RANG FASTER than Grace could answer them. As soon as she transferred a call the phone would ring again. The stack of messages from reporters across the country grew as they called to discuss their stories before the news conference in twenty minutes. Grace loved the constant drama, never knowing what each day would bring. The only thing that would make it better was adding her own stories to the list.

She spent her spare time researching and writing stories, then typing them up after Sam left the office. Practice stories about homeless families she saw in the Botanic Gardens, an interview with the men fishing off Station Pier in Port Melbourne, who turned out to be a foreign merchant crew who couldn't afford to buy meals during shore leave so they were catching their supper. Only one of the sailors spoke halting English, but she'd managed to find out that the war was making people suspicious of foreigners, so they weren't welcome in their usual cheap pubs and hostels. She'd left several stories on Sam's desk but never had a response. He was probably trying to spare her feelings. After all, she'd had no real training.

As she sorted Sam's messages and handed them over, he nodded his thanks but stayed focused on his work. That was one of the things she'd enjoyed most about working for him over the last six months: no matter how busy Sam was, he never shouted at his staff, never lost his temper. When he was busy he put his head down and concentrated on his work until the edition was safely put to bed. But so many of the reporters were signing up and heading overseas that gaps were opening on the staff roster, and the growing number of empty desks was making her restless. Twice now she'd raised the subject of a cadetship. His firm response was the same each time: 'No, not possible, Miss Fowler.' So she'd changed tack, casually mentioning stories she'd covered on her father's paper; the fireman who baked fruitcakes for the local nursing home and the elderly librarian who loved to tap dance. Colour stories, yes, but she was happy to start there before being given harder news.

'Good morning, Miss Fowler. How are you today?'

Grace felt the hairs on her arms rise. Whenever she looked up from her typing lately, she'd catch Phil Taylor staring at her. Her skin would tingle and she'd quickly look away. The first few times she'd thought she must have buttoned her blouse strangely or perhaps her hair was sticking out at a funny angle, but several trips to the ladies' room had assured her all was in order. He probably wasn't really staring at her, she reasoned, but was just lost in thought as he worked on a story and his gaze happened to be turned in her direction. After all, he seldom spoke to her unless he needed something from Sam.

'Can you let Sam know I've finished my feature article?' Phil said now, standing by her desk.

'Does he know what it's about?'

'It has to do with how the war's affecting the racing season. There probably won't be many more races after the Melbourne Cup week. Not enough diesel to transport the horses.'

'I see, well that sounds quite serious.'

Grace noticed that Phil was leaning awkwardly to one side, supporting his weight on the hand he'd placed on her desk.

'Are you all right? You look as though you're in pain.'

'It's nothing, just pulled a hamstring when I was training.'

'Football?'

'No, I'm a runner—a sprinter, actually. One-hundred-yard dash.'

'Goodness, do you need time off for treatment?'

'No, nothing like that. I've got the nationals next weekend; I should come good in time.'

'Injuries are so miserable,' Grace said, thinking of Mick's football injuries. He seemed to be on crutches at least once each season.

'Do you play sport, Miss Fowler? Netball, tennis?'

'I'm more the enthusiastic supporter.'

'Integral to any team,' Phil said with a wide grin.

Grace's blush raced from her chest to her forehead. One of her telephones rang and then the other.

'If you could tell Sam I need to talk to him, tomorrow will be fine.'

'I'll let him know.'

Grace watched Phil limp back to his desk as she answered the calls and quickly wrote messages. Phil smiled at her as he sat, but her mood sank when she realised that his gaze had probably been fixed on Sam all this time, not her. How stupid! He was just like Mick, who had always treated her like a little sister. And having met Caroline, Grace knew it was impossible that Phil could see her as anything other than a mousy little secretary. So why was she still blushing whenever he paid her any attention? She really needed to grow out of that habit, and fast!

When the last edition was finished, Sam stood and stretched, grabbed his jacket and notebook then said he was off to see Mr Gordon.

'I'll probably be there for a while, Grace. You might as well head off too.'

'Phil Taylor wanted to see you about his story on the horse races. He said it's finished.'

'Goodo. Tell him to come and see me in the morning.'

Grace looked across and saw that, again, Phil was watching. She nodded her head and mouthed, *Tomorrow*. He smiled that big bright smile of his and replied, *Thanks*.

The following Sunday after trying another church, Grace took the tram to the library in the city and climbed the two flights of stairs to the reading room with its soaring dome and wooden desks arranged like bicycle spokes. She stacked the week's magazines beneath a reading light and began to leaf through them one by one, adding to her list of possible profiles. When she opened the *Melbourne Magazine* and scanned the society page, her heart leaped painfully at a picture of Phil holding hands with Caroline in the ballroom of a Toorak mansion. He looked like a dream in his tuxedo, but she couldn't drag her gaze away from their clasped hands. The caption added to her pain: *Belles of the Ball. Miss Caroline Strickland and her childhood sweetheart Mr Phillip Taylor provide the glamour at the annual Lord Mayor's Ball. The pair remain tight-lipped about wedding plans.*

Grace suddenly ached for home, for fresh air, sunshine and a bright blue sky, a place far from the newsroom and a time before she'd set eyes on Phil Taylor. She knew it was silly to feel upset. It wasn't as though Phil had ever shown any interest in her. He was always polite, of course, but he'd hardly asked her a question about herself; what sort of reporter did that make him? One who thought she had nothing interesting to say, that was for sure. Well, that was about to change, she decided. She might not meet people he found fascinating or go to the same parties, but that didn't mean she had to live down to the stereotype of a mousy secretary. She could still have fun. Some of the girls at work had invited her to their monthly Friday night dinner, to be held the following week. She'd been invited once before but declined because she wanted to see a new Torchy film. This time she'd make sure she went.

❧

Friday night in the ladies' lounge of the Duke of Wellington Hotel was crammed to overflowing with tables of raucous women celebrating the end of the working week. Well, almost the end. Many—including Grace—would be expected to front up to work the next day, although by the looks of it some would have quite sore heads. There were four other women at her table: two secretaries from the advertising department, Del and Jo, as well as Angela from accounts and Barbara, a reporter from the women's page.

Grace glanced at the spare chair beside Barbara, loaded with their coats. She'd been looking forward to her night out with the girls all week, but that afternoon Barbara had mentioned that the women's page editor, Avril Johnson, would be joining them. Grace had spotted Avril on her first day at work: tall, platinum blonde and impeccably dressed in the finest tailored suits, she was Torchy Blane incarnate. Avril glided instead of walking and she seemed also to have Torchy's confidence. When Avril wanted to see Sam, she often bypassed Grace all together, calling his name from across the newsroom as she homed in on his desk. A slight grimace usually preceded his polite smile as she approached. He'd never said anything disparaging about Avril, but Grace could tell from the way his mouth tightened when he spoke to her that she set him on edge. Keen to make a good impression on Avril, Grace carefully nursed a port and lemonade while the other girls drank glasses of beer from a jug.

'Would you like a cigarette, Grace?' Barbara asked, offering her tin of Craven As.

'Thank you, but I don't—' Grace stopped abruptly as Barbara suddenly straightened in her seat and her gaze shifted over Grace's shoulder towards the door behind her.

'Good evening, ladies,' Avril said as Barbara whisked the entire coat pile into her own lap. 'Thank you for saving me a seat.'

'I wasn't sure you'd come to a place like this,' Barbara said.

'Nonsense. It's important for reporters to stay in touch with the hoi polloi, no matter how senior their position,' Avril purred as she removed her gloves and placed them in her handbag.

The two secretaries, who had been wearing their gloves while they drank their beers, hurriedly removed them under the table.

Avril was at least five years older than Grace. The rumour was that although she had never married, she had no shortage of men friends who took her to the city's most fashionable restaurants. She was always immaculately turned out, like something from the fashion pages. She must get good discounts from the retailers, Grace thought. Or maybe she got free samples.

'Miss Fowler, so lovely to see you away from that desk. Sam must make you work the most frightful hours.'

'I enjoy it, Miss Johnson,' Grace said. She managed to

refrain from blushing, but her skin prickled as she became the centre of the table's attention.

'Do you drink riesling, Miss Fowler? I'm about to order a bottle. I know Barbara will join me.'

'I'm fine, thank you. It will take me a while to finish this. And please, call me Grace.' Grace followed Avril's gaze down to her glass that, thankfully, looked more like red wine than the sweet drink she'd ordered, hoping it looked more sophisticated than beer.

When Avril brought the wine back to the table and poured two glasses, she proposed a toast. 'To Barbara. Congratulations on your engagement, darling.'

'Engagement!' screeched Del. 'You minx, you never said anything.'

'Avril made me promise to save it for tonight, so we could all celebrate together.'

'When? How? Tell us all the gories!' Del demanded. 'Do you have a ring yet?'

Barbara described how her fiancé Andrew had asked her father for her hand before proposing at her parents' house in Gippsland over the weekend. He'd given her his late mother's ring, marcasite surrounding a single diamond.

'And the wedding?' Del asked. 'Have you set a date?'

'We're planning on late May, when it's cool but not quite winter.'

'Very sensible, Barbara—much better for dressing up,' Avril said, before she switched her attention back to Grace.

'So, Miss Fowler—sorry, Grace—what are your ambitions? Working till you marry your school sweetheart? Fishing for a reporter? Maybe your soldier is overseas?'

'She's got a thing for Phil. You should see her blush whenever he talks to her!' Del said.

Grace felt her skin redden. She couldn't speak. How on earth did Del know that? 'I don't,' she gasped, wishing she could slide under the table.

'Oh, you poor dear.' Avril laughed. 'Our very own Olympian scores another member for his cheer squad.'

The other girls laughed. Barbara put her arm around Grace's shoulder. 'All the girls love Phil,' she explained. 'He's a complete darling, but he's never dated anyone at the newspaper, has he, Avril?'

'I'll only say that running's not the only thing he deserves a medal for.'

Grace stared at Avril, who looked far too pleased with herself to be joking.

'Don't listen to her, Grace,' Barbara said. 'She's just teasing. Avril always says he's too young for her.'

'To marry, Barbara—I said he was too young to marry! But Caroline's proving me wrong on that front. They'll be announcing any day now.'

Grace lifted her drink and drained the last inch and a half in one swallow.

'That's the girl. Here, have some wine.' Avril poured some riesling into Grace's glass.

Grace took a sip. It was surprisingly sweet and fruity, not nearly as bitter as beer.

'Well I hope they'll be very happy,' Grace said as her stomach warmed. It felt like she was blushing inside.

OLYMPIAN AND DEBUTANTE TIE THE KNOT. OLYMPIAN WINS DEBUTANTE'S HEART.

'Speaking of happy marriages, when are you finishing up, Barb?' Del asked.

'Two weeks before the wedding,' Barbara replied.

'After all the time I've spent training you, now I have to start again with someone new,' Avril said. 'Such a waste. But those are the rules: as soon as you marry you have to give up work. That's why I won't marry anyone who isn't rich. I couldn't stand spending all day stuck in the suburbs with nothing to do and nowhere to go.'

Grace's heart fluttered. She'd never told anyone at work about her dream of becoming a reporter, but she'd be crazy not to try for Barb's job. If she didn't grab this chance, she'd have to wait until the next reporter decided to marry. That could take years.

'How will you choose a replacement? Will you take a cadet?' Grace asked.

'Oh, we have a long list of hopefuls; daughters of editors and society types, girls who are already well connected.'

Grace poured herself another wine. 'You won't look at applications from outside?'

'No need. There are already plenty to choose from, aren't there, Barb?'

'Yes, you'll hardly know I'm gone.'

'Well, this party needs a lift—food anyone?' Del asked.

Grace was starting to feel dizzy. She didn't know whether it was from the wine or all the rotten news she'd heard tonight. If this was a night out with the girls, she wasn't sure she wanted to do it again. She thought of pleading a headache and leaving, putting the night behind her. But Barb seemed nice; she wanted to stay and be part of her celebration. Maybe food would help, and a bit more wine might calm her down. That was the way it worked, wasn't it? Her father always said a few drinks helped him to forget his troubles. She was beginning to feel like she had a few troubles of her own. What if Del told Phil that Grace was sweet on him? What if half the newsroom knew? How could she convince Sam to override Avril and give her a chance in Barbara's job? GLUM SECRETARY ASKS: WHAT WOULD TORCHY DO?

CHAPTER 7

September 1941

My darling Sunny,

I am delighted to hear that both of you are getting along nicely and I'm anxious to come and see for myself. I requested weekend leave for next Friday but it wasn't granted.

We all expect leave now that we are in the east, but at this point it seems no nearer than when we were in the west. I can't wait to see Katie's smile. You say she is a pretty little baby. Well that's only to be expected when she has such a lovely mother.

That is all of my news for the moment, so I will close with lots of love—all of it to you and a big kiss for the smiler.

Your devoted and loving Harry

Mae pressed on her stomach with one hand and used the other to hoist herself into a more comfortable position.

Four months had passed since Katie's birth, but moving about still required effort. Struggling to stand for more than five minutes, Mae relied on her uncles to walk with Katie when she cried.

'You forget, Mae, we looked after you when you were a baby,' William said, gently jiggling the baby on his shoulder until she burped.

'You do have a knack for coaxing wind.'

'It's not the first time I've been told that,' William said, reaching over to lay Katie down on the bed between Mae and the wall. 'Would you like me to burp you too?'

'That will be quite enough out of you,' said Mae, clutching her stomach again as she tried not to laugh.

Katie had refused to settle that night. She fed, but she refused to sleep for more than a few minutes at a time.

'Shhhhhh,' Mae whispered, as William left the room. 'You've worn Uncle William out and Et will be grumpy if you wake her too early.'

Katie wailed again. It was just after six and Mae barely heard the knock at the door.

The floor shook as Et stomped along the hallway. 'That will be the neighbours complaining about the noise,' she huffed. 'Well they'd better get used to it because babies cry, and they get louder as they get bigger.'

Mae heard the door open, but instead of raised voices, she heard a muffled squeal and the shuffle of footsteps heading down the hall. A tall figure strode into her room, threw his hat on the chair and scooped her into his arms.

'It's so good to see you,' Harry said, kissing her cheeks and forehead and her lips.

'I had no idea you were coming,' she sobbed. 'How long—?'

'Just the weekend.'

Mae hugged him tighter.

'Dear little Sunny, are you still in pain?'

She shook her head and pulled away just enough so she could see his face. 'It only hurts when I laugh. And when I walk. And lift. Really, I'm much better.'

Mae followed Harry's eyes down to the small bundle lying quietly beside her. He reached over and picked the baby up, holding her towards the window and the early-morning light. Holding her breath, Mae watched as her husband cradled his child for the first time. His eyes moved over Katie's face, taking in her tiny nose, her bow lips, her chubby little chin. He moved the blanket down and pulled out one of her hands, which wrapped itself around his little finger. Her eyelids twitched as she drifted toward sleep. He kissed her head then stood and put her in the pram, which still doubled as a bassinette.

'You've made a lovely baby, Mrs Parker,' he said softly.

'Thank you, Mr Parker, but I can't take all the credit.'

Slipping his shoes off, Harry slid under the blanket beside her and pulled her close. 'I can't tell you how worried I've been. I thought I'd die if something happened to you. And when I finally heard the news, I was desperate to see you, just for five minutes, just to make sure you were all right.'

Mae stroked his shoulder and ran her hand through his hair. 'I was so scared I wouldn't see you again or that the baby would die. If it wasn't for Claire—'

'How long till you recover?'

'The doctor says another few months. But I won't stay here that long.'

'Don't rush it, Sunny. Stay till Christmas or New Year, then I'll be home to look after you both.'

'Really?'

'That's the plan. Back to teaching on dry land. Our boys should be right to go overseas by then.'

'That's good, darling. As long as it's what you want. And you're not sad that—that we'll never have a son? I couldn't stand it if you were.'

'Of course not. You're still here and we have a beaut little girl. I'm going to spoil her rotten. I'll buy her dollies from all over the world. Do you think she'd like a train set? Or a pony?'

'I'm sure she'd love both. And you can teach her to draw and play the violin. She already makes as much noise as you do.'

Harry kissed her again. 'And I can watch her grow. If she looks like you, I'll be able to imagine you in all the years before we met.'

'She might look more like you. What will you do then?'

'I'll just have to pretend.' Harry slid carefully out of bed. 'I have something for you,' he said, rustling through the duffel bag he'd dropped on the floor. 'Close your eyes.' He placed a parcel on her lap. 'Okay, now open.'

Mae clapped her hands together like a five-year-old then carefully slipped off the string and brown paper. Inside was a Chinese box, lacquered in bright red enamel.

She flipped the brass clasp and lifted the lid. An embroidered silk pouch sat inside. Mae loosened the ribbon at the top of the pouch and removed a jade bracelet carved with Chinese dragons.

'How gorgeous,' she said, slipping the bracelet onto her wrist and holding it up to the light. 'Just lovely. Wherever did you find it?'

Harry chuckled. 'A market in Singapore. I knew you'd love it as soon as I saw it. It's almost translucent, like your skin.'

'Thank you, darling, it's beautiful and the box will be perfect for keeping your letters. Everything is perfect, just perfect.'

❦

Katie's cries roused them an hour later.

'She certainly has a powerful set of lungs on her,' Harry said, carrying the baby into the kitchen.

'We were wondering when you two would emerge,' William said, rising to shake Harry's free hand. 'What do you think of young Katie here? Bit of a treat, isn't she?'

Et grabbed the kettle off the stove and filled the teapot. 'Are you ready for breakfast? We've been waiting. I've made enough porridge to sink a ship!'

Harry walked over and threw his arm around her shoulders, kissing her on the cheek. 'With treacle? I can't think of anything better.'

Et giggled then gave the porridge another stir. 'She likes to be rocked rather than jiggled,' she said. 'Just lay her sideways and sway a bit. That will settle her.'

Harry was amazed when Katie nodded off immediately. He looked around the room triumphantly, as though he was the first father ever to stop his baby from crying.

'You look well, son—a bit underfed, but the salt air obviously agrees with you,' William said.

'The chef makes porridge but it's nothing like yours, Et. In fact, none of the food's much chop.' Harry winked at Mae's aunt. 'Three days of your home cooking will be heaven.'

'Does your mother know you're home?' William asked, glancing at Mae, who scowled as she poured the tea.

Harry sat down at the table, still holding the baby, and tucked into a bowl filled to the brim. 'I'll call her after breakfast, if you don't mind me using the telephone.'

Et pushed the cream jug towards Harry. 'I imagine Elizabeth will want to see you today. Will you go to visit?'

'I'd like to, but I'm not sure whether Mae's up to travelling.'

'Tell Elizabeth she's quite welcome here,' Et said. 'The whole family. Just let me know how many are coming before the shops close at noon.'

Mae reached over and took Katie, who began sucking noisily on her bottle. 'Et, that's too much. You can't do an open house on such short notice. Who will work in the shop this morning?'

'Mrs Green and her daughter are running the shop. I've already asked them. I'll bake a sponge with Mrs Watson's eggs and William can get a leg of mutton if we're having a houseful for dinner.'

'Don't tell me that ratty old hen's still going?' Harry asked. 'Still pecking everyone's ankles?'

'She still lays like a trooper. Lovely big golden yolks. We've got six layers now, but she rules the roost. Even crows like a rooster.'

Harry smiled. 'Et, if you're going to all that trouble, you'll be needing a special treat.' He walked to the door and disappeared for a few moments. He returned holding a parcel. 'After the way you've looked after my girls I couldn't come home empty-handed.' He leaned down and kissed her cheek again.

Et carefully untied the string, winding it into a small ball for reuse, then unwrapped the package, smoothing the paper against the table as she went. She gasped as she opened the final layer to reveal heavy black silk embroidered with red, pink and gold flowers. She stood and held the robe against herself, the dense material falling to her ankles. 'Oh, Harry. It's far too good for me. I'll put it away and Katie can have it when she's older.'

'Nonsense. It's to make you feel like a queen. Katie will have plenty of her own clothes.'

Mae had never seen Et so thrilled. Of course she deserved thanks. Mae mentally kicked herself for not doing more to show her appreciation. She'd begin by cooking dinner in the evenings, she decided, and today she'd offer to do the vegies for the roast.

❧

At lunchtime, Harry's mother Elizabeth, his younger sister Mim, and his younger brothers Richard and Eric climbed the front stairs onto the verandah, the boys calling Harry's name. When William opened the door, they almost knocked him sideways in their rush to shake Harry's hand and slap his back.

Mae walked slowly into the hallway to greet the visitors. She needn't have bothered. Harry had Elizabeth hugging him from the front and Mim hugging from the back.

'Where's my granddaughter?' Elizabeth demanded from beneath a purple velvet hat, a net veil over her eyes. 'I want to see her with her father.' Harry's mother always wore the same old-fashioned outfit on Sundays: a white pin-tucked blouse under a grey jacket and an ankle-length skirt. She hated 'peacockery' and frivolity, she declared, and everything associated with fashion. She wouldn't dream of buying anything at Et's dress shop when she still had children at home to feed.

Et handed Katie to Harry. 'Here we are, Daddy.'

'It's uncanny,' Elizabeth said, drawing a hanky from her sleeve and dabbing her nose as she looked from father to daughter. 'If I didn't know better I'd swear I was looking at you as a bub.'

'She has to look like me so I know which cave to return to after a hunt.'

'Oh, Harry, you do say the funniest things. Just like your father. It's so important to have a husband with a wonderful sense of humour, don't you think, Mae?' She threw her head back and laughed so hard Mae could almost see down her throat.

'Yes, Mrs Parker. My husband is wonderful.'

Harry leaned across and squeezed Mae's hand and grinned.

Elizabeth shifted her attention to William. 'Where's Albert this morning? I would have thought he'd be thrilled to see Harry.'

'Albert stays at his club in town on Friday nights. He catches up with old friends from his regiment.'

Mae noticed a smirk between Et and William, but the moment passed.

'I'm surprised he hasn't been dragged out of retirement,' Elizabeth said, her gaze fixed on Harry and Katie. 'The railway must be crying out for engineers with all of the younger fellows joining up.'

'If things get worse, they'll probably call him back, meanwhile he's enjoying bossing the air-raid wardens at the town hall. He's quite in his element there.'

Et herded everyone into the sitting room. Mim sat beside Harry and asked to hold the baby. Katie had just started smiling and with Mim making a fuss, she broke into a wide toothless grin.

'Harry, I brought your fiddle,' Eric said, holding up two violin cases.

'Great, I've been dying for a session,' Harry said. He removed the instrument from its case and held it to his chest. He plucked the strings to check they were in tune then he drew the bow across them.

At the sound of the familiar chords Elizabeth yipped with joy. '"Danny Boy"—your father's favourite!'

Eric picked up the other violin and joined in.

Mae had forgotten how beautiful Harry looked when

he played, and how much she loved watching him, his eyebrows lifting and falling, his mouth grimacing, as though he were summoning each note from his soul. It gave her the chance to examine his face, imprint his features on her mind without him getting embarrassed. And it didn't matter who was in the room, she always felt that he was playing just for her. When they'd first courted, he used to serenade her with romantic Italian tunes. He didn't sing; he said the violin did his singing for him. And he hated playing 'Danny Boy', because he thought it was sad, but his mother loved it so he always made the effort.

He looked up and smiled at Mae, as though reading her thoughts.

When he'd finished playing, Elizabeth leaned across and put her hand on Harry's arm. 'It's so good to have you home, dear. Tell us about the ship. Your letters say so little. What's it like at sea?'

Harry smiled. 'To be honest, Mum, it's all pretty dull. When I'm not running the men through drills, I wash and iron my clothes, write letters, play cards and chess.'

'That does sound tedious. What about when you're in port?'

'We're doing lots of repairs, so I don't have much spare time. She was damaged pretty badly in the Mediterranean. A few weeks ago I went up to the art gallery in Perth to see if I could do a class, but they don't run a school there.'

'Poor lamb. It must be frightful. Especially with Mae and Katie being so ill. You must have been awfully keen to get home.'

'That's certainly been the worst of it,' he said, pulling Mae towards him. 'It's a relief to see both of my girls doing so well.'

Mae could have sworn she saw Elizabeth frown before she smiled stiffly at Mae, nodding. 'Yes, she's a strong woman. A remarkable recovery indeed.'

Harry beamed and squeezed Mae tighter.

'So what's really happening on those sorties of yours?' William asked. 'Any sign of Jerry?'

Harry relaxed his grip on Mae's shoulders. He hesitated then looked across at Richard and Eric and back to William.

'To be honest, it's all getting a bit worrying.'

Inside, Mae's heart thudded in panic, but she managed to arrange her face into a calm mask.

'We're seeing more and more evidence of German movement in the region. If we don't stop them in Europe soon, they might help the Japs get a stronger foothold in the Pacific.'

'Do you think they'll invade?'

'No. They're spread too thin. The Germans are trying to blockade supplies and troops. But the Japs are a problem too. They've taken half of China and everyone reckons it's only a matter of time until they push further afield.'

William leaned forward, rubbing his knee. 'If they move down through Borneo and New Guinea we'll be in a right pickle. The papers say the United States must demand full Japanese withdrawal from China. Otherwise they'll just get more confident and the situation will drag on.'

Harry nodded. 'We need to shore up our defences in Singapore and Malaya.'

Richard said, 'What about here? Any activity around the coast?'

'More than you'd think, mate,' Harry replied sombrely. 'We've been racing up to ships day and night, making sure they're all above board, trying to stop the Germans picking off our merchant ships. They've already taken a few. We had a pretty exciting trip up the coast last month—found some sort of practice target, but not like anything we use.'

Mae willed her face to stay calm. She wanted to hear his story but she also wanted to cover her ears and tell him not to go back to sea. He wasn't supposed to be anywhere near danger; he was supposed to be safe.

She glanced at Harry, whose eyes had narrowed, as though he were reliving the moment. 'It was a clear day; we could see for miles. We were cruising way off the coast and out of nowhere we came across this thing bobbing around in the ocean: a big raft with trellis built up on all four sides— about fourteen feet high, very strong, built for heavy seas.

'We stopped for a while to make sure there were no subs waiting to take pot shots, then we lowered a dinghy with a few fellows to check it out. They towed the thing back to the ship and used the Walrus crane to lift it onto the deck. It looked pretty new. The enemy must have been practising with it, took off when they saw our masts on the horizon.'

William thumped his fist onto his bad leg. 'So you were within a few minutes of an enemy raider off Western Australia?'

'Looks like it. One bloke joked about a Kiwi ship being off course, but most of us were chilled to the core. To think they were that close and doing target practice . . .' Mae heard a slight catch in Harry's voice. She squeezed his hand a little tighter and pulled their clasped hands to her chest.

'Surely there can't be enough Germans around here to do any real damage,' Richard said.

'They can sink our ships and mine the ports,' William said. 'It's madness that we're not hearing the full story. That newspaper mate of yours should do more, Harry. People need to know how hairy things are getting in our own backyard.'

Harry spoke quietly: 'It's hard to know what the government makes of all this. It seems to be a case of "so far so good", but that could all change tomorrow.'

Mae nodded slowly. *Everything will be fine, just a few months more*, she told herself. The navy would never let the *Sydney* out on its own if the enemy really were that close. There was no way they'd risk losing their greatest warship.

CHAPTER 8

AFTER HARRY'S FAMILY LEFT, he sat at the kitchen table with Katie firmly in the crook of his arm, feeding her a bottle while Mae and Et did the dishes. Albert was home from his club and William could barely keep his eyes open.

'She's a trick, isn't she?' Harry said fondly, not taking his eyes from the child.

'Well, son,' Albert said, 'you've certainly taken to this fathering caper. A natural, I'd say.'

'It's not hard when they're like this, all sleepy and warm.'

'She's not always like that, you know. Sometimes she keeps us up for nights on end.'

'Albert, I can't tell you how much—'

Mae's uncle waved away his thanks. 'We're happy to have them both here. Given all of us oldies a new lease of life it has. Especially Et. She has real get-up-and-go again.'

'I don't know how Mae would have managed without you all, nor me for that matter. When I heard what happened, I just wanted to come straight home.'

'Mae's our flesh and blood, a daughter to each of us. Now Katie is too.'

'I've always been curious, Albert. You can tell me it's none of my business, but you would have been a great father. Why didn't you marry, have kids of your own?'

'That was never going to be my path, son. I was happy to raise Mae, but I was never destined to go forth and multiply, if you know what I mean.'

Mae noticed Harry's puzzled expression, but before he could question Albert further, Katie began to whimper and he returned his attention to his daughter.

❧

After putting Katie to bed in her pram, Harry stood by the mantelpiece in the bedroom. He'd already lit the fire and snaffled a bottle of brandy and two glasses. Propped on the bed against two snowy pillows, Mae drew her knees to one side, leaned on one elbow and held her glass in the other hand. Taking a small sip, she felt the hairs stand up on her neck as Harry sat down beside her and softly stroked her leg. Her body always responded to his touch in this way, sending tingles to surprising places. Once, when he'd rubbed her left foot, she'd felt her right earlobe tingle. He gazed at the section of her leg he was stroking as though seeing it for the first time, then his eyes swept slowly towards hers with a look of wanting she remembered from her dreams.

'Our first night together as parents,' he said.

She slipped off her dressing-gown, revealing her best white embroidered nightgown.

'You look positively bridal, my gorgeous, radiant Sunny.'

'A little battle-scarred, I'm afraid.'

'I think motherhood has made you even more beautiful.'

'We can try if you like,' she said shyly, 'although I don't know how I'll go.'

Leaning across her body, Harry kissed her softly, then more deeply as he lifted the glass from her hand and put it on the table beside his. Mae slid her hand inside Harry's shirt and then down to the drawstring of his pants. Harry stroked Mae's hair back from her face. 'Are you sure you're ready?'

'I want to,' Mae whispered, looking down at his fingers, which had halted above her cleavage. 'I need you to know I'm still the woman you married.'

'You're so much more than that.' He dropped his hand and ran it across her knee, lightly stroking the pale skin of her inner thigh.

Lifting his shirt, Mae leaned across and kissed his flat stomach, smooth and taut.

'I don't want to hurt you,' he said.

She sat up and raised her nightgown above her head, dropping it suggestively on the floor. He stood and removed his remaining clothes then lay beside her, kissing her softly. 'We'll take this slowly.'

Mae slid her hand over her caesarean scar and the pouch of stretch-marked, saggy skin. Harry moved her hand away and ran his tongue along the scar's length, kissing it at each end. Mae tried to relax. Her stitches were long gone but the skin was still sensitive to touch. The wet line burned as it cooled. She looked at the top of his head. How could he make love to her ugly scar, still so angry and red? She tried to push his head away, but he stayed. She gently pushed his head back. 'I want to see your face.'

Harry hovered a moment longer before he slowly moved his hips towards hers and began to enter her.

Mae concentrated on relaxing, keeping her breath even. After the first tentative thrusts, she realised she was too dry. It hurt each time he moved, as though she was being scoured with sandpaper.

Harry's eyes were closed. He sighed softly. His weight pushed her into the mattress.

Mae had thought she could do this; she wanted to with all her heart, but the pain built, like a red-hot poker stabbing deep inside. She tried to change position, to push his shoulders up and away from her, to ease his weight off her stomach. But nothing helped. Crying out in pain and frustration, she punched him in the shoulder, but his rhythm didn't change.

'Stop!' she shouted. 'Stop it!'

Harry returned from his distant place. 'What's wrong?'

'Please get off me,' she said, pushing at him.

'I said to tell me if it hurt.'

'Couldn't you tell?'

'Well, no. I thought you were enjoying it.'

'You had your eyes closed. How would you know?'

Harry sat up and ran his hand through his hair. 'You should have said something. I'm sorry, I didn't know.'

Mae pulled her nightgown towards her and yanked it over her head. 'How could you not notice?' she sobbed.

'Come back here,' he said, reaching for her.

'It's time for Katie's feed,' she said, rising from the bed. 'I have to warm the bottle.'

'I can do that; you get some sleep.'

'No, I need a cup of tea,' Mae said. She left the room.

✦✦✦✦✦✦✦

The next morning, Harry took Katie out in her pram while Mae slept.

'We've been saying hello to the butcher, the baker and the candlestick maker, haven't we, my precious?' she heard him cooing to Katie as they wheeled through the front door and down the hall to the bedroom. 'She's quite the social butterfly, smiling for them all. But I think she needs changing.'

'You might be right,' Mae said, brushing her hair. 'You go and have a shower. I'll do this.'

Harry gathered his shaving kit and some fresh underwear. 'Are you all right?'

'Of course. Everything's good.'

'I thought you might be angry about last night.'

'It couldn't be helped.'

'You haven't looked at me once this morning.'

Mae stood at the dresser selecting clothes for Katie. Her cheeks burned with shame, and she felt like she was about to cry. But she forced a smile. Remember to be gay, to be perfect, she reminded herself, turning to face him.

'I'm fine,' she said.

'What time did you tell my family to be here?' he asked.

'Around one o'clock.'

'I'm not sure how many we'll have today. There's my mother, and Mim is bringing her fellow, plus they'll invite everyone who couldn't make it yesterday.'

'Harry, no! I thought it would only be a few.'

'What's the matter? They said they'd bring all the food and drinks.'

Mae bowed her head and spoke quietly. 'I know you think I'm being selfish, but I just can't bear to share you with the whole world again today.'

'It's not the whole damned world,' Harry protested. 'It's my bloody family.'

'Don't use that language here—you're not at sea now,' Mae cried, tears streaming down her cheeks.

Harry reached out and pulled her close. 'I'm sorry. You're not being selfish. It's hard enough fitting everything in to a normal leave, but you're not well. I'll take Katie to my mother's this morning, then we can spend the afternoon together, maybe take Katie to the zoo. Later we'll have dinner with your family. How does that sound?'

'I'm ruining your plans.'

'Don't be silly. I'll ask Et to feed and bathe the bub before we go.'

❧❦❧

Mae spent a couple more hours in bed reading then set her hair in rollers and spent time ironing a dress and fixing her make-up. She hadn't used rouge or powder since before she'd had Katie. It felt good to take a little trouble again with her appearance. Slipping into her favourite pale green linen dress, she was surprised to find the zipper gliding over her waist with room to spare. She buttoned a cardigan over the dress then put on her hat and gloves, ready to catch the train to meet Harry and Katie in town. It felt strange walking along the street without the pram. She felt light, unencumbered—apart from a small picnic basket. For just a few minutes, she didn't have to think about anyone else. But as lovely as this taste of freedom was, she also felt something was missing. Handbag, purse, keys, gloves, hat; she hadn't forgotten anything but she still felt like something was lacking. She smiled at the thought of meeting her husband and child at the station. It was so lovely having people to miss.

Arriving at Flinders Street just before one o'clock, Mae walked across the concourse and waited at their usual meeting place, under the portico beneath the famous clocks. It was really everyone's meeting place, and today it seemed that half of Melbourne was there. A moment later Harry arrived pushing Katie in her pram.

'Shall we go and get a little wild at the zoo?' he asked.

Mae felt like she had when they were courting; excited and safe at once. Harry rolled the pram out onto the footpath and Mae slipped her hand through the crook of his arm as they ambled towards the tram stop on the next corner.

The tram conductor picked up the front of the pram, while Harry stepped onto the running board then into the carriage before turning and holding his hand out to help Mae on board. They settled onto a leather bench seat and passed several blocks of shops before reaching the Queen Victoria market, bustling and humming with activity as fruit sellers and fishmongers shouted their afternoon specials.

The tram almost emptied at the market, the remaining passengers, lulled into silence by the straight, flat run past the university, as dappled light filtered through the plane trees. Mae nestled a little closer to Harry.

'What's in your basket, Miss Sunny?'

'Nothing much, just a few rock cakes and some milk for Katie. I didn't think you'd need to eat after lunch at your mother's.'

'But I left room. I thought there might be a sponge or something.'

'Oh well, we'll just have to make do, I suppose,' Mae said, lifting the lid of the basket so he could see inside. Mae had filled a thermos with tea, made roast lamb and chutney sandwiches and had bought neenish tarts and cinnamon scrolls from the bakery near the station.

'You tease. I can't trust a thing you say, can I? You'd make a perfect little spy.'

'Mata Hari had better watch out.'

'Indeed. My very own *femme fatale* who is also the perfect mother.'

'Speaking of babies, how did you go feeding Katie? Does she need another bottle or a nappy change?'

'All done before I left Mum's place.'

'Did you do it yourself or did you leave it to your mother?'

Harry blushed. 'Well, Mim was dying to have a go. I couldn't disappoint her, could I?'

'Harry Parker, you're the end.' Mae giggled. 'Brave enough to go to war but you can't change a baby's nappy.'

'Not true. It's just that, well, other people offered. I didn't want to be disagreeable.'

'All right then, next nappy change is yours. No excuses.'

'Whatever you say.'

The tram stopped opposite the wrought-iron gates of the zoo. Harry bought tickets then the little family passed through the turnstile into the park with its sculpted lawns and paths winding past the giraffe and monkey enclosures.

'Birds or beasts?' Harry asked.

'I brought your sketchbook, darling. What takes your artistic fancy today?'

'Hmmm. I feel like visiting the leopards. It's definitely a day for spots, don't you think? Then maybe the platypus tank, and we can show Katie the seals too.'

A few minutes later they settled on the soft lawn near the big cats' enclosure. Two lions roamed the fence line, roaring as though they could smell the lamb sandwiches. Mae set out the thermos and the food while Harry lifted the baby out of the pram and took her for a stroll around the cages, naming each of the animals. Mae watched as Katie tried to lift her head to look at Harry, more interested in his voice than what he was saying. As he pointed out the cheetah, Katie stared at him as though he were the strangest thing she'd ever seen. Harry turned at that moment, his nose wrinkled as he held Katie away from his chest. 'Nappy time.'

Mae laughed and lifted the baby bag. 'Well you'd better get on with it before you eat.'

'Do I do it here, or do I go to the toilets?'

'I don't think they have change tables in the gents'. You'll have to do it here then empty the nappy in the toilet.'

'Oooh!'

After Harry's nappy debut and a strong cup of tea, Mae sat back against a tree and fed Katie her bottle while Harry made quick sketches of leopards lying, sitting, prowling and licking their young. He would use the sketches to do more detailed drawings later, Mae knew. She loved watching him draw. He got the same faraway look on his face as when he played his violin. He never looked more alluring than he did when sitting on the grass like that, his legs stretched out, his shirtsleeves rolled to his elbows, his back slightly hunched over his sketchbook, and making such beautiful pictures.

Despite the awkwardness of the previous night, she felt desire stir in her chest, in her stomach. She longed to be home with him, lying in his arms, getting things back on track. She'd be happy to stay awake all night, holding each other, until he had to leave for the ship in the morning. But would that be enough for him? What if he tried again? She hoped he'd be happy to wait a bit longer. After all, they had the rest of their lives to make love.

Through the trees, Mae heard the sound of a band starting; clarinets and trumpets. Harry looked up from his drawing and grinned at the same time as Mae recognised the first tune: 'Moonlight Serenade' by Glenn Miller. Harry stood and brushed grass off his pants.

'Are you in the mood for a dance, Miss Sunny?'

Mae laughed and put Katie in her pram, then let Harry pull her close as they swayed on the lawn, other couples nearby following suit. Although the melody was beautiful, Mae always felt there was something a little wistful about it too, but she couldn't be sad in Harry's arms on such a perfect day. She let herself relax against his chest, happy to be led across the small lawn and onto the pavement beneath a giant Moreton Bay fig. Bats squawked and monkeys screeched, there was even some trumpeting from elephants in the background. The music had woken all the zoo's creatures and visitors from their mid-afternoon rest. She closed her eyes and let her mind dwell on the sounds and the smells. It was one of those lovely moments that she wanted to imprint in her mind and her heart forever.

<hr />

That night, after a leisurely meal with Mae's family, she and Harry returned to their bedroom.

'Et loved it when you had a *third* helping of her lemon delicious,' she said, surprised that she felt a little shy.

'Mmm. I don't think I'll be moving for a week.'

'I wish that were true.'

Light from a candle on the mantelpiece flickered across their faces.

'It's so hard to leave you,' Harry said, stroking her hair. 'Three days is nowhere near long enough. Every time we sail past the entrance to the bay without turning in towards home I feel like jumping over the side and swimming ashore. But at least we have the end in sight. I've promised to stay till the crew is ready to go overseas, but that's only a few more months. Each trip, I think, *Well that's one nearer to leave, one nearer to Christmas.'*

'Are you sure you really want to be on dry land again?'

Harry dropped his chin to her shoulder and rested his face against her neck. 'I loved being at sea when I was younger. But everything's changed now. I can't stand the thought of being away from you and Katie one second longer than necessary. After this is over, I'm never going anywhere without you again. We have a house to build, don't forget.'

'Our own home,' Mae said dreamily. 'Do you think we should have two bedrooms or three? We'll probably need a spare room for visitors like Alice and Jim and the boys. And we'll have a sitting room and a separate dining room with space for a buffet—like the one we saw in that shop, remember?'

'How could I forget?' Harry said, stroking her shoulder and kissing her neck. 'We'll need a big garden where Katie can play with her friends.'

'And garden beds so I can grow roses and vegetables.'

'And a garage, big enough for the car and my motorcycle.'

'Albert says we should get started building as soon as the war is over, when more workers are available and it's easier to get materials.'

'He's probably right. But we haven't bought the land yet. It takes time to find the right place.'

'We can build on my mother's block here in Yarraville.'

'But we agreed to build closer to where I'm working, down near Frankston, so I can get home a couple of nights during the week.'

'If these last few months have taught me anything, it's that I can't live forty miles out of town where I don't know a soul. I can't be so far from my family.'

'You can catch the train if you want to visit and we'll come up to Melbourne on weekends to stay with my mother or here with your family.'

'So we'll never spend a weekend alone? You want me to live a two-hour train ride from my family? And what if you get sent overseas? What am I supposed to do then?'

'I just assumed you'd want to be near me. My mother always followed my father.'

'And there it is: your mother!'

'What about my mother? What's she done now?'

'Nothing, Harry. Did she remind you of that fact today, about following your father? I can never live up to her standards, can I?'

'For God's sake. Can't we have one night without a bloody argument? This whole leave I've been walking on eggshells. What's wrong with you?'

Mae bit her lip and turned away, tears welling in her eyes. After everything she'd been through and he was only thinking of himself. She'd feared his feelings for her would change now she was a mother, and now it seemed it was true. The way things were going, he'd probably decide to spend more time at sea, leaving her home alone for years at a time. She couldn't blame him. She couldn't give him her body or more children, she wasn't perfect any more.

Maybe he was going to be like her father after all, moving on to a better life.

'I'm going outside for a smoke,' he said, pulling his dressing-gown tight around his waist.

'Don't wake me when you come back.'

<hr/>

Minutes became an hour and then another. When he finally returned, Mae turned her face to the wall, pretending she was asleep. Her anger grew as his breathing deepened into sleep.

He rose at five-thirty the next morning and showered and dressed, returning to their room to cuddle Katie before laying her beside Mae.

'It won't always be like this,' he whispered to Mae, who kept her face hidden rather than meeting his gaze. 'I never knew it was possible to love two people so completely, but you'll always be my number one girl.' He kissed her goodbye and walked out of the bedroom.

Mae got up and put Katie back in the pram as she heard the front door close. It was dark outside. She listened to his steps fade and pictured him turning the corner towards the station to catch the early train. She rolled over to his side of the bed and breathed the scent from his pillow through her tears. Katie began to cry.

CHAPTER 9

October 1941

FADDEN OUT, CURTIN IN screamed the front page of the first edition. Nine subeditors pounced on the bundle that had been dropped in front of Sam's desk by the copyboy. The men thumbed through the pages, quietly commenting on smudges that looked like commas and full stops, checking for mistakes. When they had agreed the copy was clean, they lit cigarettes, drained their mugs of tea and returned to their typewriters to work on the next edition updates.

Prime Minister Fadden had been voted out of office after just forty days in the job. Labor leader John Curtin was set to be sworn in as prime minister the following week. Most of the coverage was handled by Don Porter, *The Tribune*'s chief political correspondent in Canberra and Sam's best friend, but three other *Tribune* reporters were covering different aspects of the story, interviewing backbenchers, members of the Opposition, lobbyists, the numbers men. They worked together seamlessly. Grace was continually impressed by the skill and professionalism of the news team, and the way Sam filled the paper four times over, every day except Sunday. He was like a musical conductor, drawing contributions from every part of the newsroom to cover the stories of the day. It might be a major sporting event one day, a police story the next. Today the stars were the political reporters.

'Grace, can you get Don for me, please?' Sam requested. 'I don't care where he is—I need him on the phone now.'

Grace called Don's direct line but it rang out. She tried his secretary but got the engaged signal. She tried again and again, imagining she was chasing down a major story, close to deadline, trying to land an important interview. She'd have news editors, maybe even Sam, watching as she tried to get through to her source, to get the critical quotes that would complete the story. It was exhilarating but frustrating too. She tried Don's phone number again, then all the other *Tribune* numbers in the press gallery, but no one was answering. After ten minutes she looked up at Sam and shrugged.

Determined not to let him down, Grace decided on a new tactic, calling the *Gazette* secretary in Canberra to see if she could help. Although they were officially the opposition, the two papers shared an office. Surely it would be all right, just this once.

She got through immediately.

'They're all in a press conference with Mr Curtin, dear. I don't know how long they'll be.'

'It must be exciting up there, today,' Grace said,

hoping to keep the woman on the line until the reporters returned.

'Oh, we've had plenty of exciting days here recently, but this one's more hectic than most, I suppose.'

'It must be hard to keep up with what's going on; who's leading and who's voting with whom?'

'The reporters keep us all informed, so we're always first with the latest.'

'Maybe they should interview you.'

'I'm not very interesting, dear. The reporters are much better at explaining all the strategies and alliances. Here they come now. Nice talking to you, Miss Fowler.'

Grace got Don on the first ring then put him through to Sam. She'd been in the newsroom seven months now. Barbara wasn't leaving for another four months, so Grace was writing up as many story ideas as she could for her portfolio and pitching them to Sam whenever she got the chance. Her latest idea was compiling a list of profiles of women being deployed into war jobs at factories making munitions and uniforms. 'You could use my stories in the women's pages,' she'd suggested to Sam the previous week. 'I could do the interviews after work so they don't inter-fere with my job.' He'd actually smiled, as though perhaps he approved, then a ringing phone diverted his attention. She hadn't got an answer. Maybe she should just go ahead and write the first few and give them to him on spec. If he liked them they might get a run. If he didn't, well, at least she'd know where she stood.

'Hello, Miss Fowler. Can you get me a few minutes with Sam today?' Phil asked, startling her from her thoughts.

They'd barely even spoken in recent weeks. She'd wondered more than once if he was avoiding her, entering and leaving the newsroom through the back of the building. Occasionally she'd noticed him looking in her direction again. Could he tell she was daydreaming about him? Had Del said something?

Grace slowed her voice, keeping it free of emotion, thankful that at least the flush in her cheeks didn't feel as though it had spread to her neck and forehead.

'He's really busy with Don and the Curtin story. Do you want me to pass on a message?'

'No, that's fine. I'll catch him later.'

'Is everything all right?'

Grace watched Phil consider his response. 'Sam's asked me to think about how the paper should continue to cover sport, now that so much is winding back. I might have to hand over some of my reporters to the general round.'

He was interrupted by a sharp voice saying, 'Well, well. I wouldn't have thought this one was your type, Taylor, knowing what you've got waiting at home.'

Alan Swain, one of the paper's photographers, was walking towards them. Alan's black hair was so slick it was almost reflective. He had a Clark Gable–style moustache, trimmed to the thinnest line possible, but that was where the comparison ended. While the movie star was tall and handsome with an attractive smile, the photographer had small dark eyes that absorbed light instead of sparkling, a beaky nose and a permanent sneer.

'What did you say?' Phil demanded, turning to face Alan.

'No need to slum it with the help—although you big shot society types always like a bit of rough on the side, don't you?'

'Don't say another word, you little weasel!' Phil snapped. 'And you should apologise to Miss Fowler.'

'I've got nothing to be sorry about. You're the one who needs to apologise for swanning around town like an entitled brat, not doing anything useful like joining our boys overseas!'

Grace shrunk down in her chair. A bit of rough on the side? Was that how the newsroom thought of her? She scanned the room but no one was watching the exchange. They were all busy with their stories.

'Get out of my sight now, Swain,' Phil warned.

'Or what?'

'I'll report you to Sam and have you thrown out.'

'Miss Fowler, always a pleasure,' Alan said, nodding as he stepped past her desk and continued towards the darkroom. 'Taylor, please let your lovely fiancée know that I'm looking forward to her modelling shoot next week. Best part of my job, entertaining the models all alone in my studio.'

Phil flexed his hands then balled them into fists, anger squeezing his lips tight and making his nostrils flare. As Swain sauntered away he turned to Grace. 'Are you all right, Miss Fowler?'

'What did he mean?' Grace said as tears threatened to spill from her eyes.

'Nothing at all. Don't listen to any of his rubbish.'

Grace felt her heart pounding, as though she'd been chased. 'Is he always like that?'

'He's got worse over the last few months. I heard he tried to join the army as a photographer, but he was rejected.'

'So he's taking it out on us?'

'Swain's too much of a coward to do anything, but if he gives you any more trouble, let me know immediately. I'll sort him out.'

Grace studied Phil's face. He really did seem concerned. But that was just his way, she realised. He was a nice fellow looking out for the new girl, nothing more.

'Well, if you're sure you're all right, I'd better get going,' he said finally. 'Let me know if Sam has a moment tomorrow.'

❧ ❧

The following morning, Phil arrived at Sam's desk for their meeting. Grace had glanced in his direction a few times during the day; most times he was hunched over his phone taking notes, but a couple of times she'd seen photographers and reporters slapping him on the back or shaking his hand. They were congratulating him on something; he was all smiles.

'Have you had a chance to think about my request?' Phil said to Sam, his back to Grace as though trying to block her from their conversation.

Sam nodded. 'It's a big step. How does your family feel about it?'

'My father's all for it. Mother, well, she'll go along with whatever the old man says.'

'And what about—'

'No other considerations.'

'That's not what I've heard.'

'It won't affect this.'

Though she was pretending not to listen, Grace was desperate to see Phil's expression. She couldn't tell from his voice whether he was happy or sad. And what was he asking for? Sam's face gave nothing away.

'Well, you know what I think, son. I'll take it to Gordon and see what he has to say, but I'm all for it.'

'Thanks, Sam. I appreciate your support.'

Hmm, a mystery. STAR REPORTER COOKS UP A WINNING STORY IDEA. RUNNER SHAKES UP NEWSROOM. The exchange she'd overheard could mean anything. Was Phil going away? They needed a new bureau chief in Perth; perhaps he'd applied for that? Maybe that was why he'd been so anxious to talk to Sam—he'd wanted to make his case. But what about Caroline? Surely he wouldn't just go without her. Or maybe something was going on in Canberra. Was Don moving on? No, Phil must be joining up. Maybe he'd taken to heart what that swine Swain had said. Grace knew several of the reporters who'd gone to the front, but not well. Some of the boys from home had gone too. But despite the news reports that she saw each day, the whole notion of war seemed quite distant, an abstraction rather than a reality. There'd been no bombings, hardly any rationing; the only real impact on her life was the odd empty desk in the newsroom, and that might be something she could turn to her advantage. A bit of rough indeed!

CHAPTER 10

October 1941

DUST BILLOWED FROM THE lounge room curtains whenever Mae slid them open or closed. Mae had been home at the Williamstown cottage for three days, but getting rid of the dust and mustiness needed more than a cursory tidy. The curtains needed to be taken down and washed. The thought of wringing, drying and steaming the heavy drapes made her slump with exhaustion.

Opening the windows to let in the spring breeze, Mae saw a truck pull to a stop out the front. Two young men swung out of the passenger door and immediately lit cigarettes, as though drowning on fresh air alone. An older man slowly eased himself out of the driver's side door and walked towards Mae's gate. There was something familiar about him but she couldn't place him. Without waiting for his knock, Mae met him on the verandah.

'Mrs Parker?'

'Yes,' she said, still searching her mind.

'Jeremiah Johansson, Mrs Parker. We met in my shop a few months back, in the city. You looked at a buffet in my window?'

'Oh, yes, Mr Johansson. I remember—such a beautiful piece of furniture.'

'Mr Parker came to my shop when he was home on leave. I still had the buffet so he bought it and asked me to keep it until he wrote that you were safely home.'

Mr Johansson handed her an envelope and signalled to the other men to begin unloading. As they moved around to the back of the van, Mae read the note.

Dear Mr Johansson,
Thank you again for holding on to the buffet.
Mrs Parker is now recovered and will be at home next week, so please deliver the buffet to the address below.
Regards,
Harry Parker

Mae watched as the men wrestled the buffet through the gate and towards the front door.

'He came to see me with the dear little poppet in her pram. He was proud as punch.'

'My goodness. I had no idea. Just give me a moment to clear a space.'

Mae stepped into the front bedroom and dragged the linen chest that sat opposite the bed over to the window. How odd that Harry hadn't said anything. He must have bought it that dreadful morning he took Katie to his mother's, she thought sadly, recalling their arguments. She'd been so awful to him. It was no wonder he'd said nothing. He probably regretted the purchase as much as she regretted . . . If only she'd been able to apologise properly, instead of relying on letters that took weeks to reach him.

After the men left she stared at the buffet in her bedroom, aching to hold him and tell him that she hadn't meant any of it. Mae slowly arranged her shoes and hats and handbags in the buffet. That wasn't really what it was designed for, but it would do for now, until it had a proper dining room to live in, with a dining table and chairs and a fireplace glowing in the corner.

Minutes after the truck had left, Claire arrived with Nicholas and her new baby, Ella.

'I saw from the window—what were they delivering?'

'Come and see what Harry's done,' Mae said. 'We saw it months ago but decided to wait until we'd built the house. Then, when he was home last month, he went out and bought it to surprise me.'

'Oh, Mae, it's glorious,' Claire said, opening one of the doors and inspecting the shelves. 'Look, there's room for a bar in the end cupboards!'

'Harry'll love that. I'll put a bottle of Scotch and some glasses in there for Christmas. That way he'll hardly have to leave this room.'

Claire giggled as Mae dusted a framed photo of Harry in his uniform and placed it on top of the buffet beside their wedding picture. 'I can't believe we own this!' She beamed, imagining lying in bed beside Harry, the walnut gleaming in the morning light.

'You've both got wonderful taste. It will last a lifetime.'

Mae sighed. 'Well, as hard as it is to tear myself away, shall we walk first then come back for tea?'

'We might have to have a picnic here in your bedroom.'

'The first of many, I hope—when Harry's home.'

The cloudless sky had lulled Mae and Claire into believing the morning would be perfect for a stroll to the beach with the children. Walking along their street, Mae unbuttoned her coat. She took a deep breath of damp salt air and tipped her hat to shade her face. It was months since she'd felt this calm. She smiled, thinking about the buffet, picturing Harry in Mr Johansson's shop. How could she ever have doubted how much Harry loved her, how important she was to him . . .

As the women turned onto the Esplanade, they were blasted by a chilly sou'wester. Barely able to push Katie's pram into the wind, Mae quickly re-buttoned her coat and the two women hurried to a shelter on the edge of the sand. They flopped onto the wooden bench, warming their backs against the sandstone as they caught their breath.

'I'm so glad you're home,' Claire said, laughing. 'I've missed our walks.'

Nicholas picked up a hand-sized scallop shell and started digging a hole. 'That'll keep him busy for ages. Sam once told him that if he dug deep enough he'd dig all the way through to China. He's never forgotten.'

Mae peered into the pram to check that Katie was still asleep. 'I was beginning to wonder whether I'd ever do this walk again. Whenever I started to feel better, I'd do too much and end up in bed for a few more days.'

'Well, you mustn't overdo things now that you're back. Just call on me when you need a hand.'

'That's very kind. But only a fleet of angels will save me this weekend. I had a telegram from Harry's mother this morning saying she and Mim are coming to visit on Saturday afternoon.'

'You sound upset.'

'I'm terrified.'

'But why? Harry said his family adores you.'

'His brothers are lovely, but Harry's sister Mim is fiercely protective of him and his mother . . . well, he's the eldest and the favourite. In Elizabeth's eyes, even the Virgin Mary wouldn't be good enough for her son.'

'Oh dear! But surely she just wants to make sure that you're fully recovered and managing with Katie.'

'She promised Harry she'd keep an eye on me, but I know she's just coming over to find fault with everything; she always does. And the house just isn't up to one of her inspections.'

'I can help you get things ready, do a bit of cleaning.'

'Thanks, Claire, but I'm not going to do too much this time. Elizabeth will just have to make allowances.'

'Have you seen her since Harry's visit?'

'No. I'm a bit surprised she's stayed away from Katie for six weeks, but I'm glad. I couldn't bear to listen to her prattling on about her perfect son.'

'I thought that was the one thing you two agreed on: that Harry's the most perfect man ever to walk the earth.'

'He is, most of the time. When he's home I couldn't be happier, but sometimes—oh, I don't know. Sometimes when he's been away for a while it feels like he's a complete stranger, different from what I remember.'

'How do you mean?'

Mae hesitated. 'It's nothing. I'm sure I was still recuperating. We argued a bit—actually, quite a lot—when he was home last month. I tried so hard to be perfect, and it all went wrong.' Mae's voice quavered as the tears began to flow.

'Mae! You poor thing. I'm sure it wasn't that bad.'

'It was awful.' Mae blew her nose. 'I got upset with him for visiting his family and for —well, I don't know— for being so cheerful. How silly is that? I spent months wishing him home and then I spent the whole time upset with him. He must have thought I was a mad woman.'

'Don't be silly. Look how much he cares. He sent that lovely gift today.'

'Yes, but he bought that beforehand.'

'Sometimes, when Sam's working long hours on a big story, I barely recognise him. He gets cranky, can't stand any noise from the children. He yells and stomps, just wants to be alone. But once he's had a good night's sleep, he's a lamb.'

'What do you do when he's like that?'

'I try not to get upset, let Nicholas know that he hasn't done anything wrong, that Daddy's just tired. When he feels better, he tries to make up for it by being a saint, taking in the waifs and strays that wander through the newsroom. We had a lovely young boy from the country staying with us while you were away. The poor thing was so shy, and he had the worst skin you've ever seen. He cried himself to sleep every night for the first few weeks. But then he found his feet. Sam says the lad was adopted by the police rounds boys, but I think he might have met a girl. Anyway, he moved into a flat with some of the reporters. Sam says he's really stepped up his work as well. I must bake him some sausage rolls. They're probably terrible for his skin but he loves them.'

'Claire, I don't know where you find the energy to look after so many people.'

'I enjoy it, and you'll do the same when you feel better. Just give yourself some time, build yourself up for when Harry comes home. Is he still planning to be back for Christmas?'

'He says so—New Year at the latest. Just a few more months.'

'Sam will be happy to hear that. He can't wait to take him to the football, although they'll have to wait till next season now.'

'Harry was disappointed not to see you when he was home. He wanted to thank you for helping when Katie was born.'

'I was so scared, Mae. I can hardly bear to think about it.'

Mae squeezed Claire's arm. 'I can't wait for the New Year. We'll all have so much to celebrate.'

⁓⁓⁓⁂⁓⁓⁓

Early on the morning of Elizabeth's visit, Mae surveyed the house: still filthy. She decided to bake first, then clean. As she washed and dried two mixing bowls, she heard a quiet knock at the kitchen door. Claire stood on the bottom step holding a stack of biscuit tins.

'Claire! Is something wrong? The children? Sam?'

Claire shook her head and held the tins out. 'I hope you don't mind my coming so early. I've been baking for the reporters and I made some extra for Elizabeth's visit.'

Mae opened the screen door and Claire climbed the three rickety steps. Mae prised the top off one of the tins to find a dozen fresh lamingtons. The next held a cream sponge with passionfruit icing. The third was filled with melting moments.

Mae turned and hugged her friend. 'Your timing's perfect. It looks delicious. I can't thank you enough. She certainly won't be able to criticise the catering.'

'Maybe it won't be as bad as you think. After all, you're the mother of her first grandchild. If she gets you offside, she won't get to see Katie.'

❦

Elizabeth and Mim tucked into Claire's baking as though they hadn't eaten for a week.

'Goodness, Mae, however did you find time to do all of this?' Mim asked.

'It was no trouble at all,' Mae replied, biting into a cucumber sandwich; she'd made those herself.

'You seem so much better,' Elizabeth said. 'Katie's thriving.'

Mae saw Elizabeth's eyes darting from the rim of her teacup, around the room and back to her teacup. Mae shifted sideways in her seat as she realised her mother-in-law was struggling to pull her gaze away from the cobwebs in the corner of the dirty grey ceiling. Mae had learned to overlook the grimy paintwork and the peeling wallpaper. Without their modern lounge suite, the room would have been a complete hovel. But seeing the scene through the older woman's eyes, Mae felt her stomach tighten. She took another sip of warm milky tea.

Mim tried to daintily nibble a biscuit but it fell to crumbs in her lap. Pretending nothing had happened, she used the side of her hand to wipe the crumbs into a pile and then pushed them from her skirt onto the floor. 'We were so worried when we heard you were returning home on your own against Harry's wishes,' she said as more of the crumbs settled on the rug around her shoes.

Annoyed by the mess she was making, it occurred to Mae that, at sixteen, Mim was turning into her mother. She was assuming the same haughty tone, adopting similar mannerisms, even the throaty laugh.

'I'm feeling much better, thank you, and I have wonderful neighbours who help in all sorts of ways.'

'That's very reassuring, my dear,' Elizabeth said. 'Harry will be most relieved when I let him know how well you are doing. Now tell me, did you get a letter today? We had two in the morning post.'

Mae had received a long letter earlier in the week, she told them. 'He couldn't say very much of course. He mostly talked about what a wonderful time he'd had here in Melbourne and said they've been over in Fiji and training in the Pacific. Now they're back in Perth, but hopefully not for too long.'

'It's such a shame that you can't just get on a train and move over there,' Elizabeth said. 'That way you could see him whenever he's in port. He said some of the other wives have been taking rooms in Fremantle.'

Mae concentrated on keeping her voice even. 'Did he now! Well, until a few weeks ago, I could barely walk. I couldn't possibly manage a week-long train trip with Katie right now. And we don't have the money. Not when we're saving for our house.'

Elizabeth's mouth stretched into a tight smile. Her eyes remained cold. 'Of course, dear. If only you were stronger. And you must think of the future. I wish I'd been so sensible when I was your age. But nothing could have stopped me travelling around the countryside to be near Harry's father. It did mean the children rarely went to the same school two years in a row, but we just had to make do so we could be together. I'm glad we had so much time together before he passed on. I guess your situation is different.'

Mae could feel the perspiration beading beneath the linen collar she'd fixed at her throat with a brooch. The dreadful woman had no idea what she was saying. Harry's ship could suddenly arrive in Melbourne while she was on the train to Perth. Then what would they do? Her hands tightened their grip on the sides of her chair.

'Harry says he'll be home around Christmas and back to teaching.'

'Are you sure about that, Mae?' Elizabeth said. 'Now they've got him on a ship, they won't rush to post him back to land. And I'd be surprised if he chose to give that up for teaching.'

'What do you mean? He said he couldn't wait to get back home.'

'The *Sydney*'s everything he's dreamed of. He's worked for this chance his whole life, and it's wartime. It's a lot for him to give up just to be a teacher.'

'Our plans all centre around Harry being in Melbourne.'

'Plans change, life changes. Do you want to be the wife who made her husband miss the chance to fight for his country on the pride of the fleet?'

Mae was aware that both women were staring at her, watching her reaction. They were ganging up on her, but Elizabeth's speech seemed rehearsed. What if they weren't her thoughts, but Harry's? Could he have said something to his mother about not wanting to come home?

'Harry said he wants me to start planning our new home so we can start building next year.'

'I see. And how will you go about building a house forty miles away in Frankston while living in Williamstown without a car or telephone?'

'We've decided to build on my block in Yarraville, near my family,' Mae said, aware that they hadn't agreed at all but unable to stop herself speaking.

'You are? Well, I must say I'm surprised. Harry has always been adamant that your mother's land was yours to hold on to for a rainy day; that it's his job to provide for his family. You must have a special way of wearing him down.'

Mae rose from her seat, jerked the teapot away from the small table and marched into the kitchen for more hot water. *Silly cow*, she thought, stomping down the hallway. A wife's job was to keep the home fires burning, not to follow her husband around like a puppy. To make him a beautiful home that he never wanted to leave. And to make sure it didn't have enough room for Elizabeth when she grew old and feeble and needed nursing. Mim could look forward to that lovely task on her own.

As Mae returned to the lounge room, she heard her name being whispered. She felt a headache brewing in her temples.

'There you are. Mim and I were just talking about the parcel we're putting together for Harry's birthday. I'll make his favourite fruitcake so he can share it with the crew. He has so many friends on board, it will have to be a large one. And Mim has knitted him some new socks. What will you be sending, Mae?'

Mae hadn't given Harry's birthday a thought. It was nearly a month away. She bit her lip and tried to decide what he might like. A new sketchbook? Or perhaps a book of poems; he'd said he loved the Tennyson she'd quoted in her last letter. But best not to suggest that; Elizabeth thought poetry was for dreamers and fools. 'Harry bought some lovely dark blue silk in Singapore. I've been meaning to make up a shirt for him.'

'Well do try to get it finished this week so we can send everything together. That way we'll save on postage.'

Mim looked towards the door. 'Is that Katie? Can I get her up for a cuddle?'

Mae rubbed her forehead, relieved that their attention had shifted from Harry's birthday but reluctant to have

Katie's routine upset. 'Please don't disturb her sleep, Mim. She'll be crying for a bottle soon enough.'

'Mim's getting broody, aren't you, dear?' Elizabeth said. 'She can't walk past a pram these days without asking for a hold.'

'I've been thinking,' Mim said. 'Maybe I could come over and look after Katie on Saturdays, so you can get out and about, do a few chores.'

Mae looked from Mim to Elizabeth and back again. Both women were nodding as though they expected her to jump at the chance. Another idea they must have cooked up together. It would be lovely to have some free time, but what Mim was proposing was too much. Spending her day off with Katie every week?

'Mim, that's a lovely offer, but I'm not sure every week is a good idea while Katie's so young. Maybe when she's a little older. You're welcome to visit though—maybe fort-nightly?' As soon as the words left her mouth Mae was regretting them; she didn't want to see Harry's family that frequently. 'Or monthly perhaps?'

CHAPTER 11

24 November 1941

THE FLOOR SHOOK AS the presses thundered into action below. Midday already. Grace glanced over the diminishing collection of reporters and subeditors but no one seemed to notice the vibrations. She returned her attention to typing the news list for the later editions. Grace had been at her desk since seven that morning and the day had passed much like the day before and the week before that. Most of *The Tribune*'s news was now coming over the wire from overseas. There was almost no local news, apart from police and fire stories, and anything from the state and federal governments was going straight to the morning papers. Plans for a new eye and ear hospital in Melbourne had been released that morning: important but hardly riveting. Still, it was something for the remaining general reporters to cover. Something that would get a run, anyway. Many local stories now went to the specialist pages—the women's page, the social page, the sports pages and council news—to make more space for war news. Sam's main task was deciding which of the overnight war stories would get a run in the afternoon. Everyone wanted news of the campaigns being fought by their boys: their sons, fathers, husbands and brothers.

And with so little space for local news, it was getting harder to keep the reporters interested. The younger lads were joining up, their heads full of travel and adventure despite the rising death toll. Sam had said that if they continued to lose their youngsters, he'd have to bring some of the older newsmen out of retirement, or put on some women. Grace had skipped a breath when he said that but seeing her expression Sam laughed: 'Don't get your hopes up, Miss Fowler, the subs have threatened to quit if they see any more skirt in the newsroom.' Grace followed that conversation with another request for a cadetship, but he dismissed her, saying she was the best secretary he'd ever had; it would be too hard to let her go.

'Nearly done, Miss Fowler?'

'Yes, Mr Barton. Anything I need to add?'

'Barring catastrophe, we should be set. We'll lead with the Allied victory in Libya. More than one hundred and eighty German and Italian tanks destroyed. That'll show the Kaiser!'

'Yes, sir,' Grace said, trying to match his enthusiasm as the phone on her desk rang. 'Editorial, Grace Fowler speaking.'

'Good morning, Miss Fowler, it's Don Porter. Is Sam nearby?'

'Yes, Mr Porter, I'll put you through.'

Sam nodded and returned to his desk, retrieving the handset from under a clump of copy chits. Beside the phone, a sandwich curled out of its paper wrapping, the lettuce brown, the ham grey. Sam's ashtray was full and threatening to overflow. Grace hated the mess, but she'd clean up when he went to his editorial conference. REPORTER WORKS UNDERCOVER AS CLEANER.

'How's it going up there, Stretch?' she heard Sam say. 'Yep, all good here. We're leading with the news on Libya and following with Roosevelt sending in the troops to end the American coal strike. Apparently all his talk of support in the Pacific's been a complete bloody farce. They can't help us here if they're all tied up with domestic crap . . . Too right! So, what's the news from our illustrious leader today? More taxes? Another trip to the mother country?'

Sam sat forward in his chair, lighting a cigarette as he focused on Don's reply.

'Did he say which ship?'

Grace saw Sam frown as he scanned the newsroom.

'Well, stay on it and call me at home if you hear more. I'll ring the navy bods here, see if I can get anything out of them. What else have you got? . . . Okay, we can probably run a brief on three. What else? . . . See if you can get some details and reaction from the usuals. I'll hold space on five if you can get it to me in the next hour. But, mate, like I said, call me anytime about the other story.'

Sam hung up and scribbled a note then gave it to Grace.

Possible loss of Australian warship, it said.

'Can you please add this to today's list?'

Grace drew a sharp breath. 'Which ship, sir?'

'The government's not saying yet. Doubtless they won't release details until deadline for the mornings. Too late for us, as usual.'

❧❧❧

Two hours later, Sam and the chief subeditor stood at the high layout table, finalising the book for the third edition. Grace took notes as they talked. She looked up as Sam called across the news desks to Nolan, a cadet police rounds reporter, and beckoned him over. Tall and plump with a perpetually red face, he had none of the swagger second-year cadets usually assumed from hanging out with the coppers, covering death and destruction. As Nolan sloped towards them, Grace noticed his eyes were puffy and his nose was red.

'Nolan, how's that young fellow from the lift well coming along?' Sam asked.

'Didn't make it, sir. The lift shifted and crushed him flat against the wall. Took the ambos half an hour to get him out. Said he must have suffocated.'

'All right. Have it on my desk in fifteen. We'll run it on two.'

When Nolan had first arrived Sam told Grace that he wasn't convinced the lad had the makings of a hard news man, but his uncle had been a war correspondent and a wonderful teacher when Sam was starting out. Everyone deserved a chance, Sam said of Nolan. Grace tried not to feel disheartened when he said they'd move Nolan around the newsroom over the next couple of years and see if he took to any of the sections. Features, perhaps. She could see he didn't have the hunger that some of the other cadets had—like she'd have, if given half a chance, or like Curtis, one of the fourth years. Everyone said Curtis was a brilliant writer with a keen news sense, that he'd shone from the beginning. But like so many of the best over recent months, he'd signed up and today was his last with the paper. His send-off had started just after breakfast and now he was standing on his desk, loudly relating details of the entertainment at the Waterside Hotel down near the river.

'So there's this redheaded sheila,' he yelled, swaying and nearly toppling, 'and she lifted her blouse . . .'

Grace ran to answer the phone ringing on her desk, but she could barely hear what the caller was saying.

'And she had the biggest tits . . .'

Grace covered the mouthpiece and looked to Sam for help.

'Shut up, Curtis, people are trying to work,' Sam shouted.

'Miss Fowler, it's Lieutenant Hill from the Naval Information Office. Is Mr Barton there? It's quite urgent.'

Grace put the call from the navy's chief publicity censor through to the layout table.

Sam straightened at the sound of Hill's voice. Hill was a regular contact but it was usually Sam doing the calling. 'Sorry, Hill,' he said. 'One of the young blokes is leaving today and it's a bit rowdy here . . . No, I haven't seen anything. Did you send it on the wire? . . . Well, what does it say? We've just heard from Canberra that an Australian ship's been lost.'

Grace watched as Sam banged his fist on the desk. 'The *Sydney*?' Sam said, his voice getting louder. 'Good God! Are you sure?'

The newsroom fell silent.

'What do you mean we can't mention it? Come on, man, what's happening?'

There was a pause as Sam listened.

'What about survivors?' he broke in. 'How many have been rescued? How many ships and planes do you have out searching? . . . Well, when *will* you have news that we can print?' He was silent for a few moments then said heavily, 'Yes, we'll be waiting to go to print as soon as you confirm.'

Sam looked up from the notebook in which he'd been jotting details, his face grey and drawn, the lines on his forehead deeper than they'd been five minutes earlier.

Grace watched and waited, barely able to think. Could it be true? The pride of the Australian fleet lost at sea?

The newsroom was silent as Sam picked up the phone again and dialled.

'Jamieson, mate, we've just heard there might be something happening with the *Sydney*. She's based in Perth, right?'

He frowned as he listened to the other man's response. 'Jesus Christ! Why is this the first I'm hearing of it?' he shouted. Sam ripped his tie loose and unbuttoned his collar. 'It's the biggest bloody ship we have and it's bloody missing. You're the bureau chief, for fuck's sake. What are you doing over there? Sun fried your brain? . . . Well, if you heard the rumours last night then you should have called me immediately. Tell me everything you've heard . . . All right, put a reporter and photographer at the docks and keep digging. Call me the minute you have anything—anything at all.'

Sam ended the call, then immediately picked up the phone and made another.

'Gordon, we have a bit of a problem. You might need to come down. Thanks.'

The news editor rose from his desk, buttoned his collar and yanked his tie back into place. The chief subeditor was already spreading clean grid paper on the high table, ready for a new layout.

The editor-in-chief joined the men at the table a few minutes later. Their voices were low and serious as Sam related his conversations with Hill and Jamieson.

'All we know is that *Sydney* was due into Fremantle several days ago but she hasn't been heard from since the nineteenth, when she was sighted off Geraldton. Jamieson says there's talk of a massive sea battle off Carnarvon that evening. Hill said a search began yesterday.'

'What do you think of Jamieson, Sam?' Gordon asked. 'Is he up to the job?'

'He says he started hearing about it on the weekend but he didn't say anything about it till I called him. I think we need someone else over there to back him up.'

Grace took notes as Sam and Gordon assigned tasks: crew list; photos; ship's history; timeline of recent engagements; biographies of the commander and senior crew; details of the search.

'We can run extra editions tonight, but we need to have stories ready in the next hour so we can start mocking up the pages,' Sam said grimly. 'Of course, we can't run a thing until the navy gives the go-ahead.'

'We'll worry about that later,' the editor-in-chief told him.

The telex machine behind Grace's desk rattled as a message arrived. She walked over and read the paper as it printed out.

NO REFERENCE WHATEVER PRESS OR BROADCASTING ANY STATEMENTS OR RUMOURS REGARDING ALLEGED NAVAL ACTIVITY AUSTRALIAN WATERS.

Grace handed it to Sam, who read it then passed it to Mr Gordon.

The editor-in-chief's expression didn't change. 'Proceed with your preparations, Sam.'

CHAPTER 12

25 November 1941

KATIE GURGLED AND SPLASHED in the sink as Mae sponged her pale skin and her soft, jet-black hair. At six months, Katie was already so much like her father, with the same enormous, sea-blue eyes. And like Harry, Katie loved the water, but most of it ended up on the kitchen floor at bathtime, meaning more mess to clean.

In the past, Mae had never really understood when women complained about how much cleaning children added to the day. Now with a child of her own, she had plenty of complaints. No time to bathe because the baby wouldn't sleep. No time to clean the house properly. Too tired to read in the evening. Mae missed reading terribly. It had always been her escape but these days whenever she tried, she was asleep within moments. She wondered how women managed with six or seven small children. It must get better when they went to school, but that was years away.

At least when Harry was home, he could mind Katie while she got on with the chores. Mae knew it was unlikely Harry would be home for Christmas, but he'd written in his last letter that he was desperate to be home in early January. He was counting the days, he'd said. What would Elizabeth know, the interfering old cow? Mae would make sure they celebrated their first Christmas as a family then. She wouldn't invite anyone else, it would just be their little tradition, maybe on the twenty-fifth of January every year. If she put aside a few shillings each week, she could afford a chicken to roast with all the trimmings. She'd make him some new grey wool trousers, maybe a bit bigger than last time. He always gained weight when he was at sea for so long, unable to run around on the tennis court or do his gymnastics. He could wear the trousers with the shirt she'd sent for his birthday, if it arrived in time. There was always the possibility that Elizabeth had accidentally forgotten to include Mae's gift—

A knock at the door shifted Mae's annoyance to the charity collectors always calling at dinnertime. Katie kicked and spluttered as Mae pulled her out of the water and swaddled her in a towel, her cries growing louder as the pair hurried towards the front door. Mae's scarred stomach still hurt when she lifted Katie, who was growing heavier by the day. Katie was roaring now, wailing like a police siren. Mae wrenched open the door, prepared to give the collectors an earful of baby, but her mood lifted immediately when she saw Et, Albert and William standing on her doorstep.

'I hope we haven't caught you at a bad time, my dear,' said William as he opened the screen door for Et then entered without waiting for an invitation. Albert quickly followed, closing both doors behind him.

'Being Harry's birthday tomorrow, we had a sudden urge to see you both. We thought you might be lonely,' William said.

Et bustled past with her basket and headed for the kitchen with barely a 'hello'.

'You're all very sweet, but you needn't worry about me.' Mae jiggled Katie to quiet her. 'Katie and I have been planning a special birthday and Christmas celebration for his homecoming.'

'Well, now that we're here, perhaps we'll stay for a few minutes. Albert brought a bottle of beer and Et has a steak-and-kidney pie.'

Back in the kitchen, Mae placed Katie back in the water to stop her crying.

'This is a surprise,' Mae told her relatives. 'You never just drop in at this time of night. Are you sure everything's all right?'

'I went to the races today, and while I was on the train I thought a visit might take your mind off things,' Albert said quickly.

'Katie seems happy now,' William observed as the little girl splashed more water across the floor. 'Will she cry again when you take her out?'

'The trick is to have some food ready to distract her. See? I've mashed up some vegetables. Mmm, pumpkin, your favourite.'

Between spoonsful, Mae dried and powdered Katie, dressed her in her nightgown, tied a bib around her neck, then tried her best to keep the mashed pumpkin away from little hands and freshly washed hair. Washcloth at the ready, she mostly succeeded.

'You're getting much better at that,' Et said as Albert poured the cold drinks. 'She's more fidgety than before.'

'This is a good night. Sometimes I have to bathe her again after she eats. Good sense would dictate feeding her first but I can't stand her howling when I try it that way. There, all done. Why don't you sit with Uncle William while I clean up?'

'Come here, dear girl,' William cooed. 'You can play with my pocket watch.'

Albert smiled and tickled Katie's feet as she sat in William's lap.

Et blew her nose then offered to put Katie to bed.

'Are you sure, Et? You don't look very well. Perhaps you should sit down.'

'I'm fine, dear. I could use a Katie cuddle. Come on, pet—let everyone kiss you goodnight. We might have to read two stories tonight, I think.'

Mae drained the sink and wiped up all the splashed water. 'How were the races then? Did you rogues clean up on the Sunbury Cup?'

William shifted in his chair as Albert hesitated for a few moments.

'Yes, very good, dear,' Albert said. 'We came out quite a few pounds ahead.'

'It was looking a bit grim there for a moment, wasn't it, Albert?' William said. 'Alibi was galloping towards the finish line, then Ellison's jockey just managed to edge his nose in front. Won it by half a head. Rank outsider, but we had twenty pounds on him. Sixty to one shot.'

'That means you won a hundred and twenty pounds,' Mae cried.

'Well, yes, I suppose we did,' Albert agreed.

'So, why do you both look so glum? You look like kids who lost their lollies. Bookie raid?'

The two men looked at each other then they both looked at the table. Albert was the first to look up.

'Mae, you'll never guess who we ran into at the races,' Albert said.

'Let me see,' Mae said, pretending to think hard with her finger at the side of her chin. 'Squizzy Taylor?'

'Squizzy Taylor was shot dead years ago. No, we saw Tom Wilkinson. He was there with his son Johnny.'

'That cad—we should have strung Tom up when we had the chance,' William said, polishing Katie's fingerprints off his watch.

'I couldn't believe it. He just stood there talking to us as though nothing had happened. And his son is a dead ringer!'

Mae checked the pie in the oven. 'Does Et know? Is that why she's so upset?'

'Er, it hasn't come up,' Albert said.

'I don't think we should say anything. It will just drag it all up again, don't you think?' William added.

'So what was he like? I've always wondered about him.'

'Looking at his son was quite eerie,' William said. 'It was as though no time had passed at all.'

'Et showed me his picture once,' Mae said, 'when

she thought I needed to learn that love didn't always end happily.'

Albert and William's gazes met again then they both quickly looked away, like guilty children.

'I wouldn't want to be around when Et finds out you met Tom and didn't tell her,' Mae joked. 'She'll have your guts for garters. But it's probably best you leave it be. If I were Et, I wouldn't want to be hearing about his handsome, grown children. And his name is hardly likely to come up again, is it?'

Albert took a hanky from his trouser pocket and blew his nose. He folded it carefully, concentrating on each crease, then replaced it in his pocket. Clearing his throat and straightening his back, he placed his hands flat on the table.

'Perhaps. But something else happened at the races, and he was part of it.'

Mae looked from one man to the other. Normally easy around her, tonight they were so solemn.

'What? What happened?'

Albert looked away from her face as he spoke, as if he were addressing another person standing just behind her left shoulder. 'Tom was talking twelve to the dozen as always,' he said, selecting his words carefully. 'His son barely said anything until Tom started talking about a conversation the younger fellow had overheard. He said—and I'm sure it's not true—he said he'd heard that the *Sydney* was overdue by a few days and might be missing. A young bloke at the bar was telling his mates about it. The lad was a wharfie apparently; he'd heard it around the docks this morning.'

For a moment Mae expected them to laugh, to tell her it was one of their jokes. But they didn't.

'We don't believe it for a moment,' William said hastily.

The *Sydney* overdue—maybe missing. Mae tried to tell them that it wasn't funny, but sounds refused to come out of her mouth.

William fanned Mae with a magazine and Albert rubbed her hands to keep the blood circulating. 'Do you need to lie down, my dear?' he said. 'Shall I carry you to the couch?'

'Just give me a moment,' she gasped.

'I'm sorry, Mae. Shall I fetch Et? She'll know what to do.'

'I need a glass of water.'

'It's pretty common for a ship to be overdue by a few days,' William said. 'She could have had engine problems. Maybe her orders changed. They're probably on their way to Singapore or Fiji as we speak.'

Reassured, Mae agreed, 'I'm sure that's all it is.'

'Sorry to give you such a start,' Albert said as he handed her the water. 'There was nothing in the papers. Surely there would have been if there was an ounce of truth to the rumours.'

Mae took a sip then reached over and switched on the wireless. Sunlight dappled the sink and sideboard through the vine overhanging the back porch. The room was dim but not so dark that they needed the light on yet. A few moments later the news theme filled the room.

'*Good evening. This is the ABC news.*

'German armoured forces remain trapped south of Tobruk. Allied forces are consolidating their position in Libya after trapping the Germans three days ago . . .'

William loosened his tie.

'Moscow radio says German pressure from the north-west and western fronts is increasing. Russian troops are receiving fresh reinforcements and are doing their utmost to hold the enemy, but the danger to Moscow is great.'

Don't let them say anything, Mae chanted silently. If they don't say anything then it can't be true.

'Reports from Washington say the US secretary of state, Mr Hull, and the Japanese envoy, Mr Kurusu, have begun a series of talks regarding Pacific issues. It is understood that the negotiations include the possibility of the withdrawal of Japanese troops from Indochina. Talks will continue . . .'

Mae watched the brown box intently, its valves glowing softly against the wall. She felt that if she looked away from the wireless, even for a moment, she might miss an important clue, a word, a coded hint.

The bulletin finished with news of the Sunbury Cup winner and the following day's weather, but no mention of the *Sydney*. Albert switched off the wireless, sat down and poured them each a cup of tea from the pot in the middle of the table.

William packed his pipe with a match.

The woman next door screamed at her boys to get out of the ash pile in their backyard. *Wash yourselves off in the gully trap or you'll get nothing for dinner, ya hear me?* Shrill birds rummaged in the tree outside the kitchen window, its branches scratching and scraping the roof's tin gutter.

The tap dripped in the sink—Mae had forgotten to give it the extra quarter-turn when she finished Katie's bath.

She stood and scrubbed the sink then filled it with fresh water to wash the teacups before dinner. Grabbing the soap in its little wire holder she shook it violently under the water to make suds. Numbness crept along her bones, but she reminded herself they'd heard nothing but a rumour. People spread stories all the time. Gossips like Pearl Atkinson—who spent half her life spreading stories about everyone at church—revelled in that sort of thing; it made them feel important. But there was usually little or nothing to their tittle-tattle.

'Thank you for telling me. But until we have some proof, I won't be giving it another thought.'

William smiled. 'That's the way. Nice and brave.'

Mae scrubbed at every tannin mark inside the cups. 'I think the pie's nearly ready. Albert, would you tell Et? And not a word about Tom. She's had enough starts for one day.'

❧❧❦❀❦❧❧

Desperate to be alone after a very quiet dinner, Mae persuaded Et to leave with the uncles.

'No, really, you don't need to stay on the couch. Yes, come and spend the day with us tomorrow. No I don't think we need to telephone Harry's family yet.'

After they left, she tidied the kitchen then lit a large candle, placing it beside the picture of Harry on the buffet in their bedroom. Dusting the picture frame, she thought about the day she'd introduced Harry to her family over a

Sunday lunch of roast lamb. Harry had brought beer for the men and cider for the women, and when the greetings were over Mae had taken Harry into the garden to pick mint for the sauce. That's where they had their first real kiss. Until then, there'd been only pecks on the cheek at the train station and the front door after an evening out. Albert laughed when he saw the flush on Mae's cheeks as they walked inside.

'Rather strenuous picking that mint, isn't it, Harry?'

'Yes, sir. All that bending down and standing up. It's quite taxing.'

'Not often that you see a snowflake that colour, is it?' William chimed in.

'Snowflake?' Harry said, looking at Mae, whose face had gone an even deeper shade. 'I don't understand.'

'They call me that because of my white hair and pale skin,' Mae explained. 'And they've always said that because of my size I should keep my arms down in strong winds or I might drift away like a snowflake.'

'I've always seen you as the brightest ray of sunshine,' he said. 'From now on, I'll call you Sunny.'

And he did. If it was possible for an entire family to fall in love, it happened then. Et was smitten. Even the uncles had fallen for Harry.

She picked up his letter from the previous week and lay down on the bed to read it again.

Dearest Sunny,
We had a rather nasty trip to where we are now, but I survived the ordeal all right. Two young seamen from

my Melbourne group have been horribly sick all the way. I suspect they were wishing the ship would sink! I must be getting accustomed to the sea again as the motion just makes me very sleepy.

Doesn't it seem ages since I was there to see you? I hope you are getting along all right, dear. It is a great relief to know that Sam and Claire are nearby in case you need them. And you should write to Alice, have her up to stay for a while. Please let everyone take care of you the way I would if I was there.

We are off any day now and it may be some weeks before I can write again. Sweetheart, remember that you have grown right into my heart. I will only cease to feel you there when my heart stops beating. Look after yourself, please.

Au revoir, darling, with lots of kisses for you and the bub.

Love always,

Your devoted Harry

CHAPTER 13

28 November 1941

GRACE WATCHED SAM JABBING his typewriter keys at lightning speed, using just his forefingers. Three days after the rumours broke, despite the maddening lack of details, Sam was still updating the *Tribune* editorial about the *Sydney* for when the embargo was lifted. Each paragraph was typed on a new three-layer chit, carbon-copied twice and stacked to the side of his blotter so they could be corrected and rearranged depending on the column space. Surely they'd have to release the news today, Grace thought. She'd kept careful watch over the telex machine all day, waiting for the details to appear on the wire. No sign. Two editions had already gone to bed, but the city editions would go at two-thirty and four. It was one-thirty now.

'Do you want a fresh cup of tea?' Grace asked.

Sam ignored the question and kept typing. The newsroom was a mass of clattering typewriters, ringing telephones and excited voices. As awful as the *Sydney* rumour was, it had injected sorely needed urgency and purpose into the editorial staff, each wanting to contribute stories that would get a decent run. When the phone beside her right hand rang, she could have sworn it sounded more urgent than usual.

It was the reception desk announcing the arrival of Lieutenant Hill from the naval office, here to see Mr Barton and Mr Gordon.

When Grace interrupted Sam with the news, he leaped to his feet and asked her to show Hill into the conference room and call Mr Gordon's office.

Despite numerous phone exchanges over recent months, Grace had never met Lieutenant Hill in person. She'd expected a larger and older man to match the deep authoritative tone of his voice, so she nearly laughed out loud when she saw the short, slight man in a starched uniform waiting near the lift. He looked at least five years younger than Sam, but his demeanour was that of a man with great worries on his shoulders.

Showing him into the conference room, Grace cleared the table of papers and invited him to sit opposite the window while they waited.

Sam appeared in the doorway looking as though he'd washed his face and combed his hair.

'Good afternoon, Lieutenant. I trust you've brought us some good news.'

'Sam, Mr Gordon, thank you both for seeing me at such short notice. I'm here, of course, to brief you on the *Sydney* story, but only off the record, I'm afraid. What I'm about to tell you is still confidential.'

Grace stood, thinking she'd need to leave, but Sam waved her back to her seat. 'Miss Fowler will stay to take notes, Lieutenant. I'm sure you understand we need to document the conversation in case any of the facts are disputed later.'

Hill nodded.

'So, what's the latest?'

'Most of what you've heard is true as far as we know. The *Sydney* was expected to arrive in Perth on the twenty-first, but she was operating under radio silence. There were many reasons why she might have been detained, which is why we delayed contacting her. The RAN broadcast ordered her to break silence and make contact on the twenty-third. We heard nothing. Later that day we had the first reports of German survivors from the *Kormoran* being picked up by ships and search boats.'

Grace's shorthand characters were getting looser by the moment as she tried to keep up with Hill's words.

'How many have you found?' Sam asked.

'Around three hundred. Many of them made it to shore. They're already being interrogated.'

'And nothing's been found of the Australians. No oil slick, debris?'

'Nothing at all.'

'What are the Germans saying?'

'So far they're all saying the same thing: there was a battle at dusk on the nineteenth about three hundred miles west of Carnarvon. Apparently, the *Sydney* was hit by torpedos and badly damaged but still managed to get off a couple of shots. Completely devastated the *Kormoran*. The

Germans all say the *Sydney* was burning above the water-line and heading out to sea when they lost sight of her.'

'And these prisoners, you believe them? They've had plenty of time to concoct their stories.'

'We've nothing else to go on for the moment. They say there's no reason why there shouldn't be survivors. We're searching, but no luck so far.'

Sam referred to his own scribbled notes on the pad in front of him. 'Why did you wait so long to try to establish radio contact?'

'Enemy ships have been active in our waters for some months now. We're wary of broadcasting any information that might give *Sydney*'s position away if she's still afloat. And we don't want German intelligence knowing the *Kormoran*'s been sunk.'

Sam rapped his pencil hard against his notepad. 'What about the families? Don't they have a right to know what's happened?'

'Next of kin are being informed today that the *Sydney* is missing. We're not saying anything further until we have more information.'

Sam grimaced and tightened his lips as if to stop himself from saying anything further. Gordon nodded steadily.

'I don't need to remind you, we are at war,' Hill said. 'We won't release any reports that could endanger lives. The censorship order still applies. Any contravention will result in swift action.'

Sam glared at Hill. 'One of the crew is a friend of mine,' he said, keeping his voice even. 'His wife heard the rumours several days ago. She and all the other families deserve to know what's going on.'

Hill gathered his papers and stood. 'We're doing everything we can to find them. While there's a chance the ship is still afloat, no information will be published that could assist the enemy. In the meantime, my office will help you with background information. To avoid confusion, I must insist that only one reporter from your paper liaises with my office.'

'That's it? That's all you've got to say?'

'I'm afraid so. I'll see myself out. Good afternoon, Miss Fowler, Mr Gordon, Sam.'

❧❧❧❧

'Bloody navy arseholes!'

Grace started as Sam slammed his coffee down on the desk, the dregs slopping across the first edition of *The Gazette*. She slid down into her chair, trying to make herself smaller so that he didn't turn his anger on her. She was surprised to see him this way, language getting worse, his hair rumpled and his shirt creased as he smoked cigarette after cigarette. But part of her had expected to meet this Sam too. Editor Sam, just like her father when a crisis kept him on edge in the newsroom for days on end. As far as she knew, anger went with the job; it was the only way to deal with the pressure. She needed to toughen up if she was going to survive as a reporter. Grace looked across the newsroom and saw Phil walking towards Sam's desk. He smiled grimly as he passed.

'Sam, what's wrong?' Phil asked.

127

'Bloody Hill! The nerve of him, sitting here today, banging on about confidentiality. Keeping the public calm! Then he feeds the *Parramatta* story to the morning papers. The bloody tabloids.'

'Bastards!' Phil said as Sam ripped a sheaf of copy pages in half and threw them in the bin.

Another Australian ship, HMAS *Parramatta*, had been lost off the coast of Libya earlier in the week after being hit by two German missiles. Grace and Phil watched as Sam scrawled the numbers of lost crew on his blotter. One hundred and thirty-eight sailors aboard the *Parramatta* and six hundred and forty-five on the *Sydney*; nearly eight hundred men lost in one week—and that was just at sea. More had been lost in the other services. Grace tried to picture what that many people looked like: a train full of passengers; the students from two high schools at the local sports carnival. That many people, all gone in one week— just one week! How many would die in a month, in a year? She'd know some of them for sure. They'd be the boys from the newsroom, her classmates, kids from church.

'So why's the navy buddying up to the morning papers?' Phil asked.

'No idea. Hill must have known damn well what was happening when he said the embargo applied to everyone, even the radio stations. Now, all of a sudden, the mornings can publish so that people get one last sleep before the bad news.'

'Yeah, right,' Phil said. 'Reading about it over porridge will make the news much more palatable. And what about the *Sydney*? Can they publish that too?'

Sam stared across the darkened newsroom. Everyone else from *The Tribune* had gone to the pub hours ago. Grace didn't normally work into the evening but in the five days since news broke about the *Sydney* going missing, she'd worked from six in the morning till after nine each night. She couldn't leave and nor could most of the journos and subs, who all stayed across the road at the pub until close to hear the latest news. Mind you, even without clearance to publish, nothing stopped the spread of wild rumours; on trams and in trains and bars and shops right across the country, people talked of nothing else. And why wouldn't they? The *Sydney* was supposed to be invincible. It was inconceivable that it could be lost. Everyone seemed to know someone on the ship. Everyone seemed to have heard a new snippet of information: that the search was being conducted in the wrong area; that clothing and effects with HMAS *Sydney* insignia were already washing up on Perth beaches, despite reports that the battle had occurred hundreds of miles to the north.

The stench from Sam's ashtray caught in her throat as she lifted piles of papers and heaved them into a basket ready for filing in the morning. He'd been running on coffee and cigarettes for days. The sandwiches and fruit Grace brought him at lunchtime sat untouched. She'd tidy up as soon as he left.

'Want to get a beer?' Phil asked Sam. Sam nodded and looked at Grace.

'You should go home. Nothing more to be done tonight.'

Grace imagined the taste of an ice-cold beer and thought she'd like nothing more herself, but she obviously wasn't included in the invitation. In fact, she'd never been asked to the pub with the men. The subs on her dad's paper had always shared a drink with her, first a shandy when she was younger, then a glass of beer from their bottle as she got closer to the legal drinking age.

She knew Sam needed to unwind with the boys, especially after his outburst, but she could have used a bit of company too. The thought of going home to her tiny room with no one to talk to brought a new heaviness to her mood. It was too late to ring anyone; even her landlady would be asleep soon. And Phil was all but ignoring her now. She had no idea what she'd done to annoy him, but she was almost past caring. If he wanted to be aloof, to treat her as nothing more than the person scheduling Sam's meetings, well he could just go jump in the lake. Her mother had once said that there was no one less attractive than someone who didn't want to be your friend. That was how she needed to think of Phil.

Grace collected her coat, walked downstairs and waited at the front doors for the tram.

Bruce the doorman stood with his braided cap tilted slightly to one side like an army slouch hat.

'Nasty business about the *Parramatta*,' he said as *Gazette* trucks trundled out of the loading bay a few yards further along the street. It was dusk and the hessian bags covering the streetlights cast a dull glow. The brownout had increased the number of road accidents and Grace had seen several near misses in the last few weeks as drunks wandered onto the street and were almost collected by cars and trams. It was nearly summer but coal smoke from converted truck engines hung like winter fog.

'What's happening with the *Sydney*?' Bruce continued. 'They found her yet?'

'We haven't heard anything.'

'Poor blighters. My wife heard that the Krauts pretended they were going to rescue them, then when they got up close they shot all the survivors in the water.'

Grace pulled her coat tight at the neck. Were the beasts getting ready to invade? Sam said the Brits wouldn't get there in time to help if the Germans started bombing like they had in London, nearly wiping that huge city off the map. Melbourne would be a much simpler job for them.

Grace looked at the historic buildings along Flinders Street, trying to imagine them all bombed to rubble like she'd seen on the newsreels. Sometimes she thought it was almost enough to keep her away from the pictures. It was strange to watch all that suffering then to sit back and enjoy the films. But beside the newsreels, the movies were still the best part of her week. This weekend she had a new Torchy Blane movie to look forward to. She couldn't wait. Each new film fuelled her dreams of working as a reporter in a newsroom full of tall and handsome reporters like . . . Phil. *Stop that!* But he had been so calm tonight, settling Sam down so quickly, getting him away from his desk. He certainly had a way about him, a quiet authority and confidence that made you feel as though he could steady any situation. REPORTER CALMS STORMY SEAS.

Grace settled into a seat beside the window for her tram ride home. As they reached East Melbourne, a warden patrolled the streets looking for stray house lights. Everything seemed tranquil, but underneath something was not right. The other passengers on the tram were silent or spoke in hushed tones. They seemed to be holding themselves more tightly, taking up less space, as if trying to present a smaller target to the enemy. There were hardly any cars on the road, and few pedestrians. Maybe she was just more sensitive because of her job and the news she'd heard that day, but she felt a tension in her muscles, as though she were ready to spring at any noise. Seeing Sam so wound up today just added to her unease. It was strange. He hadn't been in the last war; he'd been too young. His friend was on the *Sydney*, but surely that wasn't the whole story. Something else was troubling him and Phil, lovely, kind Phil, was the only one who knew what to do. If only he were her friend too. She missed the way he used to smile at her when she first started in the newsroom, as though he thought she was a little bit attractive.

A whimper caught in her throat as she longed for someone to hold her and whisper that everything would be all right; that she had nothing to fear from the Germans or anyone else; that she didn't have to face everything alone.

CHAPTER 14

28 November 1941

MAE BOILED BABY BOTTLES and mashed potato while William sat at the table feeding Katie. She'd had a string of visitors keeping her company all day—to take her mind off things, they'd all said. But she didn't want to stop thinking about Harry and imagining him walking through the door, throwing down his duffel bag and sweeping her against his warm, solid chest. She longed to kiss him, to smell his skin, to hear his voice; her mind was full of desire and she didn't want any other thoughts crowding those images out.

Instead, she was entertaining people non-stop; people who spoke quietly, carefully, as though they were at a funeral. Their sombre words and sympathetic tones were wearing her out. She'd barely slept since that dinner a few nights before. But she still hadn't heard anything official about Harry or the ship, so she reminded herself every few minutes that there was really nothing to worry about.

Obviously they were sitting somewhere out in the ocean with Harry leading the team to fix the broken engine. When they arrived back in port they'd wonder what all the fuss was about. Et didn't need to close the shop and come over at lunchtime. Albert and William needn't sit in her kitchen all afternoon. She knew they were worried, that they loved Harry like a son, but she'd run out of things to say and she was getting tired of making the effort. If people wanted to visit, she'd let them take over the speaking for a while.

'Tell me more about Tom Wilkinson,' she urged. 'What was he like?'

William shifted Katie on his lap to get a better angle on her rapidly emptying bottle.

'Hmph! Bold as brass, he was, as though we were old mates.'

'Well, you *are* cousins.'

'Only by blood, not in spirit, my dear. Not after what he did to your aunt.'

'Did he ask after her?'

William raised one eyebrow. 'Oh yes. Completely offhand, like she was just an acquaintance, not the woman he was going to marry. "How's the family?" he said. "Kate, Et?" I told him Kate had died but that Et was just fine and she'd been busy raising you, we all had.'

'Did he say anything about Et not being married?'

'He was pretty disparaging, actually. "What do you mean Et didn't marry?" he said. "Jeez, never took her for the spinster type. I thought someone'd snap her up real fast."'

'No!' Mae gasped. 'He didn't!'

'I can tell you, I came that close to punching him—like I should have done when he was younger.'

'How awful! Could he see you were upset?'

'If he did, he ignored it. Just said, "Well, life goes on, doesn't it, fellers?" and went straight into prattling on about his five kids.'

The clock on the mantle ticked slow seconds as its hands moved towards five. Katie stirred in William's arms and whimpered. As Mae stood and reached for the baby, there was a soft knock on the front door. It wasn't the confident knock of Et or Albert, and Claire would be at home feeding the children. It must be someone from church, Mae surmised, popping past on their way home from the shops.

Handing Katie back to William she walked along the hallway, smoothing her hair again and checking that her blouse was properly tucked into her waistband.

The person at the door knocked again, a little harder this time.

'Coming,' Mae called.

Opening the door she saw a young boy with a satchel over one shoulder; he couldn't have been more than ten years old. He wiped his nose with the back of his hand and thrust his other hand towards her. It took her a moment to realise he was trying to give her an envelope. *He's just a child*, she thought. *Why is a child delivering the post? And why doesn't he put it in the letterbox?* Then she realised it was Paul, the postman's son; she knew his family from church. She smiled tentatively, but he said nothing, just continued to proffer the envelope.

Frowning, she looked at it. It was a telegram.

She let out a tiny gasp, then reached for the edge of the door to steady herself.

Silently, Paul pushed the telegram a few inches closer.

She knew she should reach out and take it, but instead she drew back into the dark hallway.

'Telegram for you, Mrs Parker,' the boy mumbled. 'Dad said I had to give it to you in person.'

He looked so innocent, so unaware of its meaning, of what it might do to her life, her family. She waited a moment longer then reached out. For a second, the small brown envelope connected the two of them. Then Paul whipped his hand away, thrusting it deep in his pocket, as though he'd been singed.

'Good afternoon, Mrs Parker,' he said, then turned and ran down the stairs and out the gate, slamming it so hard the catch rattled.

Mae stepped back inside, closed the door and leaned against it. Over the last few days, as much as she'd tried not to, she'd begun to imagine how a telegram might look, what it might say, how she'd manage to open it if it arrived. In all the times Harry had been at sea in the past, she'd barely given a telegram any thought. And this time, well, he was supposed to be far away from the action; he was supposed to be safe. Weak red and blue light streamed through the stained-glass panels above the door. She looked again at the address, making sure the telegram really was meant for her. It was.

She slowly opened the flap on the back of the enve-lope. It was barely sealed, as though it had been done in a hurry. Her hands quivered as she unfolded the note, the words leaping about on the page, refusing to settle into a coherent sentence. She counted them instead. So few words. Just thirty-six; one for every year of Harry's life. Then she made herself read.

With deep regret I have to inform you that your husband is missing as a result of enemy action. The Minister for the Navy and the Navy Board desire to express to you their sincere sympathy.

CHAPTER 15

30 November 1941

THE KETTLE BOILED ON Mae's stovetop, steam causing condensation to drip from the ceiling into a simmering pot of soup. Neither woman noticed. Claire rocked quietly as her baby Ella slept in her arms. Mae's hands continued to work furiously at her darning. It was early Sunday evening and although Claire said she needed to get the children home soon, Mae had asked her to stay a little longer, just to listen to the news. She'd longed for peace and quiet just days before, but now she couldn't face being alone. A second telegram had been delivered that afternoon.

Dear Mrs Parker,
May I, on behalf of the officers and men of the Australian Squadron, offer you my very sincere sympathy in your recent bereavement.

    I know full well that in this dark hour, words cannot lessen your sorrow, but I earnestly hope that you may find some comfort in the knowledge that your husband gave his life for his country, fighting in the cause of right.

Yours faithfully,
Mr Norman Makin
Minister for the Navy

Sympathy, bereavement, sorrow, gave his life—it was far too soon for anyone to be saying that.

'He's an excellent swimmer,' Mae said, mostly to herself. 'An excellent swimmer. Did I tell you he made the navy swimming team three years in a row? Won his races each time. And so fit. He's a champion tennis player, you know. That's how we met. So strong and fit.'

Claire patted the baby's back as she stirred. 'The kettle's boiling. Would you like some more tea?'

'William said he'd heard the German ship was disguised as a Dutch trader. Why would they do that? They should have just backed away when they saw our ship heading towards them. There was no need to attack.'

Claire tried to sound cheerful. 'Sam says they're picking up German sailors all along the coast. They'll find our men any moment now. Just wait and see. You'll have Harry home safe any day—maybe he'll even be home for Christmas. Wouldn't that be wonderful? Then we can all celebrate together.'

'He loves Christmas, especially when it's hot. That's where we disagree sometimes, about the heat. He always wants to go to the beach and lie in the sun. I can't stand the heat, especially in the middle of the day. Sometimes I think I might melt. But I don't care now. When he comes home we'll go for as many picnics at the beach as he wants. I'll never complain again.'

'Sam likes to sit in the house with all the blinds down when it's hot outside. In summer, his favourite part of the day is walking to the station in the early morning. He says that's the only time he can breathe. But it's hard keeping children inside all day. Once they start walking they just want to run around outside. I've got an old tin tub I'll get out for Nicholas this summer. I'll put it under a tree and fill it with a few inches of water. He can cool off, then I'll use the water for the plants, if he hasn't already splashed it all out. I might even dip my feet in while I'm feeding Ella.'

'That's a lovely idea. I'll get Harry to find something for Katie to play in. I could put a washing basin out the back for her, fill it with cool water. She'd like that. You've seen her in the bath. She won't let me take her out.'

Mae felt a bump against her shoe: Nicholas playing with his train engine under the kitchen table. 'Do you remember that time we came for a barbecue? Harry loved playing with Nicholas. I know he wanted a boy.'

'That was such a nice day. Sam can be a bit shy outside of the newspaper, but he has no problem talking to Harry. Easy sort of fellow, he calls him.'

'Harry mentioned you both in his latest letter. He said how happy he was that you were nearby.' Mae's voice quavered.

'We always will be, Mae. No matter what happens. And we're praying for the best.'

For a few minutes the women fell silent, listening to the music playing softly on the wireless.

'Has Harry's mother been to visit?' Claire asked.

'No, she's sitting vigil at home with dozens of her neighbours. She's better there. I'm sure she'd find a way to blame me for this if she were here.'

'It's hard to believe such a shrew could have raised a man like Harry. He must take after his father.'

'I never knew his father. That's something else we share: our fathers are long gone. Although Harry had his for a while at least. It's hard for any child growing up without a father . . .'

'It sounds like he became the father figure in his family after his dad passed away.'

'Yes, I think that's why his mother's so possessive. And his brothers and sister just worship him.'

'But he has his own family now,' Claire noted. 'They can't expect him to spend all his time with them.'

Mae smiled faintly. 'He loses track of time when he's with them, too. One afternoon, he was supposed to be meeting me in town. I was at Flinders Street, waiting and waiting as trains came and went. There was no sign of him. I was worried that he'd had an accident. Then I worried that he wasn't coming. He'd been a bit fidgety, saying he wanted to go back to sea. Anyway, nearly an hour after we were supposed to meet, I caught a glimpse of him hurrying through the crowd. I was happy to see him but furious that he'd left me waiting for so long, so I slipped away and hid behind a pillar and watched him searching for me. When I thought he'd had enough punishment, I walked over and touched his elbow. He jumped as though I'd given him an electric shock, and he grabbed me and held me so tight, it was like he was trying not to fall off a cliff.

'We walked to the gardens after that and he wouldn't let go of my hand. When we reached our favourite seat beside the lake, he sat me down and before I knew what was happening he'd produced a ring box and he was down on one knee, asking me to marry him.' Mae's face shone as she dabbed her eyes with her hanky.

'And you said yes,' Claire added, wiping her own eyes. 'Immediately.'

Mae looked at the diamond on her finger then twisted the ring and closed her fingers so the stone dug into her palm, cutting through the numbness that had settled in her hands.

The music on the wireless faded and the announcer introduced the next piece.

'*This tune is being played by the Footscray High School band. It is dedicated to our brave boys on the HMAS Sydney. May the lord protect their souls.*'

Claire reached across the table and held Mae's hand. Both women sobbed as the band played 'Abide with Me'.

There was still no mention of the ship on the evening news that followed, so Claire and her children went home.

On her way to bed Mae let her fingers linger on the photograph of Harry and she replaced the candle on the buffet so it burned continuously. She lay down on the bed and stared deep into the flame, imagining his face and willing him home with her thoughts.

You look so handsome in your uniform, my love, just like

on our wedding day. You're trying to be serious, but you can't help smiling, can you? Always about to grin—well, except when we argue. But even then your smile's not far away. Some days you complain that your face aches from laughing. Mine too, my love, but only with you.

Mae rolled onto her side and wrapped her arms across her chest. *I can still feel the warmth of your arms holding me tight,* she told her husband silently. *Use those arms, that strength, to cling to a life raft, my love, even after your arms are numb and you're sure you can't manage another minute. Keep hanging on, my love, just a bit longer, even if you're hurt. I can hardly bear to think of you wounded, bleeding, but if it means you're alive, that's all right. Everyone's looking for you, they'll be there soon. I know you can hear me. I won't stop talking to you till you're back here beside me.*

Mae slid off the bed and opened Harry's side of the wardrobe, pressing his shirts to her face to find one that smelled of him. She tried shirt after shirt but all she smelled was the waxy soap flakes she'd used to wash them. She opened the chest of drawers and plunged her hands into a stack of his jumpers; all freshly laundered. The same with his singlets and socks. Returning to the wardrobe she grabbed his woollen dressing-gown from the hook behind the door. It had been washed too, but there was a faint smell of his hair oil on the collar. Clutching the robe, stiff from the clothesline, she rolled it lengthwise and lay on the bed beside it so it stretched from her face to her feet, her knee bent across the middle as though Harry were inside it. She closed her eyes and inhaled slowly and deeply. *I'm right here, darling. I'm staying right here till I know you're coming home.*

CHAPTER 16

30 November 1941

GRACE WATCHED SAM AND Mr Gordon as they hunched over the subs desk, reviewing the stories about the *Sydney*, which were all ready for layout and printing. They checked and measured photographs marked up with chinagraph pencil to show the compositors where they should be cropped to fit between the columns of text on the page; pictures of the *Sydney* arriving home from the Mediterranean, her decks and masts brimming with deeply tanned crew, all waving and smiling to crowds lining the harbour of the city that shared her name. Grace had been surprised to see how young they all looked; many of them were younger than her, just boys. Photos of individual crew would go with local profiles, a smiling picture of the captain sat beside the crew list, which on its own seemed long enough to fill several pages.

'We'll have to run a special edition,' Sam said. 'We've got everything for a four-page wraparound. We can have a hundred thousand copies across Melbourne in a few hours.'

'Sam, the news is embargoed until midnight. It's Sunday. The morning papers will cover it. We'll follow up tomorrow afternoon with anything they've missed.'

'I can't believe the damn morning papers got it again,' Sam shouted, picking up a clippings file and slamming it against the desk. 'The story's already been broadcast in New Zealand and Britain. There'll be nothing left for us to say.'

'I agree; it's not on. I'm already drafting another letter to the government. But the main thing now is to make sure we cover this story properly. It won't help anyone if you get us into strife.'

Sam turned and strode to the window, placing his palms flat along the polished ledge and hanging his head. Across the road, a train moved slowly along tracks in the shunting yard towards an engine. A clang, a slight shudder and a whistle from the engineer signalled it was ready to move forward. 'We have to find a different angle from the mornings'.'

Mr Gordon scanned the prime minister's statement, issued two hours earlier, then he looked again at the crew list.

'Will you write something about your friend?' Gordon asked.

'His wife isn't ready. She doesn't believe that he's gone.'

'You never know, she could be right. They might be adrift somewhere.'

'Pretty unlikely now.' Sam still stared out the window.

'You could write something about him from your perspective,' Gordon said.

'I've said everything in the leader—about them all, not just Harry. God, I hope you're right about us being premature.'

Grace tidied the letters and clippings on her desk and placed them in a cardboard file beside Sam's blotter. Gordon peered over his glasses and smiled at Grace.

'It's late. Why don't you both come to my office for a drink? There's nothing more to be done here.'

Grace followed the two men up to the editor-in-chief's office on the next floor. The ceiling soared fifteen feet high and thick carpet and timber panelling absorbed any noise. Sam motioned for Grace to sit at one end of a long chesterfield while he sat at the other end. Gordon opened a cupboard near his desk and took out a bottle and three glasses. 'Grace, would you like Scotch or dry ginger, or both?'

'Both, thank you, sir.' She'd only tried straight Scotch once before and it had burned her throat. She hoped Mr Gordon wouldn't make it too strong.

'Hell of a day,' he said, pouring the drinks and handing them around.

Sam took a large gulp of his. 'Mrs Parker, my neighbour, will have received another telegram today, just like all the other hundreds of wives and mothers. I hope they've all got a drink or two to get them through the night.'

Grace had been following the story as closely as anyone, but she couldn't understand why the navy made the situation seem so hopeless. 'There's still a possibility they'll find survivors, isn't there?'

'Of course there is, Miss Fowler,' Mr Gordon said. 'They're just being cautious.'

Sam drained his drink. 'They gave up hope days ago. There should have been some sign of wreckage by now, an oil slick, a lifeboat. They've searched every inch of coast but nothing's turned up.'

Grace protested: 'It's such a vast area.'

'That's right, Sam,' Gordon agreed. 'It will take months before they can say definitively that no one survived.'

'I hope that's true, for everyone's sakes.'

Gordon refilled their glasses. 'Let's drink a toast: to the *Sydney* and her brave, brave crew.'

The long days and the sadness had left Grace feeling miserable and scared, and she didn't even know anyone on the ship. She felt like she had no right to sadness, but this was bigger than the *Sydney* and her crew. For the first time, it felt like the war had arrived on their shores. It seemed that while the rest of the world was looking the other way, the Germans had started waging war right here, off the Australian coast. The thought of what might happen next was terrifying.

'Nothing glamorous about covering a war, is there, Miss Fowler?' Sam said glumly.

'No, sir. But it's important to tell the full story, to let people know what's happening—and, of course, to honour the lost.'

Sam rubbed his temples and leaned back in his seat. 'It's all cold comfort for the families. We just record their names, print a picture, give the mothers a news clipping to cut out and paste in a scrapbook, so they can tell themselves that people noticed their child had passed through the world. Of course, we can't help with a search, we can't contribute anything useful to fighting the enemy. Our work is nothing more than a race to the printing presses in the hope of selling more papers. Hardly edifying.'

'We keep people informed; that's got to be worth something,' Grace said, wondering whether she still believed that. She knew the only way to beat the other papers on this story was to get interviews with the families. They were all striving for exclusives. Sam told the reporters to let him know immediately if anyone came forward to speak, but he refused to pressure grieving relatives. She admired his empathy and decency. She knew most editors—her father included—wouldn't step back from a story even if it meant intruding.

Sam took a sip of his drink. 'Believe me, nothing we do will give the families any real comfort. It's the women who own the grief; the mothers and the wives. The rest of us have to swallow it, keep going as best we can.'

'I'm sorry, son, about your friend,' Gordon said as Sam drained his glass and set it on the table. 'You should head home to Claire; she'll be worried about you. Grace, we'll get you a taxi.'

Grace walked back to her desk, her head fuzzy from the drinks. On the other side of the newsroom, *The Gazette*'s subeditors were drinking beer and chattering loudly, unable to mask the satisfaction of having just put a huge story to bed. A couple of reporters and the editors stood at the chief-of-staff's desk reading fresh copies of the paper, straight off the press. She was glad Sam was still in Gordon's office, not here to see them. The way stories were being released was pathetic. The government seemed to have no regard for how demoralising their decisions were to newspaper men and women working around the clock to fill the papers day after day.

Of course, most people never gave the effort behind their papers a second thought, just like they never thought about the bottles of milk and loaves of bread delivered fresh each morning. It all happened as if by magic—in fact, that was what Grace loved most about it: the way that a huge roll of blank newsprint was transformed into printed pages trumpeting the very best and the very worst of life. It was miraculous, and why shouldn't she love it? Why shouldn't a woman be as passionate about the news as a man?

The more she saw of this game, the less she understood why men thought women couldn't do the work. Somehow she had to find a way to make it impossible for them to block her progress. Working at *The Tribune*, she was learning from the most experienced writers and editors. She was in the right place to grab any opportunity that came her way, and that included looking for work on other papers if she needed to. But days like today were a perfect demonstration of the fact that no one knew how much time they might have. If she was going to achieve any of her dreams, she needed to make every day count.

CHAPTER 17

1 December 1941

WHITE-HOT SUN BEAT DOWN on the sand as Mae sat fanning herself under a casuarina, its needles spiking light and shade across her arms and legs. She unpacked the picnic lunch; ham and pickle sandwiches, asparagus rolls and ginger beer wrapped in paper and a damp tea towel to keep them cool.

Harry raised his eyes from the newspaper and peered across the top of the page.

'Hungry?' she asked. Silly question; he was always hungry.

He pushed the paper aside, leaned forward and walked his fingers across the blanket to touch her hand.

'Yes.'

She registered his nakedness as he moved, catlike, stretching and curling until he lay on his side with his legs against hers. His hand slowly travelled up her wrist, rested briefly inside her elbow and grazed her shoulder before moving across her neck and down to her breast.

Mae closed her eyes and lay back on the blanket as he lifted his fingers just far enough away from her body to allow the heat shadow to trace shapes across her stomach and thighs. Still not touching her, he moved his body over hers, supporting his weight with his hands and knees. She lifted her head to kiss him, her tongue teasing his salty lips. He increased the pressure of their kiss, tentatively then firmly exploring her mouth. She dropped her head back onto the towel, pulling him down with a hand behind his neck. His body followed, pressing against hers, sandy skin rubbing and burning her; hot breath on her neck. His wet hair lightly brushed her face. He pulled back and looked at her again, seeking permission with his eyes. She smiled and pressed her hips into his.

She gasped as he peeled aside the gusset of her swimming costume and entered her smoothly, without haste. Delicious moments passed as her senses focused on feeling every inch of him inside her, his rhythm slowly increasing. Her fingers scraped his lower back and grasped his buttocks as her muscles clenched him tighter and tighter. The sky and the air around them glowed golden as they melted into one another in the sun. With each thrust his hips became her own, his chest merged with her ribs. She felt her spine lift as her breath caught and pleasure prickled her toes, sweeping along her legs and body. He cried out then, his breath suspended for a delicious second or two before his mouth found hers again.

With their lips still touching, he rolled slightly to the side, leaving her torso weightless, floating.

'Swim?' Harry whispered.

'I can't.'

'Let me teach you.'

'You've worn me out.'

He ran his finger along her stomach, as perfect and flat as it had been when they first married. 'Nothing like water to revive you, my Sunny.'

He grinned as he stood then ran across the sand. Plunging into the surf, he climbed the face of a perfectly formed sapphire wave with ease. Up and over he swam, further and further from the shoreline. She waited for him to turn and catch a wave, ride it back to shore, effortlessly, smoothly, a fabulous sea creature completely at home in the water.

Standing on tiptoes to see him better, Mae watched him slip beneath an enormous wave that continued to build, its crest foaming. She waited for him to resurface but there was no sign of him. The wave seemed to freeze, not moving closer to the shore but instead just tumbling and turning in place. Its power kept Harry submerged. Running towards the water she called his name. Sunlight stung her eyes as she scanned the beach, left, right, left again, shouting for help. But no one came.

Mae screamed his name over and over, but she could no longer pinpoint where she'd last seen him. Seagulls screeched and flapped in the dunes behind her as the wave continued to tumble in place. The birds' squawking grew louder, harsher, as though . . . her mind slowly registered the birds chirping in a nest they'd built in the gutter above her bedroom window. Keeping her eyelids closed, she fought to keep her mind at the beach.

He's still there, in the waves. If I can just stay asleep a few more minutes, I'll find him, I'm sure of it.

But no amount of bargaining would enable her to slide back to that dream, with its tantalising nearness to Harry. Her chest heaved as though she'd really been running along that beach.

Finally letting the morning fill her consciousness, she opened her eyes to a cold, wet and windy day. Mae got up, wrapped herself in Harry's dressing-gown and wandered to the kitchen to make a pot of tea. She felt she should have some sense by now of whether Harry was alive or dead, but all she felt was numb. The drowning dream had woken her every morning since she heard he was missing, each time a little different in the way it built but the outcome always the same, so vivid, so terrifying, leaving her helpless to save him.

What's it about? What are you trying to tell me? Am I supposed to see something—a clue? Should I know that beach? Mae closed her eyes again as she took a sip of tea, and sent more silent prayers to help Harry find his way home. *Show me how to help you. I don't understand why this is happening. If you're punishing me for that night, I understand; I can't tell you how sorry I am. I promise to be perfect next time you come home, and all the times after that. I'll never doubt you again.*

Mae rested her head on her folded hands on the table and sobbed. She felt completely drained, wrung out like a wet cloth. But she reminded herself that there had still been nothing definite in the papers or on the wireless, that no news had to be good news; she just had to keep her faith, not let despair inch its way into her thoughts.

Wobbling, she forced her hand to reach up and switch on the radio. *The dream hasn't changed,* she told herself, *today will be like every other morning: the* Sydney *won't be mentioned.*

She twisted her wedding ring on her finger, its smooth surface as much a part of her hand now as her fingernails. *Remember our wedding, my darling, when you slid the ring over my knuckle then kissed my hand, 'to seal the deal'? Remember, Harry? And the way you made me giddy on the dance floor, twirling me so much I nearly took off and flew? Remember the soft lighting, the jazz quartet on the terrace? It was all so lovely. And our first kiss as husband and wife; I could hardly bear to stop. It felt like sunlight was streaming from every pore of our skin, enough to warm us forever.*

Mae shivered and drew the lapels of the dressing-gown together at her throat. *But I'm so cold now, my darling. How is it possible to go from that day to this? People are saying you might be gone. That I have to prepare myself for the worst. I'm trying not to listen. It can't be right. They don't know how strong you are, that when you set your mind to something, nothing can stop you. You promised you'd come home, that you'd never leave, and I believe you, no matter what other people say.*

Noticing several specks of black mould in the grout behind the sink, Mae frowned. She tied an apron over the dressing-gown, donned rubber gloves and began scrubbing the tiles with bleach.

Once the tiles were clean she worked her way along the lino on the floor, using a knife to attack the corners, then turned her attention to the skirting boards.

After mopping everything clean with a wet tea towel, she emptied the cupboards and scrubbed every scuff mark from the shelves.

It's a good thing you're not home yet, Harry, she thought. *Imagine if you'd seen this mess. You'd think me the most slovenly cow.*

Mae realised she hadn't cleaned like this since before she was pregnant. The last time they'd been in the cottage together she'd been too big to get down on her knees. What if he'd noticed the dirt? She scrubbed harder. She'd just need to keep working hard for the next few days, so the cottage was shipshape by the time he came home.

The gate latch clicked and Mae saw Albert walking towards the back door. Returning the saucepans to the cupboard, she smoothed her hair and removed her apron, opening the door before he reached the steps. His face looked so serious and drawn, his skin a tired grey.

'This is early even for you. Come in, you're soaked to the bone.'

'Have you slept at all, dear?' Albert said, wiping his shoes on the mat.

'A little. Katie will be up soon. Have some tea.'

Mae tried to focus her mind on choosing a cup and saucer and pouring the tea. It was far too early for a social call even from close family. Maybe Et was sick, or William. Or perhaps there'd been a fire at the shop, a burglary? Or maybe Albert just needed company; he was worried about Harry too. Her mind flitted like a moth around a light, her thoughts never landing anywhere long enough to take the worst shape.

Albert gently steered her to a chair. 'I have to show you these.' He opened his coat and pulled out the morning newspapers, laying them on the table. 'I didn't want to disturb you and the wee one too early, but I knew you'd want to see.'

Mae looked at *The Gazette* without touching it.

CRUISER SYDNEY MISSING

FEARED LOST WITH ALL 645 HANDS

SANK ENEMY RAIDER

Tears didn't come, just hard clarity, cold and bright like crystal. She read every word, looking for information she hadn't already heard, a fact that would take the story in a different direction. Seeing the words printed in black and white didn't change her conviction that someone had made a hideous mistake. The words jumbled and shifted on the page. FEARED LOST: well that wasn't *actually* lost. Not lost for sure. And anyway, when something was lost it could be found. Gone would be more decisive and the report didn't say that. *Extensive search by air and surface units to locate survivors continues.* There it was—they were searching for survivors, not for wreckage. There would be survivors and then they would be found, not lost.

Albert stepped forward and placed his hand on her shoulder. Mae slowly rose from the table, letting his hand fall as she put one of Katie's bottles into a saucepan of hot water. Staring straight ahead like a sleepwalker, she left Albert in the kitchen while she changed the baby then brought her back to the table and fed her.

Albert spoke carefully. 'They're still searching—nothing's set in stone.'

Mae stared at the newspaper on the table, mechanically wiping the baby's face then putting her over her shoulder.

Albert blew his nose and dabbed his eyes with his hanky. 'Would you like me to take her to Et for the day? She could bring her back when she closes the shop.'

Mae patted Katie's back. 'I couldn't possibly—it's too much trouble for you, managing a pram on the train.'

'I'll survive. Get her ready and we'll give you some peace for the day. Time to collect your thoughts.'

Mae wobbled as she stood.

'Are you going to be all right?' Albert scooped Katie from her arms.

Mae's gaze returned to the paper.

'We'll come back for tea, unless you need us sooner.'

Mae nodded. 'Tea will be fine. I've got to finish my cleaning.'

'Perhaps you should both come and stay with us?'

Mae's head slumped forward slightly, as though it were too heavy for her neck. 'They'll find survivors any moment now,' she said, 'just like they're finding the Germans. They only know to send word here.'

Albert rocked Katie then laid her in the pram beside the kitchen door. 'We're all desperately worried about him,' he said, patting her hand. 'Everyone's praying and praying.'

As soon as Albert left, Mae spread the newspapers across the table. The vast number of missing men barely registered; Mae only thought of Harry. She'd heard it said that when you died your life flashed before your eyes. As she sat there staring at the paper, glimpses of her life with

Harry flooded her mind. She imagined herself walking beside him at the zoo, her hand nestled warmly between his arm and his ribs. She saw him riding his motorbike, grinning beneath his leather helmet and goggles. He loved that bike. She'd tried to ride pillion a couple of times, but it was too frightening when he leaned into the corners. It was the only time she'd struggled to trust him. They'd had to compromise, only holidaying in places Mae could reach by train while Harry rode his motorbike.

Their happiest holidays were with Alice and Jim, Harry's best friend and shipmate. Mae wondered how Alice was getting on. She'd have had the telegrams too, about Jim. She knew she should telephone, but any hint of fear in Alice's voice would make the situation far too real. She closed her eyes and pictured Alice giggling at one of Jim's silly jokes, the one about the dinosaur:

How do you ask a tyrannosaur out to lunch?

Tea, Rex?

He always snorted with laughter at his own jokes. Sometimes that was the funniest part.

Mae and Harry met Alice and Jim when they moved to Sydney just after their wedding. Harry and Jim were stationed together at Jervis Bay and Mae took country girl Alice under her wing, introducing her to city life. In the seven years that Mae had known Alice, her friend had given birth to two healthy boys but lost her mother to cancer, her father to a heart attack and both her brothers to the war. Now Jim was missing too.

Mae folded the newspapers and put them on top of the woodpile, ready for burning. She washed her cup and rinsed the teapot then wiped the table. Now that she had a day to herself, she'd concentrate on cleaning the bathroom then sort Harry's clothes for summer and stow his winter woollens in a suitcase.

She looked at the papers again, then took them from the woodpile and tucked them in a drawer under the tea towels, so she could show Harry when he came home. *You'll laugh about the whole adventure, won't you, darling? You'll brag about sinking the German ship then racing to an island to fix your engines with bamboo and rubber strips straight from the trees. You'll tell us how you drank out of coconuts and swam in a lagoon while the natives played music and let their children run wild. When we grow old, we'll tell the grandchildren your story together, finishing each other's sentences.* The dream image of Harry disappearing behind the wave flashed into her mind again. She felt the prickle of sun and the sand on her body. She heard the waves and the birds, and felt the helplessness of not being able to reach him.

Raindrops pattered on the window panes and slowly dribbled down the window towards the frame.

They're all wrong, aren't they, Harry, the papers, the gossips? You can't have given up, not yet. I know you've got all the strength you need to fight this, unless—unless you had no choice. I know the only thing that would stop you fighting is being so badly hurt that you couldn't—

A car drove past the front of the house, its tyres splashing along the wet road. There was no sound of children playing outside, no birds singing, no repairmen lopping trees or fixing fences.

You're not trying to tell me . . . goodbye . . . are you, my darling?

Mae felt a chill shiver along her spine. She belted the dressing-gown tighter around her waist and willed herself to imagine a day that was sunny instead of grey, a day that would wash this nightmare away like a wave breaking and disappearing as it ran onto the sand.

CHAPTER 18

4 December 1941

MAE AND ALICE SAT on a wooden bench under Mae's kitchen window, a wicker basket piled with damp towels, sheets and nappies at their feet. Both women sagged against the wall, staring straight ahead, no energy for pegging. Mae had spent hours the previous day boiling, scrubbing and bleaching her washing, then she forgot to hang it on the clothesline.

Alice's boys—five-year-old Josh and three-year-old Jeremy—were chasing each other up and down the narrow strip of concrete that stretched from the women's feet to the fence. It was a good idea to surround herself with people, Mae told herself. But Alice looked so morbid, with her cheeks sunken and dark smudges under eyes that constantly streamed with tears. And the boys were running wild. They didn't understand what was happening or why they should play quietly. At least Katie was asleep in her pram. Mae hoped the boys would wear themselves out then settle down.

Mae needed to gather her thoughts, steel herself for what was coming; the place and the event that had no relevance to her life. A memorial service—ridiculous! The search had barely begun; the papers had only just run the story. It was crazy, yet there were services happening right across the country tomorrow, in every city, in churches of every denomination, with guest lists more akin to a royal visit.

Alice and her children had arrived on the train that afternoon, so that the women could go to the service at Scots' Church together. Mae had rung the farm when news of the memorials arrived via telegram, just a day after the news reports in the papers. Mae recalled little of that conversation, just that Alice kept saying, *Whatever you think, Mae, whatever you think.* So Mae must have decided which service they'd attend, which nights her guests would stay. Now here they were, in what seemed like just a blink of time since Albert had arrived with the newspaper. Her life was like that at the moment: flashes of situations, as though she were in a strangely edited film with the scenes flickering to life then changing moments later with nothing to link them.

A squeal from Jeremy recalled her to the backyard scene. The boys were shrieking with laughter, treating the excursion as an adventure. Coming from the farm, the children had been up before dawn, but they showed no sign of tiring yet. But they weren't naughty. No tantrums, no making a mess of their food. Alice had taught them well. And as boisterous as they were, every now and then Jeremy toddled over to Alice and gave her a cuddle before running off to play again.

'He knows,' Alice sighed as he did it again. 'Sometimes he just snuggles up and pats my arm, like I'm his puppy. Today on the train I couldn't stop crying. He put his arms around me and stroked my hair for a minute or two then slipped away to play with the other kids. Not a word.'

'Such lovely boys,' Mae said, her eyes closed against the sunlight. 'What have you told them?'

'The day after the first telegram I said Daddy's boat was lost.' Alice dabbed her eyes with her hanky. 'Josh got the atlas off the shelf and asked me to show him where. He wanted to go and look for him.'

'I'm sure he senses that Jim's alive. They both must. That's why they're being so good, so you can tell Jim what brave boys they've been.'

'If that were true, they would have found some kind of sign by now. A lifeboat or something.'

Mae stood and picked up a sheet, began pegging it on the line nearest the fence. 'They're still searching. Harry and Jim could be holed up anywhere along the coast just waiting for rescue.'

'But the memorial services; the prime minister's coming to the one at St Paul's. He wouldn't do that if he wasn't sure.' Alice rose too and started pegging nappies. Then she pulled her hanky out of her skirt pocket again and blew her nose. 'I've got to be practical, Mae, with two boys and another bub on the way. I can't sail off to fairyland.'

'Another baby? You should have said.' Mae reached out and hugged her friend. 'Jim will be so pleased. When are you due?'

'Around the end of May or early June.'

'See? It's a sign.'

'Hopefully the weather will cool off before I get really big. I'll need to get the wheat harvest in. Get it baled and stored.'

'It's wonderful; a new life to keep your spirits up while you wait for Jim.'

Alice sat down again, wiping at her tears. 'Raising three children on a widow's pension and whatever I can eke out of the farm. I just don't know how we're going to manage.'

The boys stopped their game, ran over and squirmed into Alice's lap, little brown arms circling her neck. 'Kisses to make Mummy better,' Jeremy said as he made wet smacking sounds against her cheek before Josh dragged him off by the hand and the pair of them raced around the side of the house.

Mae returned to her washing, shaking out two pillow-cases then pegging them back-to-back on either side of the wire. Her situation wasn't so different. Alice had inherited her farm. Mae owned some land. Her family had offered to loan her the money for a house but Harry was adamant they'd manage on his salary. She hadn't told him yet, but she planned to return to work and help save for their home as soon as she could. Motherhood certainly wasn't what she'd expected. There was little joy to be had in spending endless days alone with a baby who couldn't walk or talk, who depended on her for everything. She missed working. She missed adult conversation. She missed shopping without a pram and dressing in a blouse that lasted the entire day without needing changing because of the baby. As far as she could see, the only good part about motherhood was making Harry happy. He'd said he didn't mind not having more after Katie, but had he really meant it? Was he already looking at other families and longing for more children? Would he resent her for not giving him more?

Mae shook out a towel and tried to slow her mind, silently chanting the words that had become her prayer: *He's got plenty of reasons to come home; he wants to come home. Lord, please bring him home.*

Alice sorted the damp socks into two piles for pegging, matching and odds, sighing as the odds pile grew higher. Looking towards the side of the house she tilted her head and listened. 'The boys are a bit quiet, don't you think?'

Mae looked past the sheets. 'I don't see them.'

Alice walked around the corner of the house, towards the tree where Mae had parked Katie in her pram. 'Stop that this instant!' she shrieked. 'Oh, Mae, I'm so sorry. I'm so sorry. There, there pet,' she crooned.

Alice rushed back to Mae carrying Katie, whose face and blanket were black with briquette dust, her pink mouth open as she roared her disapproval.

Jeremy joined the crying, tears wetting his blackened hands. 'Just helping, Mummy,' he wailed. 'We put coals in the barrow.'

'It's Katie's pram, not a wheelbarrow. Josh, you should know better. Get those briquettes out now and put them back in the bag. Mae, I'm so sorry. I had no idea . . .'

'Daddy said I have to be the man, I have to help,' Josh said sternly, his hands rammed deep into his pockets.

'You're big enough to see Katie sleeping in the pram. You could have hurt her. Now look at the mess we have to clean up!'

As Alice rocked Katie, Mae stood completely still, her arms hugged tightly across her chest.

'She's all right, Mae; she's fine, just a bit dirty.'

Seeing Alice holding the blackened bundle she knew she should run to soothe her child, but her feet felt like ten-tonne weights. She dropped her arms and forced herself to move towards the baby. *Pull yourself together. Give him every reason to come home.*

CHAPTER 19

5 December 1941

MAE SHUDDERED IN HER bed as wind whipped open the manhole cover in the ceiling outside her bedroom, then slammed it closed again. There was nothing she could do to stop it making her jump with fright through the night. Not that she'd seriously attempted sleep. Nights of lying awake worrying had taught her to dread the silent hours punctuated by the cuckoo clock in the lounge room striking three, four and five every morning. When sleep did arrive, it was fleeting. And of course, sleep also brought the nightmare of losing Harry in the waves. She longed for the moments where her mind let her feel him close even though it demanded the payment of loss, over and over.

Wrung out by endless nocturnal ups and downs, the best she could hope for was enough rest to keep her going, especially today. The thought of dressing and going to the memorial service to be surrounded by her family and hundreds of strangers felt dreamlike, unreal. She felt like she was on a stage, with people around her acting out a play that she didn't understand. She couldn't remember her lines. What was she supposed to do? Where was she supposed to stand?

Mae tried to keep busy. Alice had brought an old black frock to wear to the service and Mae lengthened the sleeves, replaced the frayed cuffs and mended the hem. She added black lace across the bust. It would be quite smart. She'd trimmed a hat to match with a small net veil on the brim. Quite smart, indeed.

The blustery weather reflected the women's sombre mood as they sat in the back seat of the taxi on the way to the service. Claire was minding the children. How lucky the little ones were, having no understanding about the day. Mae smoothed the pleat in her skirt. Her black woollen suit gaped around the waist; she probably should have adjusted the darts but having moved the button, it would do for today. She looked out the window and wondered how many people would be at the church. With so many services on that day across the city and around the country, it didn't seem likely the church would be terribly crowded. And surely the weather would keep the stickybeaks away. She hoped so anyway. Albert said the papers predicted there'd be hundreds of people at the Scots' service, but she wished it were just close family and friends at the local church instead; people who knew Harry, who were sending their thoughts to him. It would be stronger that way, a shower of prayer for his safe return. Larger services were being held at the cathedrals, St Paul's and St Patrick's, but the women had decided on the smaller church when they heard that the chaplain who'd recently served on the *Sydney* would be there. Pastor Symonds was on board until October, so he would have known Harry and Jim. That thought was far more comforting to Mae than being surrounded by politicians.

The taxi inched along under the elm trees on Collins Street, behind a line of other taxis depositing passengers at the Scots' portico. While they waited, Mae spotted Harry's family huddled under umbrellas. Harry's younger brother Richard nodded when he saw Mae, opened her door and paid the driver. Mae and Alice walked arm in arm through crowds of unfamiliar faces. Mae was unexpectedly glad to see Elizabeth, who awkwardly kissed her cheek while keeping her head tilted to the side so their hats didn't collide. As soon as Elizabeth stepped back, Mim grasped Mae's upper arms and burst into tears. Mae absently patted the girl's coat and made the same soothing noises she used for Katie.

Harry's youngest brother, Eric, took charge of his sister and Alice gripped Mae's hand as the group was ushered towards the door. Mae was swept along as though the footpath were moving her towards the stone doorway, beyond which she could see nothing but a dark sea of men's and women's hats. She fought the urge to turn and run away from this church where she was being dragged to say goodbye to Harry. She tried to slow her pace but the crowd propelled her forward. Her breathing grew shallow, her face hot, and her fingers started to tingle. Her mind silently called, *Stop, no; it's too soon!*

Gasping for air, her gaze landed on Sam Barton. He was leaning over to speak to a young woman beside him. Raising his head, his eyes met Mae's.

'Mae, are you all right? You look terrified!'

'I'm, I—I don't know why—'

Sam called across the crowd to Albert. 'I think Mae needs some help. Mae, Albert's right behind you. You'll be fine.'

Mae felt Albert's arm slip around her waist. Still holding Alice's hand, she let them both lead her to the reserved pews at the front of the church. Walking slowly down the aisle, she couldn't help recalling walking towards Harry on their wedding day. She clutched Alice's hand tighter. The pews were full and hundreds of people lined the walls. There were so many; how could so many people care so much about the missing crew? Still, it was nice of them all to come out on a day like this to pray for the men's safe return.

As the service got underway, Mae tried to block it out, reasoning that the pastor wasn't really talking to her; that he was just trying to prepare people for the worst in case something did happen, sometime in the future. She had to stop herself from clapping when he said the government hadn't done enough to inform the families, that the censorship had added pain on top of suffering for the next of kin. She realised her face was wet with tears.

Harry's not dead, she assured herself. *It's still too soon. He'd never leave.* But no matter what she told herself, the tears wouldn't stop.

Then the Last Post played; the service was over. Before she had a chance to decide whether to stand, to sit, to speak, a warm hand clasped her arm. Mae looked up into the round, red face of Pastor Symonds.

'Mrs Parker, Mrs Gower, I recognised you both from your pictures,' he said, sitting beside them. 'I'd hoped to meet you.' He had the calm and sympathetic voice of a man used to dealing with a stranger's grief. 'I knew Jim and Harry. I wanted to meet you in particular, Mrs Parker, knowing what you've been through this year. Do you know the entire ship followed your progress when you were ill? Not knowing your condition was so hard on Harry. But it warmed my heart to see the way all the men, even the young ones with no wives or children of their own, rallied to keep his spirits up. And Jim too. He was a tower of strength and such a great leader to his gunnery crew in the Mediterranean. Two wonderful men and terrific friends. I'm sure they would have been an inspiration to the men during their final battle.'

Alice pressed her hanky to her mouth again.

Mae leaned forward. 'Pastor, do you think they could be somewhere waiting for rescue?'

'It would be a miracle indeed, Mrs Parker,' he said, squeezing her hand. 'But of course, I'm not averse to praying for miracles.'

CHAPTER 20

5 December 1941

GRACE SURVEYED THE NEARLY empty news-
room. Phones rang non-stop but no one answered them.
Sam was in an editorial conference with the subeditors.
Everyone else was out covering the memorial services for
the crew from the *Sydney*. Even the copyboys were out at
the churches, standing by to rush back stories and films for
the first edition. The newsroom hadn't been this deserted
since Melbourne Cup day, when all the reporters had scattered across the city to cover the races, society lunches,
charity functions and even community picnics. Today had
that same feeling of a big event, but of course it was so
much sadder.

She watched as Sam walked towards his desk, shoulders slumped, face pale.

'Another problem, I'm afraid, sir,' Grace said. 'Nolan's
off sick. Tonsillitis. His housemate rang a few minutes ago.'

'Damn it!'

Grace flinched then looked towards the ringing phone on the desk.

'He's supposed to be covering Scots'. There's no one else to do it.'

'What about one of the subs?'

'They're all needed here to get the first edition out.'

Grace waited for the next outburst but Sam was quiet. She looked up and realised he was watching her. 'Grab your coat and your notebook, Miss Fowler—you'll have to cover the service instead.'

'What? Me?' Grace fought her face as it tried to split wide in a smile. 'Really?'

'Don't get too excited. Just take notes then bring them back so one of the subs can write it up. Nothing fancy. Just whatever the pastor says during the service. We'll add a few pars to the bigger story, a wrap from across the memorials.'

'I see, right.' Grace got her arm tangled in her coat as she tried to fill her handbag with pencils and two spare notepads at the same time. She tidied her hair then pinned on her hat and tied a scarf around her neck. It might be early summer but today felt wintery.

'Where am I going?'

'Collins Street. I'll walk with you and show you where to stand.'

Grace struggled to keep pace with Sam as he strode up the hill.

'We need to be there early. Get your notebook and pencil out and stand with the other reporters. That way, people know where you are and they can choose to stand near you or not.'

'Are we allowed inside?'

'Yes, you're allowed to stand just inside the door, so the copy kids can get in and out without interrupting people listening to the service.'

'I'm sending copy back?'

She'd dreamed of her first assignment in so many different settings, but she hadn't thought it would happen this way. TORCHY HOLDS THE FRONT PAGE. It was just like in the movies, she thought. All the men had gone to war and a small town girl got her big break. She just had to make sure she covered everything they'd need, but what if she forgot something critical?

'Get yourself an order of service,' Sam said, as though he was reading her thoughts. 'Write down exactly what each speaker says and make a few notes about the number of people, the hymns they sing, any psalms. The subs will take it from there.'

The crowd was so huge the church couldn't hold them. Despite the rain, they'd gathered in their hundreds, huddled beneath hats and umbrellas. Standing beside the door, Grace saw women being led through the crowds in twos and threes, clinging to each other for support and comfort. Most of them were weeping. Some women were older—the mothers or the aunts, she supposed— but the vast majority were young women: the wives and sweethearts.

Sadness stole her breath as the feeling of responsibility dawned on her. This was so much more than just a chance to write her first story for the paper. For many people, this was one of the most important days of their lives. She was witnessing history and she had to record every moment, every detail.

Two women walked towards the door, holding tightly to each other's hands. The woman wearing a black woollen suit was as thin as a stick. She stared straight ahead as she made her way along the path, as rigid as a wind-up doll. The other woman scanned the sea of faces surrounding them, bewildered, as though she didn't know where she was or how she'd got there.

'My neighbour, Mae Parker,' Sam said quietly in Grace's ear. 'Her husband was on the ship.'

'It's tragic,' Grace said.

'She looks pretty frail; I won't try to introduce you.'

Grace saw Mrs Parker lock eyes with Sam, who removed his hat and bowed his head towards her. Then he was gesturing to an older man walking behind, calling to him to help her.

'The poor woman,' Grace said, feeling a lump of sadness in her throat as she watched the women move slowly towards the front pews. 'I'll be fine if you want to head off,' she said, determined not to let Sam see her cry. She'd never be taken seriously as a reporter if she choked up on her first assignment.

Sam nodded. 'Okay then. Remember to look out for the copyboy at one-thirty, then head straight back as soon as the service is over. We'll take care of the rest.'

Grace settled against the wall just inside the doors, opened her notebook and began taking notes, describing the crowd, the rich sounds of the organ music, the beauty of the stained-glass windows. Although the church was warm, Grace saw people still huddled in their coats. At one o'clock precisely, Pastor Symonds addressed the congregation.

He led them in prayer and hymns, then spoke about the tragedy. 'A strange poignancy is added to the grief of those who have been bereaved by the fact that the sinking of the *Sydney* is attended by so much mystery. It would be some comfort to them to have known a little more; to many hearts it would have brought an added thrill of pride to have heard of particular instances of bravery in which their loved ones played a part. They only know that hundreds of brave men had given themselves for their country.'

People nodded agreement and sniffled into hankies. Grace flipped to a new page in her notebook, holding her breath as she wrote furiously, determined to capture the exact order of his words. She was amazed that he was being so critical, so controversial. Surely the paper couldn't print this? But, she reasoned, he'd said it in front of the entire congregation, so there was absolutely no reason why she shouldn't report it. She wondered whether the other priests and pastors around the country were also being so blunt.

A lone bugler sounded the Last Post then the congregation bowed their heads while Beethoven's 'Funeral March on the Death of a Hero' rumbled through the transepts. When Dyson, the freckly copyboy, appeared in front of Grace, silently waiting for her notebook, she felt a rush of fear. *I've got something extraordinary here*, she thought. *What if he loses the book? He might drop it somewhere or the rain might soak the pages.* AWARD-WINNING STORY DOWN THE DRAIN!

'I'm heading back now,' she said, sure that she had enough for the story. 'I'll take it myself.'

⁓⁓ ◦⦚◦ ⁓⁓

Grace was the first back in the office. Sam might be annoyed that she hadn't stayed longer, but the service was over and, other than eavesdropping on the families, she wouldn't get anything more. She wanted to type up her notes, maybe even craft a few paragraphs, just to make sure her thoughts were clear. She found herself transcribing the sermon then describing the atmosphere. By the time Sam arrived back at his desk, she'd written enough copy to fill ten column inches. She handed him her pile of typed chits and carbon copies then, when he said he didn't need anything else, she went in search of a strong cup of tea.

The staff cafeteria was deserted. Grace waited at the cash register with her tray, her ears buzzing, her breathing so tight she was almost giddy. As sad as the day was, it was thrilling to cover a story like this, rushing to get it written for a deadline. It was just like she'd imagined all those times sitting alone in the dark watching Torchy Blane movies. Of course, her real job was answering the phones and filing edited stories and photos—for the moment, anyway. Today was just a one-off, but it was a taste, a lovely big bite of what she wanted, being a real reporter, covering real stories. Nothing mattered more than that.

The sound of china smashing on the floor came from behind the kitchen door. 'Those teacups are coming out of your pay, you klutz!'

'Wouldn't want to be in their shoes,' Grace heard a voice behind her say. But not just any voice; as soon as she heard him every part of her brain fizzed; excitement fluttered in her chest. She hesitated before turning to look at him, not trusting her complexion to behave. Taking a small breath, she set her smile and met his lovely gaze.

'I hope no one was hurt,' she said.

'I can't hear screams of pain; that's always a good sign,' Phil replied.

Grace glanced at the corned beef sandwich on her plate. 'This might not be the best time to order a cup of tea, if everything's broken.'

'Allow me.' Phil stepped behind the counter and found a small teapot, a cup and saucer and a milk jug. 'Bushells, *mademoiselle?*'

'*Oui, monsieur. Merci beaucoup.*'

Phil used the urn to fill the pot, then placed the pot on Grace's tray and found a strainer in a basket under the bench.

'How do you know where to find everything?' Grace asked.

'We have free range at night when the kitchen closes— just for pots of tea, but they're a lifesaver at three in the morning during a bushfire. Let's sit down and wait for the cashier. Meanwhile, you can tell me all about your first big assignment.'

'How did you know?'

'No secrets in the newsroom, Miss Fowler. Besides, there's a couple of noses out of joint. Some of the cadets are annoyed that they weren't called in.'

Grace's smile slipped. 'People are upset with me? It was just a spur of the moment thing, when there was no one else to send.'

Phil smiled. 'They'll get over it. The cadets just get a bit competitive, trying to outdo each other for stories.'

'But I don't want anyone hating me,' Grace said, 'especially today.'

'So how was your first foray into the heady world of the fourth estate?'

'I can't believe how much I loved it; it was better than I'd imagined,' she blurted, then blushed, realising she sounded like a silly child.

Phil laughed. 'Uh-oh! Sounds like you've been bitten by the news bug.'

'I've always wanted to do this, ever since I could read and write,' Grace said shyly. 'Maybe if Mr Barton likes what I've done today, he'll give me a chance. I wrote a full story, all the details, not just notes and quotes.'

Phil looked at her, the skin around his eyes crinkling with amusement. 'Don't get your hopes too high, Grace. He just wanted the pastor's words. He won't run any of your colour, probably won't even have time to read it.'

Grace stared at the man across from her, so sure of himself, of his place in the newsroom. He wouldn't have ever had to beg for the chance to cover a story. She took several slow sips of her tea.

'Don't take it badly, Grace,' Phil said. 'I'm sure you did a great job. That's just the way it is on deadline. Ah, here's the cashier now. I'll pay for lunch.'

⁌⁍

'Miss Fowler!' Sam called as she returned to the newsroom. He was standing over the subs desk, rolling layouts for the vacuum tube that would transport them to the compositors' room on the floor below. She steeled herself against the criticism for not staying longer at the church. She'd probably missed something critical by being so silly about her notebook and leaving early, probably wasted her chance by not trusting Dyson. She tried to read his face. He wasn't frowning, which was good. The newsroom was full of clatter and ringing and shouting as usual, but today everything seemed more frantic. As she approached the desk, Sam's expression changed to a tired grin.

'Good job. We're using it all in a separate story. That Symonds fellow—what a character, giving the navy a serve like that. I'd love to see Hill's face when he reads your story.'

Your story! Grace barely repressed a yelp of joy. 'Do I get a by-line?'

Sam laughed. 'Don't push it, Fowler,' he said.

Fowler! Last name only, just like the reporters . . . the *other* reporters.

CHAPTER 21

6 December 1941

THE DAY AFTER THE service, Mae saw Alice and the boys off at the station, then she and Katie caught another train to Elizabeth's house for lunch. Harry's mother had planned to have the entire family over for afternoon tea after the service but Mae had begged off, saying she felt ill. But as bad as Mae felt, she'd been shocked by Elizabeth's appearance outside the church. The older woman seemed to have aged decades with deep, deep lines around her eyes and nose.

Mae stared at her own reflection in the train window, taking in the dark circles around her eyes, the hollows beneath her cheekbones, the heaviness of her cheeks that felt like they might never have the strength to form another smile. The train slowed and halted beside a row of tennis courts, full of women dressed in whites laughing and playing as though they hadn't a care.

Mae let her mind drift back to the first time she'd seen Harry, at the tennis club just near their cottage, eight years earlier. That day she'd been playing the formidable club champions, Edna and Beryl.

Edna was rumoured to be in her sixties, but no one knew for certain. Beryl was a bit younger, but she was still fearsome at the net. Mae, aged seventeen, was paired with Glenys, a friend of Et's from church. Aunt Et had signed her up for the Saturday tennis competition, saying it was the perfect way to meet her future husband, but scampering around a tennis court, getting red dust through her blonde hair and under her nails, seemed to Mae like the least promising way to meet a man.

Halfway through the third game, Edna lobbed Glenys's serve over Mae's head towards the baseline. Mae knew she'd never make it, but a rare streak of determination drove her to chase it anyway, right towards a group of young men who were watching the spectacle through the wire fence.

Lunging for the ball, Mae overbalanced and lurched forward, hitting the ground with her arm first, followed by her ribs, her hip and her knees. She skidded towards the fence through the dust, just managing to keep her head and face from scraping along the gravel, and halted in front of the young men, some of whom seemed to be exclaiming in a foreign language—German, she thought.

'My God, are you all right?' One of the young men—with a broad Australian accent—rushed through the side gate and crouched by her side.

'I—I'm not sure,' Mae said, waiting for the pain of broken bones to sear through her embarrassment. Then she noticed his unusual eyes; sapphire blue, fringed with the longest, darkest lashes she'd ever seen. It was unfair to see lashes like that on a man, especially when hers were so white it looked like she had none. She rubbed at the grazes on her knee and her right palm.

'Do you think anything's broken?' he asked.

'Just my pride,' Mae said, wobbling as she tried to stand.

'Lean against me,' the man said, cupping her elbow.

'Thank you, I'm fine.'

She dusted her skirt then dabbed at her knee with a hanky. Sensing the man watching her, she forced her mouth into a grim smile. 'Really, it's nothing. I think your friends are waiting.'

Mae watched his expression shift from concern to disappointment. He stepped back and straightened his stance. Mae noticed the naval insignia on his jumper.

She was doing it again; forgetting to make a fuss when he was only trying to be helpful. Men hated that. *Smile with your eyes, girl,* Et had advised. *You must learn to flirt a little, flutter your lashes.* Mae had always imagined fluttering her lashes would make her look simple, but she suddenly felt compelled to try. 'You're very kind,' she said, forcing herself to flutter as she met his eyes. 'Thank you for your concern.'

She looked towards the net and saw the three older women watching with interest, conducting a whispered conversation behind their hands.

'Well, if there's nothing further I can do, perhaps I'll see you at tea,' the man said.

'I'll save you a cup,' she said, then immediately regretted her inane response. The teapot was so large it would cater for an entire crew, though he didn't necessarily know that, she supposed.

He followed the other men, who were heading for the grass courts near the grandstand. Mae rubbed her aching wrist. Her knee was throbbing too.

'All in one piece?' Beryl asked.

'Yes, thanks. We should probably get on with the game before I get too stiff.'

'Sure you don't need to forfeit?' Edna said.

'She's still young enough to bounce,' Beryl teased. 'Besides, we don't want to finish too early or someone will miss the chance to see those handsome sailors again.'

Edna laughed. 'They're too young for an old bat like you.'

'Too old, you mean. I'm only twenty-five on the inside.'

Mae hobbled through the remainder of the set as her opponents lobbed balls over her head and past her limp forehand and backhand. As hard as she tried, she couldn't keep her mind on the game. She kept picturing the man's face, his perfect blue eyes, his wide smile. She wondered whether he was laughing at the spectacle she'd made of herself. Had her skirt ridden up? Had he seen her bloomers? She blushed at the thought. Maybe she should just leave after the match, slink home on the train, but she was rostered to help with tea and she'd left Et's good plate on the table with the scones. She didn't dare go home without it.

After managing to lose every game in the two sets, Mae tidied her face and hair while the kettle boiled. Powder tamed the shiny patches on her face but fluffing her hair raised puffs of dust. Close inspection of her scalp showed red lines of dirt. She'd only had her hair washed and set the night before. Now she'd have to wear her hair like this for another week.

After an hour of keeping the kettle on the boil and serving tea to the other tennis groups, Mae could barely concentrate. She'd given milk to people who wanted their tea black and poured boiling water into a teapot with no leaves. Her wrist throbbed as she tried to lift the pot to pour fresh cups for two teams of elderly gents from the local Rotary Club. Then she heard voices approaching from the main path. She nearly missed a cup as she turned towards the sound of their chatter. She couldn't believe it; they were looking at her and laughing. Unable to look at them, she arranged spoons on cups and saucers, topping up the pot, tapping out the tea strainer.

The man who'd rushed to her aid was watching when she finally looked up. He smiled. 'Still upright, I see.'

Mae raised her teapot as if she proposed to clobber him. 'Didn't your mother ever tell you it's rude to laugh at other people's misfortune?'

He scratched his jaw then slowly ran his hand through his dark, silky hair. 'My mother's never told me off for anything, but I apologise for being a clod. Are you hurt?'

'I'm quite well, thank you. Black or white?'

'I have a thing for white—and blonde; anything that reminds me of sunshine,' he said. 'Harry Parker, leading seaman and navy tennis team captain. And this is Lieutenant Detmers, sports officer from the German cruiser *Köln*. His ship is here for training exercises.'

'Yes, I read about your visit in the paper,' Mae said, hoping she didn't look uncomfortable. Her day was taking her into all sorts of uncharted territory, but she'd never imagined she'd be consorting with the enemy—well, former enemy.

'Your fall was quite spectacular,' Detmers said, his English perfect.

'I'm glad to have provided such memorable entertainment.'

The other men laughed as Detmers translated.

'They'll be talking about your acrobatics in the mess for weeks,' Harry said.

Mae forced her gaze to meet his and stay there. 'I'm sure they'll see much more interesting sights on their visit.'

Harry's smile didn't falter. 'I don't think *I* will. It's not every day that a beautiful girl flings herself at my feet.'

Mae's mind froze. She had no witty retort, no smart comeback. She wanted to keep the conversation going, but instead her mouth flapped open then closed while she silently debated whether to acknowledge the compliment or bat it away. Maybe she should say something nice about his appearance? *What nice tanned calves you have.* Or, *My goodness, your wrists look strong.* She rested the teapot on the table and straightened the cups and saucers, glancing at him quickly. His eyes really were the prettiest shade of blue she'd ever seen.

'Did you know the Germans have a lion on board their ship, and a kangaroo?' Harry said a moment later.

'They do not!'

'It's true, I swear. Gifts from different places they've visited. They live in cages on the deck.'

Mae leaned back slightly, relaxed her shoulders and

tilted her head towards him in the way Et had said men liked. Behind Harry, she could see the Germans clearing the platters of sandwiches and scones. They'd be ready to leave soon, but she already knew she didn't want him to go. There was a fluttering in her stomach and her pulse was racing. She took a breath and tried to calm her tumbling, churning thoughts. *He'd never be interested in a scrawny little bookworm like me*, she thought. *Besides, he's just being polite after my fall. He's stopped speaking. Quick, mention the weather, ask if he plays lots of tennis. Oh, of course he must— he's the team captain.* She saw his expression turn serious.

'I—I could show you around the German ship tomorrow, if you like,' Harry said, his tone tentative now. 'It's only open to the public today, but I'm sure Detmers could arrange for us to have a tour tomorrow. You could bring your family if you like . . . or your fellow.'

Mae tried to glean his thoughts. The offer of a tour was friendly, but it meant nothing. He probably had a wife and children tucked away somewhere and he was feeling lonely. And her aunt and uncles would never set foot on a German ship. The war felt like yesterday to them, her uncles' wounds still giving them grief. *Insensitive*, Albert had branded the visit by the German ship. *Far too soon*, William had agreed. Perhaps Et would come along and sit on the pier while Mae toured the ship with Harry. He looked nervous but keen. Then again, maybe she didn't need a chaperone. After all, she *was* seventeen and Harry seemed nice—very nice indeed.

She smiled. 'That sounds wonderful. I'd love to.'

When Mae finally made it to Elizabeth's house for lunch, Richard and Eric were sitting at the dining table with the papers laid out in front of them, discussing the day's news.

'Can you believe it? Those poor buggers were stuck on the *Kormoran* for five months, just sailing up and down the coast. Prisoners in their own backyard.'

Mim and one of the neighbours were in the kitchen, fussing over pots of tea and sandwiches. In the front room Elizabeth slowly rocked Katie, holding her close as if somehow the sleeping baby could absorb some of her grief. Mae sat across from Elizabeth with her back to the piano. She couldn't bear to look at Harry's photograph sitting atop the piano beside his violin, nestled in the leather case which looked like a tiny coffin lined with red crushed velvet.

'It says here that the Krauts reckon they sunk the *Mareeba* in June. The Aussie survivors were on the *Kormoran* till October. Then they got transferred to POW camps in Germany.'

'Utter bloody torture, to be so close to home for so long. They'd have been watching the coastline most of that time. How'd you be, not being able to yell for help or swim for the shore. At least they didn't have to see them sink the *Sydney*.'

'Well, if they had, we might have known what really happened. It makes no sense, the *Sydney* being outgunned like that. The Jerries must've been in cahoots with another German boat, or a sub maybe.'

'Maybe it was the Japs. A bloke outside the church yesterday said Jap subs have been hanging round up north.'

'Well, anyway, a bunch of rotten Jerry POWs won't tell us the truth.'

'Look, it says here that the German captain's been named in a communiqué from Berlin: Captain Theodor Anton Detmers, he's called.'

'Doesn't sound all that German, does it?'

An image of the German tennis player she'd met all those years ago came to mind; the one who'd spoken such perfect English. No; that would be too much of a coincidence. Detmers must be a common name, or maybe she hadn't remembered it correctly.

Katie stirred and Elizabeth rocked her a little faster. 'Did Alice make it to the train on time?'

'Yes, they had half an hour to spare,' Mae said, slowly lifting her cup of tea from the saucer, trying to stop it from trembling.

'And they had plenty of food for the trip?'

'I packed some cakes people had dropped off. I'm sure the boys would have been happy.'

'Such well-behaved children. You wouldn't really think it, considering they normally run wild on a farm.'

Mae pictured Katie covered head to toe in briquette dust and the boys chasing each other up and down the hallway when it was too wet to play outside. 'They're good company for each other, but they can be a bit of a handful.'

'Alice looked very unwell at the church. How is she managing?'

'Not well. Not sleeping or eating. She's expecting, you know.'

'Babies are made of hardy stuff; they adapt,' Elizabeth said, looking at Katie.

Mae strained to hear more of the boys' conversation from the next room. She looked down at the carpet, hoping to avoid Elizabeth's attention for a moment. Light blue cabbage roses, the size of dinner plates, seemed to lift like lily pads from the darker blue background. Blue cabbage roses—who ever heard of such a thing?

'You don't look well either, Mae. Have you eaten?'

Mae was surprised at the concern in Elizabeth's voice.

'I'm managing, thank you. Everyone's been very kind.'

A knock at the front door interrupted the conversations.

'Probably someone from church,' Mim said, returning to the lounge room. She picked up the teapot and swirled it to check whether it needed refilling.

They listened to Richard's footsteps as he walked along the hallway to open the door.

Muffled male voices, a brief discussion. Then the front door closed and a single set of footsteps paused in the hallway. Richard walked back into the lounge room with his eyes downcast, carrying a large package wrapped in brown paper.

'Who was that, dear?' Elizabeth asked.

Keeping his head bowed, Richard crossed to the piano, holding the parcel away from his body as though it might explode. As he placed it beside the violin, Mae took in the crumpled brown paper, the hole in one side where the string had pulled too tightly. She slowly registered what it was. Elizabeth gasped and Mim quietly crumpled into a chair. It was Harry's unopened birthday package, stamped with large black letters: RETURN TO SENDER.

CHAPTER 22

8 December 1941

GRACE GLANCED AT THE bank of clocks above the subeditors' desk showing times for London, New York and Melbourne. It was one-thirty pm local time. Three editions of the paper had been put to bed. The fourth edition was normally the last, but today was different. The Japanese had attacked Pearl Harbor in Hawaii overnight and America had declared war. The Japanese were also reported to be heading south towards Malaya and Australia. Darwin's naval, air force and army bases were on the highest alert. Stop News and City editions would run until six or seven.

Grace's stomach grumbled as the telephone rang. There'd been no time for lunch. She answered the phone but the voice on the other end interrupted before she could complete her greeting.

'Grace, it's Phil. I need the boss.'

'He's on the phone.'

'It's urgent. He'll want to hear this.'

'Just a moment, I'll see if he wants to speak to you.'

Grace put the receiver on the desk, stood and walked the few steps so that she was in front of Sam. He held up one finger as he finished his conversation.

'Phil says he has something urgent; he's on line two,' she said, when he'd hung up.

'What is it, Taylor?' Grace heard him say.

A few minutes later, Sam called Grace back to his desk. 'Taylor's up at the Exhibition Building with a snapper. The police are rounding up all the Japanese in Melbourne for interrogation. They'll be locked up afterwards. I need you to get up there and pick up some films for the fourth edition.'

Grace dropped her notebook on the desk and grabbed her bag and hat. Okay, it wasn't the chance to write a story, but this was a copyboy job, which was nearly as good. And Sam hadn't even hesitated about sending her.

'Let the picture desk know you're going,' Sam called as Grace buttoned her cardigan, ready to step outside. 'I'll get the press room and the compositors ready.'

Moments later, she was in the street, running up the hill and along several city blocks to the gardens on the edge of the city, only slowing at intersections. Ever since the memorial service last week, Grace felt certain that her life had begun to change. She felt a sense of lightness, lifting her feet and helping her to run faster. Sam was definitely treating her differently. This morning he'd talked to her about the major stories as though she was part of the reporting team. He'd even sought her opinion on Pearl Harbor and Malaya.

'Everyone's wondering where the next Japanese air raid might happen,' he said. 'Melbourne's unlikely, I'd say;

they'd be more interested in Sydney. What do you think, Miss Fowler? What can we assume from the information we've received today?'

'It seems to me we have nothing but speculation. No one predicted Hawaii so I doubt they have any idea about the next move either.'

Sam had smiled and nodded then turned back to his typewriter.

Each day she'd willed him to say something, anything, about another reporting assignment, but he hadn't said a word and Grace was careful not to nag him. Maybe over January, when people were still away on their summer holidays, she'd put forward some more of her story ideas. It was only a few months now till Barbara's wedding, so the timing could work well.

Running through the parkland towards the exhibition hall, she was surprised to see the entryway almost empty. There were a few police vans on the forecourt outside the huge wooden doors. Four reporters and three photographers stood in the foyer smoking and reading the papers, like they were waiting for a train. She'd heard that at least half of a reporter's life was spent waiting for the news to happen, especially on courts or police rounds, so you had to get along really well with the other press or your life was pretty lonely. Several of the group were gathered around Phil, who wasn't saying anything, just nodding and listening. But he was clearly at the centre of the men; he stood a little taller and he was slightly better dressed. The men around him talked over each other, watching to make sure he laughed at their jokes or nodded at their comments.

Grace stood back from the group but Phil noticed her and walked over, his smile more radiant than the agreeable face he'd worn with the men.

'Well, well. Copyboy duties today! This is becoming quite the habit.'

'Sam couldn't spare anyone else.'

'Well, as you can see, there's not much action at the moment.'

Grace looked through a gap between the doors, expecting to see hundreds, perhaps thousands of Japanese people lined up waiting to be questioned. But she saw nothing. There was no sound either, just the reporters and photographers asking each other for smokes, comparing race tips.

'Where is everyone?'

'The police started rounding them up about ten this morning,' Phil said. 'My running coach called me. Said he was worried about being separated from his family. He's Japanese, you know.'

'Oh, really!'

'Most of the Japs have already left the country. Fewer than twenty left in the state, they reckon.'

'That's amazing,' she said. 'What about the rest of the country?'

'Police reckon there's about seven hundred left in Australia, mostly up north in the pearling areas.'

'What happens next?'

'They'll finish the questioning then send them to internment camps.'

Graham Ross, the *Tribune* photographer, stood behind Phil reading a copy of *Life* magazine. An older man, in his fifties at least, Ross was also called Mr Front Page by the newsroom because he always managed to find the angle or the light that transformed an ordinary picture into a work of art. Grace sometimes wondered why he stuck with the paper, which used his pictures so small, when his work would look so much better in a magazine like the one he was reading.

'Miss Fowler, wonderful story last week,' he said as he slid captions beneath wide rubber bands on two film rolls and handed them over. 'As good as anything Mr Taylor could write, I'm sure.'

'Steady on, the reporters are already shaking in their boots that we're about to be invaded by a bunch of Lois Lanes.'

'Thank you, Mr Ross. It's very nice of you to say so. And Mr Taylor, you have more to fear than cartoon girl reporters.'

Graham winked at her and Phil pretended to look scared.

'Dorothy Dix, eat your heart out.'

'At the very least!' Grace smiled.

'Good girl,' Graham said. 'It's about time these lads had a shake-up.'

'Nice talking to you both, but I'd better be off. Hold the front page, and all that!'

'Grace, we're all going for drinks later. Maybe you'd like to come too, now that you're a red-hot reporter?'

Phil's grin was as warm as it had been when she first started at the paper. She hadn't expected to see it directed her way again. Oh no: prickles of heat starting in her cheeks and running down her neck.

'Perhaps. I don't know. I'll see what time I finish.'

Grace felt close to airborne as she raced back to the *Tribune* building. Her feet complained about running in heels, but she ignored the forming blisters and ran all the way through the city and straight to Sam's desk.

'Ah, there you are,' Sam said, looking up from the pages he was correcting. He peered at her over the top of his glasses. 'You're loving this, aren't you?'

'It's in my blood.'

Sam smiled. 'Tell the darkroom boys we need something in fifteen minutes.'

Grace dashed to the pictorial department to deliver the film, but no one was at the desk. The processing area was empty too, so she called out and parted the first set of blackout curtains, closed them behind her, then walked through a second set of curtains into the orange gloom of the darkroom. Letting her eyes adjust, she saw a row of enlargers set high on benches along opposite sides of the humid space. A trough in the middle of the room held trays of chemicals and water baths. The smell of acid and ammonia caught in the back of her throat. Over the trickle of running water, she heard three or four voices.

'Hello,' she called hesitantly. 'I've got films from the Exhibition Building.'

The conversations stopped and everyone looked her way. A man in a dark duster called out, 'Be with you in a tick, love.'

She recognised Frank, the darkroom technician, from his voice and then his shape: small and gaunt with a rough mop of wiry hair. Phil had told her that Frank used to be a jockey but a bad fall had crushed his back twenty years earlier. No one ever saw him sitting down. The closest he ever got was leaning against the racing desk with a cigarette wedged between stained fingers, swapping tips and gossip with the writers. The rest of the time he scurried around the darkroom mixing chemicals, processing films and cleaning the cameras.

Frank motioned for Grace to follow him out through the curtains. As they emerged into the light, Grace saw the walls for the first time; they were covered in photographs and cartoons of scantily clad women.

'We don't get too many visitors in here, love,' the technician said with an apologetic grin. 'Most people go to the office instead.'

'I'm sorry,' she muttered. 'There was no one around and these are urgent.'

'That's all right, love. I'll take care of it from here. Have you got the caption details?'

Grace handed over the films. 'The captions are attached. Mr Barton said he needs them in fifteen minutes.'

'Twenty or thirty minutes should do it,' he said. 'I'll bring 'em round when the boss has chosen the shot.'

'We'll make a copy kid out of you yet,' Sam said as Grace returned to her desk.

'I'd rather be a cadet.'

He laughed.

❦

An hour later Phil was perched on the edge of her desk, chatting easily, as though the distance that had grown between them over the last few weeks had never happened. 'You ready for that drink?'

'I'm not sure I can get away,' Grace said, thrilled but confused by his sudden attention. He was practically married. What was he doing here? Was he flirting? Surely not; he was just charming her, like he charmed all his other reporting buddies, nothing more than that. And it was exciting that he thought of her as a reporter. Maybe the others would follow his lead—maybe even Sam!

'Taking Fowler somewhere important, Taylor?' Sam said without looking up from his proofs.

'Just over to the pub for a quick drink.'

'Well, I think we all need a drink today. Make sure no one gives her any trouble.'

'I'll look after her.'

Grace wondered at the changes one week had wrought. Was this really the result of a single story? It felt like she'd crossed some sort of invisible line and now she had . . . respect. *Calm down*, she scolded herself. It was just a drink with a workmate on a day that had everyone feeling petrified. It meant nothing.

As they entered the pub, Phil placed his hand in the small of Grace's back and guided her to the upstairs bar, packed wall to wall with *Tribune* staff and several *Gazette* journalists who were having a drink before their news conference. Phil and Grace found a space against a wall.

'What would you like?'

'A glass of beer, thanks.'

'With lemonade?'

'No thanks, just beer.'

'Pot and a glass, thanks, Joe,' Phil called to the barman. He turned back to Grace. 'I didn't take you for a beer drinker. Thought you'd be more into sherry, or port wine and lemonade.'

'A girl's drink?'

Phil smiled. 'Got me there!'

'My dad used to let me have a sip or two of his beer, then I graduated to my own glass. Reminds me of home.'

'Homesick?'

'A little, especially with so much going on. But working at the paper is so exciting. I think I'm just missing having people to talk to about work and everything, especially today.'

'You can talk to me anytime,' Phil said, catching her gaze and holding it until he was slapped on the back by two young reporters. Grace had seen them in the lift but didn't know their names.

'You guys are a bit early, aren't you?' Phil said. 'Gaz, Jacko, this is Grace, our editorial secretary. These fellows work on *The Gazette*, Grace. We all started the same day as copyboys, but they're still on general—haven't got rounds yet,' he teased.

Gaz, the shorter and rounder of the two, shook his head. 'Investigative, mate. We cover the big stories, not fun and games like cricket and the gee-gees—not that you could really call them sports; just pretty-boy pastimes, don't you reckon, Jacko?'

'Too right, mate; political corruption, gangsters,

dodgy business—we get more exclusives than anyone else.'
With his narrow face and oversized suit, Jacko reminded
her of a boy playing dress-ups. In fact, the pair of them
looked like a junior version of Laurel and Hardy.

'You guys need a new routine. You've been telling
those lies for years now. No one listens anymore.' Phil
winked at Grace.

'Grace looks like a smart girl. I'm sure she's happy to
be talking to real reporters, aren't you?'

She laughed, suddenly aware of how close Phil was
standing, heat from his arm radiating through her cardigan
as the crowd gently pushed them together. She tried to
move away, but there was nowhere to go. Jacko and Gaz
were jostled back towards the bar.

'Is everything all right?' he said softly in her ear.

'Yes, thank you,' she replied.

'It's getting a bit rowdy. Maybe we should go somewhere else, get something to eat.'

This time she turned and looked at him. 'Are you
asking me out, Mr Taylor?'

'Yes, I suppose I am.'

Grace was amazed by the seriousness of his expression. There was no confident smirk, no chance that he was
joking around. He was asking her an important question.
She needed to ask one of her own.

'Phil, I—I can't. What about your girlfriend? I read . . .'

'You know you can't believe everything you read in the
paper, Grace. They got it wrong.'

Grace waited, wanting him to say more but not sure
she wanted to hear it. Was he saying that he wasn't seeing

Caroline any longer? Surely not. But if he was lying, that would mean he was being a sleaze! How was she supposed to know what to think?

'It said you were getting married,' she probed.

'We're not. In fact, that story finally made us tell our parents the truth. They wanted us to get married. We weren't interested.'

'Really?' she said.

'Yes, really. Come on, I'll tell you all about it.'

He led her down the stairs and out onto the street. Grace stopped under a lamppost where the lane met the street.

'I'm not going anywhere with you until you tell me what's going on,' Grace said, surprised to hear that her voice was steady. The beer must have calmed her nerves.

'Let's go and sit down somewhere quiet.'

'No, I mean it. I don't go out with cheaters.'

'You are very determined, Miss Fowler. You're going to make one heck of a reporter.'

'Don't try to butter me up. I refuse to be charmed.'

'All right then, here goes. Caroline and I grew up together. Our parents paired us off when we were children. It was a bit of a joke at first, I think, but we got along so well we kind of grew into their story. We were best friends, but she felt more like a sister than a girlfriend. For a long time, I kind of went along with it, but then I met someone who made me want much, much more.'

Grace almost sobbed with disappointment. So he'd fallen in love with someone. Maybe it was Avril. She was glamorous enough to turn any man's head. Or someone from his university days; a smart girl with good breeding whom his parents would adore. She forced herself to keep her expression neutral. In the most detached tone she could muster, she asked, 'So what happened to her?'

'Her? Who?'

'The girl you met.'

'You duffer. I mean you. From the moment I met you I could hardly concentrate on my work or my running, anything. I just wanted to sit on the edge of your desk all day and gaze into your beautiful eyes.'

'*Me?*'

He smiled. 'When I noticed you looking at me at work, I thought you might have been interested. But then you stopped looking. I figured I'd got it wrong.'

'I—I thought you weren't interested.'

'I couldn't be more interested,' he responded.

Grace smiled so hard her cheeks ached.

'Does that smile mean you'll have dinner with me?'

Grace didn't trust herself to speak so she just nodded.

He took her hand in his, sending the loveliest pins and needles dancing along her arm.

They walked slowly up the hill towards Bourke Street, where he led her into a bustling Chinese restaurant. Settling at a table in the back, they sat side by side rather than opposite each other.

'I hope you like Chinese,' said Phil. 'I forgot to ask.'

'We've got Chinese at home, at the pub. I love lemon chicken.'

A pot of jasmine tea arrived while Phil ordered lemon chicken, beef with black bean sauce and fried rice to share.

After pouring the tea he rested the pot on the table and took a long look at her face.

'What a day. Disaster this morning and now this— you. I don't think I'll ever forget it. But I think we need to celebrate properly. Would you like to go out for a proper dinner on the weekend, somewhere special?'

Grace felt like she'd forgotten how to swallow. Her mouth still full of tea, she worked her throat, her tongue, then realised she needed to breathe, right now. Scared that she might breathe the tea into her lungs and drown, she pictured herself having to spit it into her cup, right in front of Phil. God, he'd run for the hills. He'd take that invitation back, tell her he'd forgotten another engagement. Her eyes bulged and she tried to breathe through her nose. Nothing worked. She looked down and concentrated on swallowing. Just in time, her throat opened and the tea slid down it. She gasped then managed a weak smile, feeling a burning pain in her chest, she hoped it was muscle strain, not a heart attack. 'Thank you,' she said. 'I'd love to.'

CHAPTER 23

Christmas 1941

MAE STARED AT THE lacy shadows dancing across the ceiling. As the curtains swayed to the left and then back to centre, she imagined she was underwater, looking up at clouds scudding across the sky. She let herself float beneath the ripples, listening to the sounds of children playing in the street, little girls squealing as they played hopscotch and boys shouting as a ball thudded off a wooden bat. While the neighbourhood buzzed with light and noise, Mae's mind felt shrouded in a thick, dark fog.

Since the memorial service she'd hardly slept more than a few hours each night. Sleep would have been a relief, but closing her eyes brought nightmares of fire and blood-soaked waves. The nights crawled until dawn, when early birdsong and the clip-clop of horses pulling the milk cart announced the arrival of another day. Sounds that Mae had loved just weeks before were suddenly mournful. She wondered whether Harry would ever lie beside her listening to those sounds again. Would she spend the rest of her life alone in a bed with the other half ice-cold, undisturbed? She tried to wrench her mind back to hope, but exhaustion made it harder every day.

Every morning she wept until drained then dragged herself out of bed, dressed and fed Katie, then returned to bed fully clothed in case a knock at the door meant she needed to pretend she was managing. Once her chores were done, she spent the days lying on her side touching Harry's last letter, the one she'd placed beneath his pillow. She didn't need to read the words; she could recite them like a poem.

> With any luck we won't have to rely on letters much longer for our most important conversations. It is just over two months before I finish my time, but it seems like forever. Is it too soon to wish for a long happy summer together, my darling Sunny?

It had been waiting in her letterbox the same day the birthday package was returned to Elizabeth. Sam said the post was held back until after the services. Anyone with relatives or friends on board the ship received their post that day. She imagined hundreds of mothers and wives and sisters opening their post at the same time, the whole country awash with tears.

Elizabeth's face had turned a ghostly grey when she realised what the package contained. Then she'd buried her face in her hands and run from the room. Mim ran after her. The boys, meanwhile, had disappeared to the backyard. Half an hour passed, and then an hour, but nobody returned to the lounge room, which was still strewn with half-drunk cups of tea and barely nibbled food. Mae carried a few plates to the kitchen then gathered her things. Choking out a tiny farewell to the empty room, she and the baby caught the train home. The letter was waiting when she arrived.

Since then, Mae had passed her time staring at the wall or the ceiling or out the window, doing just the bare minimum to keep Katie calm, fed and clean. Et arrived each evening—often with Albert and William in tow—to make sure Mae ate dinner. They'd watch her pick at a few vegetables and urge her to try a chop or some custard, then they'd beg her to go home with them, but the thought of leaving her cottage was inconceivable. She needed to be surrounded by Harry, his things, their life together. And she never wanted to be out of hearing of the radio, just in case there was news of the ship. She had it playing day and night, but that wouldn't be possible if she was living with her family. Nor could she bear having to talk about things that had nothing to do with him. She didn't want distraction; she wanted to focus her full attention on Harry and any mention of the ship, even if it was news repeated from days earlier.

But mentions were few and far between now that the world had shifted its attention so quickly to the Japanese attack on Pearl Harbor and the invasion of Malaya. That was it: just days after the memorials, the loss of the *Sydney* was no longer news. It might as well have never happened. Et said it was because everyone was scared;

that they were only just realising the scale of the disaster looming on their doorstep. The Yellow Peril was coming for them; it was just a matter of time. But Mae couldn't imagine anything worse than her husband and an entire ship's crew missing without a trace. And what if the rumours were true that the Japanese were involved? Even more reason to find the *Sydney*. She'd asked Sam Barton about it a few days after the service, but he swore the navy hadn't told them anything more. She didn't believe that was possible; he had to know something. Every day since, she'd asked Claire for news. In the last week, Claire had gently urged Mae to spend Christmas with her family.

'Leave a note on your door directing visitors to us,' Claire said.

'You're not spending Christmas with your parents?'

'We'll be right here with a house full of newsroom orphans. We'll ring you the moment we hear anything at all.'

❦

On the morning of Christmas Eve, Mae placed a gift for Harry on the buffet beside his picture. She'd made grey trousers to match his blue silk shirt. She pinned the note to the front door then pushed Katie's pram to the station and caught the train to Yarraville.

Walking down the ramp from the platform to the footpath, she kept her gaze low as she walked past the old Lyric Theatre, where she and Harry had seen dozens of films during their courtship. It was at the end of her family's street. *You're a woman with the lot*, Harry would tease. *Easy access to entertainment and a fast getaway on the train if I say the wrong thing.* Well, he couldn't leave fast enough last time he'd visited, could he? She understood why he'd been upset, but he could have made more of an effort; perhaps they both could have.

A large painful lump rose in her throat. More tears. Stopping outside her family's house, she blew her nose several times and wiped her face. Trying to still her thoughts, she examined the rose bushes stretching the full width of the fence. Most of the spring blooms were long gone, but new buds were forming that would produce huge blooms in autumn. Mae preferred bold reds, oranges and yellows, but Et always went for softer pinks and purples to complement the deep pink camellias towering either side of the four steps leading onto the verandah. The house needed repainting. The brickwork and columns were holding up well, but paint peeled from the cream-coloured fretwork.

Mae pulled the pram backwards up the steps and onto the tessellated tiles. Resting in a wicker chair, she tried to summon the energy she'd need to talk to her family when she went inside. The street was quiet. Many of the Victorian and Edwardian houses and cottages were occupied by older people who'd spent their lives in the area, working in foundries and workshops—the glassworks, the rope makers, the quarry down the road. Albert and William owned numerous commercial properties and shops in the area. Mae had grown up wondering whether her family was wealthy, but Et said it was rude to ask. 'We're comfortable, nothing more,' she'd say. 'We've worked hard for everything we own and we accept our good fortune with grace.'

Mae wondered about the nature of fortune, of fate; how some people seemed to have more luck than others. Until the last few weeks she would have said she'd been mostly lucky, and she didn't know whether she had the fortitude to accept bad luck. She'd had an unlucky start to life, but it could have been much worse. Her mother's death left her practically an orphan, but at least her aunt and uncles had come to her rescue. They'd kept her safe, protected her, but she'd always sensed something was missing. She couldn't put her finger on what it was.

She'd read books by the dozen, by the hundred, as she was growing up, searching for clues as to why she felt there was a gap, a hole inside her chest. Her reading didn't reveal many mothers to admire—especially not Mrs Bennet in *Pride and Prejudice*—but some of the father figures gave her pause for thought. What would it be like to have a father devoted to your happiness? Offering firm but wise counsel, never abandoning his child, never leaving her to feel that she'd done something wrong, wondering what she could have done to make him stay.

And now Harry had also decided she wasn't worth— no, she couldn't let her mind stray down that road. Since the day they'd met at tennis, she'd imagined their life together, a lovely home with a yard lit by sunshine and full of friends. Now the only future that came to mind was more days like this, her limbs feeling tired and heavy, her eyes brimming. She longed just to fade into the cushions, but Katie had other plans. Deciding that it was dinner time, she began to bellow. Well, that was every bit as effective as a doorbell, Mae supposed.

With a weak 'yoohoo', Mae held the screen door open with her hip and manoeuvred the pram inside.

Outstretched arms appeared along the hallway, whisking Katie out of the pram and into another room. Another set of hands steered Mae to her old bedroom and put her suitcase on the chair. That's right, she didn't have to talk after all. Her family knew that just getting herself here was all she could manage. She sat on her bed and watched as Et silently unpacked her case, placing the picture of Harry on the mantelpiece across from the bed.

'See? It's not so bad, dear,' Et said, parking the pram beside Mae's bed.

Mae tried to form words, to smile, but her mouth wouldn't move. 'I—It's . . .'

Et's pitying gaze settled on Mae.

'Come and sit in the kitchen. You can shell the peas. You always liked that job as a child.'

Mae followed her aunt and sat in a chair at the table beside a basket of freshly picked peapods. Without thinking she lifted the first pod, squeezed it gently between her fingers then, when it split, she slipped her thumb inside and ran it under the peas, flipping them into the dented metal colander for rinsing. She heard Albert and William out in the garden reading to Katie from the racing guide as if it were a children's story. A tap dripped in the bathroom. Several children ran along the front footpath, calling to one who must have fallen behind, *Hurry up, slow coach, you're gonna make us late for lunch*. Mae was acutely aware of every sound, but the one she most wanted to hear was absent.

'Can I switch the radio on? It's nearly time for the news.'

'Why don't we listen to some music today? There won't be much news.'

Mae looked at her aunt to make certain she was serious. 'How can you say that? I told you I'd only come if I could hear the news. Now you've got me here, you have to let me listen or I'll turn around and go home.'

'All right, all right,' Et grumbled as she strode to the radio and turned the dial. 'I just thought we could use some time off.'

'What do you mean? There's no time off for Harry, trying to come home. And there's no time off for me from worrying about him. Surely we owe it to them not to give up yet,' she pleaded.

'All right, Mae, settle down. I'll get you a sherry.'

❧ ⬥ ❧

All the shops were closed when Mae and her family walked home from the Christmas service. Normally crowded with cars and delivery vans, the only movement in the street was a dog poking through an overturned rubbish bin outside the butcher's shop. Albert shooed it away, but it returned as soon as they passed. Mae pushed the pram as Et counted on her fingers how many chairs were needed at the table that evening.

'We'll use the Royal Doulton setting; there's enough for all of us, including Harry's family.'

'I think they'd be more comfortable with the kitchen crockery,' Mae said.

'That's not very charitable, Mae. Besides, it's our Christmas too, and I'd like to use the good china.'

'It's up to you, Et. I just don't think they're used to expensive things. It might put them on edge.'

Albert and William raised eyebrows at each other then continued discussing war news. Mae's thoughts drifted to the previous Christmas, when Harry had walked her home from church along this exact same route, carefully holding her arm as though she were an invalid. He'd spent the entire walk anticipating every moment of today, which would have been their first Christmas together as a family. *We'll spend Christmas Eve with your family then go to church with them in the morning,* he'd said. *Then we'll have lunch with my family and spend the evening alone, walking on the beach if it's warm or snuggled on the couch if it's cool. It's important that we establish a family routine from the outset, don't you think?* he'd asked earnestly. *Let them all know we want to have some of the day for ourselves, never give over the entire Christmas to other people.*

Et stooped over the pram and tickled Katie through her rug. The little girl's laugh was unusually deep for a child so young. 'I could listen to that sound all day, couldn't I, sweetie? Couldn't I? Ah, there's that smile. We should bottle those. Lovely service, don't you think, dear?'

It took Mae a moment to realise the question was addressed to her. 'Yes, lovely.'

Actually, it hadn't been lovely at all. The minister

instructed everyone to rejoice that the Lord had sent his son to cleanse their sins. Well it didn't seem to be doing much good, did it? There were plenty of sinners out there killing, bombing. With the war on, Mae thought he might have offered comfort instead of celebration, hope instead of the same tired old sermons. The children's choir sang 'Silent Night'. It had always been her favourite, but it had been played so often on the radio over recent weeks that she'd come to hate it. *All is calm, all is bright*—no, it wasn't; there might never be a calm or bright night again. Reminding herself that Christmas was a time to pray harder, to keep her faith, she'd tuned out of the service, closed her eyes and prayed for Harry's safe return. There was no reason to give up yet, no reason at all.

❧ ⁂ ☙

Back at home, Et set the suet pudding boiling on the stove. She'd bought a goose and a chicken. Both were roasting and the air smelled of clove, onion and bacon stuffing.

'What time did you tell Elizabeth to be here?'

Mae sat quietly in the corner peeling potatoes. 'One o'clock. She'll have Mim, Richard and Eric with her.'

'And she's bringing a Christmas cake?'

'Yes, she made one a few months ago when she made Harry's.' Mae hoped she wouldn't bring the one from the birthday parcel. That would be just like her. She'd wait until everyone was eating then announce its provenance. *Waste not, want not*, she'd say, insisting on leaving it behind then going home to another without the awful memories attached.

Mae's stomach churned at the prospect of seeing her mother-in-law. Elizabeth was playing the part of bereaved mother to the hilt, sobbing into her hanky at every mention of Harry, or her children, or the war, or—well, anything, really. The violence of her grief scared Mae. It was as though she were intent on winning a contest. But Mae had begun to wonder if, by comparison, she herself wasn't showing enough sadness. Of course she'd never said it, but Mae could tell Elizabeth thought Harry deserved better, especially now; he deserved a wife torn apart by grief.

'You're off with the pixies again, Mae. Why don't you lie down before lunch? William can finish that.'

'Katie needs a feed soon.'

'We'll give her a bottle. Off you go.'

Mae shuffled to her childhood room and settled on the side of the bed where she normally slept, then rolled over to where Harry had slept during his last visit. Pulling the blanket over her legs she hugged a feather pillow, curling around its softness. She knew she wouldn't sleep, but being alone was better than trying to make conversation. They meant well, and they missed him too, but the effort of trying not to talk about him took every ounce of her strength. And dealing with Elizabeth today . . . well, she couldn't imagine how she was going to get through that. And Mim would probably be just as bad. Mae knew she was expected to listen to their endless stories about Harry as a boy, before she'd known him. They weren't interested in any stories that included her. But that was fine; there were pieces of his life that she didn't have to share with them either. Still, the whole day would be exhausting. Maybe if she just closed her tired eyes for a moment . . .

❧❧ ◑◐ ❧❧

'Good morning,' Et said, rousing Mae with a cup of tea.

Mae blinked as Et opened the curtains. Her eyes no longer scratched. Her body felt relaxed. She stretched in the light and realised she was . . . hungry?

'Is lunch ready?' Mae asked, sipping the warm, sweet tea.

Et laughed and grabbed Mae's skirt, which was hanging over the chair. She shook it out. 'I took this off you last night but I think it could use a press. I'll lend you a fresh blouse. You were sleeping so soundly we hated to wake you.'

'I missed lunch?'

'And dinner.'

'What did Elizabeth say? She must have been furious.'

'Don't worry about them. Mim brought Katie the most darling little dress. She made it from a tartan remnant she found at Coles and cut up two white linen serviettes for cuffs and collar. I think she's going to make a reasonable seamstress.'

'I slept through the whole thing?' Mae smiled for the first time in a month, then she sank into the feather pillows and mattress and stared at the door. Her smile faded as she pictured Harry the last time she'd seen him. She'd vowed to be the perfect wife, but she'd broken her own rules and let him leave in anger. And now she might never have the chance to put things right.

She felt a stab of pain below her ribs. Rolling onto her back, she tried to take a deep breath, but the pain intensified and now a heaviness weighed on her chest. Maybe she was having a heart attack. Was this how it felt to die? Did Harry feel this way? In the water? When he— She gasped as the thought broke like a wave, pulling her under. As she felt herself sinking, a new question slowly took shape. *That morning, the day you walked out the door . . . was that the last time?*

CHAPTER 24

January 1942

GRACE GAZED AT THE picture strip of herself and Phil from the photo booth in St Kilda. In the first one they sat chastely side by side; in the second he had one arm around her shoulders, the other hand clasping hers. In the next photo he was kissing her cheek, and in the last he was cross-eyed with his tongue poking out the side of his mouth as she kissed him just in front of his ear. Goofy, she knew, but a precious memory of a summer night when the sunset had burned red and the wind blew hot dry desert air across the water—their last night before he left for the tropical heat of Singapore.

She kept the picture in her desk drawer, hidden from the newsroom. Not that there was anyone to see it yet; it was still early, only six-thirty in the morning. Sam would be in by seven. Phil would phone around eight. In the meantime, she had a pile of cables to sort. For the first time since she'd started at the paper she was content being

Sam's secretary. It meant she got to speak to Phil when he phoned through his stories, his voice crackly but bright, thrilled to be reporting on the Allied troop build-up and preparations to repel the Japanese.

'It sounds dangerous,' she'd said the day before, trying to keep him talking as long as possible, not wanting to pass him on to Sam. 'Are you certain you're safe?'

'Churchill says there's nothing to worry about. The city's completely protected if they try to land from the sea. Apparently there's a few bods on bicycles trying to cross the mountains and swamps. They'll never get through.'

'Has it stopped raining yet?'

'It's so bloody hot up here, and wet! The monsoon's drowning us.'

'Careful, you'll get mouldy.'

'That's what the cocktails are for.'

'Oh yes?'

'Plenty of that sort of thing. Drinks every night. There's something on at the British embassy tonight. Chance to meet the bigwigs.'

Grace immediately pictured palm trees and glamorous women in gowns and jewels swishing around a ballroom. It's a war zone, she reminded herself, changing her mental image to a steamy room full of sweaty men in heavy uniforms, smoking cigars.

'I miss you so much,' she whispered.

'Me too.'

They'd only had ten days together before he left for Singapore. The weeks when he was travelling were miserable, because she couldn't talk to him, but now at least she had his daily calls to Sam. Still, it seemed unfair that he'd gone away so soon into their romance. Some days she wondered whether it had seemed more serious than it was because he was going away. Could it really last in real life? After all, she was a country girl, and he was a society boy, privileged, well-educated, wealthy. Their first real dinner date had shown her exactly how far apart they were. She shuddered remembering what a bumpkin she must have seemed.

He'd taken her to dinner at Florentino in the city, upstairs in the dining room. She'd never been inside but knew its reputation. It often featured in the society pages, the scene of glittering dinner parties for visiting theatre stars. Walking up the stairs, the place looked like fairyland. Everything shone, from the candles to the beading on the women's dresses, the glassware and cutlery. Lacquered hair glinted as men and women bobbed their heads, talking and laughing. And everyone seemed to know Phil. He nodded at several people as they followed the waiter to a vacant table near the window.

Surrounded by silks and velvets, Grace felt incredibly self-conscious about her dark green jersey frock. She wore a matching silk hat with a small veil and her grandmother's pearls, but compared to the other women she felt dowdy. The one thing that did make her feel special though was the touch of Phil's hand on her back, protective and possessive in the nicest way, signalling to the entire room that she was the focus of his attention, at least for that night. He looked elegant and entirely at home in his dinner suit, his athlete's body relaxed, fluid in its movements. He was one of those rare people who seemed comfortable in every situation. One minute he'd be joking with the police, then he'd be drinking a beer in a dirty pub or chatting with the social elite. She supposed it was necessary for a reporter to be something of a chameleon; you never knew what the day would bring.

The waiter pulled out her chair and expertly slid it beneath her as she sat. Then he whisked the white damask napkin from her plate, snapped it to remove the folds and placed it across her lap, all before she realised what he was doing. Phil sat back as the napkin process was repeated for him, then he ordered a bottle of burgundy.

'So what do you think, Grace? Do you like it here?'

'It's magical. I've never been anywhere like this before.'

'Just wait till you try the food. I'm starving.'

'I'm not surprised. I can't imagine how you run so many heats then turn around and run the finals, all in the one day.'

'I'm used to it. I've been doing it since I was a kid.'

'Well, congratulations! Third in the state champion-ships and your picture on the back page.'

'It's pretty funny to *be* the news rather than reporting on it.' He grinned, his face shining red from the day's sun.

'Olympic trials next?'

'That's the plan.'

Their wine arrived and then they ordered their meals. Spaghetti to start for both of them, then cannelloni for Grace and veal scallopini for Phil.

Grace had never eaten spaghetti before, so Phil showed her how to twirl the strands around her fork into a neat mouthful. Within minutes her napkin was covered in smudges. Phil smiled, pretending not to notice, but no matter how Grace wound the pasta, she covered her chin in sauce each time she tried to take a mouthful. Eventually she gave up and sat back, happy to watch him eat and talk and eat some more.

She sipped the soft, smooth wine. At least she could pretend she was a bit sophisticated drinking from her crystal glass, nodding, smiling, making sure she didn't spill anything. She'd never doubted her table manners before, thinking her mother had taught her everything she needed to know, but apparently not. There'd been nothing about eating in front of a handsome, kind man who apparently liked her as much as she liked him. That required a new level of coordination: eating strange food, drinking wine and making conversation, all at the same time. She lifted her glass and took another sip. Before she was able to swallow, Phil took her hand and looked deeply into her eyes.

'I'm so happy you're here with me tonight,' he said, glancing over her shoulder and nodding to someone. Then she heard a man behind her start to sing in a rich tenor voice. 'O sole mio . . .' Everyone in the restaurant stopped talking to listen as the voice grew louder. Then Grace saw another man emerge from behind a curtain playing a violin. He stood behind Phil. Grace felt chills as the music lifted and lilted, the power of the man's voice raising the hairs on the back of her neck. They sang three songs, each more beautiful than the last.

'Have a wonderful evening, *signorina*, *signor*,' the tenor said, bowing then disappearing into the kitchen.

Grace grinned. 'Did you arrange that?'

'I told them it was a special night when I booked.'

'I've never heard anything so beautiful.'

'And you look beautiful,' he said, raising his glass. 'The smartest, most glamorous woman in the room.'

Grace felt herself relax. He seemed so sincere it was hard not to believe him. He was speaking so openly, here in front of all these people who could listen in if they wanted.

'This week has been the happiest of my life,' he said, his expression turning serious, 'but I've got something important to tell you.'

Grace felt her smile wobble then collapse. She'd been walking on clouds, barely able to concentrate at work or sleep at night. She should have known that she was being silly. Of course he wasn't interested. He could see how smitten she was and now he'd try to dampen her expectations; that's what tonight was about: letting her know that he liked her but he'd changed his mind. She couldn't possibly make a scene in a place like this, where she was at such a disadvantage.

'I don't think I can take too many more surprises,' Grace said, trying but failing to keep the disappointment from her voice as she pulled her hand away and put it in her lap.

'I'm taking a correspondent slot, covering the Pacific,' Phil said.

'You're going away?'

'I've been talking to Sam about this for months. It's the only thing that's stopped me joining up—the thought that I might be able to do this with the paper. I just heard yesterday that my posting's been approved.'

222

'Really? But the Japanese are already in Malaya.'

'Yes, but they're nowhere near Singapore. That's where I'm going, to write about our boys on the ground. Stop relying on the overseas agencies for our news.'

'And Sam thinks this is a good idea?'

'He suggested it. Most of the sport here is being cancelled. I've got little to report on, so it makes sense that I cover the build-up of the Australian forces in the region. We can get around the government censors that way.'

'When do you leave?'

'The end of next week.'

'Gosh. I've heard of some great excuses for not going on a second date, but this kind of takes the cake.'

'This *is* our second date.'

'Oh, yes, well if you count that night at the pub, but I'd like to think of this as our first night together.'

'You're my only regret, Grace. I hate to leave now. I can't believe that you agreed to go out with me.'

'I can't believe it took you so long to ask.' Grace reached over and stroked his face. 'I'll miss you, Phil Taylor.'

They'd walked all the way back to Richmond that night, pausing to kiss under every tree along the way. The next day she packed a bag and moved into his East Melbourne apartment, staying with him until he left, making love to him and sleeping more soundly than she'd ever thought possible, except for their final evening, when she'd cried all night, missing him already.

❧❧❧◈◈❧❧❧

'Good morning, Miss Fowler,' Sam said, placing his hat on the coat rack and tossing his briefcase beside his desk. 'Has he called yet?'

'It's still a bit early.'

'Claire asked whether you'd like to come to lunch on Sunday. I said you looked like you needed one of her apricot pies to keep you going.'

'I'd love to. Thanks, Mr Barton.'

'Goodo. Is that my news list?'

'Nearly finished.'

Grace finished typing the list, and when Sam went to the editorial conference at nine, she still hadn't heard from Phil. They'd agreed he would always ring before eight-thirty Melbourne time if he wasn't out on assignment. If he didn't call by then she wasn't to wait. Time to tear herself away from the desk and walk upstairs to the cafeteria. The place was nearly deserted but the tea lady was stocking the trolley for the morning rounds.

'Goodness, love, this is a surprise. Is something wrong?'

'I just couldn't wait for the tea trolley. Is that all right?'

'Take a seat and I'll fix you up in a jiffy. Here's a scone, just out of the oven. I need a taste tester, just to make sure they're up to scratch.'

Grace smiled, glad to feel fussed over. As well as missing Phil, she'd worked through Christmas, unable to face her father, who was still furious that she'd disobeyed him and was working at the paper. Well, he'd wanted her to be a secretary and she'd finished her course; she was doing everything he wanted. But the real reason she hadn't gone was because she doubted she'd be able to hide her unease from her mother. There was a chance—well, she and Phil hadn't been quite as careful as they should have been and a rubber had split. He'd laughed, saying he wouldn't mind a baby, but she'd been worried and stayed in town rather than facing her family. Two weeks later she'd discovered she had no reason for fear, so there was nothing stopping her going home, except that she didn't want to miss Phil's phone calls. Maybe she'd go at Easter, in a couple of months.

As she walked back into the newsroom, one of the phones on her desk rang. There were a couple of reporters nearby at the subs table but they seemed not to hear. She ran over and grabbed it, expecting to hear the operator saying it was Singapore.

'Miss Fowler, it's Don Porter here. Is Sam around?'

'He's in conference.'

'I see. Well, you'll need to hear this too, I'm told. It's about young Phil Taylor—he's had an accident. The embassy phoned this morning. Apparently he slipped on a step last night in the rain. Fell and broke his leg.'

'No! How bad is it? Can we speak to him?'

'They took him to the army hospital and they'll be operating this morning. I'll get a number for the doctor so Sam can call later today.'

'Operating?'

'Yes, it sounds like a bad break; but he's fit, he'll recover.'

'Of—of course. I'll get Sam to call you,' she said, imagining Phil in hospital, writhing in pain. An operation. How awful. At least he had Australian doctors. But he'd hate being stuck in bed for weeks. Still, it meant he wouldn't be tearing off into the jungle chasing stories, she consoled herself. Maybe they'd ship him home. She could visit him in hospital then nurse him when he was discharged. She went to the filing cabinet to retrieve his next of kin card. Sam would need to call Phil's parents. She hadn't met them yet and had no desire to start with that call. Best to let Sam speak for the paper, keep it all professional. Her hand rested against the gold signet ring she wore on a chain beneath her blouse. Phil had given her his ring the night before he left. 'Just till I get back,' he'd said, 'then I'll get you a real ring, if you'll have me.'

'Yes,' she whispered to herself, 'Yes.'

CHAPTER 25

GRACE SLUMPED DOWN INTO her seat, scratchy pieces of cracked leather pricking her thighs through her skirt. At least she had thighs and legs and feet that let her run as fast as she could to the dark comfort of the cinema. She watched the opening credits of the Movietone news through a fug of cigarette smoke. The audience sat completely still, their sweets untouched in bags on their laps as the screen showed vision of Australian army troops digging trenches in the jungle around Singapore, getting ready to defend the city against invasion. Grace scanned every scene intently, looking for the hospital among Singapore's cars and buildings. She was desperate to see how closely defended the building was, how close it was to the jungle. The camera panned across giant leaves and muddy tracks. Malaya, just above Australia; the Japanese were so close . . .

That morning Grace had been filing photos from the third edition ready for the picture library when Sam phoned from the editor-in-chief's office and asked her to join them. When she arrived, Mr Gordon's secretary nodded but didn't speak; she barely even looked at her, just opened the door and waved her in.

'Sit down, Grace. I'm afraid we have some more news about Phil,' Mr Gordon said.

Grace dropped into the seat nearest Sam, her heart pounding, her mind racing. *No, no. Not dead. Please not that.*

'He's still alive, dear,' Mr Gordon said kindly.

'We don't know much,' Sam added, 'but they had to amputate his leg below the knee.'

Grace felt her stomach sink.

Mr Gordon continued: 'He's too sick for evacuation, but as soon as he's well enough to be moved, we'll try to get him home.'

The floor seemed to shift beneath her feet. He'd be devastated; never able to run again, unable to compete at the Olympics after all those years of training.

Mr Gordon's secretary appeared with a cup of hot, sweet tea.

'He's still alive,' Grace repeated, 'and he's coming home to recover?'

'That's right, dear,' Mr Gordon said. 'He'll be fine. He's a reporter, smart, resourceful.'

'He's probably already persuaded a general to set him up with a typewriter so he can keep reporting from his hospital bed,' Sam joked. 'After they've beaten the Japs back from the city, then he'll come home.'

Grace lifted her teacup to her lips but lowered it again without taking a sip. Both men were trying so hard to smile, to sound cheerful, but the effort only reached their mouths; their eyes remained sad.

'He'll be fine, I know he will. It's a blow, but he'll get over losing his leg.' Grace didn't believe the words as she said them, but it seemed to be what they wanted to hear.

'That's the way, Miss Fowler,' Mr Gordon said, nodding.

'I should get back to my desk. I'd like to keep busy.'

Sam stayed seated as she stood. 'I'll see you downstairs. Keep your chin up, Grace.'

❧☙

As the day wore on, Grace's mind filled with searing images of Phil lying in bed, crying out in pain. They'd give him painkillers, she told herself. It wasn't like the old days, when doctors would fill a soldier with brandy, give him a stick to bite down on then hack off a limb. He was in a proper hospital with surgeons and anaesthetic. They'd take good care of him. She returned her attention to the soldiers on the screen. They looked cheerful enough, but they were getting ready to fight. God, what if the Japanese soldiers reached the city? Phil had said the port was a fortress, that they'd try to invade from the sea. So why were the men digging trenches?

The newsreel ended and the main feature began: *His Girl Friday.* She'd seen this film three times since Phil left, but instead of laughing, this time she wept, barely able to see the screen. She blew her nose and dabbed her eyes as Rosalind Russell bustled into the newsroom and began

229

to spar with Cary Grant. But instead of being caught up in the story, Grace focused on Cary Grant and the way he walked; tall, strong, easy, just like Phil. She couldn't look away from his glorious, healthy legs. Her tears started again. Phil had beautiful, muscular legs that he'd wrapped around hers in bed during their lovely nights together. She ached to lay beside him now, to feel his skin against hers from head to toe. It would still be the same. Once they were lying down, she wouldn't even notice his missing leg.

She tried to picture what his leg might look like. She'd seen old men from the last war, the empty leg of their trousers folded and held in place with a nappy pin. But she'd never tried to imagine what the stump inside the fabric might look like. Would it be mangled and ugly? What if she couldn't bear to look at him when he took his trousers off? What if she was so repulsed she turned away? *Don't be so shallow! It's only one leg. He'll be himself in every other way. And he's so lucky it won't affect his work. He'll be just fine, we both will.*

Grace resolved to talk to Phil as soon as he was awake, to tell him how much she loved him. She was sure of it now. Although it had seemed understood, they'd never actually said the words. But she would, the very first chance she got. She'd keep telling him until they put him on the ship and sent him home to recuperate, and then she'd tell him every day after that. GRACE LOVES PHIL, the most powerful headline of all.

CHAPTER 26

February 1942

THE SHORELINE SHIMMERED AS Mae pushed
Katie's pram along the Esplanade, desperate for a hint of
cool breeze. Here among the young couples holding hands
and children shrieking and laughing, life was continuing
as usual, but the war was edging closer. Et and the uncles
talked of little else. Albert's wardens were helping people
to prepare for the possibility of Melbourne being bombed
like Darwin or overrun like Singapore. They were attaching
shutters to shop windows and filling sandbags that sat
beside doorways. There was talk of digging trenches and
public shelters in parklands from Footscray to the Botanic
Gardens. Albert had drawn up plans for an air-raid shelter
in their back garden beside the vegetable patch. William
was frustrated because all the race meetings had been
cancelled and Et couldn't get butter. Mae felt scared and
miserable about her future, but most days she found it
easier to stay at home rather than risk running into anyone

who'd ask if she had any news of Harry. She hadn't heard anything more from the navy and she was struggling to remain hopeful.

That morning she'd been at the butcher's with Katie wailing on her hip when Pearl Atkinson appeared beside her at the counter.

'Surely you must have heard something more about the ship,' Pearl insisted.

'I assure you there's no news.'

'Well, everyone says the Japs helped the Germans shoot them all in the water. It's pathetic, absolutely pathetic. The government's afraid we'll panic if they say anything, but the Japs are already here, ready to slaughter the lot of us.'

Mae fled the shop without ordering and rushed home, where she sat in the dark, her mind seeing the scene Pearl had described. Men bobbing in the water like ducks. Japanese sailors standing over them with guns, picking them off one by one. Sharks, drawn by the blood, tearing the men apart.

When the house grew too hot in the late afternoon she'd hoped a walk to the beach might soothe her, but being near the water, smelling the salt and hearing people shout as they splashed about was only making things worse.

She made herself imagine walking along the Esplanade with Harry. It was one of her ways of keeping him close: telling herself what to remember, rather than relying on random memories to assert themselves. This one was easy as they'd often done this walk together, usually after supper. On hot nights Harry always tore off his shirt and ran in for a swim, laughing as his wet trousers squelched and slapped on the way home.

As Mae trudged on, Katie slept peacefully in her pram. Mae hadn't walked much lately and blisters were forming on her heels and toes. She sat on the bluestone wall that separated the footpath from the sand and slipped off her shoes. Her feet were burning. The water looked so cool and inviting. She stepped onto the sand and walked toward the water.

Standing in the shallows, tiny waves lapping at her ankles, she imagined how nice it might feel to lie flat in the water and float on a current that would carry her past the swimmers and out to sea. She'd drift through the water with the fish, gliding through the seagrasses, floating over ancient shipwrecks. She'd ride the current that looped out of the bay and around to the west towards Harry, who'd be sailing east in a life raft to meet her. Surely he could still be drifting, waiting for help. He was being pushed slowly by the wind, edging along the coast, closer and closer each day.

Mae opened her eyes. It had been long enough now for the tides to have pushed his lifeboat all the way to this spot. Harry could be in the bay right now. She shaded her eyes and scanned the horizon. But there were too many people blocking her view; she needed to get past them. She took several steps deeper into the water. It was warmer than she expected. Soft ripples swallowed her shins then rose to her knees and tugged at the hem of her skirt. For the first time in months she felt calm. It was getting harder to stay upright; the need to lie down and drift was almost overwhelming. She was waist deep in water when she heard someone calling her name. It was so faint she could hardly hear it.

'Mae . . . Mae . . .'

She held her breath, straining to hear.

'Mae!' The voice was louder now. 'Mae!'

'Harry!'

'Mae!'

He sounded frightened. She searched the crowd of swimmers, looking for his face. 'Harry!' she called again more loudly.

A strong hand grabbed her shoulder. She knew that hand; she'd recognise its size, its pressure anywhere. As she spun around, her chest filled with pure, exultant joy. Her face split into a smile, anticipating his sea blue eyes, his tanned face.

'Harry,' she sobbed, reaching out to him.

'Mae, what on earth are you doing?'

She blinked a few times. Sam Barton's face came into focus. What was he doing here? 'Harry,' she said. 'Where's Harry?'

Sam turned away from Mae and looked over his shoulder towards the beach.

Mae followed his gaze and saw Claire standing on the footpath, Nicholas tucked behind her legs sucking his thumb. Her friend was holding onto two prams, one with Katie inside.

'Are you all right?' Sam asked, tightening his grip on her shoulder.

'I heard him,' Mae said, feeling like a stone sinking to the bottom of the sea.

'I was calling out to you. You left the baby.'

Dazed, Mae let Sam lead her through the crowd and back onto the sand.

Nicholas bounded over and took her hand. 'We had fish and chips on the beach. The seagulls ate Mummy's chips.'

Claire stood rigid and pale, gripping Katie's pram with white knuckles. 'It was rolling into the street,' she said. 'People were running to catch it before it ran onto the road. I saw your handbag on the handle . . .'

Mae stood blinking in the light, watching Claire jiggle Katie's pram. She'd been so certain that she'd heard Harry's voice. Disappointment replaced the elation of just a few minutes earlier.

'We should get the children home,' Sam said.

They crossed the road and walked in silence. Claire and Sam lifted Katie's pram up the steps while Mae opened the door. She barely had the energy to raise the key to the lock. Her skirt smelled of wet wool and her stockings slid about in her shoes.

Claire left the babies in their prams in the hallway then took Nicholas out the back to the toilet. Mae looked around the gloomy sitting room then her gaze settled on Sam, her mind returning to Pearl Atkinson's comments.

'You know more, don't you?' Mae demanded.

'Mae, I don't—'

'You hear things from the government. Things they won't let you publish.'

'Stop it, Mae. There's nothing else to tell you.'

'We haven't heard a thing in months. Nothing! It's like it never happened. What about the Japanese? Why don't you write anything about them?'

He ran his hand across the back of his neck, rubbing the tight muscles as he chose his words. 'Mae, we only hear rumours. Nothing we can confirm.'

'What sort of rumours? What have you heard?'

'It's all too wild to believe.'

'They're still alive, aren't they?'

'I didn't say that. The German prisoners, they all say the same thing—that the *Sydney* was still afloat after the battle, heading for the horizon.'

'And?'

Sam hesitated. 'I'm only telling you this because you'll probably hear it eventually. But I have to stress, nothing's come through official channels.'

Mae felt her face trying to smile. He *did* know something. There was more. Her vision focused, her hearing sharpened. She felt more alert than she had in months.

'There's talk of a radio broadcast last week by Tokyo Rose . . .' He hesitated.

'Yes?'

'Apparently she broadcast that they'd captured the *Sydney* and towed it to Singapore.'

Mae squealed and clasped her hands in front of her chest. 'It's true. I know it. They're safe.'

'Mae, I've had two reporters digging around for days now. We don't believe the broadcast is true and neither does the government.' Sam spoke slowly, as if to a child.

'Listen to me, Mae. They were getting ready for Pearl Harbor when the *Sydney* was attacked. They weren't even in the war yet. It makes no sense.'

As Claire entered the room, Mae turned to her, ecstatic. 'He's alive!' she said. 'Harry's alive! Did you know?'

Claire's face froze. 'Sam, what have you told her?'

'I—I said it was just a rumour. None of it's confirmed.'

Mae hadn't felt such glee since the morning Harry appeared in her doorway after Katie was born.

'And even if it is true,' Sam cautioned, 'it's a dire fate. One of my reporters is in Singapore. He didn't get out in time. Now he's a prisoner.'

'But Harry's alive,' Mae insisted. 'All he needs is a chance. He's strong enough to endure anything as long as he's alive.'

'Ella's asleep and Nicholas is tired,' Claire said to Sam, her measured tone the opposite of Mae's excitement. 'Please take the children home. I'll stay with Mae for a while.' She touched Sam's hand as he passed. 'I think you should telephone Mae's family.'

'Oh yes, Sam, please do. I want them to hear the wonderful news.' Mae hurried to the kitchen to fetch Katie's bottle. 'I'll just organise Katie, then we can have something to eat. I'm starving.'

While Mae fed Katie, Claire heated a lamb stew. She stayed silent as Mae speculated about how Harry might get home. 'I suppose he'll have to wait for rescue, but at least they have hospitals, doctors. If he's hurt, they'll fix him up.'

'Mae, listen. You gave us a fright at the beach. It looked like you were about to do something really foolish.'

'Nonsense. I thought he was calling to me. I was just looking for him.'

'But letting go of Katie's pram without setting the brake. And walking off like that. Someone could have taken her. She could have been hurt.'

'I've been so tired. I just forgot where I was for a moment.'

Claire leaned forward and patted Mae's hand. 'You've been under too much strain, spending too much time on your own. Let's walk together every day.'

'We can do our groceries as well. There's so much I have to organise. I've let things slip around the house over the last few months.'

After Claire left, Mae changed into her nightgown and sank exhausted onto the bed. Drifting towards sleep she felt a deep sense of calm. Sam's news had erased her fear. Instead of curling up, she lay on her back with her arms stretched wide open, letting go of the pain and uncertainty of the last few months. Everyone had been so quick to give up on him, but she'd been right to hang on to hope. Harry would know that, he'd feel it for sure. One day soon they'd lie together and never part again. If he wanted to go back to sea, she'd put her foot down. His place was here with her and Katie. They might even think about taking in some war children, orphans maybe, build their family that way. Mae turned towards the buffet, the light flickering from Harry's candle. In the distance, the town hall clock struck midnight.

Mae was scrubbing scuff marks off the kitchen linoleum when Et arrived the next morning.

'What's this I hear about you trying to drown yourself?' Et demanded from the hallway. 'I don't appreciate being told that you abandoned your child and had to be stopped from swimming for Tasmania like some modern-day Ophelia.'

'Did you hear the wonderful news? Harry's alive. He's in a Japanese camp.'

'Sam told me all about it, young lady. We're very disappointed by your carry-on—spending all day in bed, barely leaving the house and now fixating on wild stories.'

'It's not a wild story. Sam said—'

'Stop being so self-indulgent. Do you think all the other women who have lost husbands are behaving this way? I'm sure your friend Alice isn't; she has children to raise and a farm to run. Imagine if she was off with fairies like you.'

Mae threw the scrubbing brush on the floor. 'What could you possibly know about it?' she yelled. 'What do you expect me to do? Forget him? Go out to tea dances? He could be on his way home right now.'

'Imagine him coming home to see you in this state, behaving like you're soft in the head. He'd be horrified!'

'Don't you dare—' Mae's hand whipped through the air and connected with the soft flesh of her aunt's cheek. It wasn't a hard slap, but it was enough to leave an angry red blotch. Mae sprang back as though she were the one who'd been struck, her hand burning.

'I'm so sorry,' she shrieked. 'Did I hurt you?'

Rubbing her face, Et walked to the pram parked in the doorway. 'It takes a lot more than that to hurt me, Mae.'

'I'm sorry, but you don't understand. How could you? You've never been married.'

Et sighed. 'You're right. Of course. It's not as though he meant anything to us. Oh no; we're not grieving, we're not sad, thinking of you both every minute of the day. No, the grief's all yours to bear alone. Nothing to do with us.'

Mae stared at her aunt a moment longer then lifted the scrubbing brush from its puddle of suds.

'You need to buck up, for Katie's sake,' Et said firmly. 'Come and work with me in the shop. Katie can sleep out the back. It'll keep your mind busy.'

Mae scrubbed at a black mark, picking at it with her fingernail when the brush had no effect.

'Sam should have known better,' Et grumbled. 'I credited him with more sense.'

Mae was desperate to be left alone with her happy thoughts. Whatever anyone said now, she had hope, her own life raft. She'd cling to it for as long as she could. As long as she worked hard enough, believed strongly enough, built a beautiful home, Harry would return; no other end to their story was possible.

'I'll think about it,' Mae told her aunt. 'I will, really. You're right, I have to think of the future now.'

CHAPTER 27

1 June 1942

GRACE STRAIGHTENED HER DICTIONARY, thesaurus, notebooks and pencils on her desk in the corner of the *Tribune* office allocated to the women's page. There were only two desks, hers and Avril Johnson's, but a bank of filing cabinets separated them from the rest of the newsroom, creating a small island of calm beneath sooty windows that hinged open at street level at the back of the building.

It had taken just over a year to get a job on the reporting staff, but she'd lobbied hard for Barbara's position and Sam said he couldn't find any more excuses to hold her back. He also said he couldn't stand the look on her face whenever the phone rang and it wasn't news about Phil. So she found a smart girl from secretarial college to fill her place and here she was, nearing the end of her first month as a cadet reporter. She had no intention of failing. Whatever Avril asked her to do, she happily complied. Grace threw herself into writing stories about the war effort, how to knit socks and balaclavas, the need for food rationing—tea was first to become scarce because it came from the islands occupied by the Japanese—and how new bread delivery schedules were helping to save petrol. She wrote stories explaining why butter and meat were rationed, non-essential goods like toys were outlawed and there was little fabric available for clothes. She wrote a daily tips and recipes column advising women how to bake their own bread, grow vegetables and recycle clothing. She'd never done any of those things herself but she was learning everything as she went along. She was also writing tips on how to make the American GIs flooding into the city feel welcome. SECOND HOME FOR US TROOPS, VICTORY ONE PIE AT A TIME.

Avril arrived just after ten, removing her hat and patting her perfectly lacquered blonde wave into place. 'Good morning, Grace. Any news?'

'Not since the Red Cross letter last week.'

'Well, hopefully the Americans can get the Japs out of the way and send the prisoners all back home. But we need to get the Americans out of the pubs first. The government wants people to entertain GIs in their homes, turn on a bit of local hospitality—but not too much, of course.'

'How do they plan to do that?'

'Home cooking. The Gas and Fuel have supplied recipes, we'll run them over the coming weeks; succotash and pecan pie. Irresistible.'

'Succotash? What's that?' Grace asked.

'I have no idea and I don't intend to find out. I can't afford to grow out of my clothes, not when those hideous austerity suits are all you can buy. Brown gabardine is neither my colour nor my fabric. I'll happily stick to tea during the day and a lovely piece of fish or lamb in the evenings.'

Avril covered all the social events for the paper, which suited Grace just fine. She'd seen Phil's parents in some of the photographs but still hadn't met them. Probably not the best circumstances now, but surely he'd be home soon.

'The cook's making a devil's food cake this morning,' Avril said.

'What's that?'

'I saw one at last week's afternoon tea for General MacArthur and his wife. It's a rich chocolate cake; the Americans love it. Anyway, the cook's doing a rations version. I need you to write a how-to guide with pictures.'

Grace wrote Avril's instructions on her shorthand pad. *Dev cake pic with how to's.* 'I'll get started right away,' Grace promised.

'Lovely. We'll run it large above the fold with the recipe and instructions down the side. Although chocolate always looks so unappealing in black and white, just a dark blob.'

'I'll ask the cook to decorate it a bit, but nothing so fancy the women at home can't follow.'

'Good, and get Alan Swain to shoot it in the studio. You can be the hand model, wield a spatula. Make it look like a snap to bake.'

❧

An hour later, Grace walked downstairs to the studio. She knew Alan had a reputation for taking 'artistic' pictures, whatever that meant. Hopefully he could do something artistic with the cake.

She opened the door expecting to find a room full of cameras and lights; instead she saw dull, grimy walls and high windows blacked out by patched curtains. A wide roll of crumpled paper covered in scuff marks hung from a rail and another pile of black paper lay heaped on the floor near the far wall. Two lights on rickety stands stood either side of a metal stool.

Alan swaggered into the room. 'Grace, my dear,' he said, lifting her hand to his face and lightly brushing her knuckles with a pretend kiss. 'So lovely to have you all to myself.'

Grace shuddered and pulled her hand back, feeling a mixture of shyness and revulsion. Looking past Alan, she saw several boxes in the corner of the room filled to bursting with empty beer bottles. He followed her gaze.

'Oh, yes. Sometimes the other snappers come down for knock-off drinks. Cheaper than the pub and no chance of getting thrown out if you have one too many. Don't tell the boss though.'

'I won't,' she mumbled.

'I can get you a beer now, if you like. We could both have one.'

'No thanks, I think we should just get on with it.'

She watched Alan examine each part of her body. 'You really do have the prettiest ankles, my dear. And your legs! I think I'll have you modelling for us quite often.'

'Let's just see how these shots turn out first,' Grace said, wishing she could have refused when Avril asked her to pose. But she was determined to prove her worth as a reporter; she could hardly say no to pretending she was icing—no, they called it *frosting*—a cake. The picture would be a close-up of her hands, the spatula and the finished cake. It would only take a few minutes, then she could leave.

Alan placed a table in front of the backdrop, draped a piece of white cloth over the top then smoothed it with his hands.

'This needs ironing. Do you mind?'

As he loaded sheet film into holders in the next room, Grace did her best with a clumsy old iron that left spurts of rusty water on the cloth. He returned to the studio and stood behind the bellows camera propped on a sturdy tripod. Grace removed the cake from the tin and placed it on a plate, positioning it to cover the worst of the stains.

'Okay, we'll start you off standing on the right and leaning across so that your head and hand are directly over the cake.'

Grace squinted as the bright lights flickered to life. 'Like this?' she asked, holding her hand with the spatula near the edge of the cake.

'You need to bring your head down closer to the cake and press your chest forward.'

'But the photo's only supposed to show my hand.'

'Don't tell me what to do, missy. I've been doing this for years.'

Grace leaned in and lengthened her neck, dropping her shoulder and elbow. Maybe he was just getting a better angle on her hand.

'That's much better. Hold your breath. That's it. Now, move around to the back of the cake and do the same thing. Head down nice and close. This time, touch the icing with your knife.'

Grace changed position slowly. She'd looked straight ahead for the first shot so she didn't have to watch Alan, but this time he'd be right in front. She tried looking to the side.

'Grace, look at the camera. Come on, head and chest forward. That's the way. Deep breath. Hold it . . . hold it. Now stay there while I reload.'

She stood up, stretching her back and neck. As soon as she moved he barked at her to get back in position. Grace leaned down again. The sooner he finished, the sooner she could leave.

'So how's that fellow of yours going overseas? Must be hard with him away so long.'

'He's doing well, considering. Keeping his spirits up.'

'Now, this time I need a smile. Look at the camera. Come on, you look like you're going to a funeral. Let's see some of that Grace sparkle you're so famous for. Say "panties".'

Grace grimaced then smiled with her mouth only. Grace sparkle indeed! What did he mean by that? A few long moments later, he was done.

'See, that wasn't so bad, was it?' Alan said as he removed the film slide.

Well, it didn't matter what he'd shot, she thought. They'd just crop the photo. No one would ever see her face.

He sat on a chair with his legs spread wide and lit a cigarette, watching as she packed the cake and plate. 'Well, I've taken your photo, so what are you going to do for me?'

Blood rushed to her ears and the hairs on her arms and neck prickled. Without looking at him she gathered her things. 'I have to get back,' she said, forcing herself to walk not run to the studio door.

She heard his laughter behind her. 'Little tease.'

❧❧❧

By the time she reached her desk, she felt ill. Dropping the cake and plate, she ran to the ladies' room. Looking in the mirror, she saw that her pupils were huge, leaving just the barest rims of green in her eyes. Her neck was red and her hair smelled of smoke. She let cool water run over her hands. Had he really meant that about her leading him on? He wouldn't really have tried something, would he? Maybe she should tell Avril how he'd behaved, that lascivious tone. But she didn't want to be a whinger. And it wouldn't do to get a reputation as a crybaby, she thought, willing away the gathering tears. He wouldn't have been so awful if Phil was around. Alan *Swine*, that was a much more apt name for him. She walked slowly back to her desk, checking that Alan was nowhere around.

'Grace, have you heard the news?' Avril appeared around the filing cabinets, unbuttoning her coat and dumping her handbag on the desk. 'The Japanese have bombed Sydney. Last night, in midget submarines. They slipped right into the harbour.'

The fear Grace had felt in the studio a few minutes earlier flooded back. Her hand flew to her mouth.

'I know, it's terrifying, isn't it?' Avril said, smiling. 'Sorry, I smile when I'm nervous, but I'm not smiling inside.'

247

'Does Sam want us to do anything?'

'No, I saw him on my way in and everything's covered. He said we should just carry on as usual.'

'What about the bay and the rivers? They could be in subs, steaming towards us right now.'

'Sam's got reporters everywhere they need to be: the naval office; port authorities. There's nothing more we can do for the moment. I'll get some comments from the lady mayoress at the tea this afternoon.'

'It's still on?'

'Absolutely. They're raising funds to help city schools relocate to the country. Then the Americans can use the school buildings. Only in the best areas, of course.'

'Of course,' Grace said absently, rubbing her temples.

'Oh, how did the photo shoot go?'

'Fine—I think. We'll know when we see the pictures.'

'Are you all right, Grace? You look like death warmed over.'

'Things didn't go so well with Alan.'

'Oh, don't mind him. He's irritating but harmless. Just a bit of a flirt.'

Avril strode back to her desk and checked her notepad. 'Why don't you get us a cup of tea? The trolley lady's around the corner. Then I want you to pop down to Georges. I'm told General MacArthur's wife will be shopping there with their son Arthur this afternoon.'

The poor child, Grace thought. *Arthur MacArthur. What a name.* 'Yes, of course—if we haven't been blown to smithereens by then.'

'You know, this latest attack might make people a bit

less complacent,' Avril said. 'Less prone to whining about rationing.'

Grace looked at her immaculately dressed boss and wondered what she actually knew about restraint. 'You're right,' she agreed. 'I think people have become a bit comfortable since the Americans arrived. They think it makes us safe.'

≈≈⊙∘≈≈

Walking the three blocks to the glamorous Georges emporium, Grace was amazed by the number of American jeeps roaring along the tram tracks. They were heading in every direction, three or four soldiers in each. Other soldiers patrolled the streets on foot, stopping shoppers and workers, suggesting they leave the city and go home. Faces tight with fear, the women and children walked faster, heads bowed, bags and parcels held to their chests. Waiting at a crossing for the traffic lights to change, she saw two women looking at a *Tribune* poster advertising the final edition. JAP SUBS BOMB SYDNEY, it screamed.

'I knew they were involved,' one of the women said to her friend. 'The Germans couldn't possibly have sunk her alone.'

'I think they mean the town, not the ship!'

'Lord almighty, we're done for. They're probably on their way here too.'

Georges was deserted apart from staff huddled near the lifts, far away from the doors and windows. They spoke quietly, eyes glancing about anxiously. A group of men stood near a ladder discussing the best way to take down the two enormous chandeliers. Grace walked past the perfectly arranged racks and shelves to the manager's office at the rear of the first floor.

'Good afternoon, Miss Fowler. I'm afraid you've had a wasted visit today. The general's wife has cancelled.'

'There are so few customers. Will you close early today?'

'No, we won't, and nor should any other shop. We'll go on as usual to reassure our staff and our customers. We can't let the Japanese think they've beaten us.'

'What about the chandeliers? I heard someone say they're coming down.'

'We're just removing them for cleaning.'

'How long will they be gone?'

'They'll be back in place in no time. You can quote me on that.'

CHAPTER 28

July 1942

MAE'S RACKING COUGH CAUSED her stomach, neck and back to ache. Lying as still as she could under the weight of three blankets and a quilt, she tried to summon the energy to rise. Hopefully Katie would sleep a little longer, just long enough for Mae to bathe her face and venture outside to the toilet. Reaching for the dressing-gown that always lay across the end of her bed to keep her feet warm, she pulled it around her, tied it tight at the waist and stood up.

In the bathroom, she felt inside the medicine cabinet above the sink, looking for something to soothe her cough. Several glass bottles toppled to the floor. A sob escaped her; now she was marooned, barefoot, in a sea of glass shards.

Reaching over to the towel rail, she grabbed the bathmat and towels. The long stretch set her coughing again and the room started to spin. Losing her balance, she cried out as she fell, glass piercing her knee and her hand. She used the towel to clear a path to the door then threw the bathmat down as a rug. As she hobbled to the kitchen to tend her wounds, Katie began to roar. No snivelling and spluttering as a warm-up, just full-pelt bellowing. Mae was sorely tempted to join in.

By the time she made it to Katie's room, the baby's face was swollen like a red balloon and she was hot with fever. She wouldn't take a bottle; she wouldn't be soothed. Mae tried taking the baby into her bed, but that didn't work either. She rocked and sang, but nothing helped.

For most of that day and the following night, Mae lay on the bed beside the screaming baby, only getting up to change Katie's nappy or fetch her bottle, feeling too sick herself to do any more.

By the next day, with Katie having screamed through most of the night, Mae worried that something was terribly wrong. A list of dire possibilities formed in her mind: measles, scarlet fever. Mae gathered the screaming child in her arms and staggered to Claire's house. The front door was open before she knocked.

'I heard you two all the way down the street.'

Mae burst into tears. Claire took Katie from Mae's arms and fetched a cool washer from the bathroom. As Claire wiped the baby's head, Katie reached out, grabbed a corner of the cloth and put it in her mouth, sucking fiercely.

'She's teething, Mae. Her poor little gums are on fire.'

'I had no idea,' Mae said, sobbing harder. 'How am I supposed to know what she needs? I think I'm probably the worst mother in history.'

'All new mothers feel that way. It's quite normal.'

'What if something really serious is wrong and I don't know what to do? I don't think I can do this on my own.'

'I know, Mae. I know.'

Katie had fallen asleep again. Claire gave Mae the washer to wipe her own face. 'I know it's hard, but you have to calm down, you're doing fine. Just follow your instincts.'

'My instincts are to send her back and run away,' Mae cried.

'You poor pet! Leave her with me for a few hours and get some rest.'

Mae went home and crawled into bed, bunching the blankets tight around her neck. Crying again and desperate for comfort, she closed her eyes and began a silent plea to Harry.

Darling, I can't stand it; Katie hates me, I know she does. Nothing I do calms her, but as soon as someone else picks her up she sleeps. She already senses I'm a bad mother and I'm getting worse every day. Last night I was so frustrated by her screaming I nearly shook her. I didn't, but it was so tempting. What if I really do hurt her? What if I'm not being as careful as I should? If only you were here, you'd know what to do. You're so calm, so patient. You'd know how to make both of us feel better. But now you're in a jungle somewhere, in a prison. My darling, are you hurt? Are you ill? I know you'll try to get home as soon as you can.

Mae let herself relax into the mattress as she imagined Harry kneeling beneath a tree, surrounded by lush forest, carving a stick and smiling up at her as though they were camping. She knew the prison camp wasn't like that, but she tried to avoid imagining something worse. She returned to her imagined conversation.

How different this all is from a few months ago, my darling. I used to get so jealous sometimes when you described your trips. When Katie was new and I was still sick, I'd get your letters about the films you were seeing and places you visited and, well, sometimes I waited days to read your letters. Does that sound terrible? There were times when I couldn't bear to read about what a wonderful time you were having without me. Is this my punishment, you going missing? I'm sorry, darling. I know you're not having fun now. The prison must be ghastly, but stay alive, come home to me. I don't want to be a parent without you.

✵

Early in the evening, Mae returned to Claire's house. Claire put the sleeping baby into her arms. Katie's cheeks were still a little red but she was no longer feverish.

'I've put oil of cloves on her gums,' Claire said. 'Take the bottle and apply some more in a couple of hours. Those teeth will be through in a day or two. Not long before you both get some rest.'

'You mean it's not over yet?'

Claire laughed. 'I'm afraid not. But don't worry. The cloves will help. Just make sure she has plenty of milk and water. You'll be fine, but knock on the door if things get too bad.'

Nicholas yelped from the lounge room and pushed past the women. Turning, Mae saw him run towards Sam, who was unlatching the gate. As Nicholas leaped into his father's arms, Sam dropped his briefcase and hoisted him high into the air, pretending to let go then catching the boy before he fell too far. Mae bit her lip. The routine seemed well-established.

'Nicholas watches through the window,' Claire said. 'He yells for me to open the door then tries to beat Sam to the verandah, otherwise he misses being whizzed.'

As Sam strode towards the house, he dipped Nicholas so he was almost upside down. The little boy squealed as Sam leaned over and kissed Claire's cheek. Mae knew she shouldn't stare, but she couldn't shift her gaze.

'How are you, Mae?' Sam asked. 'I hear Katie's been giving you some grief.'

'Claire says she's teething.'

'Oh, fun and games. Well it doesn't last too long. Dreadful weather, isn't it?'

Mae shuddered. 'Yes, it's been terribly cold. I'd better get Katie home before it rains again. Thanks, Claire. Goodnight, Sam. Bye-bye, Nicholas.'

As Mae trudged home, she imagined the scene inside her neighbour's house. Sam sitting in the kitchen listening to the news with Nicholas on his lap, Claire feeding Ella. Mae had only seen Sam twice since the night at the beach. Both times he'd barely made eye contact. Even tonight his expression was wary, as though he was waiting for her to lash out again, accuse him of hiding news of the ship. Claire said after the night at the beach Sam was worried that seeing him might upset her again. But Mae thought his discomfort was due more to his guilt over not pushing the navy hard enough for information. So although Claire remained a good friend, she tried to avoid Sam. In a way it was for the best. Seeing Sam and Claire and the children together only reminded her of what she was missing.

⁓⁓⁓

Within an hour of arriving home, Katie was awake and crying again. Mae gave her some milk but she brought it up. Another dose of the clove oil barely helped.

Mae walked her up and down the hallway, the baby's screams piercing her pounding head. Her arms ached, barely able to hold the squirming, fevered bundle. If only she would be still! Suddenly, Mae realised she was digging her fingers deep into the tender flesh of the child's leg. Horrified, she hurried into the nursery and set Katie down in her cot, closed the door to muffle the sound, then walked outside and sat on the step with her hands over her ears. Pelting rain on the iron roof echoed the throb behind her eyes. Sheltered from the wind, the cool air began to soothe her chest.

She looked up and down the street, hoping no one had seen her storming out of the house. A woman leaped over a puddle on the opposite footpath then cursed as she stepped into deeper water. The gutter bubbled around a drain that was clogged with leaves, water backing up into a tiny dam. Blowing her nose, Mae noticed a pile of unopened letters spilling from her letterbox. Trying to stand, her arms and hips stabbed from the effort of constantly carrying Katie. She shuffled across the patchy tufts of grass that had once been a pocket-sized lawn, lifted the rusted letterbox lid and retrieved the wad of twisted envelopes.

Katie's cries carried through the front door, so Mae sat again on the porch step to sort through the post. Bills, more bills, birthday cards from Alice and from Harry's family, another letter from Legacy, probably inviting her to a knitting circle to make socks for the troops. Harry would need socks even in the jungle if he was wearing his boots. But she could knit socks at home. The women at Legacy all had such sad stories and Mae felt terribly sorry for the few she knew from Williamstown, but Legacy was for war widows, and she wasn't one of them. Harry was only missing; he'd turn up in a camp any day now.

The next letter made her gasp. The naval crest was printed on a small, waterstained envelope with her name and address neatly typed but smudged, probably because it had been sitting in the damp letterbox for several days. She turned it over and inspected the back, felt through the paper to judge how many pages it contained. The letter was thin with a distinct ridge at one end. Probably just one page folded lengthwise and then in half. She tried to picture what it might say; something hopeful, something to confirm her dreams:

Dear Mrs Parker, it would say, *we are writing to inform you that Chief Petty Officer Harry Francis Parker has been found alive in a prisoner of war camp in Burma . . .*

The best news. She closed her eyes and tried to use her mind to force the words she wanted onto the page inside. Yes, he might be hurt, it might take him some time to get home, but they were writing to tell her he was alive, just as Sam had said last summer.

But what if the letter didn't say that? What if it said that he was . . . But surely Sam would have known. He'd have said something—or maybe not. Maybe this was another of those secrets he was so intent on keeping from her and from everyone who cared about the crew.

Holding her breath, she slid her fingernail under one corner of the flap, teasing it wide enough to fit her finger inside. Careful not to tear any of the letter, she worked her finger slowly along the seal, peeling the flap back in a neat line. The paper was damp but appeared intact. Taking what seemed like her first breath in an hour, she sandwiched the envelope between her palms and lifted it to her chest. The envelope radiated warmth into her palms. This was good news, she thought. Bad news and the letter would be cold, but warmth was almost certainly good news.

She hugged her cardigan around her and went inside. Gritting her teeth against Katie's screams, she opened the nursery door, made sure the baby was covered, then closed it again to block the sound. In the lounge room, she dropped the post on the side table and sat on the floor beneath the lamp with the navy letter in her hand. 'Please, please, please,' she whispered.

Unfolding the paper, she read the contents twice—fast the first time then slowly to make sure she'd absorbed every word. Once she was certain she understood its contents she crumpled the letter into a ball and threw it into the fire, watching until every morsel reddened, whitened, then became nothing but heat.

CHAPTER 29

March 1943

GRACE SLOWED THE CAR then gritted her teeth as she steered over a cattle grid set into the driveway. A wooden sign sat on the wooden fence: *Dalrymple*. The farmers of the Western District loved their Scottish names, but Grace doubted many farms in Britain looked as parched as their Australian cousins at the end of summer. The car's tyres raised a cloud of dust as she drove at a reasonable clip along the driveway guarded by tall poplars standing soldier-straight. Hundreds of dust-coloured sheep grazed at the far end of the eastern paddock. The paddock to the west was filled with weeds and wheat stubble, ready for sowing with the winter crop in the next month or two.

Despite her weariness after long days of driving, Grace couldn't stop smiling. Here she was, Grace Fowler, on the road as a reporter for *The Tribune*! Okay, it wasn't hard news, but it was a feature on the Australian Women's Land Army. She'd been given a week, a photographer and a car, and it was up to her to cover it however she wanted. Well, almost. She'd run an outline past Avril, a mix of stories about city girls battling snakes on the land, women farmers doing it tough, kiddies in overalls, drought, longing and loneliness; it would be her tribute to the wonderful *Life* magazine photo essays of America during the Depression. And with Graham Ross taking the photos, she felt she had a pretty good chance of producing something worthwhile. She just needed five or six solid pictures for the double-page spread; two of the stories were already in hand: shearing sheep outside Jerilderie and peach-picking near Shepparton.

Although she was only halfway through her assignment, this had already been the best week of Grace's life, better than she'd ever dared to imagine. She knew without a doubt this was what she wanted to do forever. And maybe it would also be the week she showed her father she could be a success, that he had reason to feel proud of her. Her mother too. She'd told her mother about this assignment, that she was being given free rein to choose her stories and decide what to share with the readers. But her mother was as timid as ever, fearful of provoking her husband.

'That's nice, dear,' she'd said. 'But don't be too disappointed if they spike it. There's always more important stories that come along.'

Well, this story was for the women's section, so it was unlikely she'd get dropped unless there was an emergency shoe sale at Buckley & Nunn. Or maybe Avril would decide to run a spread on General MacArthur's wife's trip to the Dandenongs; tree ferns and Devonshire teas—riveting!

Well, she'd just have to do such a wonderful job that there was no question of bumping her. And Graham had promised last night that he was taking the best photos of his career. 'Like the Farm Security Administration essays in *Life* magazine.'

'Yes,' Grace had nearly shouted. 'I love Dorothea Lange's pictures.'

Graham smiled. 'They've done wonderful work, Miss Lange and Walker Evans, capturing the stories of people struggling to survive on the land. It's not quite that bad here, but their images are an inspiration. We all strive to that level, even if it's just for *The Tribune*.'

Grace knew his images would enhance her stories. 'It's not hard to shine when you have him on an assignment,' Phil had said once. 'Even if your words aren't quite up to scratch, Graham's photos will put you in the front of the book.' That meant the prime news and feature pages, nearly always with a by-line.

She'd dropped Graham in Horsham before lunch so he could develop his films and get them on the evening train. He'd get a lift out to the farm the next morning when the light was still low—directional, he called it, best time for taking pictures. And he'd promised to bring proof sheets so she could see how their stories were building. If only she could show Phil. He'd love her feature, he'd tell her what a beautiful writer she was becoming, that he'd believed in her all along. She pictured long talks about their news stories, sharing their angst over subeditors mucking up their headlines and threats of writs when they upset the wrong people. She longed to cuddle up and hear him say she'd been right to follow her dreams, that she was paving the way for all the other young Torchy Blane fans dreaming in dark theatres about being bold, sassy reporters mixing it with the men.

The homestead roof loomed over a sparse, dusty hedge. Following the curve of the driveway, she rolled to a stop out the front of the single-storey Victorian house, skirted by a large shadowed verandah scattered with assorted wicker chairs and tables. A bit of wrought-iron lacework was the only attempt at decoration.

A woman sweeping the steps smiled and waved as Grace cut the engine. Immediately, two blue heelers leaped against the door, barking. The woman ordered them to sit.

'They try to round up visitors like sheep,' the woman said as Grace got out of the car and walked towards her. Smiling broadly, she leaned forward and offered her hand. 'I'm Alice Gower.' Her blue eyes were friendly and her smile was warm but worn. She couldn't have been more than thirty years old, but already her brown curls were streaked with grey and her brow was etched with lines.

Grace heard children squabbling somewhere near the house but out of sight.

'Did you find us easily, Miss Fowler?'

'Yes, thank you, Mrs Gower. Please call me Grace.'

'And I'm Alice. You'll meet the boys in a minute. I'm surprised they didn't follow the dogs at the sound of your car.'

Sure enough, two small boys appeared around the side of the house, one hand each on the handle of a metal bucket. 'We've got the eggs, Mama,' the taller boy said. 'Nine today.'

'I found three,' the smaller boy said, holding up four fingers.

'Josh is six and Jeremy is four,' Alice said. 'Jemima, the baby, is having a sleep. Say hello to Miss Fowler from the newspaper, boys. She's staying with us tonight and writing a story for the paper about how Dulcie and Joy help us on the farm.'

'Dulcie and Joy are a wonderful help to Mummy and Joy kicks the footy with us sometimes,' Josh said.

'Well, thank you, Josh. I'll be sure to write that in my story.'

Jeremy's spare thumb went straight to his mouth as he sidled behind his brother.

'Thumb out of mouth, right now. Out the back and wash your hands,' said Alice.

The boys dropped the bucket, ran up the stairs and disappeared into the house, a wire door slamming behind them.

'Do you think the eggs survived?' Grace asked.

'They usually do. Hardy hens out here.'

❧❧❧

Within minutes Grace was sitting at the large kitchen table shelling peas while Alice rubbed butter through flour and sugar for a rhubarb and blackberry crumble.

'I hope you don't mind me getting on with things. The children get a bit ratty if I don't get them bathed and fed. The girls can give you the tour when they get back.'

'I'm happy to just dive on in to family life,' Grace said, realising that she meant it. She felt calm, comfortable in the old house with its faded furniture and curtains. There was nothing new or shiny in the room, but it wasn't shabby either; it was just exactly what the heart of the home should be: warm and functional. Well-used saucepans hung from hooks above the stove, canisters lined the mantelpiece, utensils stood in a couple of ceramic jars right where they were needed. The kitchen she'd grown up in was much smaller and tidier, with everything tucked behind a cupboard door or kept inside a drawer, but a wave of homesickness rolled through her chest as she realised how much she'd missed sitting in a kitchen, talking to her mother—even her father when he was at home—while a meal was being prepared. So much had happened in the two years since she'd left home, but this was the first time she'd done something as ordinary as helping to cook a meal.

'Do you all eat together or do the children eat first?'

'No time for separate meals on a farm. It's all in together then get the children straight to bed. After dinner is our only chance to relax and it usually involves mending and bookkeeping, I'm afraid. Not much in the way of excitement.'

'It must be nice to have the company of your Land Army girls, though—some other adults around the place.'

'I can't tell you what a godsend they've been. I couldn't have made it through another harvest without them.'

'How many acres do you have?'

'We've got five hundred under wheat, although the paddocks are fallow at the moment. We'll start sowing in a couple of months. Meanwhile, we have to shear two hundred sheep and get the mutton to market.'

'How did you manage before the girls came to help?'

'Some of the neighbours gave me a hand after my brothers signed up, right at the beginning in '39. The older men had their own farms but everyone pitched in after my father died. Then I lost my brothers and finally Jim, my husband, on the *Sydney*.'

Grace watched Alice carefully, ready to concentrate on her peas if she needed a moment.

'My editor, Mr Barton, is a friend of Mrs Parker. I saw you at the memorial at Scots' Church. I'm so sorry for your loss.'

Alice wiped her eyes and blew her nose then turned to the sink to wash some potatoes.

'Thank you, Grace. I'd say it was one of the hardest days of my life, but it's all a bit of a haze; I barely remember it.'

Grace heard something pinging against metal outside the back door. 'Bullseye!'

'Josh is teaching Jeremy to throw stones against the rainwater tank,' Alice explained. 'Jim painted a target last time he was home.'

'Flick your wrist, like this!'

'Some people think the men are POWs; that they're coming home,' Alice said. 'But hope doesn't run a farm. The navy investigated whether some of the *Sydney* crew might have survived, might have been taken prisoner, but there was no evidence. They issued death certificates last winter. In a way, it was a relief; I started getting the widow's pension, but it wasn't enough to keep this place going. So when I heard that Land Army girls were being organised for the area, I jumped at it. Lots of blokes around here thought they'd be useless, but I know how much work women do on farms; I've been doing it all my life. I knew the right girls would be a great help. While they're out in the fields, I can look after the house and the vegetable garden and the kids. I get out there with the girls too when I can. They're wonderful. I hope they'll stay for a good while. They're like family now. I'd be pretty lonely without them.'

'When will they be back?'

'Any minute. I won't let them work past five. That's the rules. There's probably plenty who flout them, but I've got no intention of taking advantage. They're not allowed to do any work around the house and they always have Sunday off—except when we're harvesting, but that's only for a couple of weeks.'

As if on cue, a truck rumbled into the backyard. Through the flywire door, Grace saw a tall, blonde woman in dusty overalls and boots leap out of the driver's seat and walk to a shed. A smaller woman with dark hair pulled back in a ponytail grabbed hats and thermoses out of the back tray and ran up the stairs into the kitchen.

Alice introduced Dulcie, who couldn't have been more than seventeen or eighteen years old.

'Hello, Miss Fowler. Alice said you were coming today. Joy will be here in a tick. One of the fences is down in the west paddock. She's checking we've got enough wire to fix it in the morning.'

'Reckon we'll be right tomorrow, Dulcie,' Joy called as she scraped her boots outside the door. 'Plenty of wire an' a coupla posts. Oh, hey, you must be the reporter lady. Alice says yer stayin' tonight and comin' out with us tomorrow. Hope ya brought a hat and some strong clobber.'

Grace laughed. 'Don't worry, I don't always dress like this,' she said, gesturing to her pencil skirt and black patent-leather pumps. 'I grew up in the country.'

'Grace, you can borrow anything you need,' Alice assured her. 'Dulcie, can you keep an eye on Jemima? I've got to get the boys into the bath.'

Alice stepped out onto the back verandah.

'I'd love to get in there when they finish, but I reckon they'll've probably peed in the water,' Joy said.

'It could be worse,' Dulcie teased as she washed out the thermos flasks and left them draining on the windowsill.

'Eeew! You'd never know she went to a posh girls' school, would ya? Was on her way to an English finishin' school when she ran away and joined this circus.'

'I didn't run away,' Dulcie retorted. 'I talked my parents into letting me help the war effort at home. Said it was safer than sailing through a war just to go to school.'

'Did they mind you working on a farm?' Grace asked. 'Surely they would have wanted you at home, or working in an office.'

'I grew up on a farm, rather like this one but bigger, with lots of workers. I never knew how to do half the things I do here, but I could ride and drive and when it came to working I wanted to be outside. They didn't fuss about needing me at home. They sent me away to school for ten years, so I think they were pretty used to not having me around.'

'Where's your parents' place?'

'Gippsland. A big dairy farm near the south coast; beautiful and green, but it rains all the time.'

'What about you, Joy? Where are you from?'

'I'm a city girl through and through. Third-generation Fitzroy. Used to work in the munitions factory in Maribyrnong but got jack of workin' inside. Felt cooped up like I was in gaol or somethin', so I joined the Land girls. Never looked back.'

'Have you worked on other farms?'

'Just one, pickin' spuds near where Dulcie's from. Nearly did me back in, bending over to pick the taties out of the ground then lugging great heavy sacks on and off the trucks. They reckoned 'cause I was the same size as a bloke, I could do the same work. But ya gotta build up to it. Can't just turn up one day and get stuck in. Anyways, got transferred here, now I'm happy as a pig in poop! That Alice is an angel, poor love.'

'Bathroom's free,' Alice called as the boys streaked through the kitchen, around the table then down the hallway to their bedroom.

Joy and Dulcie raced to the door and disappeared. Grace heard them jostling to reach the bathroom first. She envied their friendship; it was ages since she'd seen any of her friends back home. And seeing Alice with the children, she realised how much she wanted the sense of belonging that came from being part of a family. Her own family wasn't much comfort but she could create a new family, one full of love and laughter. Of course she couldn't do that if she wanted a career. When Phil came home, they'd be married and she'd start a family, there wouldn't be a choice to make. She couldn't have both, that wasn't the way things worked, so she had to enjoy this freedom, this taste of being a career woman, for as long as possible.

Alone in the kitchen, she checked her notes. She'd written everything the girls had said in shorthand, but it was going to take more than a few quotes to convey the genuine affection within the house. She knew she needed to try to paint a word picture of the setting for her readers, but it wasn't coming naturally yet. She really had to think about the story, to select her words so carefully that it looked effortless. Phil said it got easier with practice. Easy for him to say! What represented them: a melting pot? Blah! A tiny Land Army battalion with a small team of women battling the Goliath of Mother Nature? Oh dear!

She sat back and closed her eyes for a minute then opened her eyes and listed everything she saw. Large wooden table in the middle of the room—well, most kitchens had that, at least in the country. What made this one special? The dents and scrapes made by genera-tions of the one family. Still ordinary. The clutter of salt and pepper shakers, mustard pots and sugar bowls in the middle. Again, nothing unusual there. No, she realised: it was the mismatched chairs. Large wooden chairs with arms sat alongside cream-painted metal, and there was a bench along the wall that could be brought to the table for big gatherings. None of it matched, but everything seemed related by age and paint colour, belonging despite their differences. That was how she'd frame her story. Gatherings like this one were happening on farms across the country; people of assorted skills and background coming together to feed the nation and help the war effort. She wasn't naive enough to think that every Land Army farm was this happy and productive, but it was a good place to start the story.

She made a few more notes about the huge old cast-iron stove, the collection of blue Cornishware canisters along the mantel, the worn lounge chair beside the stove with its comfortable cushions and a rug. She imagined Alice's husband would have sat there reading the paper, just like her father had done and probably his before that. She wondered if anyone sat there now; maybe Alice reading stories to the children.

Throughout the night Grace kept careful watch but the chair remained vacant; not even the boys ventured near it.

❧

Up with the chooks the next morning, Grace felt refreshed in the way that only came from a good night's sleep breathing clean country air; no car exhaust, no coal-fired heaters. While Alice dressed the children, Grace sat at the kitchen table adding to the notes she'd written the night before—a night that had ended at nine-thirty after several rowdy games of canasta. Most nights the three women were alone on the farm, so they were pleased to have a fourth for cards, although Joy let slip that Alice's neighbour John was a frequent visitor.

'He's away at cattle sales this week,' Alice said softly, quickly returning her attention to her cards.

'He was training in the air force,' Dulcie explained, 'but he had ear problems, so when his father died, he came home to run the family property next door.'

'And he's quite the helper here too,' Joy added. 'Knows his way around, doesn't he, Alice?'

'He was Jim's best friend at school, and our families have always been next-door neighbours. Makes things much easier.'

Grace had almost finished her notes when Dulcie brought Jemima, into the kitchen. 'Would you mind holding her while I get the tea ready?'

'Not at all.'

Grace lifted the baby onto her lap and marvelled at the way she already held her back and tiny neck so straight. Jemima turned her head and smiled. Grace hugged the child close, burying her face in the warm shiny hair that smelled of Velvet soap. She was shocked by her rush of affection, how much she relished the feeling of holding her little body so close. She was suddenly aware of an intense feeling of emptiness that ached to be filled. She'd heard women joke about being clucky, but it was surprising to actually feel it for the first time, the utter longing; it was similar to the longing she felt for Phil, yet different. It felt like the knowledge of it was burrowing into her bones, reaching into the most solid part of her, where it would live until she had children of her own.

'Ready, Grace?'

She stood and handed Jemima back to Alice, then went outside and sat in the ute's passenger seat as Dulcie pumped the accelerator, double-clutched then roared away from the house. Joy was in the back tray with Graham, who'd arrived just in time for breakfast.

When they reached a gate, Grace reached for the door handle but Joy was over the side of the truck in a flash, running to undo the latch then waving them through before reversing the process as the dogs barked their approval. The routine was repeated as they traversed five paddocks, each larger than the one before. After about twenty minutes of bouncing over ruts and furrows they reached the broken fence. The morning was clear and already warm, the sky as blue as Grace had ever seen. It would be another hot, dry day and, later, heat shimmer would smear the horizon so you couldn't quite tell where the sky met the fields. As the girls got to work pulling out rotten posts and cutting rusted wire, Graham went to work with his camera. First he got down close to ground level so he could focus on their hands, emphasising their strength. Later he stood on top of the truck cabin and used a wide-angle lens to show the vastness of the property and the huge job that rested on the shoulders of the two young women. Joy and Dulcie smiled the whole way through without Graham ever having to ask them to pose.

'Wanna have a go?' Joy called to Grace as she rammed a new post into the hole. 'Good for gettin' rid of your worries.'

'Thanks, Joy, but I'm enjoying watching you. It would take me three times as long.' As Dulcie rolled out lengths of wire for the new section Grace said, 'You both work like machines. Are there ever any arguments?'

Dulcie laughed. 'Only over the shower. When Joy goes first and uses all the hot water. Then I get a bit cranky.'

'What will you do when the war's over? Do you want to stay on the land? Maybe at your parents' place?'

'I'd love to, but I doubt they'd let me. Farm work is only good enough for their daughter during wartime, just like Princess Elizabeth. No. My options will be go home, get married and have babies, or go to university, get married and have babies. I'm just glad I've had the chance to do this for a while. I hate the war but I don't want to go home yet. Does that sound awful?'

'No, I understand what you're saying about the opportunities for women. The chance to have more independence, to learn new skills. I won't write anything that makes you sound bad. What about you, Joy? Any thoughts about later?'

'Well, I'm pretty keen to stay here. Alice has asked me to stay on and I think I might, at least until some of the local blokes come home. They'll get the jobs of course. Us girls'll have to make way so they can earn a living where they want. I s'pose my options'll be the same as Dulcie's: get married and have bubs. But with any luck I'll find a farm boy.'

'What will you do, Grace?' Dulcie asked. 'I guess you'll have to make way too. Give up work when you get married. Have you got someone?'

'He's in Changi. I don't know when he'll be back, but we're planning to get married afterwards.'

'Well there you are then,' Joy said. 'Enjoy your job while it lasts. We'll all be chained to the kitchen sink before we know it.'

Grace watched the women work as though they hadn't a care. Of course she wanted Phil back home immediately, and wanted to be his wife. But why did she have to give up work? Couldn't she do something part-time? Maybe a couple of stories a week when the babies were old enough for a nurse or a babysitter? Certainly when they went to school, otherwise she'd be twiddling her thumbs, all her training going to waste. But it was selfish to think this way, to think about how she could hang on to her job when poor Phil was in the jungle somewhere missing his leg; sick, fevered, miserable. The war had to end right now so he could come home, so all the men could. What did it matter if they took all the jobs?

'Sometimes it feels like the war's going to go on forever,' Joy said as she twisted two pieces of wire together with pliers.

'My father wrote that it's supposed to be over by Christmas,' Dulcie said. 'Then we can all get back to normal life.'

'Yeah, but what if it don't end?' Joy asked. 'How long are we supposed to go on like this? How long do you wait for yer feller, Grace—five years, ten years? How long do you wait to have kids?'

Grace stared at the bleached horizon. She'd been too preoccupied with her work to let these questions take shape. She wanted to get married, to have children, but time would run out eventually. Phil wouldn't expect her to wait forever, would he? And what if she waited for him to come home then found out he didn't love her anymore, or found that she no longer loved him? She remembered how she'd felt when she held Jemima on her lap. At what point would she need to see if she had other options?

CHAPTER 30

December 1943

Dear Mae and Katie,

WISHING YOU A JOYOUS CHRISTMAS FILLED
WITH MANY BLESSINGS!

We are all so excited about your visit next week.
The boys are counting sleeps and they've already
chosen which cakes they want me to bake! We will be
at the station to meet your train. Have a wonderful
Christmas and we'll see you on New Year's Eve.

All our love,

Alice, Josh, Jeremy and Jemima

❦

Heat shimmer rose from bleached wheat fields, the slightest
breeze setting off a sea of ripples, stretching to the horizon.
The sky too seemed bleached, with just the palest hint of
blue; cloudless, empty apart from a few galahs scouting for
grain. The train jolted and shuddered to a halt at Willaura

railway station, the only building visible as far as Mae could see, apart from two towering wheat silos.

Despite the heat, Alice looked fresh in a yellow cotton dress and straw hat as she and the children waved frantically from the gravel. The conductor heaved Mae and Katie's cases onto the platform then helped them down the steps. Katie hid behind Mae's skirt as the women hugged. Jemima mirrored Katie's actions, stepping behind Alice but peeping around, as though she was playing peekaboo. She was the image of her mother with light-brown curls and energy to burn; it looked like she didn't know how to stand still.

'Welcome to Willaura,' said Josh, sounding very grown up.

Mae and Alice laughed as Katie stared at Josh, her mouth gaping at the boy dressed in moleskins and a battered felt hat. He was starting second grade soon but to Katie he probably already looked like a grown man.

Katie nodded but stayed silent.

Josh and Jeremy lifted the cases and followed the women to the boot of the car, then the four children piled into the back seat of the battered old Holden.

'I can't believe you've finally made it,' Alice said, sliding behind the steering wheel.

Mae eased herself onto the passenger end of the bench seat, feeling several springs push into her thigh. 'Yes, it's been too long.'

Alice guided the car from under a ghost gum and onto the deserted highway.

'How far is your house?' Mae asked, stifling a yawn.

'About forty-five minutes if there's no stock on the road.'

'I had no idea. It's so kind of you to come all this way to meet us.'

Alice laughed. 'Nonsense, Mae. To us it's just down the road a bit. Anything under an hour is like a walk to the milk bar for you town folk.'

'Well, I'm still very grateful.'

Alice turned her head and smiled warmly. 'I hope you brought a party frock. We're off to a dance tonight.'

'Oh, Alice, it's been such a long trip. You go. I'll mind the children.'

'Not on your life. One of my Land Army girls is babysitting so you and I can have some fun.'

Fine lines had formed around Alice's eyes and there were more freckles and sunspots than Mae remembered, but she still recognised her friend's expression; she was determined. As a good house guest Mae supposed she had to make the best of it, but she also knew she'd do little more than prop up a wall.

'How are Et and your uncles?' Alice asked.

'They're slowing down a bit. Et complains that everything in her body either creaks or hurts or both.'

'Well, it's good that you're able to do more in the shop now. She'd be glad of the help.'

'There's a bit more to it than that. Et's retiring at Easter, so I'll be taking over the business, putting my own stamp on things.'

'Mae, that's wonderful. I'm so pleased for you. Will you be changing anything? Selling children's clothes?'

'I don't want to make big changes to begin with, but I'm thinking about how I might expand the business after the war ends. When people have more money to spend and we can get our hands on better fabrics, I'd like to do a little more tailoring for men and special occasion dress-making for women, along with selling the ready-to-wear.'

'That sounds like a huge job. You'll have to get some help, won't you? Any ideas?'

'We'll have to see who's around then. Hopefully the war won't drag on much longer.'

'Hopefully,' Alice echoed.

They spent the rest of the drive chatting easily about Harry's family, and the farms they were passing. It seemed like hardly any time had passed when Alice turned the car off the highway and onto a rutted driveway lined with poplars. The children bounced on the back seat, bleating like sheep, and Alice ordered everyone to close their windows against the dust.

From a distance, the farmhouse looked majestic, its dark verandahs and striped corrugated-iron roof appearing solidly moored in a tiny patch of lush green garden. But the mirage faded on closer inspection. As they drew nearer Mae noticed that paint peeled from the gutters, the roofing iron was rusted and the front lawn resembled the thread-bare elbow of a second-hand woollen coat.

The car had barely stopped before the children leaped out and ran up the stairs, Katie with them, leaving the women to carry the luggage to the guest bedroom. Mae's head hummed with the screech of cicadas. She looked out the window at a stand of dead hydrangeas and a dried-out birdbath, with the hills of the Grampians off in the distance.

'I often use this as my sewing room,' Alice said, picking a couple of threads off the windowsill.

'I should feel right at home then,' Mae said, surveying the saggy double bed covered in a faded brown chenille bedspread. A wooden wardrobe with a full-length mirrored panel between the doors stood beside a dressing table and chair stained the same dark colour. The room would have suited a nun.

Alice hoisted Mae and Katie's suitcases onto the bed.

'Katie can sleep with Jemima—unless you want her to stay with you?'

'No—of course not,' Mae stammered, not having shared a bed with anyone other than Harry. 'I'm sure she'd love to sleep in Jemima's room.'

'And we won't wake her when we get home,' Alice said.

'Are you sure we can't just stay here to see in the New Year? I've brought nothing to wear to a dance.'

'Mae Parker, I don't believe you for a second. You always have the perfect outfit for every occasion. Besides, I've already told my friends you're coming.'

❧

Mae glanced around the crowded hall and wiped her palms on the back of her brown linen skirt. Standing beside an electric fan, she watched as Alice moved from the arms of one man to the next, whirling around the room. A man in a checked shirt with dark sweat stains under his arms danced Alice to the edge of the room, ceremoniously kissed her hand, then turned and walked towards Mae, grinning so widely she could see his yellow molars.

'Gidday. Me name's Mal,' he said. 'Al reckons you're a real good dancer, real light on your feet. Wanna take a turn around the hall?'

Mae pressed her back against the wall, trying to make herself as small as possible. The smell of beer and cigarettes on his clothes and breath made her stomach churn, reminding her why she always crossed a road rather than walking past a public bar.

'Thank you, but I'm a little tired,' she said, even as Et's words rang in her ears: *Never refuse a dance. You don't know if it will be your last offer!*

'Nonsense, it'll perk you right up.'

Mae frantically scanned the crowd, hoping for rescue, but there was no sign of Alice. She looked at Mal again and gave him a thin smile. 'All right then, but I'm not sure that I'll be much good; I'm a bit rusty.'

Mal led her into the crowd of dancers. Mae saw Alice threading through the crowd in the arms of a tall, dark-haired man. 'Hello, Mal,' she shouted. 'Don't trample Mae's feet.'

The band struck up a waltz, and Mal took Mae in his arms, allowing plenty of space between them. His step was surprisingly sure as he led her confidently around the hall.

'You're very good, Mal,' Mae said.

'I used to dance every Saturday night with the missus before she passed on. She loved "The Blue Danube",' he said, humming along, eyes bright.

Mae settled into the rhythm, surprised at how easily her legs remembered the steps. She hadn't danced since before Harry left—not even with her uncles. It hadn't been a conscious decision not to dance; she'd just never thought she'd enjoy it with anyone but Harry. She didn't like small talk, and she hated the idea of being so close to another man. At church socials and dinner dances she'd always kept herself busy in the kitchen.

Alice and her partner were by Mae's side when the tune finished.

'Mae, I'd like you to meet my neighbour, John. I told him you were visiting and he wanted to meet you. Johnny, why don't you dance with Mae?' said Alice, who nodded at Mal as they swapped partners.

Johnny grinned at Mae. 'That friend of yours is wearing me out.'

'I find that very difficult to believe,' Mae said, inspecting his scrubbed but weathered face; his dark green eyes, slightly bulbous nose and high forehead looked vaguely familiar. Mae tried to recall if she had met him before, perhaps somewhere with Jim and Alice?

The band began a fast reel, the fiddle player's bow flying across his strings. Johnny seized her and took off in a crazy polka, legs and feet stomping and thrashing. Mae tried to keep her feet out of the way and her body upright as he bowled through the other dancers. Laughter and shouting egged him on.

'Go, Johnny.'

'That's it—faster, lad.'

Mae was surprised to feel him slowing, then he grabbed her elbows and started to spin. At first she thought she might trip, but he had a firm hold on her and they were pivoting on the spot, right foot planted and left pushing and flicking up behind the knee. The room blurred as they whirled, everything losing its shape as colours and lights streamed past. Expecting to feel ill, Mae was surprised to feel thrilled instead, tilting her head back and laughing. Closing her eyes, her attention found the sound of the fiddle. It sounded just like something Harry played when they went to his mother's; something Irish or Scottish. He'd get wound up and play faster and faster too, stamping his foot in time, laughing as the music swept him away.

Johnny twirled Mae faster and faster, then she felt her ankle buckle and her partner tighten his grip on her as she lurched to the side.

'Whoa there,' he called, as though she were a bolting horse.

The people around them clapped and cheered, unaware of the pain shooting up her leg. Mae gulped air, trying to catch her breath, as Johnny guided her to a chair near the door.

'Are you hurt?' he asked, concern in his voice, his smiling face serious now.

'I've just turned my ankle a bit,' Mae said. 'I'll be right in a minute.'

'We should get some ice on it,' he said, heading for the kitchen before she could answer.

Mae winced as she changed position and strained to see Alice through the crowd. No sign. She watched as Johnny crossed the floor, towering over everyone in the hall, his shoulders so broad that it was easy to imagine him hauling heavy wheat bags as easily as feather pillows. Like Alice, he knew everyone, and nodded greetings left and right. There would have been at least two hundred people in the hall, all of them like members of a big, happy family. She couldn't see a single glum face among the crowd.

Johnny returned with a cold towel and two glasses of punch. 'Wrap the towel around your ankle for a minute,' he instructed. 'It helps the footy players when they go down.' He handed her a glass and clinked it with his own. 'To family,' he said.

Mae stared at him, trying and failing again to work out why he seemed so familiar.

'You really have no idea who I am, do you?' He laughed. 'John Wilkinson,' he said with a slight bow. 'Your cousin.'

Mae searched his expression for a hint of mirth. 'You're not related to . . .'

'Yep. Tom Wilkinson was my father. He died last year.'

After what had happened between Et and Johnny's father, Mae wasn't sure how she should treat him; friend or foe? Of course, she realised now where she knew him from: Et's photo of Tom. Albert had said Tom's son was the spitting image of his father, and he wasn't kidding.

'It's a bit of a shock, meeting you this way,' Mae said, hesitating over her words. 'Does Alice know we're related?'

'She mentioned last week that you were visiting. Before that she'd only ever used your married name; told me about your family and the "racing uncles", as she put it; gave me a bit of a briefing on you. I realised who you probably were but I didn't want to say anything till I was sure.'

Mae recalled the look of grief that had darkened her aunt's expression when she told Mae the story, of how her cousin had stayed with the family while he was at university, then wooed her and eventually asked her to marry him. They'd planned to confess their relationship to their families and move to Queensland to live as husband and wife. But Pearl Atkinson had seen them holding hands one night on the train and told the entire neighbourhood. A huge kerfuffle followed and Tom went home to wait out the scandal. They wrote letters for a while, but he never returned, marrying a local girl when his parents threatened to disinherit him. Et still wore the gold ring he'd given her.

'I met your uncles at the racetrack a couple of years ago. Did they mention it?'

'Yes. Yes, they did,' Mae said, remembering the day clearly.

'I didn't even know we had cousins in the city,' Johnny said, smiling at Alice as she glided past. 'You could have knocked me over with a feather.'

'I see,' Mae said warily.

'They seemed a bit upset that day at the races, but I'd like to meet them again, especially now my dad's gone.'

'Did your father ever tell you why he lost touch with my family?' Mae asked, wondering how much she should say.

Her cousin shrugged. 'He said something about a difference over some family property.'

'Well, that's one way of putting it, I suppose.'

Johnny leaned close and whispered in her ear, 'I'd certainly like to know more about my beautiful cousin and her mysterious family.'

The hairs on the back of Mae's neck quivered. She shifted away.

'What are you two looking so serious about?' Alice asked, flopping onto the seat beside Johnny.

'Mae was just catching me up on Melbourne news.'

'There's not a lot to tell,' Mae said, feeling a stab of pain in her ankle. She looked down and saw it was swelling over the top of her shoe.

'Are you all right, Mae?'

'I'm fine, it's nothing,' Mae said. 'I might go and get some air.' She stood slowly and limped over to the doorway, where she leaned against the wall. There was no cool breeze, just a cloud of cigarette smoke.

Mae turned her gaze to the dance floor and saw Johnny pull Alice close for another waltz. They swayed in time to the music, Alice's cheek resting on his shoulder as comfortably as though they'd been married for years. When Johnny had his back to Mae, it was easy to imagine she was watching Alice dance with Jim; the two men were uncannily similar in height and shape. For a moment time stilled, as if Harry were just about to walk in the door and save her from the Mals of the night. Instead of feeling sad or wistful, Mae felt content. This was how the new year was supposed to begin: with the four of them together again.

Then Mae's heart jolted in her chest as Johnny looked at her over Alice's shoulder, holding her gaze before grinning; not an open, friendly smile, but something more sinister, closer to a smirk of triumph, as though he were saying, *Look what I've got, and you can't do anything about it*. She rubbed at the goosebumps that rose on her arm where Johnny had touched her. His hands were so large, so rough. The heat she'd felt radiating from him was probably just a trick of her imagination—but why was she so much more aware of him than any of the other men? And what had he meant by whispering in her ear like that?

Surely Alice couldn't be interested in someone already? Although he was so like Jim; his hair was much darker, his chin more pronounced, and he seemed so sure of himself; it was all wrong. But seeing Johnny dancing that way, it was also easy to picture Et with his father Tom. She wondered why Tom—whom everyone said was such a powerful man—had been so weak, leaving Et like that. If he'd married Et, Mae might have grown up on the farm. She and Alice would have been childhood friends and she might have met Harry that way, through Jim. But that would have meant less time together. Every now and then she wondered what was the one thing in their life that had needed to change to give them a different story. Could one different decision have changed everything? Well, if Harry hadn't accepted that posting, of course. But what could she have done to make him want to stay? If she hadn't been so awful on that last night of his leave, maybe he would have found a way to come home sooner.

She turned and walked out the door and down the steps and found a log to sit on in the shadows. Her ankle throbbed. Five minutes in the country and she was already reverting to her clumsy ways. Glad to miss the midnight countdown, she watched the crowd through the door, and saw Alice standing on tiptoe in the centre of the hall to kiss and hug Johnny. Several other men lined up to kiss Alice, but they only received chaste pecks.

The band played three more tunes then bid everyone goodnight. Within minutes the crowd was streaming out of the hall and into their cars. There was a rumble of motors and blaring of horns as people shouted their goodbyes.

Alice appeared with a beaming smile.

'Let's call it a night,' she said. 'Johnny's invited us to a picnic by the river tomorrow. I want to look my best.'

'You two seemed quite friendly,' Mae said tentatively as Alice steered the car around the edge of the football ground, past the netball courts and onto the main road.

'Isn't he lovely? I've known him nearly my whole life and now he says he's liked me since we were kids. Imagine that. Not knowing all this time.'

'Should you be getting involved so soon?'

'It's been two years, Mae!'

'I know. Sometimes it feels like it's just been a few months, other times it seems so much longer.'

'For me it just feels longer. The children are growing up not knowing Jim at all—it just breaks my heart.' Alice pulled a hanky from her brassiere. 'I keep hankies everywhere. The smallest things still set me off, mostly when I'm driving.'

Mae stared ahead at the white posts tracing the edges of the road into darkness. 'I often dream about Harry. When I start to wake, I try to will myself back to sleep so I can feel him with me for longer.'

'I'm too tired to dream, but Jim's always with me, keeping me company in the car. He's in their faces too;

287

Josh in particular. Sometimes I call him Jim. He laughs, but there's no joy in it.'

'I talk to Harry all the time, about the house and about Katie when she's being naughty.'

'It's not the same, though, is it? And I can't stand being alone. I'm certain Jim wouldn't want me to be.'

'But they could still be—'

'Johnny's one of the sweetest men I know. And he told me tonight that you two are cousins. I can't believe it. Why didn't you say you knew the Wilkinsons?'

'I didn't know they were your neighbours!'

'Life takes strange twists,' Alice said. 'I never thought I'd feel happy again, Mae.'

'Just be careful.'

'Of what? I've known them forever, Mae. Johnny's the one who told me Jim was missing. He was devastated, like he'd lost a brother.'

'Tom Wilkinson hurt Et very badly,' Mae explained. 'He promised to marry her. She never got over him leaving and marrying someone else at the first sign of trouble.'

Mae saw that Alice's smile had gone and her jaw was set tight as she spoke. 'You can't blame Johnny for what his father did. Besides, we don't know the full story and Tom's not here to defend himself.'

Alice turned off the main road and sped along the driveway, the car tyres crunching to a halt on the gravel at her front door.

They walked quietly up the stairs onto the front verandah and let themselves into the darkened house. The children hadn't waited up after all.

'Do you want a cup of tea before you go to bed?' Alice asked as she tidied the children's empty glasses and dinner plates from the table.

'No, thank you. I just need to get out of these shoes and get my weight off my foot.'

'There's cold compresses in the ice chest. See you in the morning,' Alice said. 'I'll make breakfast at eight so we can all sleep in.'

Moonlight streamed through holes in the curtains as Mae lay in bed, burned by the memory of Alice's dismissive tone. True, she'd spoken her mind, but Alice had no reason to be so cold. And after she'd tried so hard to support her friend at that interminable dance. She felt the cold cloth slipping off her ankle but couldn't be bothered sitting up to put it right. Instead she turned the night over in her mind, imagining that Harry had been on stage playing the fiddle, his fingers flying faster than she could see, weaving a thread of music that invisibly bound them together. As she drifted off to sleep, she dreamed she was wearing the silk chemise she'd worn on their wedding night. Harry was sitting in the bed propped against pillows and she rested her back against his warm bare chest. He was brushing her hair with one hand and using the other to smooth her hair between strokes. He worked gently, kissing her neck and nuzzling her ear.

It could have been minutes later or hours, but his strokes gradually grew harsh; he tugged at her scalp, digging the bristles into her skin. She reached up and touched his hand to encourage him to be more gentle, but his hand was larger than she expected, his skin rougher, hairier. She spun around and saw Johnny's face. He grinned and leaned down, licking her neck roughly with his broad, wet tongue. Her legs lurched and a wave of pleasure flooded her belly, her groin.

She sat up straight, panting, the unwanted pleasure mingling with panic. Her heart was racing, her nightgown drenched. Why was her mind playing such nasty tricks? She didn't desire Johnny; she didn't even like him. For the rest of the night she lay awake, fighting sleep in case her mind betrayed her again.

❧❦❧

'How's your ankle?' Alice asked the next morning. She was standing at the stove stirring a pot full of porridge.

Mae hobbled over to the table and sank into a chair, slipping her shoe off and slowly rotating her foot. She wouldn't be walking far today. 'I might need some liniment if you've got some.'

'You looked like you were having fun dancing last night.'

'A little too much fun, I think.'

'There's no such thing as too much fun, Mae. You've just forgotten how.'

'I'm running the shop and I'm looking after Katie, Et, Albert and William. There's not much time for dancing, and there won't be till—'

'Stop it, Mae.' Alice put the spoon on its rest and turned around. 'You have to face the facts: they're not coming back.'

'They're still finding prisoners in the jungle,' Mae protested. 'I read about it in the paper just the other day.'

'It's great that you have your family for support, but I don't. There's no one left. But the farm needs a man's hands and I do too. I refuse to live the rest of my life alone. I just won't.'

'I want you to be happy, Alice. Truly I do,' Mae said quietly. 'But there'll be no one else for me, not while there's a chance Harry is still alive.'

Alice sat in the chair opposite; her hands moved across the table to make contact with Mae's.

Mae sat to attention, her muscles tightening like a spring.

'You are probably the most stubborn person I've ever met,' Alice said. 'But I don't think you're managing very well. They're gone. It's terribly sad and we'll never forget them, but there's no government cover-up; they're not in a POW camp. Wishing won't change the facts.'

'That's enough, Alice,' Mae said, sliding her foot around under the table, looking for her shoe. When she found it, she couldn't fit her foot inside. 'Perhaps it's time Katie and I went home, while I can still walk on this foot. When's the next train to Melbourne?'

'Tomorrow afternoon,' Alice said with a heavy sigh.

'Well, I can't get into my shoes, so you go on to the picnic without me. I'll stay here.'

'The Wilkinsons will be disappointed. I know Johnny's mother wanted to meet you.'

'Katie can go with you, if you like. She'll enjoy another day with your children.'

'We won't leave for a couple of hours, maybe you'll feel better by then.'

Mae heard the car drive away as she sat on the back verandah reading a book, her foot up on a stool. She looked through the trees to the large dam about two hundred yards away. The air was already warm and harshly dry, so she was glad to be in the shade. The never-ending cicada shrill sounded like a scream of frustration. Mae's stomach was knotted as tight as a girdle. This trip had been a terrible mistake. What had happened to her friend? She hardly recognised Alice anymore. And now she was thinking of marrying Johnny Wilkinson! What if he was like his father, like her own father—just using Alice for a thrill, only to leave when things got serious?

A breeze carried the sharp scent of nettles from a stand of pines behind the sheds. Mae wondered how much Johnny's mother knew about Et. Nothing, she hoped. It would be too awful to know that Tom had known another woman so intimately then broken his promises. But maybe Alice needed to know what sort of family she was letting her children spend time with? Or maybe not. After all, it was Et's story to tell, not Mae's.

Large gum trees near the dam's edge softened the land-scape and a wooden jetty jutted into the air; the water level was so low that anyone wanting to get into the rowboat needed to climb down a ladder. The boys had promised to catch yabbies from the dam and Alice said she'd cook them for dinner, but unless they did it tonight, it was unlikely she'd get the chance to try them.

'Don't leave tomorrow,' Alice had implored. 'Jemima adores Katie and the boys treat her like another sister. Please, Mae; stay for the week and try to enjoy yourself.'

Mae knew it would be impossible to avoid Johnny if she stayed any longer, and the thought of seeing him . . . well, she was certain he and Alice would be able to see the thoughts she'd had about him written all over her guilty face. She thought back to dancing, to twirling and whirling and feeling free, flying like a bird. But then she recalled the way he'd looked at her as he danced with Alice, and the vivid feel of his tongue on her neck in her dream. It hadn't even happened, yet it was already tangling itself in her memories. How could her mind have made it feel so real?

She'd made a point of not looking at men, of keeping her expression distant, never speaking more than a few words to any of the fellows at church. And now, in a single night, she'd let herself go, dancing like a lunatic with Mal then Johnny. The whole town had egged them on, as though they'd all decided it was time for her to get on with life. But that was silly; they wouldn't know anything about her life unless Alice had told them her story, and as distant as she seemed these days, she couldn't believe Alice had slipped that far away. Still, it was just a matter of time until she and Alice drifted apart completely. Soon there'd be no one who had known her and Harry together, who knew the look on his face when he was with her, who had seen the way his shoulder dropped so that his hand hung at just the right height to comfortably hold hers. When she was gone, her memories would be gone too, and there'd be nothing left of Harry apart from his photo.

She moaned. Harry was gone. *Harry wasn't coming back*. She knew it, but she couldn't admit it to the world. Once she finally said it aloud, it would be real, and her life would change completely. The only way she knew how to live was with hope; huge, unwavering, against-all-odds hope. The thought of living without hope was almost impossible to imagine. Mae couldn't picture who she'd be or how she'd get out of bed each day if she let her hope go. Instead she filled her mind with memories, but only the good ones that brought her lightness, a sense of belonging. She was happy to let go of anything else, especially their last night together at her family's house; if only it were gone already. The memory of her last night with Harry still caused her breath to catch, her chest to ache.

I'm so sorry about that night, Harry, she whispered to the trees and the dam and the insects. *I didn't mean for it to end that way. I always thought I'd get the chance to make it right.*

Mae let the tears stream. There was no need to hold back; the luxury of being completely alone meant she could give in to the pain and let it flow through her. Alice was right; it was time to give up hope and make a new life for herself. But where would she start? Building the house? No, that was too big a step to begin. Finding a dance partner for church socials? There weren't many men of suitable age in sight. Stop talking to Harry so often in her thoughts? Impossible.

Mae heard a car approaching the house and stop. She tried to tidy her face and pretend she'd been reading.

A few moments later her friend approached with Jemima and Katie.

'Alice! I thought you'd be gone for hours.'

'I couldn't leave you here alone and Jemima left her

dolly here. We've both been miserable all day.'

'I'm sorry,' Mae said. 'You should be with Johnny, not worrying about me.'

'I've left him with the boys. He won't even notice I'm gone.'

'I doubt that.'

'I'm sorry, Mae; I didn't mean to upset you.'

'It's all right. I shouldn't have been so critical.'

Alice looked down at the hanky in Mae's hand then back at her blotchy face. 'What is it?' she asked. 'Is your ankle hurting?'

Katie and Jemima ran inside to look for the doll.

Mae looked squarely at her friend and summoned the strength to ask the question. 'What if Harry . . . What if he never forgave me?'

'Forgave you for what?'

'We fought, that last night. I turned my back on him and didn't say goodbye.' Mae's throat burned. She fought against her tears then gave in when she felt Alice's arms wrap around her and rock her gently like a child.

'Harry knew you loved him. And he loved you.'

'But I wasn't perfect. I swore I'd never fight with him when he was home, but then we couldn't stop arguing. I was just so tired, and I didn't want him to leave.'

'And you apologised in your next letter?'

'Yes.'

'Mae, I'm sure he never gave it another thought. I've never seen a man more devoted.'

Mae let herself relax in her friend's arms, comforted by her voice.

'Harry and Jim were quite the pair, weren't they?' Alice said.

'They—they were.' Mae took a few deep breaths. 'I just can't picture my life without Harry,' she said quietly. 'I try, but nothing comes to mind.'

'Mae, you're already living it. This *is* your life. Raising Katie, spending time with your family, working; even visiting us sometimes. You don't have to plan it all out, just try to enjoy some of it, dance a bit more.'

Tension slipped from Mae's shoulders and neck. She sat back and looked at Alice's expression, concerned, tired, but open, with no sign of grief.

'Thank you for coming back.'

'I'll always be here for you, Mae.'

Mae lifted her head and attempted a smile. 'I'll always be here for you too. I couldn't bear to lose you as well.'

❧❧❧ ❀ ❧❧❧

A week later, the two women stood on the station platform as the children ran around the suitcases.

Mae adjusted her hat and smoothed her blouse—tears threatened but she swallowed them back.

'We've been through our best and our worst times together,' Alice said in Mae's ear. 'But there's so much ahead, even if you can't see it yet.'

The noise of the train prevented them from saying much more. Mae still loved Alice, but she knew their lives were moving in different directions. 'Katie, say thank you to Alice for inviting us to stay.'

Alice bent down and hugged the little girl. 'You must

visit again. The boys will teach you to ride properly when you're big enough.'

Mae and Katie boarded the train, pausing in the doorway to wave goodbye before finding their seats.

As the train pulled away from the station and gathered speed, Mae watched the flat, dry landscape and spoke to herself: *This* is *your life. There's so much ahead, so much ahead.*

That might be true, but first she had to learn how to live without holding her breath.

CHAPTER 31

January 1944

'DON'T EVEN THINK ABOUT doing another country trip while I'm on leave,' Avril said before she left for her summer holiday to Sydney. 'I won't have you swanning off again as though you're some big-deal reporter. You're a cadet for the next few years if you are very lucky, but that can change in a moment.'

Grace chugged the remaining half glass of moselle while she waited for the barmaid to serve her. Shivering at the sickly sweetness, she ordered a pint of beer for herself and more wine for her two friends from advertising, Del and Jo. If only they drank beer too, she could order a jug.

Between the grief she was getting from Avril and the hard time her father was giving her, she was tempted to drink a whole damn jug by herself. Her capacity for drinking beer had risen substantially during her Christmas visit to her parents. A whole week of Nev huffing and yelling and breaking anything in sight. She would have returned to the city early, but she didn't want to desert her mother, who spent the entire week trying to keep the peace.

Her first night at home, two days before Christmas, had been the worst, but things barely improved afterwards. The reporters and subeditors from her dad's paper had invited her to join them for Christmas drinks after they put the latest edition to bed. They'd dragged several chairs to the loading bay, cranked up the barbecue and put half a dozen crates of beer on ice. The local firies and coppers had joined the fun, and most of the local councillors. There were a few women there too—secretaries and sales reps—but mostly it was blokes, who kept toasting her success on *The Tribune*. Grace tried to keep up with the men, all seasoned drinkers, but by the time Nev arrived Grace was pretty tipsy.

'What the devil are you doing here?' he'd roared when he saw her surrounded by her old friends and supporters. 'I'm not paying for my own daughter to get pissed like a trollop. Get home to your mother now.'

Scoop, the photographer, stepped forward to stand beside Grace. A similar height to his boss but twice his girth, Scoop was never afraid to speak up. 'She's just having a quiet drink, Nev, so we can tell her how proud we are.'

'A coupla bloody picture spreads doesn't make you a journo. She's only a bloody cadet on the women's page. It's not even real reporting.'

The rest of the crowd stood silently looking down at their boots, out the doors towards the empty railway station, anywhere but at the bloke wound as tight as the rolls of newsprint in the corner, or his poor daughter.

Determined to keep her voice from trembling, Grace gulped another mouthful of beer. 'Thank you for your warm wishes, but I'd better get going,' she said evenly. 'Have a merry Christmas, everyone.'

Murmured greetings and pinched smiles followed her progress towards fresh air and the footpath leading home. Grace heard their voices swell in conversation as she walked away, large, round tears rolling down her face. The thought of her father bringing his whisky- and beer-stoked rage home later that night made her hurry back to her mother. She'd have to warn her, but short of disappearing to her grandparents' house for the night, there was little that forewarning would do except prolong the fear.

Grace arrived home to find her mother washing a stack of serving platters and bowls and all the good china in preparation for Christmas Day. Wordlessly, Grace grabbed the tea towel and dried the dishes.

'How was the barbecue, dear?'

'Oh, just the usual assortment of movers and shakers and hangers-on drinking Dad's beer. I don't think the pub will be doing much business tonight—at least not till the drinks run out.'

'I see.'

Grace heard her mother take a shallow breath and her body tilted towards the sink as if seeking support.

'Well, we've got lots to keep us busy tonight. I need to wrap a few things for your cousins, and I need your help to finish decorating the Christmas cakes. The icing's all cured.'

'You know I'm not artistic.'

'These are all skills you need to learn while I'm still around to teach you. Your husband will expect it.'

'Don't say that, Mum, you'll be decorating my cakes for decades.'

'I'm sure you're right, dear; I'm sure you're right.'

The good crockery never made it to the Christmas table, that year or any of the following. Nor did three of the Wedgwood platters. Nev flung them all on the floor when he got home, yelling that Rosie and Grace should have waited up for him in case he needed dinner. At least he'd passed out on the couch without hurting anyone.

'Was he always like this?' Grace asked.

'It's the war, dear. A lot of them come back broken. You just have to pray for a good day every now and then to get you through.'

Grace couldn't imagine Phil ever yelling at her the way her father did, nor was he capable of belittling her in that awful way her father had. He'd been gone a whole year now, but her body still ached for him, her mind tricking her into reaching for him as she woke each morning only to force her to face his absence anew.

'Hey, Grace!'

Grace was jolted from her thoughts by the sound of Phil's mate Jacko shouting her name from the other end of the bar.

'You'll be wearing trousers any day now!' he called. 'Phil'd better be careful or he'll come home to find you've moved to lezzy land.'

Ignoring him, Grace picked up the tray of drinks

and carried them back to her friends. 'What's he talking about?' she asked Del.

'Don't mind him; he just can't stand the idea of women doing anything other than cooking his dinner and washing his clothes.'

'And playing with his tiny little doodle,' Jo laughed.

'But do they all think I'm getting too manly?'

'Who cares what they think? Here, have a ciggie with your beer, that'll really rattle them.'

Grace had never smoked, but aware that Jacko and his reporter friends were watching, she smiled and took a cigarette from the packet. Jo leaned over and lit it.

'Don't take too much. Just hold the smoke in your mouth for a second before you gently blow it out. It'll look like you've done the drawback.'

Grace took a sip of beer and swallowed then drew a small puff of the sour smoke into her mouth. Surprised by the tarry taste, she remembered she was putting on a show and stopped herself from wrinkling her nose in disgust. Pursing her lips, she released the smoke in a steady stream then smiled at her friends, leaned back and did it again.

'They've turned away. You can put it down now.'

Grace laughed. 'It's horrible. Why do you do this?'

'You get used to it, and it's great for beating food cravings. Keeps you lovely and slim.'

'I can see why. The last thing I feel like now is food.'

'Job done. Sing out if you want to try properly, although we should do that outside, just in case you chunder.'

'Eeew!'

CHAPTER 32

May 1944

KATIE TOOK A HUGE breath and blew out the three small candles burning on her passionfruit sponge. Hugging a musical doll almost as tall as the child, Et wound the small bronze key in its back for an encore of 'Happy Birthday' and handed it to Katie, who attempted to sway in time with the tinkling tune. As the last notes spluttered away, Et, Elizabeth and Mim clapped and Katie curtseyed, her dark blue, brushed cotton dress calming her pink complexion and mop of dark hair.

'She takes my breath away!' Harry's mother said, as she usually did several times each visit. 'The same dark curls; the eyes; that stocky little frame. She looks more like him than his brothers and sisters did.'

Keeping her smile fixed, Mae met Et's eyes and noted her aunt's tiny nod, reminding Mae to indulge her mother-in-law, to remember that she was grieving Harry's disappearance too. They all were. The war was already winding down in England, the Germans were being pushed back in parts of Europe, and it was only a matter of time before the Japanese were defeated in the Pacific. He just needed to hold on a bit longer, Mae told herself each day. Then he'd prove them all wrong and come home.

'She's a credit to you, Mae,' Elizabeth said as Katie held Mim's hand and dragged her outside into Et's garden in the weak sunshine. Et followed with a bucket. 'Harry would have been so proud of her.'

Harry will *be proud*, Mae said firmly in her mind. 'Thank you, Mrs Parker. My family is a great help too.'

'You're lucky to have them so close.' Elizabeth dabbed her eyes and nose with a hanky. 'I feel so far away sometimes from you and Katie. I know she's still very young, but I'd love to have her stay for a few days now and then. Mim and the boys would love it too.'

Harry's mother never made it through a visit without tears, but it didn't annoy Mae anymore. Mae felt sorry for Elizabeth, sad that she was still suffering needlessly. If only she shared Mae's faith. Their meetings were less of an ordeal these days. Elizabeth's old barbs had been replaced by a caring tone that seemed genuine. The shift occurred when Mae stopped visiting after the *Sydney* memorial service. When the next Easter arrived and Elizabeth hadn't seen Katie since Christmas, she and Mim braved a late March heatwave, caught the train to Williamstown and insisted that Harry wouldn't approve of Katie being kept away from his family. Katie had been too young to stay with Elizabeth before, but now she was three, surely a couple of nights away wouldn't be a problem and Mae was desperate for a break.

'Well, now that she's talking and she can tell you what she needs, I suppose it wouldn't hurt.'

'Exactly. And it's not like we're strangers—we're family. You could get away for a night or two, maybe go on a short holiday with your aunt and uncles, just the grown-ups.'

Mae watched Mim lifting Katie to help her pick ripe quinces for a jam-making session later that afternoon. The resemblance between Mim and Katie was growing more obvious. Despite her contribution, there was no question about the genes that produced particular jawlines, eye shape and hair colour across generations. Their kinship was deeper than marital choice; it was a physical bond. And Mim was becoming something more than an aunt to Katie—there was something almost sisterly about their bond. Mae knew it was right to let that kinship develop; she'd always wished for that relationship herself, not necessarily with Mim, but it would have been lovely to have cousins, sisters, people who knew everything about you and loved you anyway. Alice and Claire were the closest she'd had to sisters, but Alice was so far away, and now that Mae was working at the shop each day she had less time to spend with Claire.

❧∾჻∾☙

Two buckets laden with the yellow-skinned fruit sat on the lawn. When they'd picked everything they could reach, Et gathered half a dozen brilliant yellow lemons in her apron to add acid and pectin to the jam. Et showed Katie and Mim how to wash the fruit in a colander over the gully trap, squeals indicating that plenty of cold water was splashing shoes and stockings.

'They get along like a house on fire, don't they?'

Mae turned and smiled at Elizabeth. 'Yes, all three of them. Mim's going to be a lovely mother.'

'Not for a while yet, I hope. In fact, Mim was saying the other day just how much she admired you running the shop, how she'd love to follow in your footsteps.'

'That's very kind. She's quite the little seamstress nowadays.'

'Unfortunately, though, her manager is quite cruel to Mim and all of the other girls bar one. We think he might be leading that one on a bit; he favours her with overtime and extra time at lunch, but he pushes the others relentlessly and won't let them visit the ladies' room between breaks, no matter the urgency.'

'I remember working for a man like that once. It was as if he'd stepped straight out of a Dickens novel.'

'The thing is . . .' Elizabeth hesitated. 'I was wondering if you would have the capacity to take Mim on for the last two years of her apprenticeship? She could help you with Katie too. We'd both be so grateful.'

'But it's such a long way for her to travel each day. How would she manage?'

'I have an elderly cousin in Kensington who'd love some company. Mim would be just a few train stops from the shop.'

'Well, it's certainly something to think about. I'll talk to my aunt and see what she thinks, whether the business can support another employee.'

'Thank you. I'm sure she'd be a great help to you both and she'd love to spend more time with Katie.'

⁂

After Elizabeth and Mim left, Et shuffled into the kitchen and poured herself a cup of tea from the tepid pot.

'I'll boil the kettle just as soon as I finish the dishes,' Mae said, as she separated the good china from the kitchen crockery and stacked it on the table.

'No hurry. William and Albert will be home soon. I'll make it then.'

'Take a seat and I'll put the dishes away,' Mae offered.

'That's all right. You keep washing, I'll put the good ones in the hallway cupboard.'

Several moments later, Mae heard a gasp and saw Et near the kitchen door holding a card.

'How could you not have said anything?' Et asked, leaning against the wall, her face crumpling.

The invitation. Mae had put it on top of her basket on the hall table meaning to tell Et but then she'd forgotten. Et must have seen it when she was putting things in the cupboard.

Et's eyes drifted towards the card again, then she read it aloud.

'*Mrs Alice Gower and Mr John Wilkinson request the attendance of Mrs Mae Parker and Miss Katie Parker at their wedding ceremony on the twenty-second of September*. It says here that John is the son of the late Tom Wilkinson! Mae, is it my Tom's son?'

Mae reached forward to stroke her aunt's arm. 'I'm sorry. I—I didn't want to upset you.'

'When did he die?'

'Last year.'

'And you didn't tell me? He was family! You knew how much he once meant to me.'

Mae leaned over and clasped Et's hand. 'I'm sorry. I can't believe they're still entangled in our lives. But Alice loves Johnny. They're neighbours. I just didn't know where to start.'

Et bowed her head. 'I can't believe I was so stupid.'

Mae stood still, hardly believing what she'd just heard. Her aunt never admitted fallibility, about anything. If she scorched a shirt she'd blame the iron. If a sponge collapsed it was because someone had let a draught into the kitchen.

'I was silly, romantic. But not Tom! He got on with things and had the life we were supposed to have together—a home, children. It didn't matter whether it was with me or someone else. I wasted my life pining for a man who never cared.'

'Et, I'm sure that's not true.'

'I'm just an old fool. Still upset over someone who couldn't be bothered fighting for me. And I've raised you to be the same, pining for what you can't have.'

'We've all been guilty of that, Et.' Grace looked up to see that William was standing in the doorway to the kitchen. 'Albert and I are just as bad. Mae, I spent my entire adult life looking for an impossible ideal. At least Albert has chased his dream and found a little happiness.'

'It's not the same thing, William,' Et said as she wiped tears from her cheeks.

Mae stood silent for a moment. She'd never known William to show any interest in women. She'd occasionally seen women speak to him at church but he only ever responded with cool politeness. They soon gave up.

'Uncle William, are you saying you had a love affair?'

'Oh yes. I was only twenty-two; it was after the war. The summer was terribly hot and my leg wasn't healing, so Mother sent me down to Tasmania to recuperate.'

Mae realised that she'd never asked much about his life. She'd always figured that when adults wanted you to know something, they'd tell you. She'd never stopped thinking of herself as the child when it came to prying into her aunt and uncles' lives.

'Well, there was a woman at the convalescent hospital recovering from scarlet fever. We spent three months together, just talking at first, then walking and fishing as we grew stronger. She returned to Adelaide to her husband and three small children and I came back to Melbourne.'

'He was a different man,' Et added. 'So quiet, listless. He'd spend days on end barely leaving his bedroom. It took us months to get the truth out of him.'

'I was being childish. I think I even declared at one point: *I'm guarding my story like tiny soap bubbles, keeping them safe inside my chest so they won't burst.*'

Et laughed. 'We used to tease him: *William, how are your bubbles today? William, burst anything this week?* And then, of course, he compared any woman he met to his Mrs Morris—her looks, her nature—and they were all found wanting.'

'You never said anything,' Mae exclaimed.

'I was ashamed of having such ardent feelings for a married woman.'

'Did she reciprocate?'

'She never broke her marriage vows.'

'But she certainly led you on,' Et said. 'All that talk of moving to Melbourne, even writing to you.'

William's face burned bright red. 'There's nothing else to tell. Years passed and here we are.'

'What about Albert? Why didn't he marry?'

Et raised her eyebrows and William smiled behind his hand.

'What?'

'Albert's an entirely different story,' Et said. 'He's never spelled it out but I think he's much happier around horses and the men who rode them.'

'I beg your pardon!'

'That might be why he spends every Friday night at his club in town rather than catching the late train home,' William added.

Mae stared first at Et then at William, then clamped a hand across her mouth, which suddenly refused to close. She'd never suspected . . . Albert was . . .?

William settled back into his chair. 'He's never said it outright, but he tends to have an extra spring in his step when he comes home on Saturdays. Especially in the last few years.'

Mae couldn't believe her uncles had led such colourful lives. Talk about dark horses! She thought of all the hours they'd spent listening to her talk about Harry. Never once had either of them mentioned their own loves. Were they afraid of how she'd judge them? She looked at her aunt and uncle.

'Why is this the first I'm hearing of all of this?'

'It's the first time you've listened,' Et said.

'What does that mean?'

'You've had a lot to contend with, dear, and it was all so long ago, but we do understand a little about sadness and loss,' William said.

'You need to take a leaf out of Alice's book or you'll end up alone like us,' Et said, her voice quavering. 'You should find Katie a new father, someone for you to grow old with.'

Mae thought of having another man in her lovely new home when it was finally built. Harry's home! Lately she'd begun to imagine touching a man's skin, his hair, feeling his breath on her body. She was surprised to feel less horrified by the idea, but it was still something distant; there was no firm shape in her mind of how he would look, who he would be. And right now, getting the house built was enough.

'There are worse things than being alone,' Mae said.

'That's the thing, Mae,' said Et. 'I'm not sure there are.'

CHAPTER 33

September – December 1944

MAE LIFTED A STACK of plates off the drainer and dried them quickly. She heard Albert coughing. Unusually for Albert, he'd retired to his room straight after lunch. He'd had a cold for the last week but she'd been shocked by his appearance today. Normally dapper, he was wearing an old pair of trousers, leather slippers and a jumper and a cardigan over his shirt. He looked like a shrunken old man. She brewed him a pot of tea, adding lemon and fresh ginger to the hot water before placing it on a tray. Next she arranged the honey pot and a fresh cup and saucer then rattled along the hallway to his room.

'That cough sounds like it's getting worse, Albert,' Mae said, placing the tray on the table beside his bed.

Albert coughed himself upright then wheezed as he reached for a glass of water.

'What did the doctor say?'

'I just need a few days in bed,' he said, swiping a hanky across his mouth.

'You might need another visit.'

'Don't fuss, Mae. A cup of tea will fix me right up.'

A shaft of light streamed from beneath the lowered blind, illuminating the side of his face. His skin, normally as smooth as a child's, was covered in silver stubble.

'Thank you, dear, the tea is perfect,' he said, lying back against his pillows.

Squeals and giggles from the backyard drew a tired smile. 'I'm so proud of you, Mae.'

'Proud? What for?'

'The way you are with Katie, the way you are with Harry's family. I know none of it's been easy for you.' He quickly set the cup aside as a spasm seized his chest.

'I want to call the doctor,' Mae said. 'It's more than just a cold.'

'Nonsense. He'll just tell me to drink fluids and rest, which is exactly what I'm doing.'

William appeared in the doorway. 'How's the patient?'

'Ridiculously stoic,' Mae answered.

'Let's leave him to rest. I want to talk to you about something.'

Mae caught a slight nod from Albert to his brother before he closed his eyes. She followed William to the sitting room.

'Should we call the doctor back?'

'I already have. He's coming in the morning. Albert doesn't know, but it's all arranged.'

'I've never seen him so bad. He looks like he's getting worse.'

'He's just a bit downhearted, cooped up. He missed Trevor's party the other night.'

'Trevor?'

'His friend from the club. He's never mentioned him?'

'I don't think so. Did they serve together?'

William hesitated for a moment. 'No, they met a few years ago. They have dinner and drinks every Friday night, then they stay the night at the club.'

'No wonder he's upset, being too sick to go out this weekend. Perhaps Trevor could come to visit, cheer him up a bit.'

'He telephones most days.'

'How lovely to have a special friend like that. Maybe you should go to a club too, somewhere you can expand your horizons, meet some new friends.'

William chuckled.

'What's so funny?'

'It's all right, dear. Nothing at all. Albert's the more social one, likes a change of scenery, a bit of time away from all of us. I'm more of a homebody.'

'Still, you should think about getting out more.'

'Thank you for your concern, but I'm too old to change my spots,' William said. 'I'd prefer to talk about *your* plans.'

And there it was. It had been nicely done, she had to admit. No matter how much she tried to avoid the subject, she managed too regularly to walk into another of *those* discussions: the concerned family grilling her about the future, her plans, her housing situation. Why couldn't they let her be, at least until the war was over and she knew when Harry was coming home? There was nothing wrong with the cottage. The landlord had said she could stay as long as she liked.

William twisted in his chair, trying to find a position that would ease the pressure on his leg. The more uncomfortable he looked, the more Mae knew she probably wouldn't like what he had to say. She plunged her hands down beside the cushions so that she felt cocooned, braced. William met her eyes and launched into his obviously rehearsed spiel.

'The plans are all approved. In the next few weeks they'll be ready to start building new houses on the street where your mother's block is,' he said, elbows planted on the arms of the chair, hands clasped. He paused, watching for her reaction.

'You know I don't have all of the money saved yet, and Harry hated the thought of owing anyone.'

'But you can't be comfortable living in that ridiculous cottage, especially with Katie growing so quickly. She needs a tree of her own to sit under, somewhere to play with her friends.'

'Plenty of children live in small houses or even flats.'

'That's not the point, Mae. You don't need to martyr yourself like this. You've already admitted you need to move on with your life.'

No, no, no! Mae imagined herself sticking her fingers in her ears and stamping her foot, the way Katie did when she didn't want to get dressed in the morning. But he was right. Even though her every waking thought was about getting Harry home safely, the news coming

out of the Japanese POW camps was terrible. The like-
lihood of him coming home was fading each day and
she'd heard nothing since the Tokyo Rose rumour.
Harry had always wanted a house in Frankston, arguing
they should keep the Yarraville block up their sleeves
for a rainy day. But what if the rainy day had already
arrived?

It was so hard to know what to do. She'd often asked
Harry in her mind what he would do in her situation.
Would he hold on to hope when everyone around him said
hope was gone? Would he wait for a dream, or would he
do his best to provide for his family? Her mind knew the
answer, but her heart still dragged like a weight keeping
her rooted in their past. And in the end, was building the
house really a betrayal of their shared dreams, their plans,
their last days together? If the miraculous did happen
and he came home, they could always sell the house and
start again. Surely he'd forgive her—if, indeed, there was
anything to forgive. And it would be so nice to have a
project, something to keep her thoughts busy, outside
of the shop, training Mim, looking after her family and
raising Katie.

Mae straightened her back and clasped her hands
firmly in her lap. Taking a deep breath, she met William's
gaze and spoke so calmly and quietly she almost wondered
whether she was speaking aloud at all or merely continuing the conversation in her head.

'I've given this a lot of thought, and I've decided that
you're right. It's time to move ahead. It doesn't have to
be our home forever, but it's my responsibility to build a

future for all of us. I'll sign the papers. If it doesn't work out or I end up hating it, we'll cross that bridge in due course, but at least I'm doing something.'

William shook his head then smiled. 'You're doing the right thing. I'm sure he'd be so proud. And we'll be here to help, every step of the way.'

Mae leaned over and rubbed her uncle's shoulder.

'Go and tell Et the good news; she'll be so relieved.'

'Mim, you'll need to re-pin the yokes so the nap matches the rest of the front. See here? When you sew them together, the yoke nap will sit diagonally instead of straight up and down. It will look different to the eye instead of all running in the same direction.'

'I'm sorry, Mae. I didn't see that when I was laying it out.'

'That's all right, Mim, you're doing just fine. But it's a good habit to draw arrows on the paper patterns so that you know exactly where your nap sits, especially on velvet and silk, where it makes such a difference. It's so much easier with tartans and heavy weaves, isn't it?'

'I'm sorry, you must think I'm so hopeless.'

'Not at all; we all have to start somewhere. Just make yourself a list of things to check before you cut any fabric, and always ask me to double-check, at least until you're more confident.'

'How long did it take you to get the hang of this?'

'I wasn't allowed to cut unchecked until the third year of my apprenticeship, and even then I managed to cut a set of pockets in for a pinstripe suit with the stripes running horizontal instead of vertical. It was the day after Harry proposed. I could barely think, I was so excited.'

'I wish I'd been older then, and known you both as friends rather than just being the baby sister. We so looked forward to your visits, but then you'd leave and we wouldn't see Harry for weeks at a time. That's why it's so nice working with you now, and spending time with Katie.'

Katie's head appeared around the curtain to the back of the shop.

'That's right, I said your name, sweet pea. Stay there behind the curtain while we have the scissors out. That's the girl.'

'Why don't you leave the cutting and take Katie for lunch in the park? I've made her a sandwich so you can have a picnic together.'

'Picinicky,' Katie squealed.

'Well, aren't I lucky, having my other boss to keep me company at lunchtime? Get your coat and boots, Katie, I'll help you dress in a minute.'

'Thanks, Mim. I've got so much paperwork to go over today for the house; it will be great to have Katie tired out for her afternoon sleep.'

❦

Hearing the bell tinkle on the shop door a few minutes after Katie and Mim left for the park, Mae lifted her head from the house plans she'd spread on the counter. She'd been poring over the outlines that showed windows and doors and bedrooms and the kitchen. Everything looked so tiny, but outlines of beds and tables and cupboards, even the furniture on the verandah, were starting to give a better sense of scale. She couldn't quite grasp that this was finally going to be her home, but she'd met the builder and he'd patiently discussed every stage and said she'd be in the house for Christmas.

'Good morning, Mrs Parker. What a lovely day.'

Pearl Atkinson filled the doorway of the shop; she seemed to be getting bigger by the week.

'Good morning, Mrs Atkinson. You look well. What can I do for you today?'

'That new cardigan in the window, the taupe with the red fleck—it will go perfectly with the red floral dress I bought last month, don't you think?'

'I'll just have a look.'

Mae opened a drawer and riffled through the cellophane packages; small, women's, large, extra-large and extra-extra-large. 'You're in luck—this one should fit,' Mae said, unpacking the largest size. 'These only arrived yesterday. You'll be first with the latest. The finest merino wool.'

Pearl Atkinson stepped into the dressing room and Mae watched as elbows and rump pushed the heavy brown curtain this way and that, like a giant bag of puppies fighting to escape. When she eventually emerged, Mae fought to keep her expression professional.

'What do you think?' Pearl asked as she tugged sleeves into place and pulled the waistband around her rump.

The cardigan's flesh tones made her dimpled arms look exactly like pork sausages about to burst their skins.

Fighting for the right adjective to encourage the sale, Mae clapped her hands together in what she hoped looked like approval.

'You look delicious, Mrs Atkinson; good enough to eat.'

'Thank you, Mrs Parker. It's such a lift to have something new to wear to the church picnic next weekend. Are you going?'

'I plan to. Katie can't stop talking about "fairy foss".'

'Fairy floss, Mrs Parker. You can't be letting them indulge in silly words when they're so impressionable. Where is the little one today? Having a nap, I presume.'

'My apprentice has taken her to the park for a play before lunch.'

'Your apprentice? Surely she should be here working while you tend to the mothering. In my day, young people worked dawn till dusk with just the half hour for lunch.'

'Thank you for your advice, Mrs Atkinson, but Mim is a very hard worker. And when she takes Katie out, I'm able to get more done here.'

Pearl glanced at the plans. 'I see. Is that a new fitout for the shop? You must be doing well to have paid help *and* a new showroom.'

'No, this is something else entirely. That will be two pounds, six shillings for the cardigan. I'll just wrap it for you.'

Mae unfurled a length of brown paper—large enough to obscure the house plan—from the roll attached to the end of the counter. After cutting the paper at the end, folding it around the garment and tying it with string, Mae left enough paper on the work surface to conceal the plans from prying eyes.

'I'll see you both at the picnic, then, with your aunt and uncles. I trust they're all well?'

'Fighting fit, thank you. I'll let them know you asked after their health. Good day, Mrs Atkinson.'

Mae waited until Pearl had closed the door and turned towards her favourite destination—the bakery two doors along from Mae's shop—before she uncovered the plans to examine the space for the buffet. She'd originally thought it might be best in the dining room, but she wanted to see it each day. It looked like there might be space beside the couch, along the wall between the lounge room door and the French doors leading to the dining room. Using her tape measure, she measured the length of the space; two and half inches, which should translate to ten feet. Perfect, the buffet was only five foot six inches with the doors closed and another eighteen inches at each end when they were open.

Just as she rolled up the plans and put them under the counter, Mae heard familiar voices outside the shop.

'Put them down, Katie, you can't take them into the shop.'

'I want to show Mummy!'

'They're too dirty, Katie. They belong in the park with the other snails.'

'But I wiped them!'

Mae stepped out onto the pavement. 'Katie, are you listening to Mim? Good girls don't argue with grown-ups.'

'The snails were cold. I could see them shivering in the puddle.'

'I don't think snails feel the cold like we do. See? They're in their little house shells.'

'Can we keep them, please? They can live in my pocket.'

Mim looked at Mae and shrugged apologetically. 'I tried to get her to leave them behind.'

'I know, dear; she's desperate for a pet. Katie, they have to stay outside, away from the clothes in the shop. Mim will help you find some lawn, then you have to leave them to eat the grass. That's their favourite food.'

Katie looked at the two women then down at the three snails in her hands. Mae knew the situation could go either way at this point: tantrum or compliance. Fortunately, it was the latter. Seeing a sliver of nature strip outside the police station on the corner, Katie began to walk towards it, careful to keep her hands steady.

'I'll bring her back and wash her hands in a minute,' Mim said, following a step behind.

'As soon as she's settled, I'll head over to check on Albert,' Mae said. 'I shouldn't be more than half an hour.'

❦

Although Mae had told Pearl her family was fighting fit, Albert was battling his second chest infection in three months. A week of bed rest and nursing by Et had done nothing to help him. In fact, he could barely speak for coughing and he struggled to catch his breath after each fit. Mae sat beside Albert in the sunshine on the back porch. Despite the warmth, her uncle was wrapped in an overcoat with a thick blanket tucked around his neck and legs. The doctor had diagnosed pneumonia and recommended hospital, but of course Albert refused, saying he'd

322

get far more sleep at home. Hospitals were for sick people, he said, insisting that they shouldn't waste the bed on a man with a simple cold. But in the last few days, Mae felt his spark had diminished.

Today, every sentence he spoke was punctuated by coughing.

'Tell me about—' more coughing—'the plans.'

Just when it seemed like he'd never manage to take another breath, Mae heard footsteps and then a man's voice.

'Steady on there, mate.'

A dapper, compact man strode out through the door and slapped Albert on the back several times. 'Try to take a sip of water,' the man said as he rubbed Albert's neck and shoulders, a rose gold signet ring glinting on his little finger. As Albert's coughing receded, the man continued to gently stroke Albert's back before mopping his mouth and chin with a silk handkerchief. The gestures seemed familiar, gentle. Mae was amazed by Albert's submission. He held the man's hand for a moment and smiled before returning his attention to Mae.

'Trevor, meet my niece, Mrs Mae Parker.'

'Ah, Mrs Parker, the niece who runs the shop. Albert's so happy having you just around the corner.'

Albert shuffled in his chair. 'Mae, darling, this is my very dear friend Mr Trevor Green. He's visited every day this week; sits for hours at a time, just keeping me company.'

'It's very kind of you, Mr Green, giving up so much of your time to sit with my uncle.'

'Albert, you seem a little brighter today,' Trevor said, grasping his hand again.

'I'll be back at the club by the weekend, I'm certain of it.'

'Well, you make sure you are. We all miss you terribly.'

Two nights later, Albert died in his sleep.

CHAPTER 34

December 1944

MAE, ET AND WILLIAM stood beside the hole in the ground that would be Albert's final resting place. But looking at the drab surroundings, Mae thought he was hardly likely to rest in peace; the place was neither restful nor peaceful. Surrounded by factories belching smoke, roads clogged with trucks and the smells of tar works and foundries, the cemetery was the sort of place you'd only choose to go to be with family. In Albert's case, he was being laid beside his mother and sister in the family plot. His soul would be happy to be near them again. And Mae knew the cemetery hadn't always been so bleak. Albert had brought her here several times when she was a child to visit her mother's grave, and he'd told Mae that when he was a boy the setting was quite picturesque, situated near the river and ringed by market gardens. It only changed when the city grew and industries moved further out to cheaper land. He said it was always worthwhile buying as much cheap land on the fringes as you could afford because industry was always chasing cheaper running costs, especially during the worst of times, like the Depression and war.

Mae held William's arm, which was bent tight against his chest. They both swayed very slightly, as if caught in a gentle breeze, while the pastor from their church prayed and committed Albert's body to the ground. Although they'd stipulated the most expeditious service—after the last war, Albert struggled to worship a God who would allow such suffering—it seemed to go on for hours. Several prayers, a sermon and three hymns at the church, followed by the graveside visit and afternoon tea in the church hall.

Much later that day, Mae realised she was at her family's house, but she barely recalled arriving. Albert's death had rattled her more than she'd fathomed. Over the years she'd occasionally thought about her family getting older. But knowing that she'd lose them one day had done nothing to prepare her for the actuality. Numb for the first few days, she threw herself into helping Et and William plan the funeral; placing notices in the paper, talking to the minister and the undertakers, making endless pots of tea for the well-wishers trailing through the family home from morning to night. It was a little like when people heard the news of Harry's disappearance, but of course that was different; Albert's death was final, permanent. There was no mystery about Albert's loss. He was gone. Although she couldn't begin to imagine her life without him and her sadness often saw her struggling for breath, she did manage to laugh at some of the stories his friends told about his time in the war, about his air warden service, about scrapes on the railways that he'd helped to sort out.

Now that the work was done and the last of the visitors gone, she slumped into the chair beside the fireplace and felt the lump that had been lurking in her throat for the last few days begin to swell again. Tears arrived with gulping sobs. As she cried into her hanky she saw Albert turn and beam at her as he walked her down the aisle at her wedding. She pictured Albert sitting at the kitchen table feeding Katie her bottle, then lifting the baby and patiently patting her until she burped. She pictured him arguing with William over which horses were better in the wet or dry. Then she remembered him as she'd last seen him, rugged up in the sunshine looking older than his sixty-five years. Seeing him after he'd died, she was amazed to see how young he looked. His facial muscles had relaxed and there wasn't a line to be seen; he just looked like he was sleeping. That was a good way to remember him, rather than remembering his last struggles for air.

Hearing Et and William laughing in the kitchen, she told herself again that Albert would hate for anyone to be weeping over him. As Mae retreated to the bathroom to fix her face, another image of Albert flashed into her mind, setting off the tears again. This time she saw her uncle hunched behind Harry on his new motorbike, the pair of them roaring around the corner and past the house, broad smiles beneath their goggles and leather helmets. Dabbing her eyes with a wet face washer, she applied powder to her cheeks and chin. Then she began to cry again, thick, heavy sobs. It felt like every sadness from her life, even the ones that happened before she could remember, were flowing through her and she was powerless to stop them. The loss of her mother and Albert and, most of all, Harry's disappearance. She missed him so much that her chest constantly ached, as though she'd strained herself lifting a heavy weight. Of all the people she knew, Albert was the only one who'd encouraged her to keep hoping. He never failed to pass on any snippets of speculation that might help to lift her spirits. He'd quietly held her hand as she recited and dissected every precious memory, never making her hope seem futile.

Mae listened for further sounds of Et or William in the kitchen. Whenever she felt she was recovering, a fresh thought set her off again. With Albert gone, she began to imagine a time when Et and William would be gone as well. They would rely on her to see them through the end of their lives. And as long as they didn't get too sick, she could probably keep them at home. But whatever happened, she needed to make the most of every minute she had left with them.

❧

Several weeks later, after delivering Katie to Elizabeth's house for the weekend, Mae and Et caught the train to a guesthouse in the Dandenong Ranges, about an hour from town. Mae had discovered that some of her morning sickness treatments also helped to relieve motion sickness. Dry toast, Anzac biscuits and a flask of strong ginger tea kept her stomach manageable for the trip; the nausea was there, particularly as the train twisted and climbed the hills, but she managed not to disgrace herself.

Et applauded as they arrived and stepped gratefully onto solid ground, another fraught step for a person with severe motion sickness, but drawing in lungsful of the damp, pine-scented air seemed to help as Mae surveyed the dense green-upon-green forest scenery. With her worries about the travel component of their trip behind them, Mae felt her spirits lift for the first time since Albert's death. Sunlight peeked through the canopy of tree ferns surrounding the station platform, the wet leaves sparkling like jewels. A porter collected their bags and placed them into a waiting bus for the short drive to the guesthouse down a steep, muddy lane.

'You'll want to borrow some gumboots before you tackle the driveway, ladies,' the driver called cheerfully as they descended towards a wide, double-storey building. Three men and a woman carrying fishing rods and baskets stood aside to let the bus pass.

'The fishing here is second to none,' the woman told them. 'People come from all over to angle for trout. You can even catch your own dinner. Mrs Jackson will cook anything you catch, as long as it's big enough. Best to throw the young ones back for another day.'

Et looked at Mae and laughed. 'I haven't fished since I was a girl. Your mother and I used to do this every summer.'

'Harry taught me on our honeymoon. I was never going to swim, but it was something I could do without wetting my hair.'

'You never said!'

'I caught a few; he said he was impressed.'

'Well then, let's have a try.'

Mrs Jackson was happy to kit them out and an hour later the two women were at the stream running along the bottom of the garden, Mae standing knee deep in the water and Et sitting on the bank. Mae flicked her wrist and watched her blue-feathered lure float through the air then settle halfway across the surface. Water swirled against her rubber waders and crept across nearby rocks. A couple of ducks squabbled on the opposite bank, most likely over a worm.

Settling her footing and her stance against the water pressure, Mae felt herself inhale and exhale more deeply than she had in months. Her lungs felt greedy for every skerrick of sweet mountain air. For a moment, she imagined what it might be like to live where it was possible to breathe such purity every day, to fill her ears with the tinkle of bellbirds and the rush of crystal-clear water; to choose not to see people for days at a time. Could she be happy in a tiny hut beside the mountains, living on fresh fish and berries? She didn't need much; just a verandah and a vegetable patch. She could fill her days gardening, reading and going for long walks. It was certainly something to think about for when Katie was grown and married, for when she was no longer needed by her family. A retirement option, perhaps.

'Chicken and mayonnaise or ham and pickle?' Et waved sandwiches wrapped in greaseproof paper.

Normally the queasy feeling in Mae's stomach lasted all day after a trip, but the thought of chicken and creamy mayonnaise made her salivate. The ham and pickle sounded good too. But there was no need to choose; she was on holiday and could have both.

'It's a bit soon for a picnic, I've only been in the water for ten minutes. But you start if you're hungry.'

Mae felt a gentle tug on her fishing line and slowly turned the handle on the reel. She imagined Harry standing behind her, whispering in her ear. *Encourage the fish to swim towards you; don't try to drag it kicking and screaming into the basket.* She smiled at the thought of a fish trying to scream underwater. As the fish tugged the line harder, she kept it firm, reeling in the slack whenever the fish rested or changed direction. Her arms began to ache. She might have snagged a big one—hopefully a trout, not a carp. As the fish drew closer she backed towards the sandy beach near the bank. Et called out encouragement but she wasn't wearing boots so Mae needed to land the fish without Et holding a net in the water beside her. She heard more instructions from Harry. *When it's close enough, flip it out of the water and onto the grass so Et can pitch it into the basket and close the lid.*

After a few more turns of the reel, the trout was close enough to see. It was huge; at least eighteen inches long. Mae hoped the line would hold. She couldn't bear to lose it now.

'Get ready, Et. This one's full of fight.'

'Be careful not to slip, dear. You're close to the edge.'

Mae dug her feet into pebbles and bent her knees. She anchored her elbows at her sides and quickly wound the handle. When the fish was just a few feet from her legs she tilted the rod straight up. As the fish shot out of the water she swivelled her torso, flicked the fish onto the ground in front of Et then lost her balance and sat back in the freezing shallows.

Et howled with laughter but still managed to get the fish into the basket and close the lid. Mae reached out to grab the rod but, misjudging the distance, she fell sideways into the water. Gasping for air she sat up and threw the rod onto the bank then tried to stand, but her waders had filled with water. Flopping around like the fish in the basket, she managed to get onto her knees then undo her braces and slide out of the rubber pants. Her wet clothes weighed her down but she eventually hauled herself out of the water and sat shivering on the grass. Et was still laughing as she wrapped a rug around Mae's shoulders and rubbed her back.

'It's not funny, I could have hurt myself,' Mae protested, though she was laughing herself.

'That was just about the funniest thing I've ever seen,' said Et. 'And when you went sideways . . .'

'You got the fish?'

Et opened the lid just far enough for Mae to see the trout twitching in the basket. 'It must be three or four pounds at least,' Et said. 'We'll have to get a picture before it's cleaned and cooked.'

'I might need to change before I pose for any pictures,' Mae said, rubbing her wet hair with a corner of the rug and tipping her head sideways to clear her ear.

❧

After drying off, changing clothes and eating their sandwiches on the verandah, the two women walked along the river path from the guesthouse towards the town.

'Such a shame William didn't come with us. He would have loved it here,' Et said, laughing again. 'He would have loved seeing you land that trout, then land yourself, all without a net.'

'It felt like Harry was right there urging me on,' Mae said, 'just like he did on our honeymoon.'

'You've certainly got the knack. It seems fishing runs in the family. Or part of the family, anyway. William particularly loved it but Albert was never interested; hated getting wet and anything that might mess his hair.'

'I think about him every day. I still can't believe I'll never see him again.'

'You will, though, in your memories. He'll always be there.'

'Is that what it's like for you? Do you have all the people you've lost with you every day? My mother, your mother?'

'I do. I talk to them when I'm doing the washing, when I'm walking to the shops. Any time I'm not speaking out loud, I'm talking to them in my mind. Now Albert's part of the conversation too.'

'I talk to Harry all the time in my head, but I've always done that; when he was at sea, or when I was cooking his dinner. I talk to him about the house now, about all the problems we're having getting the materials, getting carpenters to turn up to build the frames.'

'That's perfectly normal, dear. Especially when you're going through such upsets.'

'I'm upset about Albert, but I don't feel too bad about the house. It's as though it's all happening to someone else, more of an annoyance than anything.'

'What's the latest estimate?'

'The builder said we should be in by February but, honestly, the thought of packing up and moving is more tiring than exciting. I don't know where to start.'

'Maybe you could start sorting a few things now so there's less to pack later on.'

'But it seems silly not to pack as I sort, and we have nowhere to put boxes.'

'Well, I'd be happy to help.'

'Look at those maidenhair ferns. Yours always grow so well but I hear they're pretty temperamental.'

'Nonsense. You just have to make sure you don't over-water them or put them in direct sun. Then they'll grow like weeds, just like they do here.'

'I'd love to put in a fern bed in the new place, along the south-facing wall of the garage.'

'That's a wonderful idea. We could borrow a spade from Mrs Jackson and dig up some of these. Pop them in pots till you're ready to plant.'

And so, later that afternoon, Mae pushed a rusted spade into the lush black soil around the plants. Taking plenty of the dirt around the roots, she laid the plants on large sheets of newspaper then wrapped them tightly in several layers, wetting the bundles as she stacked eight large ferns in a wheelbarrow.

Mrs Jackson said the bus driver was used to guests taking green keepsakes home, that he'd make room beneath the back seat and help transfer their booty to the train.

Then, after their day of exertion, the two women sat in front of a roaring fire, sipping sherry as they waited for dinner. With its low ceiling and red-painted walls, and shelves cluttered with porcelain figurines of ducks and fish, the sitting room had a cosy feel. 'Busy but quaint,' was Mae's summation when she first saw the room. Et said she hoped Mrs Jackson had help with the dusting.

'Ladies, your dinner is ready.' Mrs Jackson placed a large platter of grilled trout on the table.

Mae took her seat opposite Et and unfurled a linen napkin from its beaten silver ring.

'Doesn't this look lovely?' Et said. 'We must have this sort of outing more often. You can teach Katie to fish.'

'We could bring William too.'

'Perhaps, dear. I'm sure he'd like to be asked. Maybe next autumn when you're all settled in your new house.'

Mae smiled and reached for the utensils to serve the fish. As she carefully separated a fillet from the bones, she noticed her naked left hand. Her wedding ring was missing. She dropped the spoons and the fish portion back onto the platter and tried to recall where she'd taken it off. She only ever removed it when she washed dishes or clothes and linen, and she hadn't done either of those things today. She racked her brain, trying to recall when she'd last noticed the band on her finger. She was certain she'd worn it on the train; she never stepped out of the house without wearing it. That meant—oh no, no, no!

'What's the matter, dear? Fish not cooked?'

'My wedding ring—it's gone. I must have lost it in the river.' Mae rose from the table and rushed towards the door. 'I need a torch; I have to go look for it.'

'Mae, you won't see it in the dark. You'll fall in again and be swept away.'

'I have to try!'

'Wait till the morning,' Et said, wrapping her arms around Mae's shaking shoulders. 'We'll search the room and your suitcase. That's all we can do tonight.'

'It can't be gone, Et. I can't lose another piece of him— of us. I just can't.'

CHAPTER 35

January 1945

GRACE LET THE CAR'S acceleration press her further into her seat as she drove west out of Benalla. Dusk was the most dangerous time on the road, with kangaroos and wombats chasing food no matter where it ambled. Hitting a large animal at full speed could take out a fully laden stock truck, let alone a car. You just had to hold your nerve and not swerve into a tree trying to avoid animals. Easier said than done. Hopefully rain would keep the roads clear tonight of animals—and prisoners. She scanned the trees at the side of the road; she had no idea what she'd do if she saw anyone lurking in the shadows.

The windscreen wipers squeaked back and forth across her vision. They hadn't been used for so long that they needed oiling. It wasn't cold, but the hairs on her neck stood at attention, excitement mixed with fear. She'd never covered a prison break, but a couple of years ago she'd seen the police rounds guys buzzing in and out of the office during a manhunt for two armed robbers in the northern suburbs. The robbers were eventually found passed out in the back of a brewery. It was hard to tell how dangerous these Germans might be, but Grace knew they were murderers; they'd killed those boys on the *Sydney*. And they'd be pretty healthy after a few years in the prison camp—much healthier than if they were prisoners of the Japs. Poor Phil. How could anyone survive years in the steaming jungle as a Japanese prisoner of war, with only one leg and goodness knew what tropical diseases? She'd finally had a letter from Phil a few weeks earlier. The Red Cross had managed to get letters out of the prison camp so she knew he was alive, but he'd said very little, just that he was managing to walk with a crutch made from a branch and dreaming of a roast dinner. He also said that the thought of coming home to her was keeping him going. When Sam had rung her at her parents' house earlier that night, she was barely able to hold the phone still enough to hear; she was certain he was calling with bad news about Phil. But no, when she was able to register his words, he was asking her to cover a *real* story about twenty German prisoners of war escaping from a prison farm near Murchison, not far from Shepparton.

'Their leader's a bloke named Detmers, the captain of the ship that sank the *Sydney*,' Sam said. 'Several of his crew are with him. Police are coordinating the search from their station house at Shepparton. There's a press conference at nine pm.'

Grace drove for about an hour. When she reached the police station, she saw light spilling from the doorway as reporters milled near the entrance. Several news cars were parked near the fence. Grace gathered her raincoat and handbag from the passenger seat as Scoop, one of her father's photographers, on loan to *The Tribune* until another photographer could get there from Melbourne, approached her window, lighting a cigarette.

'Quiet out there tonight, eh?' he said, nodding back towards the road they'd both travelled. 'Almost nothing on the roads.'

'No sign of the prisoners either.'

Grace surveyed the other newsmen and policemen standing in groups, laughing and smoking as casually as if they were at the pub. You could tell they were in their element. Gallows humour they called it: a way of coping with serious incidents. Phil had once told her about a fatal car accident he'd covered as a cadet on police rounds. An entire family, including a baby, had been incinerated when they were hit by a truck that ran through a stop sign.

'One of the older reporters said joking around was the only way to deal with what you saw, especially when there were children involved. But it builds up, he said. Police rounds men have to go home and sleep, then turn up the next day and do it all again. Some blokes can handle it for years, others only last a few months.'

But no matter how long they'd done that job, Grace had seen enough over the years to know the police reporters all drank more and more each year.

With an hour to wait for the briefing, the press and the police shifted to the pub across the road for dinner. Grace was more relaxed than the blokes on the morning papers, who needed to file stories right away. For once *The Tribune* had managed to run the story about the escape first. It was good watching the others play catch-up for a change. She read the menu, which featured various combinations of lamb and potatoes. Chops and mash, curried sausages and mash, roast lamb with potatoes and shepherd's pie. At least it would be fresh.

'What are you having, Scoop?' she asked.

'Bangers look pretty good. I'll order if you like.'

'Thanks. I'll have the shepherd's pie and a lemonade.'

Grace settled at a table in an alcove beside the bar. She was the only female customer in the place. The ladies' lounge was dark through the glass panel. No one seemed to mind that she was in the wrong bar, but she was glad to have her notebook for protection.

'So these escapees have got the place buzzing,' Scoop said, nodding towards the bar. 'No one's saying anything about the cricket.'

'Nothing like a good manhunt to work up an appetite, eh?' The woman who'd been serving drinks behind the bar bustled towards them holding their plates of food. 'Are you from the paper?'

'Grace Fowler from the Melbourne *Tribune*,' Grace said, smiling at the woman whose grey-streaked black hair was unravelling from the knot on top of her head. Her face was round, her nose and cheeks red; perspiration shone on her forehead.

'I'm Shirl, love. You staying with us tonight?'

'We've booked rooms, but I'm not sure how much sleep we'll be getting. It depends on what the police tell us.'

'Reckon those Krauts'll be long gone,' Shirl said, looking towards the bar but making no move to return to the growing crowd with empty glasses. 'Had a good head start before the alarm was raised. All night, they reckon.'

'Really? How do you think so many got away without raising suspicion?'

'Well, you know they dug a long, long tunnel. But it was pouring too. That's all the guards would've heard: rain on the roof.'

'Did anyone see anything here in town?'

'Nah. Pretty likely they avoided the town and went straight for the train tracks and the highway, trying to hitch rides to the city.'

'What about today? Was anything out of place?'

'Well, our Floss, the housekeeper, reckoned there were some men's clothes missing from the ironing basket in the washhouse, but it turned out they'd already been collected by the gent who was staying last night. He was in a hurry to get back on the road. Salesman.'

'I see,' Grace said, making a few notes that she knew she wouldn't use. 'What about food going missing? Anything like that?'

'Nah, love. Reckon they would have been running like rabbits, getting as far from here as they could.' She paused to call out, 'Yeah, Merv, keep your pants on, I'll be there in a tick.' To Grace she said, 'Natives are getting restless—I'd better toddle. Let me know if you need anything else.'

Grace turned back to Scoop, who was forking gravy, mash and sausages into his mouth with his head cocked towards the police at the next table.

341

'Doesn't sound like anyone knows much,' she said, breaking the cheesy crust on top of her pie, letting steam escape.

'Shhh!' he whispered, nodding at the next table. 'There's been a sighting. Got some coppers out at a farm at the moment. People called about noises near their chook shed.'

'Great, Nazi chicken rustlers. I can see the headline now.'

'If they don't catch them soon, I'm sure the stories will only get crazier.'

All heads turned towards the door as four uniformed policemen entered the bar. Grace's breath caught as she recognised the tallest of the group; it was Mick Foster, her former girlhood crush. After school he'd joined the police and now here he was, tanned skin, hair more golden than red, the same broad shoulders, now grown into a perfectly filled-out chest. It took a moment, but when he saw her, his entire face erupted in a dazzling smile.

'Grace Fowler—my God! What brings you here, tonight of all nights?'

'The prison break. I'm reporting for *The Tribune*.'

'No! I don't believe it. All those years you dreamed about being a reporter, and here you are, actually doing it.'

She blushed redder and hotter than she had in years. Damn, she thought she might have been growing out of that habit, but here she was beaming like a lighthouse in front of all of the other reporters, including Phil's friend Jacko from *The Gazette*.

'You're not doing badly yourself,' she said, pointing to the sergeant stripes on his shoulders.

Mick continued to smile at her and she couldn't look away.

'Mate!' Scoop roared, shaking Mick's hand. 'Seems like only yesterday I was following you round the football ground with my camera. Now look at you. Still playing?'

'Afraid not. Knees aren't quite what they were. But I hear the Benalla juniors did well last season.'

'They've got some real talent, those boys. A few more years and they'll be right up top of the league.'

'That's good to know,' Mick said, before returning his attention to Grace. 'So, Grace, I've never seen a girl covering a story like this. What gives?'

'Right place, right time.'

'Well it's good to see you giving the blokes a run for their money.'

'Were you at the chook shed incident?'

Mick laughed. 'Whoa. Interrogating me already.'

Grace smiled and tapped her notebook.

'Okay. Yes, we went out to the farm and looked around, but we didn't see anything out of the ordinary. It was probably just a fox, but everyone's on edge.'

'Are we likely to hear anything new at the press conference?'

'Probably not, but I'll introduce you to the boss afterwards if you want to hold a few questions back.'

❧❧❧

Grace joined nine reporters, five photographers and six policemen in the hall beside the police station an hour later. Inspector Frank Wiles stood in front of the stage, looking like he was melting. Following the rain, the night was humid and sweat dripped down his cheeks and neck.

'As you know, twenty male persons of German descent absconded from Dhurringile Internment Camp sometime after twenty hundred hours on Wednesday,' he said, projecting his voice to fill the hall.

'Their absence was not discovered until assembly at eight this morning. It's believed the men, led by Captain Theodor Anton Detmers, tunnelled from a disused crockery room within the main house for a distance of about four hundred yards under the garden and the barbed-wire security fence. From there, the men decamped in as yet unconfirmed directions.'

'Inspector Wiles, do you believe they're heading for Melbourne or Sydney?' Jacko from *The Gazette* asked, smirking as he waited for an answer, clearly pleased that he'd fired the first question.

'We can only speculate at this point, but we believe they probably split into small groups—twos and threes—and headed towards locations where they might find transportation via trucks, trains and private vehicles.'

'Do you have the dogs out tracking their movements?'

'Last night's inclement weather erased any possibility of detecting either scent or footprints.'

'Sir, are any of the prisoners considered dangerous?'

'These men are already responsible for killing hundreds of our naval men and imprisoning others. We have to class them as desperate at the very least.'

'Are you saying they might try to kill people in their beds?'

'No, I'm not saying that—who asked the question? Oh, Turner from the *Truth*, I might have known. No, let me be quite clear. We think they will try to get to ports in the major cities and get themselves on ships heading back to Europe. They'll be looking for a way to rejoin their forces and complete their missions.'

'Do you know if they have food and suitable clothing?'

'They are likely to have some cash and maps, maybe a few tins of food, but nothing much else. They may try to buy things they can't easily steal.'

Grace stood silently near the back of the crowd, hoping Mick would remember his promise to organise a private chat with the inspector. She glanced across to the group of policemen. Mick was already watching her; he nodded. She relaxed and focused on the briefing, trying to think of a fresh angle she could use to build a story for the morning.

A local reporter asked the next question: 'Are there extra patrols at the ports and train and bus stations?'

'Yes. We're also asking for help from the community. If they see or hear anything out of the ordinary, they should call their local police, no matter what the time. We'll be manning our stations around the clock.'

'That's a lot of extra manpower. You must be really concerned about these fellows.'

'We've never had a POW escape on this scale before. We have to recapture them quickly and put everyone's minds at ease.'

'Is it true that you had police at a farm tonight checking a disturbance in a chook shed?'

'As I said earlier, we need to investigate every disturbance large or small until we find these men.'

Mick waved Grace over after the briefing ended. Grace
signalled Scoop to follow.

Inspector Wiles gripped her hand far too hard and
shook it vigorously.

'Miss Fowler, I've met your father many times. How is
Nev? I bet he'd love to be covering this story.'

'He's keeping an eye on things in Benalla, sir. He
thought some of the men might head in that direction.
Do you have any idea how well they might know the area?'

'Most of the men have navigational experience, having
been at sea, but we don't know what sort of access they've
had to maps of this area and the nearest coastline.'

'What about clothing? Do you know what they're
wearing?'

'I believe some of the men are in their uniforms and
others are in sportswear. Officers have the choice in camp.'

'I guess the uniformed men might be looking to steal
clothes then, to blend in.'

'Possibly. But their grey uniforms look like our air force
uniforms from a distance, especially if they've removed
their badges.'

He glanced at another policeman and nodded. 'I must
go now, Miss Fowler. But stick with Sergeant Foster. If you
need anything else, he'll be able to help.'

Mick stepped forward as the inspector left the hall.
'You're very impressive, Miss Fowler. No sign of the shy
little girl I knew at school. You handled the inspector like
you've been doing this for years.'

'In my head, I've been reporting my whole life. I'm just loving the chance to do it for real.'

'Well, I'm happy to help. Do you have everything you need?'

'I do for the moment. I'll write this up tonight then check in first thing. Will someone be able to give me an update before nine in the morning?'

'I'll make sure of it. Do you have time for a cuppa now? It would be good to catch up.'

Grace found herself smiling again as she tried to keep her gaze from straying across his shoulders, snugly encased in the dark blue of his uniform jacket. The shiny silver buttons strained against his chest, just below his tie and crisp blue shirt. Mick had always been attractive, but there was something more now; he radiated confidence and manliness. She felt the delicious grip in her stomach that she used to feel looking at Phil. Grace quickly returned her gaze to her notebook, trying to think of any more questions about the story, but her mind was blank.

'I'd love to, Mick, but I have to write up my notes and get this story ready for filing in the morning. Maybe afterwards—if you're not investigating a disturbance in a pigpen.'

'You mean a pig *sty*,' he teased. 'But I shouldn't be correcting you. You were always the smartest girl at school.'

Grace blushed again. 'You make me sound so dull.'

'Not at all. Grace Fowler was always going to be a star.'

She was really going to have to find a way to keep her colouring in check.

'So how's life on the beat, Fowler?' Sam asked with a chuckle after she'd dictated her story to the copy taker the next morning.

'I love it. I'll be badgering you for a permanent police rounds spot after this.'

'Steady on. You've only been out there for one day. Besides, the women's page needs you.'

Grace tried to keep her voice light. 'The police are holding another press conference at three. We'll base ourselves here and follow up any leads through the day. Do you want Scoop to hang around?'

'Graham Ross should be there mid-afternoon, then Scoop can get back to Benalla. It was good of your father to loan him to us.'

'Thanks, Sam. I'll call if anything more happens this morning.'

Grace could see the police station through the front window of the main bar. She supposed it was designed that way to keep the patrons in order. The street was nearly empty of moving traffic, but every parking space was occupied by police vehicles and cars sporting the livery of every newspaper and radio station in the state. She wondered if Mick would be on duty yet. He'd been on the afternoon shift yesterday so maybe not. Grace straightened her hair neatly over her ears, touched up her lipstick and made sure none of the colour had stuck to her teeth. Dropping her notebook into her handbag she marched across the road, determined to be courteous to Mick if he was there but to keep things professional. No smiling at him, no blushing, and no flirting under any circumstances, not when Phil was suffering so badly, desperate to come home to her.

'Good morning, Grace,' Mick said, smiling from ear to ear as she walked in the door. He was standing behind the counter reading *The Gazette*. 'You're the loveliest vision to walk through that door this week—maybe even all year.'

Trying not to match his grin, Grace kept her voice cool and even.

'Good morning, Mick. Any new activity?'

'Just the usual: lights in the distance, strange noises.'

'Front-page news in *The Gazette* and *The Argus* this morning.'

'I saw! Those Germans have certainly put us on the map. If people hadn't heard of Dhurringile before, they'll all be talking about it now.'

'You're probably right. Well, I have to write the story for our evening edition. Do you have time to fill me in on the search plans for today?'

'Of course, come through,' Mick said, lifting a section of the counter and opening a low door. He led her into the staffroom at the back of the police station. The table was strewn with newspapers and ashtrays, chairs at various angles, much like the *Tribune* newsroom.

'Sorry, we don't entertain much,' Mick said, attempting to tidy while the kettle boiled on the stove.

'At least I'm in the right place if something happens.'

'You'll certainly be the first to hear if there's a sighting. Got your notebook ready?'

Grace undid the clasp on her handbag and retrieved her notebook and pencil. 'Always.'

'Okay, so while we're waiting for news on the escapees, what else would you like to know?'

Grace had tossed and turned much of the night, nervous about filing her story but also wondering about Mick. It was deeply unsettling to think about any man other than Phil, almost like she was being untrue to him. Of course that wasn't the case. Mick would obviously be spoken for, probably with a young family. He was just enjoying seeing someone familiar, someone from his past. She'd missed that herself, living in Melbourne, so far from everything and everyone she'd grown up with. It was silly feeling shy around Mick; he was practically family. And anyway, now that she was covering serious stories, she was determined to be more like her heroine Torchy; to ask every question applicable to every story.

'So, how's life? Married? Children?'

Mick dropped a plate into soapy sink water so that a few drops splashed his jacket. 'You really do have this reporter thing down pat, don't you?'

'Are you stalling?'

'Not guilty on all counts, I'm afraid. There was a nurse, but she met a Yank.'

'Ah, blinded by silk stockings and chocolate bars. I'm sorry to hear that.'

'Last I heard she was living in the nurses' quarters and waiting to sail to the States. But enough about my pathetic life; what about you, Grace? Being chased by half the blokes in the newsroom?'

She took a breath. It was never easy talking about Phil, and she felt the need to take extra care in choosing her words for Mick.

'I met someone special, a reporter on *The Tribune*—'

A constable appeared in the doorway. 'There's been a sighting just out of town. Murchison.'

'On our way,' Mick said. 'Is Scoop nearby?'

'He's waiting with the press guys at the pub.'

'All right, grab him and follow us as best you can.'

As Grace stood and walked towards the door, Mick leaned down and looked at her squarely, seriously: 'It's really great to have you here. Stick close to me—I'll do everything I can to help.'

CHAPTER 36

THE FIRST ESCAPEE WAS caught walking along the road that morning, barely six miles from Dhurringile, right in time for *The Tribune*'s second edition. Two more prisoners were captured in Murchison the following day, including one who was drinking beer at the pub while he waited for a train. Grace interviewed dozens of locals crowded into the bar. They were amazed that none of the captured men had got any further away. The pub's landlord said the man was alone and kept to himself.

'He didn't say much. No, I couldn't hear an accent. He just said, "Beer, please," then nodded when he wanted another. Put some coins on the bar and I took what he owed.'

'What made you suspicious?'

'Well, he's a stranger. And all strangers are a bit sus at the moment, so I figured it wouldn't hurt to tell the coppers about him.'

'What do you think they've been doing?' Grace asked two ruddy-faced farmers.

'Well, they're salties, aren't they? Useless at navigating on land and not much distance in their legs after being cooped up so long.'

'Yeah, they put all their energy into digging themselves out but forgot to plan what came next. They've pretty much lost their war, got nowhere to go; probably too ashamed to go home.'

Over the first few days, Grace filed multiple stories detailing sightings and arrests. The police and the army released more information about the escape, saying the floorboards had been carefully lifted and replaced each night for months while the prisoners dug the tunnel. No one knew what the prisoners did with the dirt and soil they removed, but the guards said that was something they always watched out for. The story was giving Grace a great run on the early pages, but she was amazed she hadn't been replaced by one of the senior reporters.

On the fourth night, Grace huddled under an umbrella at the front gate of yet another farmhouse in the middle of nowhere, while six policemen searched a tractor shed. Graham waited near the gate with two photographers from other papers. There was no real reason to think tonight's farm disturbance report would be any more fruitful than the others over the last few days, but still they were ready with their cameras, flash guns charged, lenses polished. The other reporters had opted to stay dry at the pub and eat their dinner. Grace wished she were there too. As the rain dripped steadily off

her umbrella, she realised she needed to use the toilet—
not urgently, but soon.

The farmers, Merle and Perce Boyd, stood nearby
recounting to Mick everything they'd heard in their garden.

'So what made you think there was someone outside?'
Mick asked the pair, who were dressed almost identically
in flannel shirts and overalls. They were of almost equal
height, with short grey hair plastered to their skulls. It was
sometimes said that couples grew to look alike, but these
two could almost be siblings. Best not to let that thought
run, Grace told herself.

'Well,' Merle said, 'we were just sitting down to supper
and we heard a tin bucket topple over and roll down the
back steps. The dogs were all inside and there was no wind.
It had to be someone snooping round.'

'I see. And what about other animals? Goats? Cats?'

'All in their pens. Nothing's out.'

'Anything else that you've noticed?'

Merle answered again: 'The chooks were squawking a
bit earlier.'

'Could it have been a fox?'

'We've got the baits out. Haven't lost any layers for
ages.'

'Well, the boys'll have a good look around, make sure
there's no one there.'

Grace shifted her weight from leg to leg, her bladder
uncomfortably full now. She looked at the house about a
hundred feet up the driveway. If only she could use the
Boyds' outhouse, but it wouldn't be safe until the search
had been completed.

Mick closed his notebook and introduced Grace, who offered her hand to Merle.

'Thought you must have been from the papers,' the older woman said. 'Where's all the others?'

'They're on deadline, filing their stories,' Grace explained, not wanting to disparage anyone in her profession, even though they probably wouldn't do her the same courtesy.

'So, we gonna be in the paper?'

'Maybe. It all depends on what happens tonight.'

'I just can't believe how long this is dragging on. I was just saying to Perce while the vegies were boiling that no one feels safe anymore. Never had to lock our doors before. Now we're all scared of having our throats cut while we sleep, aren't we, Perce?'

Perce nodded—he hadn't opened his mouth the whole time. Maybe he'd forgotten his teeth.

'What else are people doing differently?'

'I heard a few people saying they've been checking their vegie patches every morning. If the prisoners are still around, they'll be hungry by now. Like us, eh, Perce?' She chortled. 'Must have been like this when Ned Kelly's gang was on the run.' Her eyes were shining with excitement. 'It's making us all nervous wrecks knowing Nazis are on the loose. What if the Ities and the Japs get out of their camps too and they all join up? Then we'll really be in it. Our very own world war right here.'

Grace scribbled shorthand notes. Maybe the night wouldn't be a total write-off.

Merle continued: 'Someone said in town yesterday that

the escapees were looking for radios to contact German ships for an all-out invasion, a last gasp before the war in Europe grinds to a halt.'

'Do you have a radio? Are you worried that's what they were looking for tonight?'

'Our son used to muck around with a small radio in the shed, but he took it when he left.'

Grace's bladder complained again. She looked around to see if there were any trees nearby that might do for an emergency, but the roadside was clear. She might have to squat by the car, in front of the Boyds and Mick and the photographers. She could just see it now; they'd all have their backs turned, of course, but they'd be able to hear her, and what if someone drove past right at that moment, headlights blazing? REPORTER IN COMPROMISING POSITION. TORCHY BARES ALL. No, she'd have to grit her teeth and think of other things, at least until the search was over.

The Boyds moved closer to the gate. Mick sidled over.

'Lovely night for it.'

'How much longer, do you think?'

'Could be a few minutes, or hours, depending on what's back there.'

Grace sucked in her stomach against another insistent wave. 'Anything new on the escapees today?'

'Just a few details about Detmers and some of his funny little speaking quirks.'

'Like what?'

'Well, apparently he spent time in Melbourne between wars. They say he speaks excellent English but he's got a bit of a lisp, and he sounds like a toff.'

'I wonder where he picked that up?'

'Join the navy, see the world.'

Not just the navy, Grace thought, picturing Phil in the jungle. At least he'd be warm in Singapore. She squeezed her legs together. Things were past urgent.

'Mick, I have to go.'

'Don't you need to wait for Graham?'

'No, I mean go to the toilet.'

'Oh. I see. Can you hang on a bit? I'm sure they won't be much longer.'

'I've been hanging on,' Grace said, gritting her teeth as another wave brought perspiration to her forehead.

'The joys of the stakeout, Miss Fowler. Don't let on to the boys over there.'

'Can you keep an eye out while I duck behind that car up the back?'

'Okay, but let me offer some advice gleaned from my years of service.'

'Make it fast.'

'Point your feet downhill, towards the edge of the road, and only use gum leaves to—'

'That's enough,' Grace said, hastening towards the furthest car from the Boyds' gate. 'And don't listen.'

'What's that? I can't hear you!'

❧

The following Thursday, more than a week after the escape, four escapees were still on the run and more than one hundred sightings had been investigated by police from Melbourne to Sydney. Grace was exhausted from a week of poor sleep in her creaky bed at the hotel, hours of sitting or standing around waiting for something to happen, miles of driving from one sighting to another and a diet of greasy pub food. Sightings of the prisoners were still being reported across several states. That morning, Sam said police had arrested a suspicious man on the train to Adelaide overnight who wouldn't give his name when he was questioned. It turned out he was a deaf and dumb cleaner, travelling from Melbourne without a ticket.

Grace spent the afternoon in what had become her private office, the ladies' lounge of the hotel. None of the men ever entered despite all the vacant tables and chairs. It just wasn't manly to cross that particular threshold, it seemed. Grace wasn't complaining. She settled into a chair at a table beside the window, the perfect spot from which to see any activity at the police station and to watch Mick coming and going. She couldn't help it; she was constantly aware of his movements and his face popped into her mind every few minutes when he wasn't by her side, which was rarely. He seemed to always be on duty; at the police station, at every briefing, at every wild-goose chase. He was always available for dinner or morning tea, and he'd fed her so much information that she was beating the competition on every story. She'd almost forgotten the lovely feeling of spending so much time with a man, even though he was just a friend. Having his full attention made her feel special, wanted, attractive.

'Your stories have something extra,' Mick said, when he joined her for a lemonade an hour or so later. 'The way you get people to open up to you—they tell you things the other reporters don't get. It breathes life into your reports, more than just the facts.'

'It's all thanks to you, Mick. I couldn't have done any of it without your help.'

'We make a pretty good team, Miss Torchy.'

Grace stared at him. 'How do you know about Torchy?'

'I used to see you coming out of the cinema looking so happy. I snuck in one day to see what was so great about it.'

'I can't believe it! You sat through a whole Torchy Blane film? Why didn't you say something?'

'I was a bit embarrassed. It's not really a blokey kind of film, and I didn't want you to think I was some creep following you. But she was great—and now you're just like her.'

Grace fumbled for something to say. He'd watched a film because of her. He understood her dream. He was here, close enough to . . . 'I, um, I don't think the other newsmen share your opinion of girl reporters. They're not speaking to me.'

'Don't worry about them. Just concentrate on your stories and keep showing them who's boss!'

Mick slowly reached over and clasped one of her hands in his. 'When do you have to go back to the city?'

'On the weekend. I need to be in the office on Monday.'

'I'll miss you, Grace.'

Grace felt her heart leap in her chest. She pulled her hand back, not with a jerk, but as she slipped from his grasp he slumped back in his seat. She'd been so careful until now not to let the conversation get too personal. Instead she'd concentrated on the manhunt and swapped stories about their families and school mates. She'd told him about Phil, but not about her fears that he might never come home— or that he might not love her when he did. But the longing she felt for Mick was confusing; if only he wasn't so damn handsome. And he had the most wonderful smell: warm, slightly soapy, with a hint of spicy nutmeg.

'Mick, I'm sorry, but you know my situation,' she said softly, placing her hands in her lap. 'You're a wonderful man and a great friend, but while Phil's still alive, still trying to come home . . .'

Out of the corner of her eye, Grace noticed two officers race out of the police station, jump into their car and speed along the main street, siren blaring.

Graham called to her from the doorway to the main bar. 'They've found two more. Let's go.'

Grace grabbed her handbag and notebook and ran for the door. Mick followed, heading for his patrol car.

'Where are we heading, Graham?'

'Tallygaroopna. Just a few miles away.'

Her skin still felt warm where Mick had held her hand.

'Oh, they're going to love that back at the office,' she said. 'Sam said the subs were hoping some of the prisoners would be found in Poowong. They wanted to print banners saying "Nazis in Poo". They'll have to settle for "Nazis in the 'Roop", instead.'

Graham accelerated, trying to stay close to the police cars. Grace smiled, relishing the thrill of travelling so fast with the police. She hoped it wasn't another false alarm. There was still time to get this into the city edition today, even if it was just a stop press.

Steam from muddy puddles rose into the clear sky. The heat and the rain had been intense all week—tropical conditions, according to those who'd travelled further north. Tallygaroopna came into view: a tiny farming town like so many others in the area, with a few houses, a pub, several shops, a school and a football oval. Several cars from the morning newspapers had joined the convoy. They slowed and parked in the deserted main street as the police cars drove a little further and stopped outside the general store. A small crowd of onlookers gathered outside.

Graham and Grace tried to enter the store but Mick stood guard, his arms folded across his chest.

'Sergeant, have they got the prisoners?' Grace asked, trying to peer around him into the dark shop. She couldn't see any movement.

'Nice day for it,' he said with a smile as other reporters yelled questions. 'Look, there's nothing here,' he said, holding his hands up. 'There's been a development, but you'll have to go back to Shepparton for a statement.'

Grace felt her face fall as her chance to wrap up the story disappeared. The perfect ending to the story had slipped away while she was sitting talking to Mick at the pub and now the mornings were going to win. She watched as the competition ran to their cars. 'Another wild-goose chase?'

'Not quite,' Mick said with a smile. Lowering his voice so no one else could hear, he said, 'The two ringleaders surrendered about a mile out of town. The shopkeeper here recognised them from the paper and phoned it in. They were picked up a few minutes ago and taken back to Shepparton for questioning.'

'Can I quote you?' Grace asked.

'Sorry, Grace, I'd love to help but you'll have to get confirmation from the inspector.'

They were interrupted by a voice coming from a passing car. It was Jacko from *The Gazette*. He'd wound down his window and yelled: 'Tough luck, eh, Grace? All that flirting with the coppers for nothing. You *Tribune* sheilas don't belong here anyway, trying to show up us real reporters.'

Mick waited till Jacko and the others had driven away, then he smiled at her. 'You'll be safe saying they've got Detmers and Bartram, if you've got time to make the evening edition. Phone it through from here then go into town for the rest.'

'Thanks, Mick,' Grace said gratefully. 'I really appreciate everything you've done to help me. You're not upset about earlier?'

'Don't be silly. I understand you need to see things through with Phil. He's a lucky fellow.'

She touched his arm. 'Thank you again. It means more than you'll ever know.' She looked at her watch, then ran to the phone to call Sam.

She only got a few inches on the front page, but it was enough. The evening radio news bulletins would run it too, then the mornings. They'd beaten *The Gazette*. That suddenly felt like the only thing that mattered. Of course Jacko would hate her even more, but she could live with that.

Grace returned to Melbourne that night. The last two escapees were captured quietly over the weekend.

As tired and happy as she was with her stories, other thoughts kept Grace tossing and turning at night; the smell of soap and nutmeg, the perfectly proportioned chest, that smile, and how wonderful it might feel to kiss those firm lips.

Joy's questions from the farm also rang in her mind: *What if he doesn't come home? How long are you going to wait?*

CHAPTER 37

August – September 1945

THE MORNING OF AUGUST fifteenth felt strangely different outside the shop. As always on a Wednesday, the main street was lined with trucks parked along one side, leaving just enough space for traffic to ease past. Most shops were open for business, but many of the shop-keepers stood on the footpath, smiling and waving as people streamed towards the train. As the morning wore on, the shops emptied and the shopkeepers pulled their blinds and locked their doors to join the drift into the city to await the announcement. The papers had said it would happen today: the end of the war in the Pacific.

Mae watched the backdrop of activity behind Mim, who worked quickly inside the shop window, deco-rating a display of mannequins in red, white and blue knitted twin sets. She'd made crepe paper rosettes in the same colours, which she pinned to their lapels and strung as garlands around the window edges. A bit of bunting here and there completed the display, ready for the surrender.

Et stood on the footpath with the sisters from the bakery two doors along. They still looked and sounded awfully German, although they swore they were Austrian. It didn't matter to most people, who'd feared a Japanese rather than a German invasion in recent years, but it mattered to Mae. She was coolly polite to the sisters but she kept her distance, believing Harry was still imprisoned somewhere by the Germans and their Japanese helpers. The truth would soon come out now that the war was over. Rumours had run rife for weeks about a Japanese surrender, and especially after the US bombings in Nagasaki and Hiroshima. A cruel loss of life, but nothing more than they deserved, she thought. And springtime seemed just right for a peace treaty. A new beginning, new hope. Leaves were budding on the trees and the wattle was already blooming. The sun shone and a cool breeze whipped dresses and ties of the people hurrying past.

'Mim, that looks wonderful,' Mae said, turning her attention back to the window display.

'That does look wonderful, dear,' Et agreed, walking back into the shop. She resumed folding the cardigans and pullovers on the counter. 'It's like a carnival out there, so exciting.'

'I don't think we'll be doing much business today,' Mae observed.

'I'll look after Katie if you want to go into town,' Mim offered.

'Thanks, I'm happy here, but you go if you'd like.'

Before Mim had a chance to answer, Pearl Atkinson's formidable, floral-clad bosom barged through the shop door.

'Have you heard the news?' Pearl heaved. 'They've surrendered! It's all over!'

'Good morning, Mrs Atkinson,' Mae said calmly. 'They've been saying things like that for days.'

'It just came over the wireless. Ten minutes ago. Prime Minister Chifley announced it. Turn it on and listen!'

Pearl always reminded Mae of Henny Penny: *The sky is falling, the sky is falling!* Rarely did her pronouncements of doom and disaster result in anything but a belly laugh for those privy to them. But today she might have brought good news for once.

'Well, that's a relief,' Mae said, making a sash out of the remaining paper and pinning it across the middle mannequin. 'That will do, I think.'

'You seem very calm, Mrs Parker. I'd have thought you'd be celebrating, especially after what the Japs did to your poor Mr Parker. H-bombs were too good for them.'

Mae glanced at Mim, who stood near the window with her mouth agape. 'We're closing the shop now, Mrs Atkinson. Good day.' Mae ushered her out onto the street and closed the door behind her.

'I came to pick up my skirt,' Pearl yelled through the door.

'You'll have to wait till tomorrow,' Mae called as she shot the bolt, flipped the closed sign then drew the blind. 'She'll be back first thing tomorrow unfortunately. Cuppa anyone?'

'That would be lovely,' said Et. 'You put on the kettle, Mim. I'll do the pot.'

Hateful woman, Mae thought. She couldn't bear the thought of Pearl discussing Harry, especially on a day like this—and in front of his sister, too.

'I'll finish her hem,' Mae said.

'Are you sure?' asked Mim. 'I can do it.'

'It's fine. Besides, it'll take hours to get around that length of fabric.'

Mae picked up the skirt and began to sew. When she reached the back, she neatly sewed several tiny pins into the seams, covering her handiwork with meticulous invisible stitches.

'No, you can't do that,' Mim laughed, spilling tea into the saucer as she set the cups on the counter.

'I can and I have. Now Pearl can feel tiny pricks of conscience whenever she sits down—that's if the pins can penetrate all that padding, of course.'

'Here's one from me,' Mim said, handing a pin to Mae.

'Why don't you finish up for the day, go and meet your friends in town? I'll go to the house and do some cleaning.'

'I can't believe you're so calm about it,' Mim said as she pulled on her coat and hat. 'That builder should be shot.'

Mae smiled. 'It's fine. He couldn't get the materials then he ran out of money. I need to dust and sweep out the mess so the fellows William found can sand the floors next week.'

'I'll take Katie home with me for the afternoon,' Et said.

When everyone had gone, Mae felt glad to have a day alone with her thoughts. Bells clanged in the distance; the train was approaching the station to take revellers into town. It would be crowded and stuffy and Mae didn't mind missing the party. Although there was plenty to celebrate, she felt certain she was exactly where she needed to be, exactly where Harry would find her one day; not today, but soon. Since the war in Europe had ended in May, prisoners were being released from the German camps and slowly making their way home. Depending on where he was, he must surely be on his way back. If he was in the Pacific, it might take longer, but eventually the navy would have to let her know and she could prepare. There was no need to close her eyes to imagine him walking towards her from the train station; she could see it clearly. He could be huddled in an overcoat, his face swamped by a hat, but she'd still know him from the way he walked and the way he swung his duffel. She'd see his jaw first, then his wide, bright grin; he wouldn't need to say a word, she'd know him anywhere. Everyone would be so surprised—they'd all given up—but she still felt his presence, especially at the house. It wasn't until she'd started clearing the workers' rubbish after they walked off the job because the builder hadn't paid them that she realised she sensed Harry nearby, just like when she used to walk into the cottage and knew he was home before she saw him. She felt closer to him than she had in the four years since she'd seen him last. He was right there beside her, urging her to finish their dream.

❧ ❧ ❧

Several weeks later, Mae walked along a narrow footpath bordered by long, barracks-style buildings at the new

Repatriation Hospital. Men sat on shaded garden seats staring blankly ahead as they dragged heavily on cigarettes and winced with the effort of trying to move their bandaged limbs. Beneath the sounds of warbling magpies and ringing bellbirds several patients sat silent as their visitors talked across and around them, desperate to reconnect with the strangers in the bodies of their loved ones before they took them home. But saddest of all were those men with no visitors; the same fellows sat alone week after week. Mae glanced at the figure of a man behind a cyclone-wire fence, steadying himself with a walking frame, as though he was learning to walk. The sign on the fence said the area was for prisoners but she felt sorry for him, wondering if he was far from home.

Feeling safely concealed behind her dark glasses and simply dressed in a dark green wool suit, she sensed the men watching as she passed. Elegant restraint was the way Et described Mae's style; Mae felt her outfit was more like a suit of armour, protecting her against life's buffeting, especially here. She couldn't understand why some women allowed themselves to be so open to life's ebbs and flows. Harry's mother, for instance; she could certainly do with a little more strengthening. When Mae and Katie had arrived at Elizabeth's house for lunch earlier that day, Mae was surprised by Elizabeth's appearance. Her hair was completely white and her back seemed to grow more hunched every week. She no longer needed to bend to hug Katie. Instead, she held her so tightly that the child bent backwards and looked like she might snap in two. Mae brought Katie to visit Elizabeth on Sunday afternoons then left them all to play music and dance for a few hours while she spent precious time alone, walking along the river and reading under a tree. When the new hospital opened nearby, she was glad to take the train further up the line to Heidelberg to be among the returning men. You never knew what you might see or hear.

'You look so tired, Mae,' Mim had said over lunch. 'Why don't you spend the afternoon with us instead of racing off?'

'I have to go—I need to read to the men.'

'Anyone would think you were off to meet someone,' Mim teased.

'Of course I'm not; I'm married to Harry,' Mae said, glancing at Harry's violin and photograph still sitting on the piano.

'Mae, I didn't mean to upset you. You're entitled to a little happiness. If you *have* met someone . . .'

'I'll have all the happiness I need when Harry is home.'

Hurrying to the third building along the path, Mae felt a tingle of excitement in her chest. It's just another Sunday visit, she told herself as she removed her gloves, stepped onto the verandah and walked towards the nurses' station.

'Good afternoon, Mrs Parker. It's lovely to see you again. The men are in excellent spirits today,' Sister Gibson said. 'It must be the sunshine. It lifts them immensely.'

'It is a beautiful day,' Mae agreed. 'Just beautiful.'

'We have three new men in Four West; they've come from the Pacific. We've put them in adjoining beds. One of them is blind, another has lost a leg, the third is badly scarred. I'm sure they'd all love to hear you read.'

Mae held her breath and entered the ward, her heart thumping fast under her ribs. The blinds were set low so the men could rest. Despite the relatively mild day, all the windows were shut tight, their curtains hanging still. The babble of conversation hushed as the patients and their visitors watched her carefully scan each of the new men's faces.

The first patient she saw was the one missing his leg; tall with brown wavy hair and haunted eyes, he was much younger than Harry. The man turned his head away when she studied his face. The second man's eyes were covered in dressings, his hands restrained to stop him from ripping away his bandages. His curly hair was sandy blond— nothing like Harry's straight dark hair. The third man's face was disfigured by burn scars, his mouth and eyes a sickly blur of pink melted wax. Mae steadied herself against the end of the bed. He was much shorter than Harry, only five foot six or so. Harry was nearly six foot.

'Don't worry, love, you'll find him,' said the skinny man missing an arm in the next bed.

'Mr Armstrong, I was looking for you,' Mae said, smiling quickly. 'How are you feeling today?'

'Fair to middling, thanks, Mrs Parker. The doc says I'll be able to scarper in a few weeks.'

'And where will you go? Do you have family?'

'Me sister Bev lives in Ballarat with five rug rats. Hubby died in Libya so I'm gunna mind the kids while she goes out to work.'

'You're very lucky having somewhere to go.'

'I thank the Lord for it every day, ma'am.'

Mae opened her handbag and pulled out a small cloth-covered book. 'Shall I sit here today, Mr Armstrong?'

'I'd be honoured,' he said, pointing to the chair with his stump. 'It's good of you to come again. Most of us don't get many visitors after the first few weeks.'

'Your sister sounds terribly busy and it's such a long way.'

'That must be it. But you're good for bothering.'

'It's the least I can do. When the hospital advertised for volunteers to read to the men, I was pleased to assist. I love reading, especially the classics. I used to read this to—'

'To Mr Parker?'

Mae swallowed. 'Yes. He loved me reading this book aloud. Also *Twenty Thousand Leagues Under the Sea* and *Robinson Crusoe*. Anything about adventures at sea.'

'Well then, we'd better get into it. How's that bloke in the book gettin' along, findin' his way home?'

Mae carefully opened the book, removed a hand-embroidered bookmark and began reading Homer's tale of Odysseus trying to sail home to his wife and son.

'This is where Odysseus speaks to his dead mother,' Mae said, trying to project her voice clearly so the whole ward could hear.

'"*And tell me of my father and the son I left behind. Is my kingdom safe in their hands, or was it taken by some other man when it was assumed that I would never return? And what of my good wife? How does she feel and what does she intend to do? Is she still living with her son and keeping our estate safe? Or has the best of her countrymen already married her?*"

'"*Of course she is still living in your home,*" my royal mother replied. "*She has schooled her heart to patience, though*

372

her eyes are never free from tears as the slow nights and days pass sorrowfully by. Your fine kingdom has not yet passed into other hands."'

Mae looked around the hushed ward. All eyes that were still awake were on her. She turned the page and read some more to the shattered men and their families, who at least had each other and time to say whatever was needed. Even after all this time, she would have given anything to have that one night over.

CHAPTER 38

September 1945

GRACE ENTERED WARD FOUR West at the Repatriation Hospital and smiled as she walked towards Phil, her eyes never leaving his face. She knew that if she let her gaze drift to his stump she'd cry—again. *He needs your strength, not your pity*, her mother had counselled.

Leaning over to kiss his cheek, she realised she was being too coy, even in front of the other patients. She quickly kissed him on the lips then sat on a wooden chair beside his bed.

'Hello, my darling. You look well today.'

Phil didn't say anything. His grim, hollow face barely registered her arrival.

'Can I get you anything? A drink, or something to eat?'

'I'm fine. The nurses do everything.'

'Sam sends his regards. Everyone's glad you're back.'

'In one piece?'

'Yes, one piece.' Grace searched his face for any sign that he was pleased to see her. He'd been home for three weeks but he was still too frail to stand. He was barely more than skin stretched over bones. The infection in his leg was improving and the doctor said he might try walking with a crutch in the next few weeks. But sadness flattened his face, his hand gestures, his voice, even the way he breathed; every movement and sound was slow, heavy, sad. He'd said he was glad to see her when he first arrived home a couple of weeks earlier, but his lips barely responded when she kissed him. When she tried to talk about the future, he drew further into himself. Discussing the Japanese surrender was the only thing that sparked a reaction. *They should have obliterated the entire country, rid us of the whole evil race*, he'd said several times, his voice rising.

'The woman reading has a lovely voice,' Grace said.

'She's here each week, looking for her husband.'

'Well, now the war's over, it might happen, you never know.'

'He was on the *Sydney*.'

'Oh. I see.' A chair scraped but the rest of the ward was silent, listening to the woman read to the man with the missing arm. *Armstrong*, Phil had said. *Ironic*.

'Some people believe the ship was towed to Singapore by the Japs,' Grace explained. 'They're still writing to the paper asking what the government's hiding.'

Phil winced. Grace wasn't sure whether that was from pain or the mention of the newspaper. He stared at the woman reading the book.

'One of the chaps captured after us said there were reports that the Nips towed the ship. I asked one of the Jap guards about it, in Changi.'

Grace willed him to speak more, to hold an actual conversation. His eyes seemed more focused, his mouth firmer. 'What did you ask him?'

'I said straight out: "Did you blokes capture the *Sydney*?" He said, "Yes." So I asked: "Did some of the crew survive?" He said, "Yes." Finally I asked him: "Did you capture Luna Park?" Again, he said, "Yes."'

'That doesn't prove anything.'

'We never came across anyone in the prison who'd met any of the crew after the battle.'

'But they could have been sent somewhere else. It could take years to find everyone and bring them home.'

'They should just ask the bloke in the prison ward.'

'What bloke?'

'The nurses said the captain of the *Kormoran*'s here. He had a stroke apparently. He's having to learn to walk again.'

'No!'

'They don't want anyone to know . . .' Phil's voice trailed off.

'Especially not the woman reading?' Grace asked.

There was no answer. She glanced at Phil but his eyes were closed.

'See, you're still the best reporter around, even while you pretend to sleep.' Grace watched for a flicker of reaction, but his expression stayed blank. 'You'll still be able to work, you know; write features or work on the subs desk. You could even be a news editor like Sam.'

His bony chest hardly moved. She wondered how he could bear sleeping on his side; his shoulder seemed so sharp, any contact with the mattress had to hurt. Her touch might have hurt as well. He flinched whenever she tried—or maybe after all this time he just didn't want her near him.

'We could go and work on Dad's paper,' she whispered. 'Both of us, together.'

Phil whispered without opening his eyes: 'I need to sleep now.'

CHAPTER 39

October 1946

MAE DIPPED THE BRUSH in the paint, wiped the excess on the side of the bucket and lifted the brush to the wall. She was so tired, she longed to lie down and rest.

Come on, Sunny, you're almost done. Just a few more feet and you'll be there. It was as if he was beside her, whispering in her ear, his voice was so clear.

'Mummy, can I have some more paint?' Katie stood looking up at Mae, paint spatters on her overalls and through her hair. She'd been painting the skirting boards behind where the couch and buffet would sit, places that wouldn't be seen but that kept her busy while Mae did the walls.

'We're nearly finished now. You don't need any more paint.'

'But I want some, there's still a hole.'

'A gap?'

'A hole in the painting.'

'Just a minute; I'll look when I finish this.' To Mae's surprise, five-year-old Katie had proven to be quite the little helper. 'Daddy will be so proud of you.'

'And Santa?'

'Yes, Santa Claus will be impressed too.'

'How many sleeps?'

'There's still lots—about sixty sleeps till he comes.'

'Will he find us here?'

'We'll send the letter in plenty of time so he knows exactly where you are.'

Our first Christmas in the new house, darling; hurry home to us. Be our Christmas miracle.

Mae was only vaguely aware of the sound of the car as it hurtled around the corner; the loud crash as its axle hit the stormwater drain was the first indication she had that something unusual was occurring outside her home. A deafening smash. Splintering wood. Metal twisting and grinding. A fog of dust. Car exhaust. Steam from the radiator. Debris raining from the ceiling. Mae dashed over to shield Katie.

The car's headlights shone in her eyes through the hole in the dining room wall where a window had been moments earlier. The car's bonnet and windscreen were draped with branches and splintered palings from the fence. Steam rose from the engine as Mae lifted her head to see if the car was still moving. She felt Katie move then heard her whimpering. 'Katie, don't move, darling. Stay still.'

Lifting Katie and holding her tight to her chest, Mae bolted towards the hallway and the street, imagining the roof caving in, the walls falling down. Smelling gas, she yelled silently: *Don't let it explode, Harry, don't let it explode.*

'Get him out of the car before the house collapses,' Mae heard someone calling in the distance.

'The car's gunna catch fire.'

'Someone call the police.'

'Get an ambulance.'

'Give him space. His head's bleeding.'

Everyone was concerned about the young man in the car but no one seemed to have noticed her. Mae looked up as a woman ran out of the house across the road.

'Oh, you poor dear, were you in the house? We didn't know anyone was inside.'

Mae ran to the corner still clutching Katie then sat down in the gutter to examine her. She checked her head then her arms and legs. No blood. Nothing seemed broken. Katie blinked up at her without making a sound. Trembling with shock, Mae wrapped her arms tightly around Katie again. She was safe; they both were. That was all that mattered.

Fire trucks, tow trucks, police, ambulance. As each arrived the rest of the neighbourhood followed in their wake. Mae and Katie were checked by the ambulance men, while the driver, a young man, was rescued from the car.

'You really need to come with us, Mrs Parker. The doctors need to examine you and the little one.'

Before the ambulance driver closed the doors, she surveyed the accident scene. The car was wedged firmly halfway along the wall of the house. Seeing the damage, Mae shook her head in disbelief. *Look at that,* she said to

Harry. *How could we possibly have walked away? Were you watching over us? That's it, isn't it? You helped us escape. Our very own guardian angel, aren't you, my darling? It's all right, everything can be repaired.* Mae hugged Katie closer. 'You're safe now. Daddy's looking after us.'

'Santa's chimney's broken.'

'We'll fix that too.'

CHAPTER 40

February 1947

'PUSH THE STARTER BUTTON, Grace.' Phil called from the back of the printing press.

Grace leaned forward and pressed the button but nothing happened.

The gears and drums roared into life. 'Look, it's our paper, Simon. Isn't Daddy clever, fixing the printer like that?'

She stepped back and held the baby tight as paper fed through the inked plates and rollers. The entire room rumbled as the printer settled into its powerful rhythm.

'I don't know how long it's going to last. Hopefully we'll get through this edition,' Phil said, wiping grease from his hands on a tatty old rag. 'The gears are pretty worn.'

'Can we get second-hand parts?'

'It'll take more than a few parts. We'll need a new press if we want to keep going. We have to decide once and for all . . .'

Phil limped towards the control panel and adjusted one of the dials. In the eighteen months he'd been home, he'd had three operations on his leg to cut out the remaining infection and clean up his stump so he could be fitted with a wooden leg. Then he'd learned to walk again, surprising everyone when he hobbled down the aisle without crutches during their wedding in Benalla early the following year. Nev gave Grace away but didn't tell anyone during the wedding that he was feeling unwell. The night before Grace and Phil arrived home from a week at Bright, Nev collapsed in the pub from a heart attack and died in hospital.

The staff kept the paper going over the next few weeks while Grace and Phil finished up on *The Tribune* and moved to Benalla. They'd agreed to take over for two years to see whether it would pay its way. It had broken even under Nev, but since the end of the war, several papers had expanded in neighbouring towns and the competition for advertising had to be shared with new radio stations as well.

'It's in his bones, isn't it?' Phil said, smiling tiredly at his infant son, who stared as the paper whirred through the rollers.

'If we don't stay here, we'll have to find another paper for him to play with,' Grace said, smiling at the little boy. 'Do you want me to stay and do the inserts?'

'Time to get him home,' Phil said as Simon squirmed to get down on the dirty concrete floor. 'I'm meeting some of the cops for a beer after I finish here. June can do the inserts in the morning.'

'It's no trouble, it won't take me long, then the driver can get going first thing.'

'I said no. Jesus, Grace, do you have to argue every point? Get the boy home and fed. I don't need him screaming when I get there.'

The press rattled and clunked, whirring to a halt as the paper roll tore.

'Damn, damn, damn!' Phil yelled, whacking a spanner against a metal casing. 'Worthless piece of crap!'

Grace stroked Simon's back as he started to cry. 'There, there, Daddy's not yelling at us.'

'Get him out of here, I can't hear myself think.'

'All right, I'm going. See you at home.'

As she hurried to the car she murmured, 'It's all right, Daddy didn't mean to yell.' Was she trying to reassure Simon or herself? she wondered. 'He can't help it. He's just tired.'

Settling Simon in the back seat, Grace sat quietly in the car with the engine running to soothe him. *Phil's just tired*, she repeated to herself, *always tired*. It was no wonder, given his nightmares. Night terrors her mother called them. *Your father came home with them too*. Grace asked how long they'd lasted, and Rosie replied that they'd never really disappeared completely—though they were worse when Nev drank. Well, at least her mother was getting some rest now that Nev was gone. But Phil was waking several times each night, drenched in sweat, shaking, sobbing. Grace often woke to find Phil clinging to her like he was drowning and she were a life buoy keeping him afloat. They were both tired, but how was she going to fix him, to take away his anger? It was exhausting for him and for her.

She drove slowly along the street running parallel to the main road so she didn't have to stop and chat to anyone as she passed the shops. Some days it was just too hard to pretend she was half of a happy couple, especially when she felt fear gnawing a hole in her stomach. At least her stomach pain wasn't caused by another baby. Phil said he wouldn't have any more until they'd sorted the paper out. But as time wore on it seemed like just another excuse not to make love.

When Phil first came home he was quiet and withdrawn, especially as he recovered from his operations. But then he'd seemed to come good. He told her how much he'd missed her, how much he loved her; how the thought of her had carried him through his worst times in the prison camp. But even in his best moods, he refused to say anything about what had happened in Changi. *I don't want to think about it, let alone talk about it with someone who wasn't there. You'd never understand.* Her mother advised her to let him be; he'd tell her when he was ready or he might never say much at all. But he was moving further and further from the Phil she adored. Her Gary Cooper was gone, replaced by a sullen, angry stranger. Worse, he was turning into her father, yelling about the most trivial things, blaming her whenever things didn't go his way.

Her mother had seen Phil's temper too; one day when Rosie had popped around to the house unexpectedly, she'd heard Phil in full flight. Grace still cringed at the thought of what her mother had heard. Rosie had brought strawberries and ice-cream for their tea and was slipping them into the ice chest on the back porch when Phil slammed through the front door, unaware that his mother-in-law was outside.

'Well, I've just heard how you got all your prison break exclusives, you unfaithful bitch!' he shouted.

Simon screamed from his playpen in the lounge room.

'Stop it, Phil. It's not true.'

'Don't you lie to me, you whore. Jacko told me all about it.'

'Jacko's just annoyed because he was too busy drinking with his mates.'

'Mates, hey? I know all about you and that copper and how you slept with him every night to get your scoops.'

'It's not true, he's just a friend,' Grace had sobbed as she saw her mother try to sneak past the window towards her car. 'It's not true.'

The next day, Rosie had tried to console Grace, assuring her that Phil would get better, but she couldn't hide the sadness in her voice. *It just takes some men longer to settle back into their old lives. After all, he's one of the lucky ones.* Grace knew he was lucky; they both were. He could still walk, he could work, and they had Simon.

Grace slowed the car as she passed the cinema. *Torchy Gets Her Man.* She gripped the steering wheel as her stomach ached again. Taking a deep breath, she waited for the stabbing pain to ease. *Life will be good,* she told herself as she exhaled. *No, life is good. Life is good and Phil loves us.* She leaned forward and rested her head on the steering wheel. *Life is good and he loves us.*

CHAPTER 41

April 1947

MAE COULDN'T HAVE ORDERED a better day for moving into her new house. The sun seemed to shine a little brighter than usual, birds sang louder and a warm breeze blew away the overnight chill of autumn. Children playing in the street parted to let cars drive slowly past the row of new California bungalows painted in different combinations of blue, cream and grey. Et flitted from room to light-filled room plumping pillows and placing ornaments.

'I think they'd be better in the buffet,' Mae said, pointing to a small collection of Wedgwood plates Et was arranging on a side table.

'Are you sure, dear? I think they look quite the thing here beside the chair.'

'They'll just catch dust if we leave them out.'

Mae's house was painted a rich cream inside and out. It had a large verandah with double doors opening onto a wide hallway, making it easy to move the outdoor furniture inside. The doors at both ends of the house were open to air out the paint fumes. Two bedrooms sat on the right-hand side of the hallway, and the lounge and dining rooms were joined by French doors on the left. A sunny, north-facing kitchen ran along the back of the house opposite a bathroom. The back door led out to the toilet and laundry and a generous yard dominated by a large, corrugated-iron garage.

Surrounded by boxes, William sat at the kitchen table polishing cutlery. Mae joined him for their first pot of tea together in the new house.

'Well, dear, you've finally done it. Albert would be proud.'

'I suppose he would,' Mae said, imagining him sitting at the table, reading the paper. Her heart still skipped a beat when she caught herself thinking of him or of Harry.

'Now you and Katie can spend more time at picture shows and the like. You mustn't waste so much time with us oldies. Have a few people of your own age over for dinner and cards. Your lovely dining room is made for parties.'

A clock ticked on the mantelpiece over the stove. 'It already feels like home, doesn't it?' she said, trying to keep her mood light as she handed William a pile of teaspoons.

'Albert would have been so pleased to see you and Katie here; they both would.'

Mae silently thanked Albert for leaving her the money for the house. She caught a shine in William's eyes more likely caused by sadness than joy. She knew William missed his older brother just as much as she missed her uncle. He was quieter these days, spending more time listening to the radio and reading. Et said she sometimes caught him commenting on something the radio announcer said as though he were speaking to Albert, then he'd glance at his brother's favourite chair and his smile would drop, he'd blow his nose and go back to listening.

'Mummy, can I take this to school?'

Katie walked into the kitchen clutching Mae's framed picture of Harry in his uniform, fingerprints all over the glass. 'I have to take something for show-and-tell.'

Mae reached for the picture then forced her hand into her apron pocket. Katie's face shone with excitement but Mae wasn't ready to let the precious picture outside in such small hands. 'How about you take a different picture? I'll find one for you.'

Mae crouched on the dining room floor in front of the buffet. She took out a box of photos, and found a small black-and-white photo of Harry holding Katie on the steps of his mother's church. Elizabeth had taken it on his last visit home.

'See? That's you,' she told Katie. 'You have to be very careful. We'll put it in a card and then an envelope so it doesn't bend.'

As Katie skipped off to show Et and William, Mae stacked the dinner setting on the upper shelf and the silverware and tablecloths in the drawers. She'd embroidered all the linen before her wedding, but Harry had never seen them on a table. She was saving them until they had a proper dining setting. Mae had caught him poking through the tea chest one night. He'd pulled out a napkin and held it close to the light, inspecting the fine stitches.

'There's more than one artist in this family,' he'd said, running his finger along the edge. 'I love watching you do this.'

Mae fought a wave of sadness. No, today was a day of celebration. Spending the last few weeks painting the house in her spare time, she'd felt Harry close by, willing her on. She spoke to him each night in her head. No one knew; it was just their private time together. Over the last couple of years she'd felt her hope slipping away like a slow, gentle exhale. But she wasn't prepared to let go of him completely. And as long as she pretended to accept that he was gone, no one could judge her.

Mae took the empty packing case to the back porch then stretched and surveyed the garden. An apple tree and a Hill's hoist stood side by side on bare dirt.

'A blank canvas,' Et said behind her. 'One day soon you'll be having picnics on the lawn.'

'Speaking of picnics, Harry's family is coming over for lunch tomorrow. The second time this week. Elizabeth brought dinner over while we were painting the other night.'

'It's good for Katie to see you two getting along so well. And Mim—what a treasure she's been for the business.'

'And for me. She's come along very well with her work.'

'Speaking of work, shall I bring the ferns out the back or put them in the garage?'

'I think we'll give them some air today. Maybe keep them in their pots but line them up in the shade there,'

Mae said, pointing to the shaded part of the garden along the garage wall. 'We'll see if they like it there.'

Mae imagined a fernery or maybe even something more tropical in that area. 'Harry always talked about the plants he saw on his trips: bromeliads, orchids, cycads. He drew them too. I might frame some of his drawings for the hallway, a sort of gallery.'

Et smiled. 'That sounds lovely, dear.'

A few minutes later Mae was stacking towels in the linen press when a large crash caused her to freeze. The noise had come from the backyard. She ran into the garden, expecting to see clouds of dirt and dust and another car through her fence. 'What happened? Katie? Et? Where are you?'

'Calm down, Mae, we're fine. I just dropped a pot. See?'

Mae looked down at the shattered terracotta pot. Her heart still pounded madly in her chest, but she was able to take a breath. Katie leaned over and picked at the rubble.

'Leave it, poppet,' Et said. 'I dropped it so I'll clean it up.'

'Well, that's one way of making sure it's not pot-bound.' Mae laughed.

'The fern will be fine, dear, but we'll need to plant it today.'

'It can be the first plant in the garden, then.'

'Look, Mummy—there's a fairy ring in the roots.'

Mae looked down to where Katie was pointing and saw something glint in the sunlight. Kneeling to take a closer look, she reached forward and teased the fine roots apart.

There, nestled in the fibres, was her wedding ring: the ring she thought she'd lost while fishing in the Dandenongs.

Et put her hands to her mouth. 'I don't usually believe in signs, dear, but . . .'

'Yes, I know. He's absolutely here with us, isn't he? Harry's home.'

ᕫᕒᕘ ᕘᕫᕒ

Later that afternoon, William took Katie for a walk to the milk bar and Et nodded off on the couch. Mae sat for the first time on a wooden slatted seat that they'd placed under the apple tree. Admiring the wedding ring safely back on her finger, she lifted her teacup to her mouth. The action reminded her that she'd used every muscle to its limit during the move. The early spring sun carried just enough heat to soothe her aches. She rubbed her knees then swung her legs onto the bench. It wouldn't hurt to lie down for a few minutes. She let herself feel as though she were melting onto the hard wood beneath her back and legs. Looking up at clumps of fluffy clouds against the sky, she imagined she was flying. When she closed her eyes the sun shone orange through her lids.

'It's your turn for a dip,' Harry said, standing between her and sun.

Mae smiled without opening her eyes. She loved this dream. She stood, removed her hat and dress, then walked with him to the water's edge. Following him into the tepid water, she felt it rise against the fabric of her bathing costume. It wasn't nearly as cold as she'd thought it would be.

'This time we're getting your hair wet. No arguments.'

Harry had always wanted to teach her to float and today she felt brave. She was certain she felt one of his hands supporting the small of her back, while the other rested between her shoulder blades as her feet and legs rose to the surface. As she leaned back a little further, the water crept higher around her neck and the sides of her face, lapping gently against her head as her arms floated by her side. It was like magic; she was weightless. She felt the pressure of his hands recede.

'Don't worry, I'm still here.'

'I can't feel your hands.'

'You're doing it on your own. Just breathe gently, in and out, in and out.'

She was aware of him floating beside her, holding her hand.

'It's all right darling. Just keep your eyes closed. You're doing beautifully.'

She felt her body rise and fall with her breaths, her hair brushing the sides of her face. Sunlight softly prickled her skin as she relaxed into the warmth.

ACKNOWLEDGEMENTS

THIS STORY IS INSPIRED by my grandfather who was one of the 645 crew lost on *HMAS Sydney* and my grandmother who died before the ship was found. The loss of the Sydney in 1941 and the subsequent mystery and controversy have affected thousands of Australians in the decades since. Thanks to the exhaustive research by Barbara Winter, Michael Montgomery, Dr Tom Frame and shipwreck hunter David Mearns among others, I've had the writings and resources to help bring this story and period in our history to life. I am incredibly grateful for the support of the teachers and my classmates in RMIT's Professional Writing and Editing course and my wonderful writing and book buddies: Michelle Deans, Kerry Munnery, Jennifer Hansen, Ann Bolch, Di McDonald and The Book Babes, Jacquie Byron and The Mrs Underhill Book Club, and Kathryn Heyman at Australian Writing Mentors. I'd also like to thank the team at Allen and Unwin, including

1-19

publisher Jane Palfreyman and editors Siobhán Cantrill and Ali Lavau, who have patiently guided me through the publishing process. The title for this book comes from 'For the Fallen', a poem by the English poet Laurence Binyon, that was published in 1914:

> They shall grow not old, as we that are left grow old;
> Age shall not weary them, nor the years condemn.
> At the going down of the sun and in the morning
> We will remember them.

I hope that I have done this story justice for my family and the many other families touched by this dark chapter in our collective past.